A Heart Unbound

Jen Caruso

Jen Caruso

Monee, ILLINOIS

Jen Caruso
P.O. Box 579
Monee, Illinois 60449
www.jencaruso.net

Publisher's Note: This is a work of fiction. Names, characters, places, and incidents are a product of the author's imagination. Locales and public names are sometimes used for atmospheric purposes. Any resemblance to actual people, living or dead, or to businesses, companies, events, institutions, or locales is completely coincidental.

Book Layout © 2017 BookDesignTemplates.com

A Heart Unbound/ Jen Caruso. -- 1st ed.
ISBN 978-1-7362168-0-4

For Alex and Jasmine

All dreams spin out from the same web.

—

Hopi Proverb

Contents

Chapter One 1

Chapter Two 13

Chapter Three 27

Chapter Four 35

Chapter Five 49

Chapter Six 63

Chapter Seven 85

Chapter Eight 91

Chapter Nine 113

Chapter Ten 135

Chapter Eleven 153

Chapter Twelve 173

Chapter Thirteen 207

Chapter Fourteen 245

Chapter Fifteen 277

Chapter Sixteen 293

Chapter Seventeen 307

Chapter Eighteen 323

Chapter Nineteen 337

Chapter Twenty 349

Chapter Twenty-One 361

Chapter Twenty-Two 379

Chapter Twenty-Three 391

Chapter One

Island of Croatoan, Area of Chacandepeco

Region of Ossomocomuck

June 1586

"NO one is to speak of the English we attacked," Ompeu cautioned his friends as they entered the village. An exuberant mother-in-law was among the group that converged upon the returning men. Ompeu and his small hunting party were relieved of their burdens of fresh meat amid happy chatter, whooping, cheering, and words of congratulations, and blessings. The hunt was good. This was a reason to celebrate, and among the joyful voices, he discovered that three days prior, his wife, Sequan, gave birth to their first child, a boy.

"Sequan?" he asked for anyone to answer as the small crowd followed him toward a dome-shaped dwelling. He searched their faces in the dusky glow of a fading summer sun, thinking to find his wife among them.

"It was an untroubled birth," his mother-in-law, Poussu assured him, a grin splitting her face. "She and your son are well."

Paukunnawaw gave his friend some breathing room, genially dispersing the crowd of friendly faces, allowing Ompeu a moment to gather himself before entering his wife's *yeehaukan*. The reality seemed to hit him all at once, and his feet became leaden and rooted to the ground beneath him. Paukunnawaw laid a hand on his friend's shoulder, noting the happy but anxious look on Ompeu's face. "Go to your wife and son," he encouraged.

Ompeu returned his friend's look with a blank stare, causing Paukunnawaw to chuckle. "Go," he urged, giving Ompeu a good-natured shove toward Sequan's dwelling.

Ompeu moved as though in a dream. A man of twenty winters, he had experienced much. An accomplished hunter, he fought enemies, he faced the *Tosh shonte* without fear. Now he was a father. *I have a son.* The thought caused his lips to curve in a smile, and his heart swelled as Poussu lifted the door flap for him, urging him to go inside.

A small fire glowed in the center pit. Ompeu remained still as his eyes adjusted to the dimness, finding his wife seated, nursing the infant.

Sequan's face was radiant. "Come husband," she beckoned with an outstretched hand. Ompeu never failed to make her heart flutter. Tall, lean and well-muscled, his long black hair hung loose about his shoulders, draping above his waist. His dark eyes reflected the glow of the fire, which cast the angles of his handsome face in light and shadow. Full, sensual lips were slightly parted in wonder. She studied his expression, swallowing the lump that lingered in her throat. She had loved him since they were children. They grew up together. He was a steadfast friend who matured to become a good and honorable man. Though his affection for her did not match her level of passion, Sequan chose to accept this.

Her thoughts fled as Ompeu knelt before her. His son's eyes were closed as he nursed contentedly. Sequan gently pulled the baby from her breast, the break in suction creating a smacking noise. Ompeu laughed softly as he took the infant in his arms. He studied the child, stroking the fine, black tufts of hair, touching the soft brown skin of the baby's cheek. The infant's pursed lips continued to make sucking motions as Ompeu lifted the infant's hand with a forefinger. His son gripped tightly. "You are strong, little one."

Sequan relaxed, breathing an inward sigh of relief, at her husband's contentment. She knew Ompeu married her out of a sense of honor and obligation to her family, who raised him after his parents were killed in a tribal war, long since ended. Many seasons passed, and after the Englishmen had come and taken away her brother, Towaye, Ompeu made an offer of marriage. Though he would never say it, she knew it was for this reason that they were joined. Ompeu perceived a responsibility for her, as well as for his missing friend, Towaye. It no longer mattered. Now their marriage bond would be stronger with the coming of the child, and perhaps in time her husband's love for her would deepen.

Ompeu tore his gaze from his infant son to look up at his wife, his admiration evident. "You are well?"

"Yes, husband," the corners of her mouth turned up in a tender smile.

His eyes flitted down to the child. "*Nuqisus*," My son, he murmured softly. "I am honored."

"As am I," she replied, taking the boy from him. Now that the initial anticipation of meeting his son passed, Sequan noted Ompeu's tired expression. "Sleep now," she said, motioning for him to take his place on the sleeping pallet. "The child will not awaken yet, and you've been away. The hunt was good?"

"Kupi," he answered. *"Winganouse."* Taking her suggestion, he undressed quickly, and moved toward the indicated spot.

"And the *Tosh shonte?"*

He knew she asked about the English, in the hope there would be news of her brother. "We did not see them," he winced inwardly at the lie, but rationalized that keeping the truth from her would protect her.

Sequan joined him in the blankets, and as she listened to the soft masculine voice of her husband talk of the hunt and the days he'd been away, she dozed, lulled into sleep.

Ompeu lie awake listening to his family's soft breathing, and the sounds outside the *yeehaukan.* A camp dog yipped. The voices of the few people who dwelled outside in muffled conversation drifted to his ears. Different, fleeting thoughts filled his head. Thoughts of fatherhood, and responsibility, and how he would teach his son the ways of a man. Thoughts of his friends, Towaye and Manteo who had gone away with the English, left him empty. The *Tosh shonte* were a strange, pale people, who arrived in great ships, and spoke a strange language.

The English previously kidnapped and interrogated a few of the young native men about the land, and game, requesting information about the chiefs. Manteo, son of the Croatan *werowansa* twice went willingly across the great water to live among them. He told stories of the

English lands. He knew the English words and gave some to Ompeu, who's curiosity about the white men, induced a desire to learn their language. Most of the Croatan were friendly toward the *Tosh shonte*. Ompeu grew wary of them.

An Englishman named Grenville took Ompeu's friend, Towaye and sent him across the great water. Towaye went willingly with Manteo, but no one had seen either of them since. Though she did not speak of it, Sequan mourned the loss of her brother, and Poussu, the loss of her son.

Wherever the Englishmen went, death followed. Some of the People became sick with illnesses and died within days of the white men leaving the villages. The medicine people could not cure the sick ones. It was thought that the *Tosh shonte* could shoot invisible bullets which caused the sickness. The English took this as a sign that the People were weak and beneath them.

Wanchese acquired a different view. He, along with Manteo also lived with the *Tosh shonte* in their land. Wanchese did not wish to return. He warned Ompeu not to believe all that his friend, Manteo told him. Wanchese had no love for the English.

Some thought that the strange visitors were sent by the spirits; men who died but returned to earth. At first contact, the People made the newcomers welcome. The English claimed to be friendly but were distrustful and overly suspicious. Sometimes they took food without asking. They were greedy and child-like in their helplessness. Ompeu did not understand them. They had powerful weapons and gadgets not seen before. When they arrived, they set about building a fort on the island to the north they called Roanoke and wanted the People to feed them. Two years before, Grenville and his men explored a great deal of territory and visited the villages of Roanoac, Pomeioc, and Aquascogoc. A silver cup went missing. The English burned the entire village of Aquascogoc to punish the natives they suspected of theft. Later, Grenville sailed away, taking Manteo and Towaye with him. He left a soldier, Master Lane in charge of the men who remained on the island.

The Roanoac *werowance* Wingina initially welcomed the English, but as tensions grew, he gave himself a new name. He called himself Pemisapan and came to understand that the *Tosh shonte* were not spirits, but merely human beings incapable of feeding themselves. Pemisapan took his people away, moving the village, refusing to feed the English. Master Lane learned of this, suspecting conspiracy. The white men attacked Pemisapan's village, murdering him, and taking his head. When a passing ship stopped, Master Lane and the remaining starving *Tosh shonte* returned home. Weeks later, another English ship arrived finding the Roanoke fort abandoned. They left fifteen Englishmen behind to guard it.

Ompeu rolled to his side, careful not to wake Sequan with the movement. He exhaled in frustration, unable to sleep, then rose quietly from his spot to kneel next to the tiny, sleeping bundle. With gentle fingertips, he stroked his son's head. A fierce, protective resolve swelled in his heart. He would shield his family and do what he must to protect them from the *Tosh shonte*. There were things Ompeu did not tell his wife. Things that happened on Roanoke Island.

Ompeu lifted his eyes to the piece of night sky visible through the open smoke flap of the dwelling. The winds were warm, yet there had been little rain to quench the crops. Yes, the hunt was good. Ompeu and the hunting party brought meat for all. The Croatan hunters came upon a war party of combined Roanoac and Secotan warriors, bent on revenge for the murder of their chief, Pemisapan, and others who were killed by the *Tosh shonte*. Ompeu and his friends joined them. He watched as Wanchese greeted the Englishmen using the words he knew. Upon his signal, the war party emerged. Ompeu did not tell his wife of the white men they killed on Roanoke Island, nor did he tell her of the subsequent attack on the remaining Englishmen at the fort, whom they chased and scattered to the winds, leaving the English settlement on Roanoke, abandoned once again.

Ompeu's heart was uneasy. More English would come from across the great water. As surely as the tide rushes to meet the sands, he knew more English would come. Ompeu left his son's side and crept quietly back to the sleeping pallet. His eyelids closed over as thoughts of the *Tosh shonte* dissipated, and sleep claimed him.

Ompeu found himself in the darkened woods. His body was not his own. He looked down to find himself transformed into a large wolf; huge paws, thick, dark gray fur. A rustling in the brush drew his attention. He raised his wolf head, pointed ears perked up, turning sideways, then forward. He waited, wolf nostrils flaring, sniffing the night air until he caught the scent of her. His piercing wolf eyes found her through the leaves; a doe with a spotted fawn curled at her feet, both quiet and still. Her doe eyes stared back at him in silent defiance.

"She waits for you," a voice said.

A pang of hunger burned his gut. He salivated, hoping to kill the doe, taste her blood. He panted lightly, sensing her fear, her breathing, and rapid heartbeat in his ears. She remained motionless, as they held each other's gaze. When his wolf paws suddenly pushed against the earth, his body leaping forward, she darted, leading him away from her fawn. He chased her. She ran through the brush, past trees, over hills in mindless circles. He grew tired, for she was as elusive as the wind.

One last leap. He nipped a back leg causing her to stumble. He growled, his powerful wolf jaws snapping. He captured her. Snarling, his wolf teeth pierced her neck, her blood seeping onto his tongue. He shook his wolf head fiercely from side to side. His jaws locked crushing her windpipe. He held her there for long moments until she no longer struggled, then he released her. She was dead.

Or so he thought. She twitched and moved her cloven hooves. He tipped his wolf head to the side curiously. He watched as her deer's body changed, growing larger. He yelped a wolf yelp and jumped back, watching as the transformation continued. Bushy tail, long snout, silver-light fur, large paws. The doe was gone, and in her place appeared a beautiful she-wolf. She stretched languidly, her front legs outstretched, her rump in the air. She yawned as though awakening, revealing sharp wolf teeth.

She took a tentative step toward him and whined. Ears flat, body hunched low, tail wagging furiously in greeting. He knew from her scent that she sought a mate. He went to her, unable to stop himself. She trotted around him, flicked her tail into his face, and ran from him in invitation. He chased her. They rolled and frolicked, and bit each other playfully. She turned her rump to him. He mounted her, and as he did so he became human again, the she-wolf became woman. His fingers grasped the smooth pale flesh of her woman's hips as he entered her. A hand pushed against his shoulder. From far away, he heard someone whisper his name.

"Ompeu. Husband." Sequan nudged him.

Ompeu sprawled on his back breathing heavily. He could not open his eyes. His enlarged manhood throbbed painfully.

"Husband," she nudged him again. "You were dreaming," she whispered.

Ompeu's eyes obeyed his command and he blinked them open. He felt his body immobile, as though he had drunk a sleeping concoction. He could not speak.

Sequan snuggled close to him as his breathing gradually slowed, but the engorged male part of him remained evident. She wondered what he dreamed of but did not ask. "Ompeu? I will help you," she murmured, her hand skimming over his lean belly, to the part of him that ached with need. She stroked him rhythmically.

His eyelids closed over as she touched him, the image of the she-wolf-turned-woman appeared, unbidden. He finished quickly, and Sequan rested upon him, her long, dark hair fanning over his chest. They did not speak. He lie there with her, the drug of sleep still strong in his veins. He did not know what the dream meant, or who the woman was; he could not see her face in the dream. But somewhere in the fog of his troubled mind, he knew that she was not his wife, Sequan.

Chapter Two

Voyage to Plant the Third Colony in Virginia

*June 1587, Aboard the **Lion***

"**M**Y husband believes Fernandes should be flogged for his refusal to obey the Governor's orders," Rose Darby said quietly, as she picked several maggots from the flour sack.

"Fernandes is a privateer, not a planter," Jayne Mannering responded. "He would rather be raiding Spanish ships, and cares nothing for establishing the settlement." The women kneeling around the flour sacks responded with murmurs of agreement.

Elizabeth Cooke sat in silence. She had little care for conversation this day. She wished her feet to be planted firmly on the soil. If Fernandes knew how to pilot this ship to retrieve the fifteen men left on Roanoke Island, so be it. The women talked on about Fernandes' insolence. Elizabeth stopped listening. She imagined hardtack made with maggot-ridden flour. A wave of nausea washed over her. She took a slow, deep breath and dabbed the sweat from her brow with a sleeve. Her fingers trembled slightly as she wiped them on the worn apron of her dress, her thoughts drifting to her son. Elizabeth felt on the verge of insanity. They had been at sea nearly two months, her son took ill the entire voyage. She observed his boyish enthusiasm for their adventure across the sea, fade dramatically within a week of their departure.

Their talk meandered, the women chattering on, their voices intermingling and distant. Her mind elsewhere, Elizabeth tuned in and out on bits of conversation, as she continued with the disgusting chore, sifting through more flour. They spoke of nothing new. She had heard it all before.

"Sir Walter was not pleased with the last planting. Master Lane left amid much chaos."

"If it were not for Master Drake, Lane's men would have perished. I have heard that Drake left a rather large company of slaves on the island. Men from various lands. Promised freedom if they aided the colonists.

Perhaps they shall greet us and settle with us at Chesapeake."

"Master Ralegh's supply ship arrived within weeks of Lane leaving with Drake. Had they but waited, all would have been well."

"It shall be different for us. We are settlers, intent upon building new lives, not soldiers for hire who receive payment whether or not a colony succeeds or fails."

"I heard our soldiers razed an entire Indian village over a missing silver cup, and that more recently they killed a chief. I pray there will be no trouble."

"Manteo and… and Towaye are with us, they would not allow the Indians to harm us." This from the usually quiet Emme Merriwerth, an indentured servant girl of Governor White and the Dare family.

"I'm certain they've taught the Indians a lesson. Any sign of weakness to the heathens would be our undoing."

"I shall be happy once we've arrived at Chesapeake. The promise of 500 acres is no small matter. We could never imagine being the proprietors of such a tract of land."

The endless prattle worked Elizabeth's nerves. They had already endured much on the voyage. Conditions aboard the ship were harsh. Only the highest-ranking officers retired to individual bunks. The remaining passengers slept on blankets on the floor between decks.

Some of the food turned rancid, and the flour became infested with maggots which required the current chore.

During storms, the colonists stayed below decks, where rats and cockroaches crawled over them. Seawater leaked into the ship and mixed with vomit, feces, and urine creating an unbearable stench. The passengers were unable to bathe regularly, and many of them were lousy. Being in close quarters, created tensions among them. Everyone detected the animosity between Governor White and the navigator, Simao Fernandes.

Three ships set sail months before. Governor John White worried over the smaller ship. It separated from the larger ships during a terrible storm near the Azores six weeks before. The inexperienced pilot of that ship had never crossed the Atlantic and would not know the way.

This caused one of the first arguments between Governor White and the pilot of the ship, Simao Fernandes. White wanted to wait for the lost ship, but Fernandes, not wanting to tarry further, refused, leaving the small ship behind. Others aboard *The Lion* wondered why Fernandes went unpunished for blatantly disobeying the Governor's orders, and this perhaps became the first sign of White's inability to govern with a firm hand.

Elizabeth felt a brief touch on her arm, rousing her. "Elizabeth, are ye not well?" Rose asked concernedly. "Ye seem terribly pale."

"Not very well today," she shrugged helplessly. The ship lurched, causing her nausea to intensify. She placed a hand over her middle, as though the action would soothe her rebellious stomach. "I cry your mercy. I must go above decks."

Rose wiped flour from her hands onto her brown, drab skirt. "I shall accompany ye."

"Nay, 'tis nothing." Elizabeth attempted a watery smile. "I simply require a bit of fresh air."

Rose tucked errant strands of blonde hair beneath her coif, green eyes followed her departing friend concernedly. The past few weeks, Elizabeth spent caring for her eight-year-old son, Phillip. Rose knew that Elizabeth did not sleep well either, plagued by dreams she would not speak of, but so vivid and real, that her husband refused to sleep near her.

"I pray she will have courage enough," Alice Chapman commented absently.

"She will," Rose defended her petite friend calmly, staring at the space Elizabeth vacated. "She has endured more than we can imagine," she sighed. "She will carry on."

Once above deck, Elizabeth found a private spot and gripped the wooden rail, her hands trembling. She saw nothing but sea and sky. The day simmered warm and rather humid, the welcome breeze blew tendrils of dank, fawn-colored hair from their pins. She turned her face to the wind, breathing deeply of the salty air. It did not help. The contents of her stomach erupted suddenly. The strong sea breeze caused some to splash back in her face. Still hunched over, Elizabeth glanced around quickly, wiping her face with her skirt apron, relieved that apparently, no one witnessed her seasickness.

Perhaps her fear was confirmed. She missed her monthly courses, and the combination of poor food and rest added to her discomfort. She could not recall feeling so horribly during previous early stages of pregnancy. Elizabeth did not wish for another child currently. She did not envy Eleanor Dare or Marge Harvey who were both eight months pregnant. She could not imagine traveling to a strange land across the sea in their conditions.

During her ten-year marriage, Elizabeth weathered four pregnancies. Two resulted in miscarriage. The most recent occurred the year before. She gave birth to a girl. The infant, born prematurely, did not live but two days.

Elizabeth endured the heartbreak at the death of the child she'd held in her arms. Even now, her heart wrenched at the loss. After a time her husband thought sufficient for grieving, he berated her for carrying her mourning too far. She was to cease her moping, he'd said, for he would coddle her no longer.

"Mistress Cooke!"

Her husband's gruff voice startled her. She turned, her posture rigid, forcing herself to meet his gaze. His blue eyes were glassy and unfocused. Sparse, dark blonde hair covered the lower portion of his face.

"Why are ye not below decks?" His voice cut sharply. "I forbade ye to be out here alone. There are sailors about."

The strong ale on his breath assaulted her nostrils. "I merely needed to, to…," Elizabeth started.

He grasped her arm roughly before she could finish, forcibly leading her away from the rail. "See to my son," he ground out between clenched teeth. Walking briskly, he held her arm with a bruising grip, forcing her belowdecks where the heavy, stifling air filled her lungs. Several passengers and crew took notice, but turned away, not wishing to involve themselves in private marital concerns. "You neglect your duties, whilst prattling away with the women. When will you heed my words?" he hissed in her ear. "When!" He shook her. "Woman in her greatest perfection was made to serve and obey man."

It was a quote he used from time to time, and one she knew. *"The First Blast of the Trumpet Against the Monstrous Regiment of Women,* a tract written by John Knox in the year of our Lord, 1558," she countered, to remind him that she was also well-read.

Her response served to increase his fury. Cooke moved to strike her. Instead, his eyes bored into hers in warning. She returned his stare, refusing to look away in submission. Her education made her bold and insolent in his view. Cooke blamed her father for being far too indulgent of the younger Elizabeth, an only daughter, who would sit at her brothers' lessons when she should have been more learned in the domestic arts; cooking, cleaning, stitchery, caring for children and managing a household.

Elizabeth wrenched her arm free, her hazel eyes turned fiery, daring to glare up at him in defiance. "He is asleep. The women needed help sorting through the flour. My son is my first duty, sir. Always."

Before she could turn away from him, Cooke reached for her, pulling her up short against him. "Apparently so, for you've not performed your wifely duties of late. We shall remedy that as well, soon enough." His words were more threat than promise.

Elizabeth blanched, attempting to pull away from him, for his cruel nature during intimacy left her body bruised and cruelly marked. 'Wifely duties' were not something she relished.

A satisfied smirk curled his lips, for he knew he had gained the upper hand. Cooke shoved her roughly toward the makeshift bed where their son slept upon soiled blankets. "I will not see you above decks alone again. You are my wife, and I want no sailors gawking at you. I will not tolerate such disobedience. Is that not clear, my pet?" Angry blue eyes leered at her, awaiting a response.

Elizabeth lifted her chin but said nothing as she watched Cooke secure his hat upon his head and turn away, leaving them.

"Mother."

Elizabeth cleared her throat, collected herself and knelt at her son's side. She pressed her lips to his brow. "Your fever has lessened considerably," she smiled, relieved.

"I am better."

"I'm glad of it." Elizabeth rose to ladle a bit of water from a nearby bucket, offering him several sips. She studied her son's face as he drank greedily. While he favored his father in appearance, dark blond hair, blue eyes, his temperament was far different. The younger Philip was quiet and shy. Elizabeth worried that he was too withdrawn.

The younger Phillip also experienced his father's wrath on occasion. Mother and son could not predict when Cooke's outbursts of anger would occur, or what triggered them. His temper seemed to grow worse over the years. Nothing pleased him. He would notice the smallest of errors and turn them into horrible affronts to his person. It drained them to carry on a life this way, and Elizabeth hoped that arriving in a new land and starting a new life would change him.

She glanced at her son, who sat up, tossing off the blankets. She helped him remove his soiled shirt, trading it for a cleaner one. She wanted her son to grow to be an honorable man. But what did she know about the ways of men? Her life was not her own. Her path was decided by and ruled by men.

When Elizabeth reached the age of ten, her mother became ill and died shortly after. Her father lost his anchor. In his grief, he grew restless and aimless. A dreamer, he plotted, scheming new ventures for the sake of profit. The next business opportunity on the horizon would inevitably be the one to make him wealthy. Often, he lost money. When her father met Phillip Cooke, he found a man after his own heart. Her father convinced Cooke to lend him a large sum of money and promised that this new venture would make them both richer than they could possibly imagine. Cooke, a member of the Tilers' Company was a brick maker and tiler. He agreed and gave all his savings.

Unfortunately, her father's business deal proved to be a disastrous one, and when Cooke demanded that his money be returned, Elizabeth's father could not repay the debt. Phillip Cooke threatened her father with prison. Fearing this, the older man offered his daughter as a wife, hoping to appease the angry younger man. Though not completely satisfied with the transaction, he accepted. And so, at the age of fifteen, Elizabeth became the wife of thirty-year-old Phillip Cooke.

Their financial woes stemming from her father's poor business dealings left Cooke in enormous, constant debt. Along with the added burden of a wife and child, he became increasingly angry and bitter over his predicament as the years passed. When the opportunity arose to escape the debt and settle new lands across the sea, he took it, selling nearly all their possessions to pay for passage aboard ship.

"Are you hungry?"

When the boy nodded, Elizabeth unwrapped cloth-covered hard biscuits she stashed away and gave him one to nibble, grateful that his appetite was restored. She filled the ladle once more for him to drink. Once he finished, she helped him up to relieve himself, then changed out his blankets. Her son returned to the makeshift bed, the effort exhausting the small boy. He wrapped thin arms around his mother, snuggling against her breast. She tucked his head beneath her chin, absent-mindedly stroked her son's hair, and hummed an old tune her mother often sang to her as a child. She rocked him. If Cooke were to enter, he would complain that Elizabeth coddled the boy, and that he would grow too soft. This did not concern her. The day would come when her son grew to manhood and left her. Now, he was her only joy, and if the sick child wished to nap in her arms, she would gladly allow it. He comforted his mother as much as she comforted him. The seas were calm this day, and the movement of the ship lulled them both to sleep.

The dream. A high-pitched hum, a buzzing in her ears that surged to a vibration, radiating throughout her body. The hum grew increasingly louder, the vibrations stronger. Her body became paralyzed. She could not make the slightest movement of the smallest muscle.

Then a presence. Someone. A man, she thought. She could not see him clearly, a shadow perhaps. She never saw his face, only a vague form, but somehow, she knew him to be male. She feared him. She thought that if she could move a finger, a toe, some part of her body, that the vibrations would cease, the presence would disappear, and the terror would end. He came to her and stood near her as she slept, but never spoke.

This time, he touched her. Her heart raced in panic, she attempted to force herself to awaken. She screamed in her mind, the paralytic terror increasing. He touched her again. Elizabeth felt the sudden whoosh of a tidal wave enter her. His whole being seemed to fill her, swirl around her, through her. What did he want of her? He permeated her entire being with his. Whisking, flying, passing through her as though she were a vaporous substance, moving his essence in and out of her like undulating waves.

In that twilight stage between consciousness and deep sleep, Elizabeth's world spun, dizzying, whirling, in a timeless, limitless pulse. The essence of the man stayed with her, and she clung to him, for he was the only thing to hold onto in this wild dream journey. They flew over the ocean, dipping past a sandy shoreline, through deep woodlands, above green and gold prairies. They spun beyond, through harsh desert and majestic snow-capped mountain ranges. It all happened so quickly, that she closed her eyes against the whirlwind and buried her face in his chest.

He vanished. The high-pitched humming stopped. The vibrations ceased. Elizabeth felt as though she had fallen a great distance, landing softly upon the blankets. She labored for breath. She found that she could move again and stretched her legs, testing them. Inhaling deeply, she sat up and noticed that her son changed his sleeping position, turning onto his side. She placed a gentle hand on his shoulder, leaning over him. He slept soundly. Elizabeth turned away suddenly overwhelmed with emotion, a vast emptiness engulfed her. She wept silently for reasons she did not understand.

Chapter Three

Hatorask and Roanoke Islands

Mid July 1587

"Do not tarry Governor. 'Tis late in the season to wait much longer. It will take weeks to unload these vessels. I must return to England before bad weather sets in," Simao Fernandes warned.

"Return to England? Or return to privateering?" White asked.

"That is none of your concern. Master Ralegh would not wish to endanger his ships."

"We will return after seeing to Grenville's men," the governor replied. "After we have gathered the men at the Roanoke settlement, we shall all continue on to the Bay of Chesapeake."

White and forty men, including Manteo, boarded the smaller pinnace, and set out for the island to make contact with Grenville's fifteen men. Unbeknownst to him, Fernandes ordered the larger ship to begin unloading at Hatorask in order to send goods and passengers across to Roanoke Island.

Philip scrambled below decks, to where his mother sat with her basket of sewing supplies, along with Rose Darby and Alice Chapman. They were mending torn shirts and trousers already threadbare from overuse. "Mother!"

The women looked up from their work, but before the boy could utter another word, they heard the distant voices of men arguing. "I am the master of this ship. Sir Walter entrusted his vessels to me, and I will not sail onward, to be delayed by the coming weather." It was Fernandes. "There is not time to sail farther. You must all disembark here, now."

Disgruntled voices followed, protesting this change of plan. Fernandes walked away and would not entertain further questions from the gathering crowd above decks.

Cooke entered shortly after his son and addressed his wife. "Put the mending aside. Pack what we can carry. That bastard Fernandes is ordering us to disembark."

"We heard a disagreement." The women looked to one another with bewildered expressions. "But why?" she asked.

"I know not why. Do as I say," his gaze moved to include the other women in the group. "That goes for all. Gather your belongings."

On the shores of Roanoke Island, Governor White and his men walked along the beach and nearby woods, shouting "halloos" and calling for Grenville's men. They searched the area for some time. By sunset, they made a grisly discovery.

"Governor!" George Howe used one hand to keep the broad brimmed hat from flying away as he ran toward White. He gasped for breath and appeared visibly shaken.

"What is it?"

"You must accompany me, sir."

White and the others followed Howe toward a group of men who gathered around some object in the sand. He gazed down at what was once a flesh and blood man.

"Savages," Ananias Dare said as he picked up a weathered arrow and rose to his feet, passing a hand through his dark hair. Brown eyes cast about, searching the shoreline.

White stepped forward and squatted on his heels next to the partially bleached bones wearing fragments of English clothing. He studied the remains for a time before rising. "Let us look after him," he said. He turned to Howe. "See whether there is something in the pinnace with which to wrap the bones. We will bury him in the woods." Addressing the group of men, he said, "We shall set up a camp. On the morrow, we will walk toward the north end of the island where Master Lane had his fort the year before."

"Sir."

Governor White turned questioning brown eyes toward his son-in-law, Ananias.

"What if no one is at the fort?"

White rubbed his graying beard, considering the possibility.

Ananias continued. "If the others were alive, would they not have buried their own fallen comrade?"

If the men were attacked, there may not have been opportunity. "Unless they were affrighted or killed. An excellent question to be sure. And one we shall have answered soon enough."

The following dawn, Governor White and his party walked to the north end of the island. They found the fort in ruin. Some of the houses remained intact, but the entire area was overgrown with vegetation. Deer grazed unconcernedly about the compound. It was obvious to all that the fort remained uninhabited for some time. John White realized that any hope of finding Grenville's men was slim. He ordered his men to board the pinnace.

Upon their return to *The Lion*, they watched the flurry of activity as shipmen loaded the smaller boats with goods and supplies. White grew livid but there was no chance against Fernandes and his entire crew, who stood by their pilot's order to leave the colonists at Roanoke Island. It was mutiny, but Governor White had no recourse. He returned to his cabin aboard ship and called a meeting of his assistants.

He described what they encountered on Roanoke Island. "We shall have to rebuild parts of Lane's fort and make suitable habitation for those with families." White pointed to the map he had drawn, laid flat upon the small, rough-hewn table. "We will set about re-establishing friendly relations and trade with the Indians as soon as possible."

"We must question them about the fate of Grenville's men," George Howe interjected.

"Aye, Manteo will assist us in this."

There seemed to be nothing left to say. They had to be on about the business of unloading ships and setting up Lane's old fort. They would spend the winter there, and then move onward toward the Chesapeake Bay in the spring.

The assistants agreed with this plan. There were few options. However, most of them silently questioned their governor's leadership. Fernandes not only disobeyed White, but Sir Walter Ralegh as well. Fernandes should have been severely punished, perhaps hung for his outright disobedience. White's indecisiveness in dealing with Fernandes was cause for concern. Since the incident involving the lost ship off the Azores, White had effectively relinquished his control over the mission. This latest blatant disobedient action by Fernandes, and White's inaction was an indication that White lacked the most important characteristic of a colonial governor, ruthlessness. It demonstrated that he was unable or unwilling to impose his own rules and conditions where the settlement was concerned, and this could affect the entire success or failure of the colony.

*   *   *

"They have returned." Paukunnawaw trotted toward Sequan's *yeehaukan*, stopping where Ompeu sat repairing a reed fishing net.

Paukunnawaw's words required no explanation. Ompeu looked up from his work. "When?" He set aside the net, rising to his feet.

"This day. Wobsacuck and others saw the great canoes. A group of them were on the island. Wobsacuck thinks the white men were searching for the ones left behind."

Ompeu and Paukunnawaw shared a look, each recalling the summer before, when they helped the Roanoac and Secotan warriors in the attack upon the Englishmen. "Have you seen or heard from Nussacun or Wanchese?" Ompeu asked.

Nussacun was a minor war chief of the Roanoac. He and Wanchese organized the attack on the fifteen white men in retaliation for what Lane's men had done to their village and their *werowance*, Pemisapan. Ompeu did not particularly care for the company of Nussacun but joined him because they shared a distrust of the *Tosh shonte*. Wanchese traveled across the great waters with Manteo. Wanchese, though he lived among the English in their far away land, carried no friendly feelings toward them, and was instrumental in the attack on Grenville's men.

"No, but they may have already seen the great ships as well."

"Have you spoken to our *werowansa*?" Ompeu asked.

"*Kupi*. She and the council believe we should wait. Her son Manteo may be with them, and Towaye also."

Ompeu ran out of questions for the moment. His dark eyes grew hard as he gazed to the north, in the direction of Roanoke Island.

"You do not agree?" Paukunnawaw questioned.

"I do not know. Perhaps we should move inland." He looked back at Paukunnawaw. "Or perhaps we should fight them."

"There are more *Tosh shonte* this time," Paukunnawaw shook his head. "I do not believe it would be wise to attack them now. They will be well fortified with weapons and supplies. You have a wife and child to think about," he reminded his friend.

Ompeu thought of Sequan, who worked in the nearby fields with the women. He nodded in reluctant agreement with his friend. "They are only men who bleed and die as we do. But we will wait."

Chapter Four

The women did what they could to unpack and set up suitable living quarters as belongings and supplies were gradually unloaded from the ships. The process was slow. Men continued unloading the vessels, rebuilding the earthworks and palisades that encircled the compound, and repaired cottages and other structures. Another group of men worked on setting up the brew house, the armory, and the gaol.

Elizabeth and Rose washed clothes in a large bucking tub outdoors, while some of the women prepared food for hungry workers. The intermittent sounds of hammers against wood and the clank of metal interspersed with mostly masculine voices served as background noise. Men worked in the sawyer's pit, producing planks from freshly cut tree trunks, the friction of the saw creating a latent scent of burning wood.

Rose hung her husband's breeches on the line to dry. "Do ye expect we are in danger from attack by the Indians?"

Elizabeth wiped her brow under the heat of the noonday sun, sweating in her gray wool dress and linen aprons. She swayed lightly on her feet. "I've heard the Governor and Manteo have plans to travel with a troop of men to speak with the area chiefs. I do not believe we are in any immediate danger."

"Master Ralegh wishes us to minister Christian belief to the Indians. I'm not certain they would accept our ministry if their intent is to harm us."

Elizabeth pondered the truth of this as her hands moved vigorously, rubbing over a particularly stubborn spot on her son's shirt. She silently wondered over the sincerity of her English compatriots at any missionary work. "The conflict between the Spanish Catholics, and the English Protestants grows daily. Though I've not a mind for religious or political intrigues, it seems that Christianizing the indigenous people; turning them into good Protestants and making them subjects of Her Majesty would serve English interests. Creating a colony and forming alliances with the people here, gives us an advantage and creates new enemies for Spain." Elizabeth twisted the shirt in her hands, wringing out the remaining water. "Settling a colony here also gives the English opportunity to conduct military privateering raids against Spanish ships."

Rose remained quiet, and when Elizabeth glanced up at her friend, she saw that her green eyes were wide, her delicate face revealing silent surprise. Elizabeth knew she had said too much. Claiming that the English would use native peoples as pawns for political gain could be misconstrued as treason. Her husband said that her education was a curse. Now she had possibly offended her friend with her opinions. Elizabeth chastised herself, clamping her mouth shut. She reminded herself not to voice her personal beliefs. She wiped the sweat from her brow once again. "Forgive me," she said, returning her attention to the wet shirt in her hands. "I misspoke."

"Nay." Rose took note of Elizabeth's pallor and went to her side, taking the shirt from her hands, and leading her to a nearby tree stump. "Come. Sit. I can see yer not well again today."

"No, Rose," Elizabeth protested half-heartedly. "I am well, I assure you. My husband...,"

"Would have his wife swoon over soiled laundry?"

"He will be angry," Elizabeth admitted.

Rose pressed her shoulder gently until Elizabeth sunk down, sitting upon the stump. She ladled a cup of fresh water from the wooden barrel and gave it to Elizabeth. "I'll finish yer washing. Rest."

Elizabeth relented. "For a moment. I can work, there is no need for you to be troubled." She silently berated herself for her earlier speech about political issues regarding England and Spain.

"'Tis no trouble." Rose returned to the tub, taking a few articles of clothing from Elizabeth's pile. She wondered why Elizabeth spoke of the English as though she were not English herself. Rose rubbed the cake of soap on the spot of fabric Elizabeth was working and proceeded to scrub little Phillip's shirt. Silence stretched between them. Rose continued scrubbing and covertly eyed Elizabeth who sat watching the activity in the compound, sipping a bit of water. She thought Elizabeth lovely, with wavy caramel hair that she wore pulled back and tied in a fat knot at the back of her head. Her expressive eyes reminded Rose of a young doe's, large, soft and slightly almond-shaped. She wondered how Elizabeth came to marry Phillip Cooke. Everyone aboard the ship could see the ill manner in which Cooke treated his wife.

While at sea, after most of the passengers settled in for sleep one night, Rose overheard Cooke berating and insulting Elizabeth. His cruelty toward his wife tore at Rose's heart, and she understood why Elizabeth often kept to herself, never speaking much of her husband, or of others the way some women tended to gossip. Rose imagined that her new friend was quite reserved and would not speak of private matters. Perhaps, she was simply embarrassed at her husband's vile behavior. Rose did not ask. If Elizabeth wished her to know, she would tell her in time.

Rose hesitated before she spoke quietly, "I've seen that ye can read and cipher."

Elizabeth hardly swallowed the water in her mouth. Her eyes grew large momentarily, as though the statement panicked her, and she glanced around, searching for her husband in the group of passing men carrying a large wood log on their shoulders. Satisfied that he was not among them, she answered. "Aye. I learned from my elder brothers' tutor, much to my husband's agitation," she admitted.

Rose cleared her throat. "Would ye... would ye teach me?" she ventured.

Elizabeth cast about in her mind for an answer. "I'm not certain he would allow it."

"He need not know." Rose quirked a golden eyebrow, her lips curved slightly in a conspiratorial smile. "No one would. It shall be our secret."

Elizabeth seemed unconvinced. Her husband consistently shamed and derided her, insisting that she was too outspoken for a woman. He was easily riled, and Elizabeth did not wish to provide further reason to draw his wrath. Lately, he'd been occupied with the work at the fort. When he arrived home in the evenings, utterly exhausted, he ate in silence and then retired for the night. He had not made good on his threat to seek out her wifely attentions, and for that, Elizabeth was grateful.

"I have wished to learn since I was a child," Rose continued. She lifted her eyes to some far-off place in the distance. "I come from poor stock, ye see. Put to work with my mother as a domestic servant at the age of seven. The mistress of the house possessed a small library. I would often sneak into the room and open the volumes there and touch the pages, wishing I could read the words." Rose seemed to remember herself and smiled at her trajectory of thoughts. "I loved the smell of the ink and paper. I know that some girls are afforded tutors such as yourself, but... Lord forgive me for my envy, but I envied them their ability to read." She paused, rinsing the shirt, swishing it around in the rinsing tub. She raised beseeching green eyes toward her friend. "Please think on it, Elizabeth. I would be indebted to ye."

Elizabeth returned her friend's smile, a soft sympathetic expression in her eyes. She rose from her spot, returning to the washing tub. "I shall be honored to teach you."

Rose's face beamed with joy. "I thank ye." She reached for Elizabeth's hand, giving it a gentle squeeze.

Elizabeth returned a brief smile, then grew silent. "Rose," she swallowed convulsively. "I believe I know why I've been ill of late." She hesitated, not wishing to say the words aloud. She reached for another article of clothing and dunked it into the tepid water. She washed it with more vigor than necessary, as though she could wash away fears and doubts. She was afraid. It seemed that telling her husband or anyone, would confirm her condition, and some small part of her wished to deny it. Telling someone would speak it into existence, and Elizabeth was not certain she wished to face reality yet.

Rose saved her the effort. "Yer with child," she said simply.

Elizabeth's expression grew anguished. She pressed her lips together, casting her eyes downward. "Aye".

"I thought so," Rose comforted. "New land, new life," she said softly. "Perhaps this will be a blessing to ye. A new babe to love." Rose hung the clean shirt to dry. "I know it has not been easy for ye, but yer blessed, for I've not been able to conceive a child of my own. My husband says he's not concerned over it, but I know how men can be about such things."

It was Elizabeth's turn to take her friend's hand. "Forgive me, Rose. I did not mean…."

"How could ye've known?" Rose smiled, patting Elizabeth's arm, reassuring her that she was not offended.

"I must appear to be an ungrateful, uncaring woman. I beg your forgiveness once again."

"Do not think of it. Truth be told, I would be afeared as well. So much uncertainty here. It will take all we have to survive. But ye must not dwell on what ye think may be unfortunate or disagreeable, or things ye cannot change. Have faith. All may turn out well in the end."

"Thank you, Rose. From this moment, I shall endeavor to keep my thoughts high-spirited." Elizabeth smiled genuinely, and her heart seemed lighter. It felt liberating to share a confidence with a friend. The first friend Elizabeth recalled having since childhood.

Their moods lightened; the women continued their work. Conversation flowed more freely between them, and in no time, it seemed, all the clean laundry hung in the warm, summer breeze.

*   *   *

To the relief of the entire settlement, three days after their arrival at Roanoke, the lost ship commanded by Captain Edward Spicer arrived safely. To Simao Fernandes, this meant more waiting offshore as the smaller ship was unloaded.

Two mornings after, one of Governor White's assistants, George Howe, went out alone to fish and hunt for crabs along the beach, using a small, forked stick. He removed his shirt and shoes and left his weapons on the bank. What Master Howe did not know, was that a group of Pemisapan's men from the mainland were also nearby. They attacked him, riddling his body with no less than sixteen arrows. After Howe was dead, they mutilated his body in barbaric fashion, clubbing him about the head, smashing his skull.

The group of Roanoac and Secotan, led by the minor war chief Nussacun, were concealed in the tall reeds. They slipped away silently, jumped into their waiting canoes, and made haste for Desamunkepeuc, their village on the mainland.

Governor White was greatly disturbed by the murder of George Howe. He called a meeting of Captain Stafford, Manteo, and his assistants in his quarters. "We must journey to the Croatoan village at once." He turned to Manteo. "We will need the help of your people. Though one of our own has been murdered, I wish to avoid further bloodshed. I do not wish to repeat the mistakes of my predecessor, Master Lane. We must journey to speak with the *werowansa* and the council." White recalled Lane's recent ill treatment of the Roanoac and the beheading of the Roanoac *werowance*, Pemisapan, as well as Grenville's order to burn the Aquascogoc village over a missing cup years before. White did not want to repeat history. The killing of Pemisapan was a serious transgression. It put the Roanoke settlement in a dangerously uncertain position.

Governor White, Captain Stafford, Manteo along with forty men boarded the pinnace and journeyed south to visit Manteo's people. White wanted to repair the friendship, organizing a goodwill mission. White also wished to question them about Grenville's missing men.

Manteo's Croatan people lived on the south side of an inlet called Chacandepeco on Croatoan Island. The *werowansa* was Manteo's mother, and White hoped the natives would agree to be ambassadors for the English, helping them to establish relations among the local tribal groups. White also wanted to establish trade and receive assistance in the planting of crops. The Governor was fully aware of the past indiscretions made by Master Lane, and he hoped the Croatan did not side with the Roanoac and Secotan. He counted upon the presence of Manteo to help move negotiations along peaceably.

Upon the arrival of the English in the Croatan village, women grabbed up their children, and men took up their weapons. All were scattered, running, hiding from the *Tosh shonte.*

Soon a familiar Algonquian voice bellowed amid the confusion. "My brothers! It is I, Manteo. I have returned to my people. I bring my English friends, who come in peace."

Manteo and the rest of Governor White's party waited inside the village entrance. Nothing. Silence.

"Brothers! We come to speak with you, to renew our friendship. We bring gifts to show our good feelings. We bring gifts to my mother, our *werowansa.*"

More waiting. White and his men shuffled about nervously, knowing they were surrounded. Some of the men grew restless, muttering amongst themselves as the tension grew thicker. A few of them unsheathed their swords and raised their shields in anticipation of a possible battle.

The *werowansa* and several fierce looking warriors emerged cautiously from their various hiding places.

Ompeu thought this would be the perfect time for the *Tosh shonte* to kill him. With a cursory glance, he checked to assure himself that Sequan and the baby were safe, then he stepped forward with the others. He held onto his bow, arrow nocked, ready to fly.

Upon the appearance of the warriors with their weapons drawn, the remainder of White's men unsheathed their swords and drew their muskets. Apprehension and distrust filled the air. The Croatan surrounded the Englishmen from various positions and distances. Many more were still hidden. One unsteady hand could start a battle. One small movement would cause death. White's men looked about frantically, searching the trees for possible hidden enemies.

Manteo feared that one of the Englishmen might become unhinged and recklessly initiate what could prove to be a bloody skirmish. "*Matta!* My brothers, we come in peace!" Manteo turned to Governor White and shouted in English. "Governor, tell men lay down their arms! Now!"

Ompeu's gaze did not waver from the *Tosh shonte*. Some were dressed in a strange type of armor, most carried long knives, and weapons that would shoot fire. Manteo shouted something to them in their language. Ompeu was surprised to find that he understood most of it.

Reluctantly, the white men slowly lowered their weapons, placing them on the ground. Ompeu glanced quickly at Paukunnawaw, Wobsacuck, and the others. They lowered their weapons uneasily as well, but Ompeu held fast to his bow.

Governor White stepped forward; his hands outstretched in front of him. "We come peacefully," he called. "We are friends here."

Manteo translated his words, and the *werowansa* stepped forward. She spoke to her son, taking note of his English clothing, and the hand-held musket strapped to his body.

Governor White could not help but think her a graceful creature. An attractive woman, she carried herself as a true queen. Her dark hair grew lightly interspersed with strands of gray, long and loosely tied at the back of her head. Large copper disk earrings hung from her ears, touching her shoulders. She wore a light deerskin mantle, and various tattoos adorned her arms.

"Welcome my son," she said, speaking to Manteo in their native tongue, her lips curved in a smile. She embraced him warmly. "Much time has passed since you have gone to live across the great water." She stepped back, her eyes sweeping over him, taking inventory of her son from head to toe. "Since you have come in peace with these men, come and sit by our fire and share our food. We will make a feast for our guests."

Manteo translated this to Governor White and the others. An apprehensive, collective sigh of relief sounded among his men. All were grateful at the avoidance of bloodshed. This time.

After the feasting, White explained to the *werowansa* that he desired a meeting with the leaders of the area. The *werowansa* told him that she would send messengers to the area *werowances*, and that perhaps in six or seven suns, a meeting could take place. At this meeting, White would assure the People that the colonists had no intention of taking any food from them, nor did they want further bloodshed. The English wished to establish trade relations and to live in cooperation with the People.

The *werowansa* asked that the English not take their corn. Due to the drought, they had but little. She could not promise that the chiefs would agree to this meeting, but she and her people would be among those to attend.

White also inquired after Grenville's men, and the murder of George Howe. The *werowansa* told him she believed the attacks were carried out by remnants of Pemisapan's men seeking revenge for what Master Lane had done to them the year before. It was said that Wanchese tricked the men, calling to them in English, and embracing one man in greeting. It was the signal to attack. Wanchese killed the man who welcomed him.

It was as White suspected. His colonists, though innocent of the crimes committed against the Roanoac people the year before, would possibly pay with their lives for the violence done by Master Lane and his men. White worried for their safety. He knew that the assistance, cooperation, and friendship of the surrounding indigenous groups was paramount. Too late in the year to plant crops, the settlement would need to trade, bargain, and rely on the goodwill of their native neighbors to survive until they could become self-sufficient. The governor worried and waited.

Chapter Five

Roanoke Island

August 1587

E lizabeth tugged mightily on the obstinate storage trunk left in front of her family's small cottage. Too unwieldy to lift, she first decided to push it. That did not work either. She emptied some of the contents, then tried pulling it from the handle. She managed to move it about a foot or so.

"May I help ye, Mistress?"

Startled and flushed, Elizabeth looked up to see the handsome face of a soldier. His dark hair and lashes contrasted startlingly with his light blue eyes. He wore a soiled linen shirt, the sleeves rolled up to the elbows, evidence of his labor this day. "Well, I... yes sir, I suppose I do require some assistance."

The young man gave an exaggerated bow, smiled a dashing smile, and put on his best British. "John Bridger, at yer service, milady."

Elizabeth stifled a smile, hidden behind her hand at his antics. He called over to two men standing nearby.

"Where would ye like this trunk delivered, milady?" Bridger asked as the men approached.

"In my cabin, if you please, sirs."

"Ready, mates?" The men hoisted the trunk, carried it the few yards to the cabin door and then inside. She followed them, unaware of another pair of blue eyes that followed her from a distance.

Phillip Cooke removed his hat, wiping the sweat from his forehead with a sleeve as he watched the doorway to his cabin. He wondered what the devil that young pup, Bridger was on about. He would have to keep an eye on them. He watched closely as they exited the cabin. She said something to the young soldier. He bowed his head slightly and smiled. She smiled too. Cooke seethed. He watched John Bridger and his companions walk away unconcernedly. Elizabeth entered the cabin again.

"Cooke! We are in need of those frames!" A booming voice interrupted his musings. Cooke continued on his way to where the men worked. The scene he witnessed plagued him the entire day. His fellow laborers silently wondered why the usually indolent, grumbling Cooke put in his first day's work without so much as a complaint.

*   *   *

John White and company spent several days among the Croatan people. All but a few of the warriors who remained aloof, welcomed the white visitors. The Englishmen reiterated their assurances to the Croatan that they did not wish to steal their corn. During their visit, the Croatan expressed a desire to receive a badge or mark indicating that they were friendly to the English. Apparently, the year before, Master Lane encountered some Croatans on the mainland and attacked them, thinking them to be hostiles. Governor White agreed to find some way to accommodate them in this request.

After the Englishmen departed, the *werowansa* called a meeting of council members and warriors. They sat around the fire in the longhouse, and each passed the sacred pipe filled with *uppowoc* to pray for guidance and wisdom, and so that their words would be true. Some of the finely crushed *uppowoc* leaves were tossed into the fire to ensure the blessing of *Kiwasa*.

The *werowansa* wished to speak to some of the warriors regarding the disappearance of the men Governor White inquired after. She also wished to know the opinions her people held concerning the white men.

"My friends and brothers." Her gaze encompassed those present. "The *Tosh shonte* say they have come to stay. They say they wish to be friends of the People, and we have welcomed them. I have spoken to my son Manteo, who believes there is goodness in them. He says they possess great *mantóac*. Perhaps it would be wise to keep peace with the whites and trade with them. I believe we may benefit as a result of good relations. I wait to hear what others may say."

Poussu, Sequan's mother, and respected elder was first to speak. Poussu, a pleasing, thick-set middle-aged woman, possessed great wisdom.   People sought her advice as well as her abilities in the healing arts. She possessed the uncanny ability to observe people with a discerning eye. She seemed to understand and know others, better than they knew themselves.

"My friends," she said, her voice strong. "I agree with our *werowansa*. I believe we can learn much from the *Tosh shonte*. They possess much knowledge of things we have yet to learn. I believe it is best to keep the peace between our two peoples. We will lose much if we do not try to live in harmony with these men." Poussu sat back, waiting for another response.

Ompeu could no longer be silent. "I wish to speak," he said. All eyes turned to him, and he continued confidently. "You say that we should welcome the *Tosh shonte*. You say that we should be friendly toward them. I hear your words, yet in my heart, I do not trust these men. They have been here before. Nothing I have seen gives me reason to rely on their goodwill. They have killed. Death walks in their shadow. Many have died from strange illnesses. They have no regard for others. I say we should tread cautiously among these men. We should not trust them completely." He looked at Poussu, addressing her directly. "Mother of my wife, your son, Towaye went across the great water to live among the *Tosh shonte*, and he returns to his homeland to escape them, not to come home to his mother and sister, but to live among the people of the dead Roanoac *werowance* with Wanchese."

"My son Towaye is his own man. He has made his choice," she answered. "Though I have hope he will return to us, he is my son. I have taught him well. He will know where his heart lies. I believe this."

Ompeu dipped his head slightly in deference to his mother-in-law, respecting her words.

Paukunnawaw stood beside his friend Ompeu. "I agree with my brother-friend. I have seen the white men and know what they are capable of. I also know that if we were to fight them, we would lose. They have weapons that shoot fire to kill a man from a great distance. For this reason, I also think we should try to keep the peace, but we should be wary of them. If they wish to make war with us, we will move our village inland, and join with others against the *Tosh shonte*."

"The *Wutahshuntar* have been welcomed among the Croatan before. They have stayed in our village without incident. We have always treated them kindly. There is no cause for them to take up arms against us," the *werowansa* continued. "They may also be valuable allies against our enemies, and trade with them would benefit us."

Several people spoke, and at last, they reached a consensus. The Croatan would maintain friendly relations with the *Tosh shonte*, but cautiously. The *werowansa* would send messengers to nearby tribal groups telling them of the meeting the *Tosh shonte* wished for, to take place on Roanoke Island in a week's time.

The *werowansa* spoke again. "There is also the question of the white men that were left on Roanoke Island the summer before. I told the *Tosh shonte* leader that I believed our brothers to the north, the Roanoac were responsible for the death of one man, and the disappearance of the others." The *werowansa* turned her gaze to where Ompeu, Paukunnawaw, and three other warriors sat. "I believe my words to him were true. The Roanoac and Secotan wish to avenge their many losses, including the murder of their chief." She gazed pointedly at the seated warriors. "But I am not aware if others were involved." The woman's eyes told them she suspected they joined the war party. "I am certain that if a man was killed, there was reason for it. The Roanoac seek balance."

Ompeu stiffened slightly. *Kupi.* There was reason to kill the man. Though it was not a Croatan arrow that pierced the Englishman, Ompeu still believed the *Tosh shonte* needed to know that the people of the area would fight back if forced to do so.

After all had spoken, the *werowansa* tapped out the pipe, signifying the end of the meeting. Ompeu hoped the decision they made today proved wise. He had no desire to be involved in more killing, but he was a warrior, and if required to protect his family and his people, he would do what he must.

*   *   *

Elizabeth tended the fire in the hearth, stirring the embers to life. She checked the thin soup consisting of bits of dried meat and some edible greens found to grow near the compound. She planned to make some flat biscuits with the ration of flour. Leaving the soup to boil, she returned to the makeshift table; two flat pieces of wood, set upon braces. Gathering her sewing basket, she searched for scraps of saved cloth to use as a patch for her son's breeches. He had worn through the knee of one leg. She set about mending it. As if the mere thought of him conjured him up, seconds later Phillip came running into the cabin.

"Mother, I hear that groups of Indians from everywhere are coming here. Is it true?"

Elizabeth looked up at her boy. Though now fully recovered from the illness he suffered aboard ship, he had lost weight, and his clothing hung from his slight frame. She was unable to discern whether he was frightened by the prospect of visiting natives, or excited. "I believe so," she replied. "But we've seen Manteo, and friendly Croatans about the compound before, it should be nothing to worry yourself over." She pulled the thread through the fabric, maintaining her calm. Truthfully, since the murder of George Howe, everyone was on edge, herself included. Manteo, the only indigenous person she knew, adopted many of the English ways, and so did not seem vastly different from any Englishman.

The stories Elizabeth heard of the native people could be either terrifying or comforting, dependent upon who told them. She heard they tortured their human quarry by flaying the skin from their victims with sharpened shells. Other torture included fingers and toes sliced off one by one. There were rumors of cannibalism among some groups. She also heard that they were loving and generous, giving away their possessions to anyone in need, or giving up their own beds so that a stranger might sleep comfortably. Their children were well loved and cared for by all.

"Do not worry, love. No one will harm us here," she said, thinking him to be afraid.

"Harm?" Young Phillip's brows came together in confusion. "I do not worry over that. I wish to see them. I should like to meet them and talk to them. I wish to learn how they speak and learn to shoot a bow. I would ask them why they hurt Master Howe."

Her eyes widened in surprise. His answer quite unexpected. "Oh."

He turned to exit the cabin. "I'm off to help the boys gather wood."

"Is that how your shirts are torn?"

He shrugged, offered his mother a smile and then ran off.

Elizabeth smiled after him and watched him run out of the cabin. "Coming here seems to agree with him," she thought aloud. The settlement offered more freedom to move about and develop friendships with some of the boys. He remained somewhat quiet and withdrawn, but hopefully with time, he would outgrow it. Consciously, Elizabeth's hand moved over her still-flat belly. Rose's words about having a new babe to love, came to mind. Somehow, it brought her comfort, and she began to think that having another child, could indeed be a blessing.

Her husband's temper seemed to have improved. Elizabeth noted his modest and restrained demeanor in the cabin. His abrupt change in mood was puzzling. At times, when he thought she was unaware, she would find him staring at her, his expression inscrutable.

"Mistress Cooke?"

Elizabeth stood and placed the mended breeches on the wooden table. She went to the door and opened it, surprised to see John Bridger carrying two buckets of water. "Hello again, sir. How may I help you?"

John smiled brightly. The healthy shade of golden tan bespoke the hard labor he performed outdoors. Once again, Elizabeth was struck by his startling light blue eyes, rimmed by dark lashes. "Bringin' water to some o' the cabins. I thought ye might need some for cookin' and what not. I brought ye some."

Elizabeth looked down at the buckets. "Thank you, Master Bridger. Please put them next to the hearth."

John choked out a laugh as he entered with the buckets. "Please Mistress Cooke, I'm no master. John will suffice." He set the buckets on the floor and turned to her. "Anythin' ye need milady, I'll be happy t' help, 'tis what they put me to do here."

Her mouth eased into a grin she could not control. "Thank you again, John, but do not put yourself out on my account. I am certain that I, or my husband can manage."

At the mention of Cooke, John Bridger's smile faded. He witnessed Elizabeth's poor treatment aboard ship. He also knew the man to be of an obstinate nature, grumbling and complaining about the work he was tasked to perform about the fort. "Yes Mistress, I mean no disrespect. 'Tis my job to assist the people here."

"And I am most grateful." She did not wish to hurt his feelings but worried that if her husband saw them speaking to one another alone in the cabin, he would erupt into a fit of rage.

John moved toward the door and gave Elizabeth a slight bow. "At yer service, Mistress."

"Good day, sir." After the cabin door closed, Elizabeth returned to her sewing.

John Bridger strode toward the front of the compound. He was a soldier assigned to assist the colonists in setting up their homes and offering help where needed. He also spent shifts guarding the compound against attack since the death of Master Howe. He felt especially concerned about Mistress Cooke, though he could not say why. Perhaps he felt pity for her. She seemed to be a kind woman. Her husband was a bastard who treated her horribly, though why John should care, he did not know. Cooke would not be the first man to mistreat his wife, nor the last.

He thought of his parents, and how much they loved one another. John hoped that one day, he would find a love as great as that of his parents, but alas, it had not yet come to pass. He was young, twenty-two. Certainly, there was time. Perhaps when he returned to England, he would find a wife.

Phillip Cooke stopped dead in his tracks. That young soldier, Bridger exited his cabin, promenading through the compound without a care, for all to see. He would kill the bloody scoundrel.

Cooke's eyes flew back to his cabin door, narrowing dangerously. She knew better. She belonged to him, bought and paid for. Her father saw to that. Cooke walked purposefully toward his home.

*   *   *

"Governor White, it has been more than a week with no reply from the savages. We must act. We cannot remain at their mercy until they decide to attack." Captain Stafford's determined voice filled the meeting of assistants in White's cabin.

White pulled up a wooden chair next to a dusty, wobbly table. "I do not wish to make a hasty decision," he responded evenly, then took a sip of small beer from a thick mug.

"Hasty? Sir, these savages are unpredictable. I say we advance on Desamunkepeuc and teach them a lesson. Only then will they understand that we will not tolerate the killing of our own. Have you forgotten the murder of an unarmed, innocent man? One of your assistants?"

"I am well aware of what transpired, Captain Stafford! A curse upon Master Lane for placing us in this predicament. It is his unnecessary, violent actions against the Indians for which they seek retribution upon us."

Stafford continued, undaunted. "Sir, there are women and children here. What of them? Would you place their lives in danger, your daughter's life, this very mission in danger? No sir, I believe we need to act. Now. We have given them time. Time is not a luxury we have if we are to survive this place."

Roger Baillie, White's second-in-command spoke up, "Governor, if they are not to meet with us to discuss peace, then they must mean to war against us. They could be planning our demise this very moment. We cannot stand here idly, waiting for them to attack."

"We must make a preemptive strike," Stafford added.

They took a vote. The assistants voiced their agreement with Stafford.

Governor White paused for another slow sip of small beer, thinking carefully about what Stafford said. He thought of his daughter, Eleanor, who was near to giving birth to her first child, his first grandchild. The food supply would not last. They needed to act. They would either receive cooperation from the local tribes, and live under a peace agreement, or make a show of force. The governor sighed heavily, as though breathing pained him. He closed his eyes. "Very well, Captain."

Chapter Six

Croatoan Island

August 1587

"**L**ook how he walks like a warrior." Ompeu sat watching his son toddle around the *yeehaukan*, little unsteady legs pumping as he ran toward his father, shrieking happily. Ompeu fell onto his back as his son jumped into his arms. Waacoh perched on his father's hard belly, baby toes digging in to stand. He held his son's hands, pulling him upward. The baby bounced on chubby legs, gurgled, and gave a baby screech of delight. Ompeu laughed. "Did you not hear his war cry?"

Sequan busied herself about the dwelling, packing for the journey to Roanoke Island. She paused to gaze at the two males she loved most in the world. She laughed too. "Like his father," she said. Waacoh had begun to walk and was a precious force to be reckoned with since he discovered his own mobility.

The baby inched up Ompeu's hard chest, babbling in baby words, and then proceeded to put part of his fist and his father's finger into his mouth. He drooled, then lost his balance and landed hard on his bottom, nearly knocking the breath from Ompeu's body. This caused peals of laughter to erupt from Waacoh, as he continued to bounce his bottom on Ompeu's stomach, enjoying the exaggerated reaction he received from his father.

"Ooof. Not like his father yet. But soon," Ompeu croaked. He sat up, putting his son on his lap. Ompeu became quiet and thoughtful, staring into the cooling ashes of the fire pit.

Sequan glanced at her husband. "You do not wish to go to the Island of Roanoke." It was not a question.

Waacoh hummed an intermittent baby chant as he gnawed on Ompeu's pearl beaded necklace. "I do not trust them," he answered evenly. "The *werowansa* says this is a meeting for peace. The English want no more killings." Waacoh grew tired of the pearl beads and stood up on Ompeu's lap, turning and wrapping little arms around his father's neck. Ompeu distracted him with his favorite rattle, seating his son in the vee of his legs once again.

"Will the Roanoacs agree?" she asked, as she fastened a deerskin bag.

Ompeu gazed at his son and stroked the child's fine, dark head with a gentle hand. "I do not know if the fire has gone out of their anger. We can hope," he replied, opening the baby's hand to remove a fistful of his long hair from his son's grasp. Somehow, Ompeu knew that the Roanoac war chief Nussacun, and Wanchese who had joined him, would continue to taunt the English. If there were peace, he doubted it would last.

That afternoon, a small band of Croatans embarked on the journey to Roanoke Island. Entire families traveled together by land and water. Among them were Ompeu, his wife, and their son. By evening, they were close to the village of Desamunkepeuc. The *werowansa* sent Paukunnawaw, Wobsacuck, and three others ahead to confer with the Roanoac about the impending meeting with the English. They returned with interesting news.

"They are gone," Paukunnawaw told the group. "They left everything, food, clothing, cooking pots. Their fields have not been tended."

"They left quickly," the *werowansa* surmised. "Perhaps they feared the English anger."

"Let us go to Desamunkepeuc," Sequan interjected. She adjusted the black baby sling on her shoulder that held her sleeping toddler on her back.

"No," Ompeu answered. "Let us continue on to Roanoke."

"We have need of the food and tools they left behind," Paukunnawaw said. "They have been gone for many days. If they left all behind, it is ours to take."

"What harm can there be?" asked Wobsacuck. "We will share what we take, offer gifts of food to the English to show our good faith."

The *werowansa* and the others decided to investigate the Roanoac village. If indeed it stood abandoned as they assumed, the Croatans would help themselves to abandoned crops and items they needed. They would share their spoils with the English.

When they arrived, it appeared as Paukunnawaw said. They commenced picking, packing and wrapping up corn, squashes, *uppowoc*, utensils, and medicinal herbs, tying them into packs. The hour grew late, and so they decided to remain in Desamunkepeuc until morning when they would continue to Roanoke Island, and the peace meeting with the English.

*   *   *

On the night of August 8, Governor White took the pinnace under the command of Captain Stafford and twenty-three men, heading for Desamunkepeuc under cover of darkness. Manteo guided them. The men were heavily armed. Pistols, calivers, with bows and arrows in reserve. They wore leather jerkins, wood shields, and body armor. Most were anxious. They landed and went ashore. They crept through the woods and surrounded the village. Captain Stafford gave the signal. Without warning, they burst upon the camp, finding some natives sitting around a fire, some sleeping.

It all happened so quickly, that later, Ompeu would hardly remember the moment as it occurred. He would always recall this night as though it were a terrible dream, wrapped in mist.

The English stormed the village, firing and drawing swords, startling the inhabitants. Some of them, still incoherent from sleep, scattered in confusion, hiding in the deep woods. People were screaming, running, falling. Light from the English torches seemed to swirl, appear and disappear at random.

The report of musket fire rang in Ompeu's ears. He could not find Sequan in the melee. She must have fled into the woods, the baby on her back in his sling. He could not tell friend from foe. The darkness and the smoke from the English weapons hindered his vision. He ran, his bow in hand, not knowing whom to shoot. Too many people, too much confusion, too much darkness, too much noise and thick smoke. In the turmoil, he recognized Captain Stafford, who lived among the Croatan the year before.

Ompeu caught sight of Sequan in the chaos. He saw her running to hide behind a tree. He saw a *Tosh shonte* with a musket, pointing it in her direction. Ompeu ran toward her, shouting her name. She did not seem to hear him. He called to the Englishmen. "*Matta*! No! Captain Stafford! Cap-tain Stafford!"

Somehow Stafford heard his name. At that moment it became apparent to him that this was not a group of warriors. One of the women carried an infant in a sling on her back. A young mother, not a fierce warrior. "Cease fire!" Stafford yelled.

Too late. Too late. The Englishman with the weapon fired. Bright sparks spewed from its end as it discharged.

"Stop! They are Croatan!" Manteo shouted.

Sequan shrieked, then fell to her knees, the impact of the fiery ball hitting her through the back. She tried to remove the sling with frantic fingers, her only thought to save her child. Shock and pain coursed through her. She could not feel her hands. They would not work quickly enough. Tears of pain and frustration came to her eyes, clouding her vision. Weakened, she fell to her side, a numbing coldness seeping into her bones. Her last thought was of Waacoh, who had not cried at all.

"Cease fire! Cease fire!" Stafford bellowed once again.

Gunfire fell silent. Smoke floated on the air along with the scent of gunpowder, and the distant voices and cries of people. Ompeu stood momentarily rooted to the spot where he watched Sequan fall before he could reach her. His eyes did not stray from her unmoving figure, curled around Waacoh beneath a tree. He could not move. He could not breathe. No. It could not be! In a dark, smoky haze Ompeu walked to where his wife and son lay, his gait unsteady. From far away, he thought he heard someone call his name. He thought he heard people moaning, weeping, talking. His bow slid from his fingers as he walked closer to his family. His body trembled. The baby did not cry.

Sinking to one knee beside her, he touched Sequan's shoulder, turning her. Sightless dark eyes stared at the night sky. His son looked as though he were sleeping. Dead. They were both dead.

*   *   *

Most of the Croatan were escorted to Roanoke, fed and ministered to by the English. This did not ease Governor White's anguish over the appalling incident.

"For Christ's love! What have we done?" White cried as he paced the floor of his quarters. Captain Stafford and a troubled Manteo were present.

"Governor, it was a grave error. A misfortune, a mistake. They will understand," Stafford said.

"A mistake?" White yelled. "The killing of innocents is not a mistake! I do not see how we can repair this. We have attacked the very people who were friendly to us." White turned to Manteo. "Your people!"

"Master White," Manteo said, anguish choking him. "We did not know they were my people. I am sad also. I must live with what I have done. I led you there!" Manteo lowered his head and shook it. "We thought they were Roanoac, not Croatan."

White sobered somewhat at Manteo's words. He softened his tone. "I cry your mercy, Manteo." White sighed and looked away. "I do not know what can be done now. But we shall do what we must. I hope we can rely upon your assistance."

"Yes, Governor," Manteo replied softly, uncertain there was any course he could take to set the situation right again. Never before had Manteo felt the pull of two different worlds upon his soul as he did now. He did not relish the feeling.

*   *   *

Elizabeth slept fitfully through the night, her entire body an aching, pulsing thing with no relief. She bled heavily, knowing she lost the babe. She would not tell Cooke. At daylight, her husband left the cottage without concern. Elizabeth wept silent tears, the salt stinging the cut on her bottom lip. She rolled slowly to her back, her muscles aching with the effort.

As she dozed upon the blankets, the high-pitched sound buzzed, then roared in her ears. It vibrated throughout her body, growing more intense, somehow easing her physical pain, numbing her. She felt a calming presence, then found herself kneeling in the sand on a dune overlooking the sea. A dizzying sensation filled her, as gusts of wind tore at her hair. She looked down to find herself completely naked. She covered her eyes against the harsh sand that blew in her face and stung her body. Overwhelming vertigo caused her to sway and sink to the ground. Landing sideways, she curled herself into a fetal position.

The wind slowed, and Elizabeth felt a warm, tender hand on her shoulder. Frozen with fear, she dared not look. The hand moved over her skin, yet it seemed to touch her everywhere at once, the tingling sensations causing shivers. She rolled to her back. There was no pain. She could not see him clearly, for he appeared shrouded in fog, yet somehow, she knew he reached for her.

"I need you. Come with me?" he whispered wordlessly. "Together we will fly."

His thoughts soothed her. Unafraid, she allowed him to help her to her feet. Feeling as though he wrapped his arms around her, Elizabeth closed her eyes, leaning against his strength feeling protected and loved. When she opened her eyes again, everything was gone. The dune, the trees, the ocean, everything. She saw nothing. Nothing but a soft, suffused light, yet everything existed in the light. He was with her, lending his calm strength. She felt warm and safe, as though they were both wrapped in the arms of something all encompassing, all knowing, all loving. Space and time did not exist. Somehow, she understood it all. Everything made sense. She saw a glimpse of the enormous macrocosm. She understood everything that had ever happened in her life. Everything was as it should be, and everything on earth was everything else.

She looked to the masculine figure in her arms and though she could not see him, she felt she knew him, knew everything about him, had always known. She knew his soul, and he knew hers.

Knocking. Someone pounded on the cottage door, calling her name. She must have dozed. She blinked, attempting to rise, her aching body reminding her that quick movement was impossible. She dressed, thinking the voice at the door belonged to Rose. The pounding continued as Elizabeth made her way slowly from the loft.

Rose had not seen Elizabeth at all yesterday or this morning. When she came to the cabin for her usual reading lesson the day before, she found Cooke standing in the doorframe. In his usual, brusque manner, he told her simply that Elizabeth was not well. Rose offered to help, but he blocked the entrance and ordered her to leave, and not return. She still had not seen Elizabeth yet today, and an unsettling feeling in the pit of her stomach caused her to worry.

She and Elizabeth devised a daily routine. The two women met in the early mornings, after Cooke left for the day. They would spend an hour or so practicing the letters and words, and then were ready to share in the work that needed to be done. Rose found that her time spent with Elizabeth helped to make the drudgery of chores much more pleasant.

Rose wished to speak to her friend of the tragedy that occurred at Desamunkepeuc. Certainly, Elizabeth would wish to be informed of this news, but she remained indoors during the entire visit from their Croatan neighbors. Rose found Elizabeth's absence unusual, and when she mentioned it to her husband Henry, he simply told her not to worry her pretty head over it. Something seemed amiss. Rose knew that Elizabeth would have her own opinions about the heartbreaking, dreadful incident.

She decided to attempt another early morning visit. She waited until she saw Cooke leave the cottage. Rose stepped up to the Cooke's cabin door and knocked. She waited a moment, then knocked again. "Elizabeth? 'Tis I, Rose." She waited. No response. "Elizabe…"

The door opened slowly, halfway. Elizabeth stood with her head lowered, her long, wavy unbound hair cascading forward, attempting to curtain her face. Rose glanced about quickly for any sign of Cooke, then took Elizabeth's hand, guided her inside and closed the door. She sat Elizabeth in a chair next to the table and knelt in front of her. Elizabeth winced slightly at the pain the movement caused, but remained silent, keeping her head low.

Rose glanced about the cabin. "Where is the boy, Phillip?"

It took a moment for Elizabeth to think. "Helping... some of the boys."

"Rose looked up into her friend's face, gingerly touching her chin, bringing it up. "How do ye endure it?" she whispered, unable to keep the anger from her voice. "How do ye endure that man?" She searched her friend's eyes, then reached up to brush the tawny curls of hair from her friend's face. One of Elizabeth's eyes swelled reddish-purple, the lid partially shut. The left side of her face was bruised, her bottom lip puffed and reddened from where one of her teeth cut into it on impact of the blows.

"Please," Elizabeth entreated softly. "Please tell no one."

Rose sighed and stood. She wanted to do something, anything. But she knew not what. She held no position to do or say anything. It invoked rising fury in Rose to know such helplessness. Feeling the need to act in some way, she removed her coif and untied a ribbon from her hair. She stood behind Elizabeth gathering the soft curls, smoothing out her hair, and quickly working a single fat braid down Elizabeth's back. "What was it this time?"

she asked, unable to keep the sting of sarcasm from her voice. "Did ye over boil his soup?"

Elizabeth shook her head. "Bridger." She looked over her shoulder at Rose and fidgeted with the folds of her skirt. "He brought water… and Cooke, he…."

"He thought ye were having a scandalous tryst, with a handsome, young soldier," Rose finished for her, tying off the braid. She paced about briefly in agitation. "Does Cooke know that Bridger also brings fresh water and wood to all the cabins? No. I suppose that's not entered his feeble mind." Rose tipped her head to the side, thoughtfully. "Though I daresay, Bridger has caused a scandalous thought to enter the minds of half the women in this fort." She crossed her arms over her chest and turned to her friend. "Including my own."

Elizabeth spared a small smile at her friend's attempt at humor. "Still, 'tis no cause for this," she gestured to her face, breathed deeply, and continued. "I thought arriving here would alleviate our circumstance. I had such hope. Though now Cooke is free of his debt, life here is not what he expected. He is a bitter, frustrated man."

"Ye be ill-used, and that is no excuse. It is sinful for a man to treat his wife in this way."

"There is no help for it," Elizabeth shrugged. "I must remain strong for my son." She stood up slowly, and turned away from her friend, wrapping her arms around herself. "Accept the things we cannot change, remember? I sometimes wonder if this is God's plan for me. To hide my education, to be shamed because I have opinions and thoughts and ideas of my own, simply because I am a woman born into a lower class and station that frowns upon me. I am an oddity." She turned back to Rose. "The truth is my husband is a man, unhappy with his lot in life. He blames me for his lack, fears me because I have my own mind, and so he seeks to control me in all things, in the only way he knows." Her lips trembled, and an unwanted tear slipped down her cheek. She brushed it away angrily. "It becomes harder for me not to believe that I am what he claims. Something bought and sold, worthless. 'Tis an effort to feel I am worth anything." She sniffled. "Yet each day, I fight. I will continue to fight, if for no one but my son. I will not surrender."

Rose took a tentative step toward her, uncertain Elizabeth would accept comfort. She opened her arms and Elizabeth stepped into them, weeping. "All things come to pass for a purpose," Rose soothed. "We may not understand in the moment. We may never understand the right and wrong of things."

They clung to one another for a time before Elizabeth whispered through tears. "I... I lost the babe."

"Nay." Rose stepped back, her ire growing more fiercely. "He beat it out of ye."

Elizabeth pressed her lips together not wishing to speak, for it was entirely possible, and she had already said too much. Cooke sent a few well-placed kicks to her mid-section. After he beat her, he dragged her to the loft, lifted her skirts, and forced himself between her legs. Elizabeth wiped at her eyes with her apron, gently dabbing the wounded eyelid. "My greatest shame is for my son to see me this way." She blew out a breath. "Unfortunately, it would not be the first time. I would not have him carry on the ways of his father when he is grown."

"I wish to do something, but I know not what," Rose whispered. "If there is anything ye need... help with chores, an ear to listen, anything, do not hesitate to call on me." Rose wished she had more to offer her friend.

Elizabeth clasped Rose's hands. She lowered her head and shook it. "Nay, you have done more for me than you know, my friend."

Rose left the cabin to seek out Manteo before he left to visit Croatoan. She would find a delicate way to ask him whether there were native remedies to alleviate pain for women who miscarried.

*   *   *

Manteo sat in his mother's *yeehaukan*. They were alone, but this was not a friendly visit between mother and son. This was a meeting of *werowansa* and English ambassador. The sacred pipe was filled and offered to the four directions, raised to the sky above and touched to the earth below. *Uppowoc* was cast into the fire.

"My son, you have come to discuss a matter of importance." She offered the pipe to Manteo, once again taking note of his shoulder-length hair and the English clothing he wore. Had they changed him so much?

Manteo smoked. His eyes moved over his mother's face. She appeared tired, as though she had aged much since he last lived with her. He shook his head sadly. "My mother, I come to you with a heavy heart. What happened at Desamunkepeuc was a terrible thing. My English brothers did not mean to attack our people. They believed a band of men, responsible for killing Master Howe occupied the village."

"Did not the white men say they wanted peace? Yet it is they who break this peace."

"My mother, why were the Croatan at Desamunkepeuc? Had the English known that our people were about, they would not have attacked. Master White and the English are very saddened. You and others should not have been there."

"Did we not ask for a badge so that we would be known as friendly to the *Tosh shonte*? They are quick to judge and kill without question."

"No badge would have saved the Croatan in the dark of night."

"No badge will save any of us from the *Tosh shonte*, it seems."

"This is not true. Our people must also share the blame. Had you not been at Desamunkepeuc, this would not have happened. We believed you were hostile Secotan and Roanoac. The English beg our people for forgiveness over this terrible mistake."

The *werowansa* remained silent for a long time. She saw for herself how distraught Governor White and the *Tosh shonte* appeared at Desamunkepeuc when they recognized their grave error. White expressed his anguish over the incident to her, and she believed him to be sincere. He invited them to come to Roanoke to care for the wounded. "I hear your words, my son. But I wonder at the honor of the English, who claim they want peace, yet do not act in a peaceful manner."

"The English do want peace. I know this in my heart. Please consider what I have said. The English are prepared to make amends. They have promised to assist the Croatan people in any way they can."

"I cannot control every warrior here. One you know well, may be eager to shed English blood. He has friends who would follow him. I will do what I can."

Manteo knew she spoke of Ompeu. At one time he and Ompeu were like brothers. Manteo taught him English words, but since his return to Croatoan Island, there was no opportunity to speak with him. He hoped Ompeu would not act impulsively or try to seek his revenge upon the English for the loss of his wife and child.

"What of Towaye? Why has he not returned to us?" she asked.

"Towaye's heart is good," Manteo said. "He is lost in between worlds, and so he lives apart. He will soon find his way again. His mother understands this."

The *werowansa* tapped the *uppowoc* from the pipe, tossing the remainder into the fire. Manteo rose to leave. "Manteo," she called to her son, using the name he chose for himself. He turned expectant eyes toward his mother. "You have been away a long time," she said. "You are also in between worlds. Perhaps you should spend time with your people."

He could not disagree with her assessment. "*Kupi, nek*," he affirmed, and left the *yeehaukan*.

*   *   *

Ompeu had not taken food or water in days. He wore no clothing. He had not slept. On this, the fourth morning, he knelt on the sacred dune, overlooking the sea. For four days he chanted. He prayed. He slashed himself in anguished mourning and watched his blood trickle and drip into the sand.

Why? Why did this happen? All things come to pass for a purpose. It seemed there was no purpose in this loss and suffering. Ompeu struggled to rise on unsteady legs, lifting his arms to the morning sky. Seabirds squawked and flew overhead, unconcerned by his presence. The intermittent roar of the surf filled his ears as he shouted his prayers to the skies until his voice left him. He grew dizzy. The world spun around him.

He thought he heard a voice on the wind. Turning toward it, he staggered through the sand, deeper into the trees behind him. He needed water and sleep, but more than that he needed answers, and he prayed that *Kiwasa* would grant him a blessing. He stumbled, falling against a tree. He slid down its length, the rough bark scratching his skin. He did not feel it. Ompeu fell to his side, and sleep overcame him. He felt the calming presence of a woman in his dreams.

When he awoke, the sun had moved across the sky, dusk settling upon the island. He heard the voice again, muffled and distant. A wind stirred. Ompeu's hand ran over the tree trunk seeking purchase. He braced himself against it, leaning upon it to give him the strength to stand upright, his palms pressed against the tree for support.

A cool breeze swept passed him, then another, stronger, causing him to shiver. The wind kicked up violently. It tore at his hair. Ompeu squeezed his eyes shut and braced himself, turning his face away from the blast of air. He clung to the tree with the strength he had left. The wind stopped.

"*She waits for you,*" a voice from his dreams said. Did the wind speak to him?

It blew again more gently this time, caressing him like a lover. Ompeu sucked air into his lungs, moved the hair from his eyes and turned his head in the direction from which the wind had come.

A shock coursed through him; for a doe stepped into his line of sight. She drew closer, taking tentative steps toward him. She drifted close enough to touch, showing no fear of him. Instead, her beautiful doe eyes watched him curiously. Gradually, Ompeu's breathing slowed, becoming even and relaxed, her presence seeming to create an odd calm that permeated him, easing his heart. The sense of peace radiated throughout his entire being, taking away his anguish and pain. He lifted his arm slowly, reaching for her, thinking she would dart away if he tried to touch her. She did not. She waited silent and still, and the moment his fingers touched gently upon her soft fur, Ompeu swayed on his feet, collapsed and sank into oblivion.

Ompeu's entire being became infused; bathed in a soft, calming warmth. She came to him, as solid as the earth he lay upon. He felt her essence surround him and seep into his soul. Unable to move, Ompeu let her in, surrendering himself to her, feeling a oneness with her that went beyond ecstasy, beyond words. She held him, and soothed him, swirling around him, gently touching the parts of his soul that no one had ever touched. She called to him wordlessly in the euphoric language that only the soul understood, and he answered, communicating the complete depths of all his anguish, his fears, and his desires. Together they soared over the sacred dune clinging to one another tightly.

Ompeu slept, holding the woman close to him in the sweetest of dreams.

Chapter Seven

"How long?" A groggy, light-headed Ompeu asked Poussu. He found himself on his own sleeping pallet. His fingers splayed, brushing against the soft bearskin beneath him. He saw that his wounds were dressed.

"Your friend Paukunnawaw searched for you. He brought you home," she answered somberly. "You have slept most of the day."

His memory fogged. He vaguely recalled seeing Paukunnawaw. Ompeu noted that Poussu cut her hair in mourning. Her dark hair was cropped at a sharp angle, reaching her chin. He noticed the sparse strands of white in her hair for the first time. She knelt next to him and handed him a cup. He struggled to sit, but he managed. Ompeu drank the strong medicinal tea, and gave the cup back to Poussu, his hand unsteady.

She offered him a wooden bowl, filled with a corn and squash soup she prepared especially for him. It was thin and bland so that it would not upset his stomach. He ate slowly, and just enough to fill the emptiness without causing his stomach to reject the food. Placing the bowl down, he lifted his head to survey the *yeehaukan*. It looked the same as when he was in it last, playing with his son while Sequan packed. Pain stabbed at his heart, and it became an effort to sit up. He lie back again, staring at the designs painted on the woven mats that served as ceiling and walls. The smoke flap was open. He thought it to be early evening, yet the village was oddly quiet. Poussu watched him, divining his thoughts.

"Perhaps you should speak to our holy man," she suggested quietly.

"*Matta*," he answered simply, his voice gravelly from overuse.

"You may wish to ask him of your vision, and your dreams."

"I did not dream." Ompeu turned his head to look at her, then wondered. "Did I speak as I slept?"

"You spoke of a doe."

Ompeu sat up quickly, too quickly. It made his head throb with pain. "Did I speak of anything else?"

Poussu sat back, surprised by his reaction at the mention of the doe. "You spoke of a wolf."

Ompeu rubbed his eyes with the heels of his hands, as though trying to clear the images in his mind. Poussu moved to take one of his hands away from his face, to study him. She raised him as her son from the time he was eight winters. She loved him as any mother would love a son born of her body. Now they were only two. All were gone from her, including Towaye who had not chosen to return to his family. All but Ompeu remained.

She held his hand. He looked tired and worn. Too young to look this way. "You do not remember?" she asked delicately, her dark eyes shining with unshed tears.

Ompeu thought of the first time he dreamed of the doe, and how the dream ended. This time, he did not remember. He did not know if the dream unfolded the same. "No," he replied. "I do not."

"You must heed the vision that has been given to you. The doe will come to you again, and when she next appears, you will summon the vision to mind." Poussu released his hand and sat back on her heels. "I wish my son to be well again in all ways so that he can care for us," her voice broke with emotion. "You are needed by your people," she said softly, wiping at her eyes. "Now that the *Tosh shonte* have returned, you are needed more than ever."

Ompeu studied her and wondered at her strength. She survived a husband and two children, and she cared for him as though he were her own son. Her fortitude shamed him. Somehow, she managed to go on living. Somehow, he would too.

       *   *   *

On August 18, 1587, the colonists had reason to celebrate. Eleanor Dare, daughter of Governor White, gave birth to a baby girl. They named her Virginia, in honor of the Virgin Queen, and of the land they inhabited. She was the first known English child to be born in the New World.

In the month the colonists spent on the island, Simao Fernandes waited for all the supplies and belongings to be transported to the settlement. He used this extra time to clean and repair the ships. He grew impatient to be away, and by month's end, Fernandes would wait no longer. Before the ships departed, White's assistants urged him to return to England for more supplies.

"I do not think it wise that I leave the settlement at this time," White said.

"Governor, who better than you? You have more influence at court than any of us. Sir Ralegh can certainly acquire funds from the investors. You can return here in a matter of months," new father Ananias Dare said.

"And if there is further trouble with the Indians?" White asked.

"Possible trouble with them is exactly why you should return. In the event there are poor relations, we would not have to rely so heavily upon their good will.

We would care for, and feed ourselves without their assistance," Roger Bailie added.

White could not help but feel that the colonists, thinking he was not an acceptable leader, simply desired him gone. True, he bungled the incident involving the Croatans, and his lack of disciplinary action against Fernandes brought concern. A new settlement needed a strong hand to govern it. His indecision and vacillation were not valuable traits for the success of a colony. But his governorship remained intact, and he would be the one to decide. The meeting continued, and White could see that every one of his seven assistants wanted him to return to England. Two days later, they presented him with a signed petition.

In order to prevent the same mystery and confusion they encountered when trying to find Grenville's men, the assistants devised a signal for the governor. In the event the colony should be evacuated or moved, they were to carve the name of their destination into a fence post or tree near the fort. If they left the settlement under duress, they were to carve a Maltese cross above the name of their destination.

Governor White dawdled over his good-byes. He detested the idea of leaving his daughter and new grandchild. He needed assurances that his belongings would be kept safe in his trunk, buried in a location that only he and the assistants knew.

On August 27, White sailed back to England. In his care, were letters and tokens the colonists sent with him for their families back home.

A sense of finality and loss coiled in Elizabeth's chest. The ships were the last reminder of home. As she watched them sail away, uncertainty crept into her expression. Biting her lip, she turned away. At this moment, she would not know how true her thoughts were, for neither she nor any of the Roanoke colonists would see England, or Governor White again.

Chapter Eight

A s the months wore on, life in the colony became routine, but not settled. Seven assistants to Governor White were left in charge, including his son-in-law, Ananias Dare. The group met to discuss issues and concerns of the colonists, settle disputes, and worry over the dwindling supplies. They decided to strictly ration not only their food stores, but musket powder and shot. Though the colonists found the water in the new world suitable for drinking, they drank small beer, or ale, as was their custom. With little rainfall, the fresh water supply had become a problem as well. This also meant that the crop yield would be low. The natives had little to spare. The women planted small gardens, but as it was late in the year, they produced little. Since they were unable to procure more livestock in their earlier stopover in the Caribbean, they relied on meat the hunting parties could provide, such as squirrels, conies, and deer.

Some discussed splitting the colony, with the majority moving on to the Chesapeake Bay area as was originally intended. Those who remained would await Governor White's return, and then join the others at Chesapeake with supplies and new colonists.

Manteo divided his time between the Roanoke settlement and his own people during the winter months. After the incident at Desamunkepeuc, the English bestowed the title of Lord of Roanoke upon him and baptized him as a Christian of their Protestant faith.

In England, Manteo saw things beyond his imagination. There were countless people, crowded streets, buildings and structures he had never seen before. There were castles, and street merchants, and horses. He and Wanchese were presented at court to Queen Elizabeth. Manteo wished to share all he knew with his people. He wished to be the instrument that joined the two groups, and to act as a bridge between cultures.

Somehow, it had not turned out as he expected. Though he lived among them, helped them, was Christianized, and made a lord, Manteo knew the English did not consider him a true equal. While there were many things to admire about the English, when in London, he saw despair and squalor. He and Wanchese were put on display; gawked at, laughed at, they were the topic of curious discussion. Manteo chose to rise above, to see himself as an ambassador of his people and ignore the discomfort. He vowed to learn all he could and bring this knowledge to his people. Wanchese was insulted.

Manteo was disturbed by the apparent rejection of his friend, Ompeu. It weighed heavily on his mind since he returned to his homeland. He recalled Ompeu's desire to learn about the English after the first voyage. He listened to Manteo's stories and wished to learn English words. Manteo, though still a student himself, taught Ompeu what he knew.

It could be delayed no longer. Until now, Ompeu took no action against the English, but Manteo needed to speak to his friend.

Since the killings at Desamunkepeuc, Ompeu kept his own council. He found he preferred solitude above all else and would often disappear for days. Poussu, as well as Ompeu's friends worried over him, but hoped that in time he would heal. He gave most of his possessions away. He burned anything belonging to his dead wife and child, praying over the smoldering objects as he did so. He hunted alone, bringing game and fish for those who were most in need.

Manteo found himself at Poussu's *yeehaukan*, where she sat in front, pounding and grinding dried *pogatowr* on a flat grinding stone. He watched her for a few moments, as she crushed the colorful grains into a coarse flour.

Without looking up, she said, "You will not find your friend here." She continued to crush a few errant kernels, then looked up at Manteo. Squinting, she shaded her eyes against the autumn sun. "He goes to the sacred dune. Perhaps you will find him there."

"Thank you, Mother," Manteo said, addressing her in the way of the People to show respect.

Manteo followed a worn wooded path away from the village, hoping to have an opportunity to speak to his friend. He walked for some time until he heard a rustling noise. He turned. Ompeu emerged from the brush behind him.

"You have gone soft living among the *Tosh shonte*. Were I an enemy, you would be dead," Ompeu said, his expression unreadable. "I had to make a big noise for you."

Manteo released a breath. "My brother. We must speak."

"What do you wish to say to me?" Ompeu asked suspiciously, noting that Manteo had traded his English clothing for buckskins.

"Come, let us smoke the pipe."

The pipe was sacred, and words spoken in its presence were sacred as well. Ompeu nodded. He wondered when Manteo would seek him out to speak of what occurred at Desamunkepeuc. "As you wish," Ompeu replied, and the two walked toward the village.

They sat in Ompeu's dwelling and after the ceremonial lighting and presentation of the pipe to the four directions, the sky above, and earth below, Ompeu spoke. "I wait for Manteo to speak."

Manteo took note of the new scars etched into Ompeu's forearms. "My heart is saddened at your loss. I remember the woman who was your wife. A good woman." Speaking the name of one recently dead was frowned upon, for to do so would disturb their soul, or call their spirit back to earth.

Ompeu nodded once.

"I am also deeply saddened by the loss of your son," Manteo continued.

Ompeu remained silent, waiting.

"I know you have anger in your heart toward the English. You must believe me when I say that what happened at Desamunkepeuc was a terrible accident. The English had no desire to attack Croatans." Manteo passed the pipe to his friend and waited for him to speak.

"It may be as you say," replied Ompeu. "But it changes nothing. Croatan blood has been shed. Would the English be so understanding if we were to attack them, even in error? No. I do not believe they would. Perhaps we shall see what they do when English blood is shed."

"This you must not do my brother. Where will the killing end? If you kill English, they will kill more Croatan. It will not stop until the last man is left. Is this what you wish?"

"If the last man is Croatan, then yes. My family must be avenged. Where is my recompense?"

Manteo thought to try another tactic. "Ompeu these English are good people."

"Good people would not have killed my wife and child. If the *Tosh shonte* have such love for us, why do they greet us with weapons drawn?"

Manteo skirted the question and asked one of his own. "Have you never killed a man? To defend your home, your family, your people? These men thought they were doing the same. Defending their families from the Roanoac and Secotan. To avenge the death of one of their men, and to show their enemies that they are not weak." Manteo's voice softened. "Ompeu, you must know there are good and bad in all men. It is the same for the English."

Ompeu remained unconvinced. "The English are afforded vengeance, yet I am not? I understand, Manteo. But it does not soften my anger against them."

"I ask that you do not continue the bloodshed. There has been enough."

"If a *Tosh shonte* walked into our village this moment, he would be a dead man."

Manteo lowered his head and gazed into the glowing embers of the fire pit between them. He did not know what else to say. His heart was torn, his identity stretched beyond what most could endure. He wondered whether he was Croatan or Englishman. He was both, and neither. He hoped he would never be forced to make the choice. Perhaps in time, Ompeu's anger and pain would be eased. It was all he could hope for at this moment. "Please consider my words, Ompeu. You are an honorable man. You will do what is right."

"What are you? Croatan, or *Tosh shonte?*"

Manteo lifted his eyes to Ompeu's wondering how the other man could voice his recent thought. "I am simply a man. One who walks between worlds. Moving among villages of Ossomocomuck for the benefit of all people, English and Croatan." He purposely chose the name Manteo, in order to have the strength of the *mantóac*. He was a mediator, a difficult position he did not choose, but one he accepted.

"I do not envy you, my friend. You must take care not to lose yourself. One day you will not know which side is yours," Ompeu forewarned.

With that statement, the discussion ended. Before he left the *yeehaukan*, Manteo turned to his friend and spoke in English. "Do you recall the *Tosh shonte* words?"

Ompeu's eyes narrowed with disdain. He replied with a single English word. "Yes."

*　　*　　*

All were concerned that Governor White had not returned. Over the winter of 1587 the assistants bickered over governance of the colony as many of the settlement's men grew insolent and disorderly. Several men deserted, taking one of the longboats. They had stolen a large quantity of food before they departed and were not seen or heard from again. The keeper of the store and the master of victuals complained to the assistants, demanding action. Now armed guards stood vigil over the food stores as well as the armory. The assistants argued that the only way to keep strict order was through fear. They would make examples of anyone who disobeyed orders by striking quickly and without mercy. Anyone caught stealing from the storehouse or the gardens, anyone caught deserting, or running away to seek shelter among the native peoples, did so on pain of death.

Fights broke out among the colonists frequently. Most rebelled against the harsh rules set by the assistants, who lashed out from a place of weakness fearing the loss of total control. Many of the men imbibed in a strong brew they made from corn mash. On ration days, they received increasingly smaller quantities to eat, which caused further disputes among those in the ration lines.

Since they made enemies of most of the neighboring tribes, the colonists became fearful and paranoid, untrusting of any of the friendly natives who may have offered food, even Manteo's people, the Croatan. As for Manteo, he continued to divide his time among the colonists and his people, traveling to neighboring villages, working tirelessly to maintain the thin shred of peace. He knew his position was a tenuous one, doubting that neither the English, nor the native peoples trusted him completely.

Emme Merriwerth, the Dare's indentured servant, and Alice Chapman joined Rose for reading lessons. Mostly, they hid away from the growing ugliness they witnessed with greater frequency. On certain mornings, after some of the men were gone to hunt, or working in the compound, the four women sat around the firelight and warmth the hearth provided in Elizabeth's cabin. Usually, they practiced reading and writing, at times they bade Elizabeth read to them from her Bible or from a book of Aesop's Fables, or from her collection of poetry. It was a small book she hid away that passed from person to person in England years prior to their departure.

Her few books and writing slate were treasures she hid from her husband, whom she had detached from so completely, that he was merely another presence in the cabin. He grew ever more irresponsible and unsympathetic, often spending his evenings drinking with a few men outside the brewhouse, or in their cabin, where they talked of their exploits back home, and lamented their decision to come to Roanoke. Whenever men came to their cottage, Elizabeth went to the loft, feigning sleep. She heard bits of her husband's conversation with someone regarding the supply of corn, and how he knew a way to remedy the problem. Cooke became involved in numerous quarrels and spent time locked up in the gaol until he sobered, and disputes were settled. She feared he would cross some unimaginable line and doom his entire family.

The time she spent in shared interest with friends reading and helping them to learn lent her strength, for she felt valued for her abilities, rather than shamed. This precious time became an escape from the bubbling turmoil around them, the bitter cold outside, and the frequent pangs of hunger. It kept her grounded with a sense of normality.

> *"The shepherd swains shall dance and sing*
> *For thy delight, each May-morning:*
> *If these delights thy mind may move,*
> *Then live with me and be my love..."*

Elizabeth finished the poem, and closed the thin, worn collection, tying it with string.

"So lovely," Emme sighed dreamily, then looked away sadly, staring off into some distant place and time. "*'Come live with me and be my love, and we will all the pleasures prove','* She quoted the line that seemed to affect her most deeply.

"'Tis most favorable," Rose agreed.

"I cannot disagree," Alice murmured. "The work is lovely."

The women were silent, basking in the afterglow of the beautiful love words of the poem, when they heard a commotion and shouting outdoors. Elizabeth rose from her chair to return her books to their hiding place, while the other women grabbed up their wraps and capes, scurrying to the front door, opening it, and spilling out of the cabin. The ice and snow-covered ground crunched with every hurried step. Under a gray morning sky, a crowd gathered near the armory.

"What is happening?" Elizabeth asked a passing soldier as the women lifted skirts, trotting toward the crowd.

"What are ye women staring at? Get yerselves home. There's trouble. The pinnace has been stolen in the night. Damned savages." His words were slurred, indicating his state of intoxication.

Gasps of surprise from the women followed. "How will we sail onto Chesapeake?"

"No Indian would do this," Emme whispered, her blue eyes searching the crowd of faces, as though she would find natives among them.

"Why should the pinnace be stolen?" Alice Chapman asked Elizabeth, giving half of her attention to the gathering of people.

"I say, 'twas the savages that made off with our pinnace in the night!" Cooke's voice boomed over the others, his breath misting the cold air.

Elizabeth wove her way through the milling crowd toward her husband as he continued to incite the captive audience. She clasped the ends of her cape against her throat, shivering. "'Twas no savages that stole the pinnace," Elizabeth said, once she reached him. "They have their own vessels, much quicker and smaller. I daresay they know not how to navigate a small English ship. 'Tis our own Englishmen that would be the thieves. They're off to steal corn from the Indians." Elizabeth's eyes dared her husband to deny it. Several people spoke among themselves, debating the truth of her words.

"Take account of the men that remain," said assistant, Roger Bailie, who arrived upon the scene. "We shall see who is missing."

"'Tis the damned savages, I say!" Cooke shouted. "The guard witnessed the theft!" All the people present spoke, murmuring among themselves, some turning suspicious glares to Cooke, who removed his hat and used it as a prop, his hands outstretched in appeal. "My wife knows not of what she speaks. I will deal with her in due course." Blue eyes flashed in anger at his wife, his expression murderous. How dare she speak to him thusly, calling him a liar, in full view of everyone? Had she lost all sense? It was inconceivable to him that she would bear witness against him. He did not expect this. This foul land poisoned her mind, as it had done to them all. "Mind yer words, woman," he warned.

She felt a cool hand take hers and squeeze gently. It was Rose, standing beside her, offering her courage. Elizabeth's voice grew stronger, filled with conviction. "Nay. I heard you speaking of it to someone. The supplies are low. There is not enough to eat, nor to brew the strong drink you men have come to favor. 'The Indians have grain in abundance'. Is it not true those words came from your lips?"

More chatter and debate sounded from the crowd. "What do ye know of this, Cooke?" someone shouted. Cooke had already earned a tarnished reputation among them. Whatever he claimed would be closely scrutinized.

"Get thee back to the cottage," Cooke ordered, low and menacing.

"I will not," Elizabeth countered. Though her heart pounded wildly in her breast, she was unafraid. This incident was an injustice she would not abide. "You would blame the Indians, incite more bloodshed, all for the theft of their corn for your precious brew, while we grow thin from hunger. The drought has left all with little corn, yet you would allow these people to believe the tribes possess great stores of it."

"Obey me and get thee home!"

"Cooke! That will be enough. We shall investigate this matter, at once," Ananias Dare said. "Escort Cooke to the Governor's quarters, for questioning. Guard him and be certain he's made comfortable."

John Bridger and another soldier quickly divested Cooke of his weapons and led him away.

He struggled against their hold. "You've lost your sense, woman! Elizabeth! Fie on thee! I shall kill ye for this!"

"You will do no such thing," Bridger said, as he helped lead Cooke away.

Ananias Dare turned to Elizabeth. "My thanks, Mistress Cooke. I will call upon you if further questions arise."

Elizabeth nodded her assent. She felt the chill of winter air as she watched the crowd disperse.

"She spoke against her husband. She must wish to be rid of him," someone cackled.

"Aye, would not be trusting her to prepare me victuals," said another.

"But what if she speaks true?"

Elizabeth covered her face as the voices faded. She and Rose turned away and walked back to her cabin. "What have I done?" Elizabeth trembled, exhilarated that she spoke out against the men responsible for the theft of the pinnace in front of the entire colony, yet terrified at the consequences she might face for doing so. He was her husband. Had she taken the right course in exposing his treachery? Had she sealed her own fate as well?

"Ye did no wrong," Rose answered. "Why did ye not speak of this?"

"I was uncertain. I heard whisperings and pieces of conversation. But now that the pinnace is gone, it all corresponds logically."

Elizabeth visited Cooke once during his sequester in the Governor's quarters. He was kept in a smaller room with a blanket on the floor for a bed. A wooden table and two chairs were placed in the room for her visit. They went unused. Cooke remained under guard by an armed soldier. When she entered, they each silently appraised one another. Cooke's eyes betrayed the animosity he felt toward his wife.

"Why did ye do it?" he asked, unable to keep the venom from his voice. Elizabeth noted his disheveled appearance. Though he did not have an opportunity to drink the corn mash brew, his blue eyes remained bloodshot and tired. "They shall hang me. Did ye not realize?" he demanded. Fists clenched at his sides, his face was a glowering mask of rage.

"Why did you do it?" she countered quietly. "Your actions and those of your companions have placed us all in danger."

Cooke eyed her. A muscle ticked in his jaw. She was too outspoken for his liking, but this wretched country made her brash and disrespectful. He diverted his gaze.

"What did you expect the outcome of your actions to be?" she continued. "That no one would notice our men missing along with an entire large boat? That anyone would believe the story about Indians stealing it?"

Cooke bowed his head, shaking it, sardonic laughter escaping him. "I suppose conspiring while intoxicated is never a good idea." He grew silent. His expression softened. Though it cost him to tell her the truth, he gave it to her. "'Twas a foolish thing. Desperation drove us." His eyes found hers again. "Would not be the first time I've done something foolish, but it *will* be the last. Meeting your father. Believing his schemes. Aye, we were a pair. Would have made something of myself, except he burdened me with a girl, thinking that sufficed as payment enough for what I lost."

Her mind refused to register the significance of his words, but they closed like a fist around her heart. She clasped the edges of her cape, gathering them. That is all she ever was to him. A burden, nothing more. An excuse. A reason why he could not better himself. She had been and unwanted, unasked for responsibility. Her eyes glittered with unshed tears. "I am truly sorry," was all she could manage before she turned to exit the room.

"Elizabeth," he called after her. When she looked over her shoulder, he continued. "If ye can find it in your heart, pray for my soul."

Eight men including Cooke devised the impulsive plan to sail the pinnace in search of native villages with the intent to steal corn. Since most of the tribes moved their villages inland during the winter months, the men were not as successful as they hoped. When the pinnace returned two weeks later, all involved were charged with desertion, treason, and insurrection. They were all hanged, including Cooke for his role as a conspirator.

Elizabeth wept in the silence of her cabin that night while her son slept, a maelstrom of conflicting emotions swirling in her mind. She cursed her situation and wished she had not come to this place. She prayed for her husband and hoped that while he had not found peace in life, that perhaps he would find it in death. It was this cursed land. She witnessed the effect this environment had on other men. The effect it had on them all. It stripped them of civility and everything that made them staunchly English.

Phillip Cooke drifted, a lost soul, and a part of her felt a sadness for him. She had been married off to a man not unlike her father. A dreamer, nay, a schemer more the like. Always searching for the next money-making, under-handed venture.

Her mind filled with sour thoughts. Should she have remained quiet? Had she sealed her husband's fate?

Had she purposely exposed him out of spite? The questions plagued her, for a small part of her could not help but feel a guilty sense of relief at his passing and she felt little remorse at exposing his scheme. His actions were reprehensible. With the colony in disorder, and on the verge of starvation, he brought this fate upon himself. He became a vile, scheming drunkard. He knew the consequences his actions would bring. One element was certain. She would never marry again. At the age of twenty-six, she would be content to remain a widow. She would never have to give her life over to caring, cooking, cleaning, or enduring the intimate attentions of a husband again. She would not miss any of it. Perhaps this land had taken her civility as well. Perhaps she had become as vile as her husband. The disturbing possibility was sobering.

Her son would not speak of his father, or of his death. He knew his father did something terribly wrong, but whatever his thoughts were, the boy kept them to himself and no amount of gentle prodding from Elizabeth could get him to speak of it. Once again, he became fearful and withdrawn. As her mind searched for ways to help her son, she would have to endure and do what was needed for them to survive. If for no one else, she would be strong for her child. Were it not for her son, Elizabeth doubted she would have the will to carry on. He was her reason for living.

Still, Governor White did not return. Some colonists wondered if Spain won the war at sea, and now ruled over England. Others theorized that perhaps a great plague swept through their homeland. If Governor White died, there were others who would surely send for them or send ships with supplies and new colonists. Had Master Ralegh forgotten them? No one wished to reason that they were abandoned by their own countrymen, though with every passing day, this sentiment grew. It pained them to consider that English men and women were expendable.

If Governor White did not arrive soon, they would all be dead by spring. There were mysterious offerings of fresh meat left on the Dare's doorstep throughout the winter. No one knew who left these gifts, or when. Were it not for this, and the occasional visits from Manteo and their Croatan friends, who supplied baskets of acorns, walnuts, and fish; Elizabeth felt certain they would not live to see the new year.

More than half of the remaining colonists decided to take matters into their own hands. When the winter weather broke toward the end of March, they would sail the full-rigged pinnace and travel onto the Chesapeake Bay. They took minimal food and supplies, reasoning that there would be time for planting. They would ration the rest. Though saddened to see some of her friends leave, Elizabeth refused to join them. She chose to wait for Governor White and return to England with her son, praying that one of her brothers in London would be charitable, perhaps take her in.

Since the death of her husband, Elizabeth's dreams became more frequent, though she hardly remembered them. The presence in her dreams spoke to her, but she never recalled his words. Nearly every night she fought the high-pitched hum and the vibrations that coursed through her body, paralyzing her.

"I am here," a soft, masculine voice whispered in Elizabeth's head.

"Why do you come? Leave me!"

His essence swirled around her. "Do not be afraid."

"I am not afraid. Ghost!"

"I am no ghost. I am a part of you." He moved his being through hers, to prove his point.

"Leave me here to die," she pleaded. "I would welcome death. We will all die here soon."

His vaporous being settled above her. "You will not die."

Elizabeth felt his tingling weight pressing above her. Somehow, she knew he sensed her despair. She knew he felt the same.

"You will not die. You will be strong again. Soon you will awaken. You will know who I am."

Upon awakening, she tried to capture elusive pieces of the dream, but always they escaped her.

At the end of April 1588, natives attacked the Roanoke fort. Led by Nussacun and Wanchese, this mixed force of Secotan and Roanoac destroyed most of the few crops the colonists managed to plant with the help of their friend Manteo. Seven men of the settlement were killed, before small canon fire frightened the hostile warriors away.

Manteo received word of the impending attack from his friend Towaye. "The English are already near dead," he said, worriedly. "I have been watching them. Their numbers are depleted. They are hungry, and so I have left food for them without their knowledge. There is no honor in attacking them." By the time Towaye spoke to him, however, it was too late to warn his English friends. "There is something more you should know," Towaye hesitated, then added somberly, "Ompeu is with them."

Manteo made it his mission to bring Towaye back to his people, and to spend time with his friend, Ompeu. Towaye returned as his joyous mother predicted. For Ompeu the circumstances were different. Manteo felt partially responsible for what happened at Desamunkepeuc, and in his heart he wished to make amends. He, along with Poussu and other friends, worked to keep Ompeu from joining Nussacun, but apparently had failed.

"So that is where he goes when he disappears, away from our village," Manteo mused aloud.

Towaye merely nodded in affirmation.

Chapter Nine

May 1588

In the Flower Moon, what the English called early May, Manteo shouted a greeting upon entering the opened compound gates of the Roanoke settlement. Towaye joined him, insisting upon accompanying him to the fort. Manteo thought to question it but accepted his companionship. The fort loomed eerily quiet. He strode toward the storage shed and the armory, peering inside through the wooden slats. Both were sparse with supplies. Manteo noted that some buildings were dismantled, and a wood barricade erected.

"Halloo! It is I, Manteo!" He called out again as he walked through what appeared to be an empty, desolate fort. The sun was high. The weather was fair. People should be out and about. He noted small gardens near some of the cabins but with little rain, they appeared pitiful. He turned in a slow circle, searching for any sign of life, while Towaye investigated the boarded-up brewhouse and several of the closest cabins. When Manteo looked his way, Towaye shook his head.

"Manteo?"

Manteo and Towaye turned toward the sound of the voice. Master Dare emerged, wielding an iron handled rapier in one hand, and a matchlock musket in the other. John Bridger appeared at his side, weapons drawn. Recognizing their friend, Dare sheathed his sword. A wan smile of relief appeared on his lips, though dark smudges of exhaustion lay under his eyes. Bridger followed suit replacing his weapons, also greatly relieved.

Before they could speak, a cry of recognition startled the four men, as Emme threw open a cottage door from the far side of the compound. She lifted her skirts, running toward them, her golden curls flying behind her. "Towaye! Towaye!" she cried.

Manteo, Master Dare, and John Bridger watched in disbelief as Emme flew into Towaye's waiting arms. "I thought ye were dead," she sobbed into his buckskin tunic.

His arms enfolded her, and he spoke softly in her ear. Emme sniffled and collected herself, as though she realized she had broken a strict conventional rule. She moved slightly apart from him, and brushed away her tears, dipping in a slight curtsy. "Forgive me Master Dare," she said. "He… he is my friend."

"'Tis all right, child," Dare said, curious about what he witnessed, but also distracted as he noted that the remaining colonists emerged from their cottages.

Manteo spoke to Towaye in their native tongue, as others approached. "This is why you went away?" He asked, indicating Emme with a lift of his chin.

"*Kupi*," Towaye answered, suddenly uncomfortable. He needed time away to mourn his sister and to sort out his feelings toward the English and particularly, for Emme. He wanted no trouble with the English. He understood that they unjustly looked upon the People as inferior, considering them of the meaner sort. They thought nothing if some of their men took native women to their beds, but flipped around, well, it seemed forbidden. He wanted to spare Emme from censure and possible punishment from her people, but also, to spare himself from the torture of being near her, yet unable to have her. Seeing her again brought a shock to his system. The situation here was worse than he imagined.

"And this is why you have returned?" Manteo wondered how he had not known of what simmered between Emme and Towaye; a friendship that must have begun in secret back in England.

"*Kupi*," Towaye said again. "Mostly. My sister is gone from us. My mother did not need to mourn another child. I came back for my mother, my people, yes, but for Emme as well. The loss of my sister lay heavy on my heart. I did not wish to lose another that I love. It is a story for another time, my friend," he finished, wishing to avoid further explanations. Towaye and Emme shared a look that bespoke their great fondness for one another. She was too thin, her angelic face too wan and pale, but still she was beautiful to him.

Manteo returned his attention to Master Dare and the others who gathered, switching to English words. "How many are here?"

"We are but twenty and two," Dare answered, deeply saddened at the dwindled number. "There were more of us, but, about seventy or so took the pinnace and sailed onto Chesapeake. A few... we lost. We wished to wait for Governor White."

"Master Dare, all of you must come with me, and with Towaye. Come with us. We will take you to my people. You will live with us on Croatoan. You will be welcomed."

Ananias Dare turned tired, questioning eyes toward the bedraggled group. He still held out hope that Governor White, or more English ships would come.

"Not safe here," Manteo urged. Twenty-two remaining, with women and children among them was suicide. There would be no way these people could defend themselves against an attack. Manteo knew they lived on false hope. They would die on it, too. Though there were no further attacks by native peoples since the month prior, Manteo knew the settlement would not hold.

Henry Darby stepped forward. "The Spanish ship we saw days ago is reason enough to leave this place."

"Our best chance of survival is to live among our friends," Elizabeth interjected. "There is nothing left for us here. If our own country has abandoned us, I say we abandon it in kind, and call this land our home now." Her gaze dropped to her son, who nodded his agreement.

"I believe my father would come for us if he could," Eleanor added. "But I must agree with Elizabeth. Something has happened to delay him. We must move onward. Father would wish it of us. He will know where to find us upon his return."

"Our lives are held in no high regard to those who command us. Apart from Governor White, who left his beloved daughter here, I daresay we have been forsaken," Henry declared. His wife Rose slipped her arm through his in a supportive gesture.

"You will all be one with us," Manteo continued, noting Master Dare's hesitation. "Among our peoples, there is a custom of making relatives. All of you will be our relatives."

"Please Master Dare," Emme spoke. No longer concerned about what anyone thought, she reached for Towaye's hand, holding it against her like a treasure, among the folds of her skirt.

Ananias rubbed a tired hand over the dark scruff of his beard. He looked at each of the faces closest to him. The three boys Phillip Cooke, Thomas Smart, and James Warren all wide-eyed, and somehow still full of life, excited for the possibilities and the assurances Manteo had given them. John Bridger, who remained steadfast in his service. Emme, a sweet and loyal young woman, indentured to his family. Elizabeth Cooke and her son, who remained strong through their many trials, along with Rose and Henry Darby, and his own wife Eleanor, holding their sleeping daughter, Virginia in her arms.

"What say you, Bridger?" He asked.

"I say we've stood 'round long enough, and should get to gatherin' our belongings, sir." Bridger's reply was met with enthusiastic agreement from the remaining colonists of the Roanoke settlement.

They carried what they could, loading the canoe and the remaining longboats. They agreed to return at a later date to the settlement for the remainder. They could still transport materials for rebuilding homes and other structures if necessary. Too unwieldy to manage on any of the watercraft, they left the small canon behind. Before leaving with Manteo and Towaye, Ananias Dare remembered the sign agreed upon. He carved their destination, CROATOAN into a wooden barricade slat, and the letters CRO into a tree trunk. No Maltese cross was carved beneath it. They would be among friends.

*　　*　　*

Manteo led the group past scattered dwellings and fields planted with corn, beans, and squash, where young boys kept watch for crows and animals, keeping them away from the precious crops. Crows were never killed or injured, for it was the crow that first brought the corn seed to the People. Towaye ran ahead to call out to the sentries and villagers to advise them of the coming visitors. The *werowansa* as well as the shaman and a few of her closest advisors exited their dwellings, in anticipation. The group entered the village proper, where Manteo turned to the apprehensive white visitors. "Wait here. I will speak to our *werowansa*. Towaye stays with you."

Elizabeth watched as he strode toward an older, elegant woman. Her graying hair was long and tied. Small copper disks dangled from her ears. A larger disk hung from her neck. She wore an intricately decorated cape of feathers and fur over her slender form. She smiled as she greeted her son, Manteo. As he spoke, she shifted her eyes from him to the group of *Tosh shonte*. She did not seem disagreeable to whatever Manteo said to her. At best, that was Elizabeth's hope.

Ompeu and Paukunnawaw watched from several feet away as the bedraggled group of English entered the village. Ompeu stood with his arms folded across his chest. His dark eyes narrowed, wondering why they had come. He hoped it was not to ask for food. The corn barns held enough for his people; no extra could be spared. Why the *Wutahshuntar* could not feed themselves, he did not understand.

Paukunnawaw's gaze also followed the group. "They bring their women," he mused aloud. "Look," he motioned with his chin toward the group, "There are some with hair like the sun."

"Hmph," Ompeu grunted in disapproval.

Elizabeth and Rose stood close to one another as they drew the attention of the Croatan. Phillip clutched his mother's skirts. People emerged from everywhere it seemed, to view their *Tosh shonte* neighbors. A middle-aged woman approached Towaye. Her voice and manner indicated a fondness toward him. Her gaze swept over the English people, her dark eyes pausing momentarily when she reached Elizabeth. The woman's expression was kind, and Elizabeth offered her a small smile in acknowledgement. The matron smiled in return and then said something to Elizabeth. Knowing she would not understand, Towaye stepped in and answered, speaking to the older woman at length.

When he motioned toward Emme, the woman acknowledged her with a grin to put her at ease, touching Towaye's arm as she spoke further. She led him to Emme, and took the surprised girl's hand, pulling her from the group. She strode around Emme purposefully, assessing her, shaking her head over some flaw. Emme looked to Towaye for an explanation, but he merely shrugged. The woman then spoke to Emme in a sympathetic tone, taking her hand, patting it gently, and reaching up to stroke and touch her hair. She turned once more to Towaye and said a few more words. Satisfied with their conversation, the woman glanced Elizabeth's way once more before she left them. Elizabeth watched as Towaye took Emme aside to speak with her privately, presumably to explain all that transpired.

Elizabeth put an arm around her son's slight shoulders and surveyed her surroundings. She observed their dome-shaped dwellings. Their houses were large, and some were elongated. They were constructed of saplings that appeared to be bent over to form a frame, which then were covered with woven reed mats, or bark. A communal fire blazed, with coiled clay pots of various sizes placed into the flames. A much larger building stood somewhat apart from the others near a circle of posts. Elizabeth wondered how the posts were used and thought to ask Manteo about them later.

"I pray we've made a wise decision," she heard Ananias Dare say to his wife. Several of the village wolfish dogs pranced about tails wagging, barking and growling. A young woman shooed them away.

"This will be our opportunity to educate and minister to the people here. Teach them to abandon their false gods and show them that our ways are far superior," Eleanor answered, her gaze following the movement of various passersby. "They certainly need to be educated on proper dress." Several laughing children bounded past. Few wore clothing.

"We've just arrived. Surely, we should refrain from any attempt at religious conversion until we learn more about their beliefs, and have established our place among the people here," Elizabeth responded before she could stop herself.

Brown eyes flashed as Eleanor sent her a reproving glance. "Manteo has embraced our true religion and our way of life. I'm certain with his help, the others will follow suit."

Elizabeth looked away, deciding to keep her thoughts to herself, effectively ending any further disagreement with Eleanor Dare. Most of the community cast curious glances toward the English newcomers as they returned to their daily activities. She breathed deeply, attempting to quell her nerves. She offered cautious smiles to the few Croatan who made eye contact with her. The people wore little; a breechclout made of skins that formed a kind of apron. It was all they wore, including the women. Most were tattooed, with designs of various geometric patterns on their arms, legs, and chests. Both men and women wore necklaces and bracelets made of pearls or shells, both wore earrings. Some of the men's heads were shaved on one side, while the opposite side grew long. Others had their hair cropped short in front so that it spiked upward. Some wore their hair long and tied.

"Lord deliver us," Rose whispered, as she caught sight of two warriors standing off to the side, watching them. "I have not ever sensed such hostility."

"All will be well," Elizabeth said quietly. "The Croatan have been constant and steadfast friends. Some of these have visited us." She followed Rose's line of sight, settling on the warriors Rose spoke of. Her eyes locked momentarily on one particularly powerful, exceptional looking young man. Strong arms were folded across his chest. His ebony hair flowed, extremely long and loose. His forearms appeared scarred and tattooed with dark lines. She noted parts of a thin tattoo design across his chest.

When Elizabeth lifted her eyes to his face, she blushed to find herself caught in her curious perusal of him. She looked away, mortified as embarrassment flooded her. She attempted to focus on other objects or people, but the sensation that he continued to watch her became overwhelming. When her eyes turned to him again, she found him staring at her defiantly. The heat of his dark gaze settled on her, deliberately moving over her figure, assessing her from head to toe. A blatantly lustful once-over. A challenge that set her heart racing. She realized he mimicked her actions, doing to her, what he thought she had done to him.

She did not mean to offend him with her rude staring, yet she had done so. She appraised his form as though he were a beautifully sculpted statue in an English garden. Though ashamed of her actions, she could not look away, and met his eyes with her own woman's challenge, full of curiosity and wondering. Only when Manteo returned, did she tear her gaze from the warrior's, grateful for the distraction.

"Come. We will council," Manteo said when he returned to the group. "The *werowansa* wishes to speak with you and the others of our village, but first, you will eat and rest." The group of English followed him.

The colonists were divided among various dwellings. Emme, Elizabeth and young Phillip were ushered into the longhouse. Several Croatan women of varying ages and sizes entered, gesturing for their English clothing. The older woman who initially greeted Towaye instructed these women, and she appeared to be greatly respected. They spoke in their native language, making hand motions that Elizabeth and Emme understood to mean their clothing would be washed. The English women modestly insisted on keeping their undergarments, but their hosts would not allow it. Covered with trade blankets and animal skins, they were swept up by the group and led to a stream. They were bathed then, and their hair washed and combed. Chants were said over them. There seemed to be a ritualistic air about the entire process, one Elizabeth did not fully grasp, though she was certain held some meaning. She wondered if this was akin to baptism, or rebirth. The entire exercise proved quite overwhelming to the confused English women.

The Croatan women chatted in amiable, pleasant tones as they worked. Elizabeth wished she understood their language. A few of them shook their heads in lament. Through facial expressions, gestures, and body language, she assumed they spoke of the sad condition of English bodies, bony and thin from hunger. The Croatan were a handsome people, vital and healthy. Their lovely brown skin shone with what Elizabeth assumed to be a type of ointment, lending a soft glow to their complexions. Wrapped in their coverings, they returned to the longhouse where they shared a meal.

Two evenings later, twenty-two colonists, fed and refreshed, found themselves standing together in a large longhouse, where a central fire burned. They were treated well. Elizabeth, Phillip, and Emme lodged in a longhouse headed by a caring woman named Poussu, who delighted in feeding them. She was the mother of Towaye, the same woman who approached him the day they arrived. She oversaw their care. "My mother thinks you are all thin like sticks," he had said.

The council lodge seemed filled beyond capacity, with every soul in the village present. Elizabeth watched in fascination at the ceremonial nature at the start of the meeting, and the passing of the sacred pipe. She noticed the man she had seen on the first day. He studied her intently, his expression indecipherable. The *werowansa* spoke, giving Elizabeth an excuse to divert her attention away from him.

"My friends, *Tosh shonte* visitors have been welcomed to live among our people. These are all that remain from their village on the Island they call Roanoke." She paused, indicating the *Tosh shonte*, and presenting them to the community. "My son, Manteo, and our own Towaye are friends to them. These *Tosh shonte* are weary and hungry. It is their wish to remain and live among us as our relatives. I wait to hear what others may say."

What transpired next, Elizabeth could not say with certainty. The conversation that followed, happened so quickly that translations were few. Though she did not understand the words, she understood the hostile tone of the warrior she had embarrassingly stared at two days ago.

"Matta!" Ompeu said abruptly. He knew it was inappropriate to speak out thusly, but continued, amid the murmur of the people in the council lodge. "I do not agree. Did they not cross the great water to live in their own village? They should stay on their island, and care for themselves. If they cannot survive, then so be it."

Poussu knew he would be angry, but she did not expect this. Just yesterday she succeeded in convincing Ompeu not to leave Croatoan Island to join the Secotan and Roanoac. He said he could not abide the presence of the English, but Poussu pulled out a bit of motherly guilt from her repertoire and made him understand that his people needed him, especially now that the *Tosh shonte* arrived with hopes of living as Croatans. One less hunter and warrior would affect them greatly. His rudimentary knowledge of *Tosh shonte* words would help cultivate good relations.

Ompeu wanted no part in helping the English to assimilate, but he agreed to remain in the village for her sake, and admittedly for his own curiosity. Poussu gathered her thoughts and rose to speak. "These few people are harmless. They need our help. There are women and children among them. Would you condemn helpless ones to die of starvation, illness or an attack by our Secotan and Roanoac brothers? No. I believe we should welcome them."

"It is not right," Ompeu's gaze encompassed the group. "Do you forget that these same *Tosh shonte* killed Croatan last summer?"

"We all remember. What happened at Desamunkepeuc was bad. Those responsible are now dead, or have gone back to England," Manteo interjected. "These people here are friends." He gestured toward the group. "I know them well. They have been abandoned by their countrymen and wish to be our relatives. Your friend Towaye seeks to take one of their women for his wife."

Others took turns speaking, weighing in on the debate that would last into the night. Even Ananias Dare, John Bridger, Henry Darby, and a few more Englishmen were given the opportunity to speak. Manteo translated their words. They told of how a cooperative living arrangement would be beneficial to the entire village. They would bring tools, weapons, and gifts that remained on their island and share all they knew with the people. They would use their talents and skills for the benefit of the village. They would accept and live by the rules and customs of their hosts and show them new ones if they so desired. Together, they would grow strong and be feared by enemies who might trouble them. They would create a new and greater people. Many Croatan were impressed by the English speeches. Manteo argued that the English *mantóac* would benefit them all.

During the numerous discussions, Ompeu found his gaze returning to the small, tawny-haired *Tosh shonte* woman he had seen upon the arrival of the English. At her side, stood a young, sun-haired boy, whom she kept close. She stared at him that first day. Her actions were bold, but her eyes, the color of honey, were soft and full of curiosity, some fear, and more than a bit of feminine appreciation at what she saw. At this moment, she looked unsure about all that transpired, for she could not understand their words. There was something about her, something familiar, though he did not know why there should be. She turned her eyes to him, as though seeking answers, as though she wished to understand the reason for his anger. And then he knew. Those beautiful eyes, her delicate face. She reminded him of a doe. The stark realization fueled his anger, for if she were the doe come to him again, it would be a cruel twist that *Kiwasa* bestowed upon him.

"Brother Ompeu," the *werowansa* said, bringing him to present. "We all know you have just cause for not wishing the English to live among us. There are those who would agree with you. But if it is the decision of myself and this council to welcome these *Tosh shonte*, then you must accept it."

Ompeu remained silent, reveling in his own anger. He said what he needed to say. There were no more words.

While the people talked amongst themselves, the *werowansa* signaled, beckoning her son Manteo. She spoke in his ear. Manteo feared that Ompeu would react in this manner, but his mother noticed something Manteo did not. She saw the way Ompeu's eyes watched one of the women, called Elizabeth. Manteo looked back at his friend, who even now, stared sourly at the woman. The *werowansa* read the look beneath the layers of Ompeu's bitter anger. Yes. It was there. Desire? Fascination? Something about the Englishwoman drew Ompeu's profound attention. Whatever it meant, the *werowansa* urged Manteo to use this to appease his friend, and perhaps restore balance.

When the final decision was made to welcome the English as Croatan relatives, the *werowansa* directed her son to speak.

"My brother Ompeu, you have suffered a great loss, a wife and son. Here among the English, is a woman and her son." He gestured toward Elizabeth. "This woman has no husband, for he is now dead. She needs a man to provide and care for her. The boy needs a father to teach him the ways of a man. Take them into your home, so that your heart is healed." The suggestion was a great risk; one Manteo was certain both parties would see as outrageous, and refuse. He did not translate his words to English for this reason.

To most of the Croatan people, this made perfect sense. Equilibrium would be restored, and the need for vengeance and recompense would be satisfied. They murmured their agreement, encouraging Ompeu to accept.

Confusion clouded Elizabeth's features. Manteo did not translate the Algonquian words, but she knew they spoke of her. She drew her son closer, her eyes darting from Manteo to the angry warrior. "I fear I have offended him," Elizabeth murmured to no one in particular.

Ompeu did not want the woman. No. Not at all. How could Manteo insult him by suggesting such a thing? How could *Kiwasa* play such a cruel trick? This could not be. This is not what he thought the vision to mean.

To take a woman whose people were responsible for the killing of his family? No. He did not want her.

The day the English arrived, the woman they called Elizabeth caught Poussu's attention. Knowing something of Ompeu's vision, she wondered if the doe he dreamed of had returned to him. Fearing Ompeu would reject Manteo's perfectly good suggestion, Poussu stood. "I will take them in. I will treat her as my own daughter, and the boy as a beloved grandson." She then turned to Ompeu, for she also sensed his cloaked interest in the small *Tosh shonte* woman. "Ompeu will teach the boy the ways of a Croatan hunter and warrior. As a mother who has lost a daughter and a grandson, I am satisfied. Let us go forward in peace." Her eyes fixed boldly upon his, daring him to refuse her. He did not, choosing to seethe in silence.

The meeting ended, and the people dispersed. The hour grew late, and most headed for their dwellings. Manteo approached his English friends, explaining all that transpired. Until new homes could be built, they would live with various families, who would teach them and care for them. The Croatan hosts led their English relatives out of the council lodge.

Poussu took a confused Elizabeth's hand, bringing her and the boy directly in front of Ompeu, who stood rigidly at their approach. She motioned for Manteo to follow so that he might translate her words.

The doe-eyed woman stood a few feet away from Ompeu. She looked up at him, wary and uncertain. Up close, she was more unusually stunning than he had first seen at a distance. He was unaccustomed to seeing women with her coloring; yellow-brown hair that coiled in loose curls down her back, and golden, expressive eyes that seemed to change color, from honey, to chestnut, to amber. He wondered if her strangeness was part of his unwanted fascination. No. Other *Tosh shonte* women were present. None drew him, only this one.

Elizabeth kept her gaze from drifting over the half-naked male in front of her, and made certain to look him in the eye, for she had been correct in her previous assessment. Though his expression remained closed, he was indeed, a handsome, sculpted work of art, but she had no wish to further offend the young man or embarrass herself.

Manteo came to speak with the woman. "Poussu says you stay with her as a daughter. Your son will be her grandson. She teach you and care for you both. This man is called Ompeu, he is like a son to her. He teach your son."

She turned to Manteo. "I understand. Please thank Poussu for me. But he… Om-pe-u seems most opposed. Are you certain my son will be safe? I may have done something to offend him, please express my regret to him, Manteo," Elizabeth said, as she looked from one man to the other.

Manteo translated for Poussu's benefit. Ompeu understood many of her words. Her concern for his sensibilities surprised him but changed nothing.

Manteo half-smiled, knowing that in all likelihood, Ompeu understood most of what Widow Cooke said, but for some reason refused to reveal his knowledge of English. "Ompeu is good and honorable man. He has reason to feel as he does toward the English, but he would not harm you or the boy." He gave Ompeu a pointed look.

"Tell her she has done no wrong," Poussu said, giving Ompeu's arm a motherly, chastising shove.

"Tell her I will come for the boy when the sun rises," he said bitterly to Manteo, refusing to utter a word of English. "We will take a group of *Tosh shonte* men, and make Croatan hunters of them," Ompeu uttered, his voice laced with animosity. He turned then and left the council lodge.

Chapter Ten

Ompeu remained aloof and apart from the
hunting party, but for the boy, who seemed to
follow him everywhere since he retrieved the
child from the woman that first morning. The child
spoke little and was not troublesome. When the Croatan
took their daily morning baths, a practice with which the
English were not accustomed, the boy followed Ompeu
unconcernedly, joining the Croatan. Manteo struggled to
convince the English that daily bathing was good for
their well-being and kept their scent at bay from the prey
they hunted. As the days passed, more Englishmen
joined in the daily ritual as the Croatans celebrated a new
day and the rising of the sun with prayers and the casting
of *uppowoc* into the wind.

Manteo and Towaye answered questions, showed the
Croatan way of setting snares to catch rabbits and small

animals, and allowed the Englishmen and boys to practice shooting with bow and arrow. They shared the ritual of offering *uppowoc*, casting it into the air along with words to appease the deity *Kiwasa,* so that the animals surrendered themselves.

John Bridger and a few of the men were already good with the bow, outperforming Ananias Dare and the older boys. "All that soldier trainin' was good for somthin'," Bridger quipped good-naturedly.

Ompeu produced a practice spear with a dull end, and Towaye fashioned a hoop from a sapling. The men practiced in a clearing, throwing the spear through the hoop as it was rolled past them at varying speeds and angles. The Englishmen had some difficulty with the spear and hoop game, but laughed at their own foibles, for the Croatan were experts at bow and spear. The hoop was then used for bow and arrow. The ability to shoot a moving target proving slightly more difficult with an arrow, but also more important to master.

"Deer, rabbits, squirrels; all run fast," Manteo said. "If you miss, no one eats." Hunting for the Croatan was not sport; it was survival.

Towaye tightened the sinew around the hoop, repairing a part that had come undone. "The small boy needs a small bow," he commented absently, referring to Phillip Cooke.

The mixed group of Croatan and English camped over many days, told stories in front of the evening fire, and slept under the stars, or makeshift shelters. They taught each other Algonquian and English words, offering names for objects and places. They laughed at each other's awkward mispronunciations; the overall mood jovial. Manteo possessed his own musket, given to him by Master Ralegh. He and the Englishmen showed the Croatan how to load and fire the weapons. Ompeu had to admit, the muskets were impressive. In the evenings when they made camp, he worked on a new, smaller bow and blunt arrows. When he spoke, he continued to use his native tongue. He slept away from the others, for the doe turned she-wolf turned woman, came to him in his dreams more frequently.

Several mornings later, Ompeu presented the completed bow and set of three arrows to the child. Eyes the color of sky grew wide with delight, as the boy smiled up at him. It was the first genuine smile Ompeu had seen from him. The smile reminded him of the boy's mother. He shook the thought away, hardening himself against it.

Unexpectedly, the boy, who barely reached Ompeu's hip threw his arms around his middle and held tight. "I thank thee, Ompeu," the child said.

Ompeu, surprised and uncertain, placed an awkward hand on the boy's head, ruffling the blond curls.

Manteo, Towaye, and Paukunnawaw watched the exchange from a distance, as the group of men packed up the campsite. "He should have taken the Widow Cooke and the boy into his dwelling," Towaye said, indicating the pair with a nod of his head.

Manteo watched them thoughtfully before answering. "Give him time. Perhaps he will."

Ompeu showed the boy how to hold the bow and position the arrow, bringing his elbow up, pulling back the bowstring near his cheek, taking careful aim, and letting the arrow fly. Phillip listened attentively to Ompeu's instructions, though he did not understand his words. He looked to Ompeu, awe and admiration clearly written on his face.

Ompeu thought that in a few years he would have taught his own son this very thing, and a wave of sadness overcame him. But he could not find it in his heart to be displeased as he watched the English boy shoot. Another arrow sailed, landing beneath an overgrowth of foliage. The boy ran happily to retrieve the arrow, searching in the brush. He stopped suddenly; his gaze fixed upon something on the ground. He turned and silently motioned excitedly for Ompeu to come.

"Look, Ompeu," he said, his child's voice barely above a whisper, as he pointed to a concealed spot.

Ompeu squatted on his heels, peering into the overgrowth. He lifted his eyes to the boy, the joy of discovery and barely contained exuberance shown on the child's face as he tried to keep silent, so as not to frighten the three kit foxes curled around one another, at the entrance of a den.

"*Onxe*," Ompeu said, and touched the boy's shoulder lightly to draw his attention. "I give you name. Good name," he said carefully, quietly, using the English words so the boy would understand.

Phillip turned questioning blue eyes to the kit foxes, then back to Ompeu, his innocent face displaying his surprise. "You speak English?"

"*Kupi*," Ompeu said, then paused, brows knitted. "Not Manteo. Not Towaye. Not good."

Phillip seemed to understand that Ompeu's command of English was not as extensive as Manteo or Towaye. "What is *Onxe*?"

Ompeu thought a moment, searching for words. He pointed to the kit foxes, who remained still and quiet in hiding until their mother returned.

"Foxes? Fox?"

"*Kupi*. Fox. New name. *Onxe*."

"*Onxe*," Phillip said, testing the sound of the word and the way it formed in his mouth. He looked at the baby foxes, then back at Ompeu. "'Tis a good name. I thank thee, Ompeu." He grinned, then pointed to himself proudly. "I am Onxe."

"Say, *Nuturuwins Onxe*," Ompeu instructed, repeating the words slowly, twice. "I am called Onxe."

Phillip's mouth twisted around the difficult words, repeating them. "Nu… nuturu-wins Onxe. Nuturuwins Onxe." His lips turned up in an uncertain grin, his anticipation evident as he sought Ompeu's approval.

Nothing on Mother Earth could keep Ompeu from returning the smile. *"Wingan.* Good." He gathered up the stray arrows and led Onxe back to camp.

*   *   *

Once Elizabeth made the decision to abandon England, she did not look back. Accepting this new land as her home, she threw herself into learning all she could, and becoming some new combination of an English-Croatan woman. Rose and Emme followed her lead by adopting this sentiment, Emme being the only one thus far to abandon most of her English clothing, trading it for a simple doeskin mantle. Eleanor stood fast in her mission to teach the Croatan what she could to Anglicize them with Manteo's help. She insisted that one of the first structures to be built as soon as the men returned, should be a place of Christian worship.

Elizabeth opined that they should first learn tribal customs and beliefs as well as their language before attempting to Christianize them. After all, these people survived millennia in this land before the English arrived. Much could be learned from them. Only when mutual trust and understanding were cultivated, could a deeper exchange of ideas take place, including religion. After all that transpired between the two peoples, trust and understanding was still in short supply on both sides.

She counted herself among those with concerns regarding trust.

She missed her son. The men in the hunting party were gone two weeks, and she could not help but worry over him. Manteo assured her that everyone in the group would look after the boys, but she was not certain she could trust Ompeu. She instructed her son to behave appropriately, and to seek out Manteo or Master Dare if he should feel unsafe. She did not wish to frighten him, but she admitted that there were some shameful, learned biases she possessed about the Indians, particularly one who seemed as angry as Ompeu.

Manteo and Towaye traveled with the hunting expedition. Without anyone to translate, efforts at deeper conversation with Poussu proved difficult, and asking questions about when the men would return or where they had gone would be futile. It must not be unusual for hunters to be away for so long, she reasoned, since none of the Croatan seemed concerned.

Though they communicated through gestures and a mix of English and Croatan dialect, Poussu saw that the young Englishwoman she chose for her daughter possessed a good heart. The doe-eyed one appeared to be respected by the other *Tosh shonte* women, as they often came to her to talk and ask questions. One called Rose was a frequent visitor, and they often worked together. Sometimes they talked from what Elizabeth called a book. They used a black flat piece of thin rock to make more talking words. Poussu did not know how to ask about it. When Elizabeth showed her, she merely shrugged her shoulders, not comprehending.

Welcoming the *Tosh shonte* women was a good decision. Having them with her helped to ease the pain at the loss of her daughter. Poussu took Emme under her wing and into her home, as her son Towaye confessed to her that he loved the girl since he visited the place across the great sea. Now she was gifted with two daughters to help lighten her heart.

Poussu taught Elizabeth and Emme how to prepare various Croatan dishes. Much of their food consisted of turtles, fish, shellfish, clams, oysters, fowl, and game such as deer, rabbits, and squirrels. They ate a versatile, colorful grain called *pogatowr*, as well as beans, squashes, roots, berries, and nuts. She taught the women how to grind dried *pogatowr* into a fine meal for making a kind of porridge as well as a type of bread. Elizabeth, through words and gestures, expressed an interest in learning about the healing herbs Poussu dried and hung inside the home. She also asked about the small pots filled with healing salves of all kinds, including a greasy, unpleasant scented mixture they used to keep mosquitos at bay. Poussu, pleased by Elizabeth's curiosity over these things, decided to teach her new daughter all she knew of medicines.

The *Tosh shonte* women were apt students, and eager to please. Elizabeth treated Emme as though she were a younger sister. Poussu would sometimes see a sadness in Elizabeth's eyes, and she wished they could communicate beyond gestures and words that were difficult to understand. She wanted to ask Elizabeth why she had no husband. Why had she not married after his death? Why was she sometimes sad? Did she miss her husband, her homeland? Only the passing of time would allow them to communicate with more ease, as they learned new words and phrases in each other's language.

Elizabeth and Emme were bringing firewood back to the longhouse when they heard shouting and whooping. The group of men were entering the village. People halted in their work and left their homes to swarm the hunters. She and Emme were swept up in the excitement, and trotted toward them, stopping at the edge of the circle. She scanned the hoard of people, searching for any sign of her son.

"*Nek*! *Nek*!" It was the voice of a blond-haired child, pulling on the hand of a tall Croatan warrior, leading him toward his mother.

His glee was contagious. A joyous sound left her lips as she crouched, reaching for her son to hold him close as he leapt onto her, nearly knocking her off-balance. He wrapped his arms around her.

Ompeu allowed himself to be led to where the woman waited. He watched as she closed her eyes and pressed her lips to her son's hair.

"*Nek*," he said, stepping out of her embrace. "Look. My very own bow and arrows. Ompeu made them for me," he beamed, sliding the bow from his shoulder, presenting her with his prize.

Elizabeth looked up at Ompeu, who stood behind Phillip quietly, his face impassive. "Thank you, Ompeu" she said. "Truly."

She smiled at him, her beautiful face aglow. She took his breath away. Ompeu said nothing, though his expression softened.

"*Nek*," Phillip tugged on her arm.

Elizabeth blinked, tearing her gaze from Ompeu and returning her attention to her son. "Yes, love."

"We built snares, and caught rabbits, and there were deer. We must give an offering to *Kiwasa*, and thank the animal's spirit, for giving its life to us. And Ompeu will show me how the Croatan build a canoe. I can take you fishing. I have already caught fish. The boys and I, we threw spears through a hoop. I have some new friends. My name is Onxe now. Do not call me Phillip. It means Fox. A good name, don't you agree? Ompeu is teaching me how to track. Yesterday we saw bear tracks. Ompeu can catch fish with his bare hands! I saw him do it. Do you have a new name as well? I will call you '*nek*'. That means 'my mother'."

Elizabeth blinked, closing her opened mouth. Phillip barely took a breath as he spoke. She had never witnessed her son this animated and excited. It was difficult to keep up with him. She nodded and smiled as he spoke. He was simply jubilant.

"I know you've missed me. I've missed you as well," Phillip continued. "But you know, I must be a man now. Ompeu says I am a little man, but I have much to learn so that I can take care of my family. That is what a man must do, he must take care of the people he loves."

"I see," she said, and then, "Yes. I agree." Elizabeth could not keep the smile from her face, deeply grateful to Ompeu for his care of her son. She lifted her head to speak to the Croatan warrior and thank him again, except he was gone.

Phillip talked of Ompeu the entire day, as though he were more than a mere man, causing Elizabeth's curiosity about him to grow. She wondered again at his anger toward the English. What caused him to be so adamantly opposed to their presence here at Croatoan? Ompeu was a mystery to her. Yet, despite his refusal to welcome the English, he not only accepted the council's decision but took responsibility for her son, an English boy. Nay, he went above and beyond that. It was evident in her son's changed demeanor and the stories he told, as though Ompeu were the hero of an epic poem. She realized that her son found a father figure of sorts, in a young Croatan man, and not in Cooke, his true father.

After he visited Poussu, Ompeu sat cross-legged beneath a tree, watching Onxe and his mother. He wondered about her husband. What fragments Onxe mentioned, were not favorable. He wondered why a man who had such a wife would mistreat her. She did not appear to be dishonorable. She seemed to have a good and loving heart, as evidenced by the affection she displayed toward her son. She was concerned that night at the council meeting that she had possibly offended him. This told him that she cared for how she treated others. Poussu told him that Elizabeth had shown her great respect.

According to Poussu, the one called Elizabeth attempted to learn the ways of Croatan women, without complaint. He could not deny that she was beautiful to him in a unique way. Something about her drew him. Before his thoughts could take him further, he looked away.

Paukunnawaw appeared and dropped beside Ompeu. "Our time with the *Tosh shonte* was good. The musket is a fine weapon."

"*Kupi*," Ompeu agreed. "The boy learns fast. He will be a fine hunter someday. And the musket is good, but arrows can be shot more quickly. What happens when they run out of powder and shot?"

"They make more?" Paukunnawaw followed Ompeu's gaze, realizing that he watched the boy with his mother from a distance.

A few moments of silence passed. "Why did you not take the woman and the boy into your *yeehaukan*, my friend? You are too much alone and apart."

Ompeu picked a long blade of grass, twirling it between his fingers. He shrugged. "I did not want the woman."

They both watched mother and son. "She is pleasing to look at," Paukunnawaw commented off-handedly.

"She is small," Ompeu gestured with a hand, demonstrating her height. He imagined the top of her head would reach the tattooed lines of his chest.

"Small yes, but she is….," Paukunnawaw searched for words, then said, "She is well made," he raised a mischievous black eyebrow.

It did not take much effort for Ompeu to envision how well made. "She is a *Tosh shonte* woman," he scoffed, as though that explained everything.

"She is still a woman."

More silence as they watched Onxe take his mother's hand. They ran together away from the longhouse, so that the boy could demonstrate shooting his arrows for her. He then allowed his mother to try, showing her how to hold the bow as he was taught. Ompeu's eyes lazily followed the curves of her body. She had gained some weight since living with the Croatan and no longer resembled a stick. A healthy glow returned to her features. Her dress no longer hung considerably on her small frame. Though difficult to discern what secrets lay beneath all the English skirts, there was nothing wrong with his imagination.

"Perhaps I would court her," Paukunnawaw said more to himself than to his friend. He watched for Ompeu's reaction from the corner of his eye. It was known that the handsome Paukunnawaw favored both men and women, but he had not yet chosen a mate, electing to spend his time with partners as freely as he wished.

Outwardly, Ompeu grunted noncommittally and shrugged. Inwardly his gut clenched at his friend's words. It should not matter to him whether Paukunnawaw took an interest in the woman. Then why did the thought cause him discomfort? He wished to end the conversation. "I must go," he said abruptly, rising from his spot, and walking away.

After Ompeu left, Paukunnawaw chuckled. "You do not fool anyone with eyes, my friend."

Ompeu saw the *Tosh shonte* woman later that day before the feast. One of the large village wolfdogs, tail wagging happily, followed her as she carried a basket, no doubt containing something edible. He watched her curiously as she stopped, picked something from the basket, and spoke to the dog. When the animal sat obediently, she fed him a piece of food. She spoke sweetly, ruffling the gray fur between the ears, and laughing lightly. The woman then strode to where the others worked, giving the basket to Poussu. She turned then, her eyes somehow finding his. She looked as though she wished to speak to him, her lips turned upward in a faint smile, but she dared not approach.

Again, her woman's eyes looked at him appreciatively. Ompeu walked away.

The women spent the rest of the day preparing food for the evening's festivities. Manteo explained that they would celebrate their new relatives and blessings of the hunt with a banquet and dancing. At dusk, after the feasting, a great bonfire was lit in the center of the circle of poles, each with a carved face. Men and women milled around the great fire chanting and singing, some shaking gourds filled with stones or seeds, keeping time with the beat of the drum. The hunters danced around the fire with acrobatic flair, their feet keeping the steady, pounding rhythm. Elizabeth felt both exhilarated and frightened by the display. The beat of the drum seemed to echo in her own breast, and she bounced and swayed lightly, bending at the knee as she followed Poussu's lead. Rose and Emme joined her at the outer circle, at first tentative and unsure. When Poussu showed them, they all moved fluidly, with more confidence.

Elizabeth caught sight of Ompeu, who danced around the bonfire, leaping and twirling. The firelight played on his skin and the contours of his body as he danced, his powerful, lean-muscled form moving with an easy grace.

"We celebrate our good fortune in the hunt, and give offerings to *Kiwasa*," a masculine voice said beside her, above the din. "I hope you and the others be not afeared."

Elizabeth looked up to find Manteo standing at her shoulder. "I admit, it is quite unusual, yet fascinating at once."

"You are not afraid."

Elizabeth stopped swaying with the drumbeat. "I would not say afraid, well, perhaps a little." She indicated her son among a group of boys, now playing off to the side of the circle. Elizabeth smiled up at Manteo. "There seem to be no ill-effects, as my son has already danced."

"Mistress Dare was…," he paused, searching for the correct word. "Unsettled. She and Master Dare went back to the *yeehaukan*." Manteo offered her a slight smile. "I know what it is to feel as she does. It is as I felt in England. All that I saw good and bad. Sometimes I was afraid, until I understood."

"I suppose 'tis not uncommon to fear things we do not understand." Elizabeth imagined Eleanor objecting to what she would consider a savage, heathen ritual. "And yet, you are Christianized."

For Manteo, it was not difficult to incorporate Christian ideology with his own beliefs. He simply chose those ideas that were similar in nature and made connections. Between the two systems, he could find commonalities; ones that could be adopted to fit with his upbringing. "The English possess much *mantóac*. I see many good things from them. From the English, I now have much *mantóac* as well."

They were silent, watching the dancers. Elizabeth thought to ask Manteo what *mantóac* represented, when Ompeu danced near them. This time he stopped momentarily to dance in front of her. He gazed down at her with smoldering intensity, his eyes meeting hers with an allure as tangible as a touch. Elizabeth forgot to breathe, drawn in by something raw and mysterious. She drew in a breath, blinking rapidly as Ompeu moved away again.

"My friend makes a show for you," Manteo uttered, unable to keep the amusement from his voice. He noted the way Elizabeth watched Ompeu, mesmerized. "This is good." Manteo secretly hoped that Ompeu's unmistakable attraction to Mistress Cooke would grow and ease his friend's heart. Evidently, she seemed equally taken with the troubled warrior.

Elizabeth continued to follow Ompeu's movement across the fire. "He does?"

"*Kupi*, for you."

Ompeu never spoke to her. She wondered why he would bother to dance for her. "Why is that good?"

Manteo hesitated, turning toward her. "Ompeu has suffered much. He has lost much." Elizabeth sensed that there was much more Manteo wished to say. "It is good that he dances with his people," he finished vaguely.

Elizabeth wanted to ask why Ompeu would not speak to her, why he seemed to avoid her, and a myriad of new questions, but when she tore her gaze from Ompeu, Manteo was gone.

Chapter Eleven

July-August 1588

The Englishmen wasted no time in setting up some semblance of their previous lives. They made several trips with canoes and the longboat, gathering useful materials from the Roanoke settlement. Henry Darby, a gunsmith and armorer by trade, set up his forge and workshop. Using discarded and old metal scraps he crafted knives, swords, arrowheads, and even cooking pots and utensils. Ananias Dare inquired about where he might find suitable clay in the area for brick making. He brought along his wooden brick molds and constructed a few more frames. Men helped him dig a pit in order to temper the clay. It was an arduous process, taking months for proper bricks to cure long enough to be sturdy and usable, but it would all be worth the effort to fortify homes and structures. In these endeavors, English and Croatan worked side by side, and each would benefit. The Croatan men especially, valued and admired the enhanced weaponry.

Most evenings, Poussu would send the doe-eyed woman to his *yeehaukan* with food. Usually, villagers ate outdoors weather permitting, but Ompeu had grown accustomed to keeping himself apart, choosing the solitude of his dwelling, away from the others. Since Poussu welcomed the *Tosh shonte* women into the longhouse, Ompeu made himself scarce. He never spoke to the woman. He knew his silence made her uncomfortable. Several times she attempted to initiate conversation with him. He knew she wished to speak to him and ask questions he had no desire to answer.

He took the boy hunting and fishing. They spent time together gathering crabs along the beach, helping to set up fishing weirs, and tracking various creatures, both two legged and four legged. Ompeu practiced English, and in turn taught the child the Croatan dialect. Ompeu grew fond of the boy and could not harden his heart against him, for he was an innocent. Children were precious to the Croatan, even English ones. It was the woman he sought to guard himself against. It was the woman who caused him to feel an odd sense of guilt, as though he were throwing away the memory of his wife and betraying the anger he felt toward the English who had slain her and their child. Since the events at

Desamunkepeuc, anger and solitude became comforting companions. It was a dark place he lived in and had grown to know well. His superficial attraction to the *Tosh shonte* woman threatened that place inside him, and he was not willing to let it go. Not yet.

Ompeu and the boy, now called Onxe, were seated near a rocky outgrowth overlooking the shore. The sound of the surf, the calling of seagulls, and the pelicans skimming over the foamy waves lent an air of calm as Ompeu showed the boy how to fashion arrowheads. The sea breeze captured and lifted Ompeu's long, night-black hair, and ruffled the boy's shorter, wavy blond locks.

They sat close together. Onxe looked on intently, practically resting his chin on Ompeu's shoulder as he chipped the piece of flint with a sharp instrument, and the arrowhead took shape. He handed the leaf-shaped, triangular stone to the boy. Onxe grinned, testing the weight and sharpness of the cool stone in his hand. He then looked up to Ompeu, his face serious.

"I wish to ask you something."

"I wait to hear," Ompeu replied.

"I'm worried about *nek*. What if someone harms her?"

Ompeu's brows knit. "No one hurt. Why?"

Phillip sat back. His gaze followed the shoreline, and he watched a pelican glide close to the surface, dive and come up with a good-sized fish in its large beak. "My father, I mean... my father that was," he said, speaking of the dead in the manner of the Croatan. "He would hurt her. Badly. I think he almost killed her once. I do not want anyone to harm her."

"Why she not put things out-side? Throw away." Ompeu imagined Elizabeth, a small woman, brutally beaten to the point of near death. He was surprised to find the disquieting picture troubled him.

"I do not know. I think the English cannot do that. My father that was, said that a wife belongs to her husband. She must obey him. But my mother, she did not listen. She did not believe my father was right. He was angry. My father said he can do what he wishes with her. He said he owned her." Onxe looked up at Ompeu. "Is that true?"

Ompeu thought for a moment, in order to gather the English words he needed. He then spoke gently. "How many arrow you have?"

Philip's face crinkled in confusion, wondering what arrows had to do with anything. "Two left. I lost one."

"Hmm." Ompeu was silent for a time. "Have three. Lost one. Now you not own."

"I do not understand." Onxe continued to be puzzled by the talk of arrows.

"All good thing is gift." Ompeu gestured with a sweep of his arm, to indicate the land, the sea, the sky. "We not own. Woman is gift to man as wife, but he not 'own' like arrow. Arrow can be lost, then you not 'own' it. Croatan woman choose him, and man honors her gift." Ompeu's lips curved slightly. "In most ways," he amended with a light shrug. "You under-stand?"

The boy remained thoughtful, then declared, "I think so. All good things are gifts, given to us. A wife chooses to give herself, and a husband must honor her gift." Onxe's eyes lit suddenly. "If something is a gift, we must care for it. I did not take care for the arrows, and I lost one."

Ompeu eyed the boy, a faint smile on his lips. A nod of his head was the approval Onxe sought.

"You would not hurt *nek*," Onxe blurted.

"You know this?"

"You are not him. You listen. You teach me things. He never did. You are different. I know you would not harm her."

Once again, Ompeu wondered about Elizabeth's husband. His heart went out to the boy. Ompeu's parents were killed when he was Onxe's age, but he was fortunate to have been raised by Poussu and her husband, who acted as a true father to Ompeu. When he died, Ompeu was heartbroken. He missed him still.

He wondered how a man would not wish to teach his son. How could he not wish to guide his son in the ways of men? Ompeu looked at the boy Onxe, "*Kurustuwes nir.*" Ompeu waited for the boy to look at him before speaking. "If man hurts woman, is no true man. You under-stand this?"

Onxe nodded and tried to keep from crying like a helpless babe. He wiped at his tears angrily. He did not wish to cry. He wanted to be a man, like Ompeu.

Ompeu placed a comforting arm around the boy's shoulders until Onxe was ready to return home.

*   *   *

"You, my good sir, must remain outside," she spoke to the large wolfdog as he followed her happily. Elizabeth was uncertain if the Croatan named their canine companions, but she chose to call him Ajax, after the mythological Greek hero. Ajax, who looked more wolf than dog, seemed to know when it was time to bring food to Ompeu's *yeehaukan*. It became their routine. Ajax waited outside patiently, and she rewarded his patience with a bit of meat. She refused to consider that he may one day end up as a meal.

Each time she entered Ompeu's dwelling, she attempted to speak to him, and made a few prior efforts at communication. His silence and aloof disposition dissuaded her from further attempts. She wondered if he reserved his disagreeable mood for her, for his temperament with her son was abiding, generous and benevolent. She scratched on the door flap. Ompeu lifted the flap, then stood aside allowing her to enter.

"What cheer? *Wingapo*," she said as she brushed past him, eyes cast downward. Ompeu stepped inside, lowering the flap. *"Sa kir winkan?"* She asked, not expecting him to answer.

Elizabeth placed the large, wooden bowl of turtle stew in the usual place near the fire pit. She rose and turned to exit, surprised to find herself so close to him that their bodies touched. Elizabeth took an awkward step back. Ompeu followed. She attempted to side-step and move past him to the door. He blocked her. Suddenly she became ever aware of his size and strength. He usually ignored her presence. If this were not an attempt to intimidate, then perhaps this was his way of telling her he would entertain her words. Whether he understood or responded did not matter. She would no longer suffer male intimidation, and she would express her thoughts. "Will you speak with me?"

Ompeu did not respond, holding her captive with his gaze. A slight shift of his head indicated the affirmative.

She waited, and when he did not speak, she released a frustrated breath. "Then I shall begin," she pronounced. "I wish to thank thee for all you have done for my son," she said, all too aware that she had already thanked him.

Ompeu tipped his head slightly, watching her intently as she spoke. Her delicately shaped features bewitched him, calling to mind the doe of his vision. Something about this small *Tosh shonte* woman held a sweetness to which he was inexplicably and powerfully drawn.

Now that he offered his full attention, Elizabeth pressed onward. "My son, he is, well, he has changed."

She smoothed her skirts and clasped her hands together in front of her, to keep them still. "He is a quiet and shy boy, and when he returned that first day after the hunting expedition, well...," a brief, nervous laugh escaped her. "Well, you were witness to it. So animated and joyous." She cleared her throat. "His participation in the dance was surprising as well."

One of her hands flitted briefly to smooth her hair, wound in a fat knot at the nape of her neck. Ompeu wondered if her hair felt as soft as it looked. Her hand then settled to rest; fingers splayed against her heart. His eyes followed the movement to the swell of her breasts. Ompeu found her nervousness amusing, but his face betrayed nothing.

"His, his father...," she trailed off, her eyes lifting to a back wall of the *yeehaukan*, as though she were studying the designs painted there. She shook her head, "I am loathed to speak of it, but his father was not..." She folded her hands in front of her again, examining a fingernail. "I think... I think if he gained all that he desired, he would have remained a miserable creature." She made a dismissive gesture, not wishing to discuss Cooke further. She lifted her doe eyes to him, looking up at him in earnest now. "Phillip says you've acquired some English. I know not whether you understand my words, but I needed to say them. Please know that I am deeply grateful for your kind acceptance and tutelage of my son," she finished, pressing her lips together, her mouth tilting into a small, watery smile before she moved to leave his *yeehaukan*.

Before she could do so, Ompeu's hand closed over her wrist, gently pulling her to him. "*Pyas*," he whispered. *Come here.* He heard the catch in her breath at the surprise movement, a hint of unease in her expression. A thought came to him. Perhaps he had found a way to keep her from invading his mind and his dreams.

It was the first word he had ever spoken to her. She understood the word, for it was one she heard Poussu use often. Elizabeth could barely breathe. She remained silent and still as he raised his other hand slowly, capturing her chin, effectively silencing what she might say next. She diverted her eyes to find his bare, tattooed chest directly in front of her face.

Ompeu nudged her chin upward. "*Matta*," he whispered. He wished to look at her, see her beautiful eyes. He wanted her to look at him. His dark eyes traveled over her face. His hand left her chin, and his forefinger traced a slow line, smoothing an eyebrow, and trailing over her cheekbone to her chin, as though he were attempting to learn her features. His hand lingered, fingertips tracing the curve of her neck.

Her pulse quickened as she peered up at him. Somehow, she knew that this man would not harm her. One hand captured her wrist, but there was no force in his grasp. He touched her, but gently, like a butterfly alighting onto a flower. His gentleness surprised and confused her. She searched his handsome face and found no malice there, only intense curiosity and fascination. She understood that she was a novelty to him as he was to her, each of them a different and an intriguing mystery to the other.

Ompeu knew the boy spoke the truth of his father. He must have been a man undeserving of Onxe and this woman. Still, Ompeu did not understand this strange attraction to her, nor did he want it. He wished to hold fast to the notion that desiring a woman whose people murdered his family, was somehow a betrayal; not only of those he lost, but of himself.

"Ompeu?" she asked, on a soft breath. "Manteo says you have reason to hate the English." His fingers strayed to her hair, bound up and twisted at the back of her head. He found a pin and withdrew it, examining it briefly before tossing it aside. "Why do you despise us? Why are you angry? I have often wondered this. I know I should not ask these things, and... I admit my curiosity about you is ..."

"Eng-lish kill," he interrupted soberly, and continued to search her hair for pins. "Eng-lish steal." Another pin fell from her hair. "Eng-lish do not speak true."

Though she should be affronted by his actions, she was not. She, Emme, and Rose discovered their hair and eyes were a source of fascination for some of the Croatan. It did not offend her. His demeanor was not threatening, but inquisitive. She knew too well the fear and pain a man's touch could bring. This, however, was a new experience, for beneath the surface, the air hummed with something raw and sensual between them. "You understand my words. Phillip... Onxe said that you could."

"*Kupi*. Yes. I hear Eng-lish word. I under-stand most. Some I do not." He flicked the last pin away and ran his fingers from her scalp through the cascade of hair as though testing its length through touch. Her hair reached the small of her back. This pleased him. She did not cut her hair in mourning for her husband.

His fingers in her hair sent tingling sensations down her spine. "Why did you not speak to me before?"

"I speak now," he answered, and watched in fascination as strands of her hair curled around his finger.

"Will you answer my questions?"

"You, much ques-tion," he said, lifting a large section of her hair from her neck with the back of his hand. He brought the mass of waves over her shoulder to fall draping past her breast, momentarily admiring the image before him.

"I wish to understand. To learn. I do not mean to intrude."

"In-trude?" He groomed her, running fingers through the silken strands made reddish-gold in the firelight.

"To ask a question I've no right to ask, to do something without permission."

He scoffed. "As Eng-lish do. In-trude."

"Forgive me."

"Hmm. No sorry." Dark eyes met hers. "I in-trude, as the *Tosh shonte*. I help Wanchese and Nussacun. I burn *Tosh shonte* crop so have no food. I make you stay in my *yeehaukan*. I touch with no ... per-mis-sion." A primitive force inside him demanded that he reach for her. He placed a strong hand at her waist, the action causing her heart to flip and beat erratically. "I can take," he whispered, nudging her toward him, his hand sliding to the small of her back, anchoring her against him, testing the feel of her and how she fit with him. "I am not sorry. That is bad thing?"

Elizabeth's eyes widened. "You attacked our settlement? Our corn?" she asked in disbelief, acutely aware of his body pressed closely to hers. It pained her to think that this man participated in the decimation of their newly planted crops, and the deaths of Englishmen. It felt like a betrayal of all she had been told about his character.

Ompeu said nothing, his expression daring her to believe that he was capable of such a thing. Yet the look in her golden doe-eyes struck something inside him. Guilt? He was not certain, but suddenly, he felt some unease over what he had done. He did not regret attacking the English, but he found that doing so did not ease the pain of his loss as he thought it would. And now, his attempt to make her fear him with his words and intrusive actions appeared to backfire, for he sensed no trepidation on her part. Instead, she seemed to have the upper hand. Ompeu felt lost in her.

Her eyes searched his, sensing his discomfort at the confession. "I understand that we are intruders in this land, but we seek to live here peacefully. I do not believe you will harm me. No man who has treated my son with such kindness and care could be detestable and vile. He speaks of you often. He tells me what you have done for him, and how well you treat him. I was wrong to distrust you. I know you are attempting to frighten me now. Manteo says you are... *winkapew,* a good and honorable man, that you would not harm me," she said, more to reassure herself that the man she was pressed against was of no danger to her.

She spoke so quickly, that Ompeu struggled to understand her many words. "No. No hurt," he admitted softly, realizing that his plan to create fear in her was useless. He would never harm her. She knew this. His gaze roamed downward to the hint of full breasts that pushed against the fabric of her shift beneath the bodice. There were things he would like to do to her, but hurting was far from any of them.

She thought of something. "Are you angry with me because I stared at you that first day? I know it was terribly rude of me to do so. I asked Manteo to please beg your forgiveness…"

"Stared?"

"Looked at you, perhaps in a way that was improper," she clarified.

"*Matta.* You see me, I see you." They both stared that day.

"Perhaps we can form a truce?"

He gently placed the wrist he held captive against his chest, her palm against the smooth, hard-muscled warmth of his flesh. "*Ka ka torwawirocs yowo?* What is this 'truce'?"

Her gaze fell from his face to where he placed her hand. It was her turn to give in to fascination and abandon propriety. She observed the contrast in their skin tones, light against dark, and swallowed hard over the sudden and unfamiliar ache of longing in her throat. She became aware of him in every pore of her body; his nearness, the breadth of his shoulders, the scent of him, the heat of his skin. The hard pressure of his body against hers caused her heartbeat to quicken, as she experienced a warm rush of feminine awareness. She fought the urge to touch him as he had done to her. Her fingers flexed lightly over the lines of his tattoo, a slight caress. "An agreement. So there will be peace between us."

Her touch sent a spike of heat that hit him low in the belly. "I am not friend to the *Tosh shonte*," he said, slipping his hand to her waist, his thumb resting beneath her breast.

"You are a friend to my son. He is English." Somehow her other hand found its way to the hard curve of his bicep.

"*Matta*. He is Croatan. He will be Croatan warrior."

"I am Croatan as well. We have been made relatives, family."

"You wish to be my rel-ative?" he asked, stumbling over the word.

"Yes. I wish to be a friend, *nitáp*? Or... perhaps not hostile toward one another? You cannot pretend that I do not exist. Croatoan is my home now, I could not go back to England if I wished it."

"Is not a good thing," he whispered. He leaned in, touching his forehead to hers. "*Crenepo...* wo-man," Ompeu swallowed hard against the words he would utter next. "You must go," he said, his voice an aching rasp that curled through her on a wave of heat. The hand at her back pressed her body closer. His hips arched, ever so slightly.

His sensual movement against her was enough to send odd, fiery sensations sluicing to her feminine core, a new kind of yearning, moistened the place between her legs. "You wish me to leave?" she whispered.

"*Matta. Kupi.*"

Elizabeth felt his desire for her pressed against her skirts. Her body responded to his, a coiling arousal she had no idea how to stop. She slowly stepped out of his embrace, her fingers trailing away from his chest, willing herself not to look at his breechclout. She could not be offended by his body's reaction, for in mere moments, his nearness aroused and awakened unexplored sensual and erotic sensations in her as well. It was all too overwhelming for her. There was something between them that could not be denied, but she would not act upon it.

The entire encounter with him felt both strange and oddly familiar. She took a moment to gather herself before she spoke again, for he had shaken her sensibilities and muddled her brain. "Please consider what I have said, Ompeu. I would ask no more of you. My son is my life. His well-being is of the utmost importance to me. You are good to him, for him. I do not seek a husband, nor do I seek to harm. I have found a freedom, a peace and contentment among the Croatan people. Something… something I have not known in my life until I arrived here." Tawny hair fell forward shielding half of her face as she looked down, surprised to find herself fighting the sudden, hot ache of tears. The memory of her abusive, controlling husband was still too raw. "I am not your enemy, but if you are opposed to my friendship, I shall not trouble thee." She turned toward the entrance of the *yeehaukan*, lifted the flap, gave him one last look over her shoulder, then disappeared through the doorway.

Ompeu heard her voice as she left. "Come Ajax, good boy."

He ran an agitated hand through his long hair, ashamed of his behavior toward her. Elizabeth Cooke was not as he expected. Ompeu thought to create a fear in her that would have her running from his *yeehaukan* like a frightened maiden, effectively keeping her away from him. Instead, she met him head on, offered him friendship, and ignited a fire in him that sparked a disquieted yearning. That night he dreamed again. Since the English arrived, the dream came to him in some variation more frequently. No matter how the dream story began, it always ended the same.

He stood proud, four paws firm against the earth, his ears forward and erect as the she-wolf licked his snout and wagged her plush tail. She nipped him playfully, then jumped back and stood waiting, urging him to chase her. He could no longer ignore her. His desire for her became too great. He chased her, but she would not be caught. He ran. She stopped suddenly, and they rolled together. As they rolled, their bodies changed. Paws became hands and feet. Fur became smooth skin. He was a man again.

The she-wolf was gone, and the woman Elizabeth lie beneath him. He gathered her in his arms, touching her, joining his body with hers. Their souls entwined, comforting and soothing one another in good times and in bad. Somehow, he knew they would belong to each other. It was good. Their life was good. It would always be good with her.

Ompeu awoke in the darkened *yeehaukan*, a thin sheen of perspiration layering his skin, his breath hurried. He raised up on his elbows and looked down to find the evidence of his seed spilled. He sat up, rubbing his eyes with the heels of his hands. He wanted the dreams to stop their torment. He knew what the dreams meant. He knew when he held the woman in his arms. The war of emotions raged in his heart. His mind and his body were in terrible discord. He desired her. His mind did not wish to accept this. He did not want the she-wolf to be the *Tosh shonte* woman.

He pushed off from the sleeping pallet, cleaned himself, then sat at the edge of the bed. The moon had long since made its journey across the sky. The dawn would come soon. He fell back upon the soft furs, one word escaping his lips on a breath. "E-liz-a-beth."

Chapter Twelve

"What do ye think?" Emme sat back and waited expectantly. She and Towaye were seated in a grassy clearing this warm, late-summer morning. After she left the longhouse to gather wood, he surprised her, stepping from behind a tree. They walked hand in hand until they reached the secluded spot. He sat on the ground, pulling her beside him and offering her some sweet berries. Afterward, she thought to try something she had been wanting to share with him for some time.

Towaye's brows knit together in deep thought. A ghost of a smile played on his lips. "I do not know. Do it again."

"Hmm. I shall try something different," she said mostly to herself. A determined Emme rose on her knees and placed her arms about the seated Towaye's neck. She pressed her lips to his and kissed him more passionately this time. "Well?"

Towaye tried to put on a serious face and look as though he were considering a matter of grave importance.

"Ye must soften yer lips more," she said, and squeezed his cheeks lightly with one hand. Sudden laughter rose from his throat. She silenced him with an open-mouthed kiss and moved her hands from his face and neck down to his broad bare shoulders. She slowly pushed him back on the grass, not once breaking the kiss. His arms lifted to wrap around her.

"Mmm," he murmured. She tasted like berries.

She kissed and kissed him. She nibbled his bottom lip. She coaxed him with gentle swipes of her tongue. Suddenly she stopped. "Ye must close yer eyes," she instructed, and then kissed and kissed him again. "Well?"

"Mmm. It is not easy to learn," said a breathless Towaye. "Show me again."

Emme kissed him again. He untied her hair and ran his fingers through the long sun-gold strands, allowing it to fall around his face. He moved her slightly to rest directly on top of him.

She broke the kiss and smiled knowingly. "I think ye do like it," she whispered. "I can tell." She referred to his arousal, felt through their clothing.

He grinned up at her. "If Emme wishes to kiss, she will make Towaye wish for something more," he breathed huskily.

"Do ye like it? Is it not pleasing?"

"*Kupi*," he whispered, and quickly reversed their positions so that she was beneath him. He kissed her. His hair fell forward, a black curtain shielding their faces, and blocking out the rest of the world.

When he lifted his head, Emme traced a fingertip over his bottom lip, her eyes filled with love. "Mistress Dare is against our plans to wed," she whispered sadly.

Towaye rolled away from her, dark eyes scanning the puffy clouds. "I have spoken to Master Dare," he said, reaching for her. Emme snuggled against his shoulder. "He has given his blessing. We are not in England. She cannot stop us. No one can."

Emme lifted her head, moving her body over him. She kissed him once more. "I love you."

"Say this," he grinned up at her. "*Kuwumáras*."

"*Kuwumáras*," she repeated carefully. "What does it mean?"

"I love you," he said, and then kissed her.

*　　*　　*

Weeks passed, Elizabeth thought it must be early August. She had given up trying to keep track of exact dates. The Croatan called it the Green Corn Moon.

Neither of them mentioned that evening in Ompeu's *yeehaukan*, but Elizabeth noticed his demeanor toward her had softened. He still did not speak often, but she was no longer completely ignored. It seemed to her that Ompeu was not a man of words, unless he felt he had something to say. He allowed his actions to speak for him. When he did speak, she noted his English improved daily. He remained an intriguing mystery to her, and anytime she was in his presence, she felt drawn to him. But after Cooke's death, she did not wish to consider involvement with any man, English or Croatan.

She loved living among the Croatan. There was freedom here that she would not experience in England. Croatan women occupied their roles separate from men, but were not measured by the same metric as English women. They oversaw the home, including working in the fields, cultivating crops, cooking, and caring for children. Elizabeth assumed, as most English had, that aboriginal women worked tirelessly, while their men were lazy. While true that women were the backbone of the agricultural society, women also held a powerful role as they were the owners of the village assets. Homes belonged to women. Bloodlines were matrilineal. The men hunted and fished, providing the family with meat, and protected the village, or waged war. They also helped clear fields for planting. Men and women retained the final say in their choice of marriage partner. Elders might have some influence out of respect, but

Elizabeth believed that if she were a Croatan woman years ago, she would have refused to be Cooke's wife, and married a man of her own choosing.

One aspect of Croatan life she found initially unsettling was that men and women were allowed sexual intimacies before or outside of marriage. She suspected that some women also traded sexual favors for gifts or food. And no one in the village seemed to care that a few couples shared the same gender. Elizabeth was not so ignorant to believe that such people did not exist in England. Croatan society openly accepted such arrangements, whereas English society would not. *'Judge not, lest ye be judged.'* It was not for her to condemn anyone. Croatans measured people by their character, and their contributions to the community for the benefit of all. Ultimately, it was this belief that she supported as a woman with newfound liberation.

Eleanor, as promised, established her mission of Anglicizing the Croatan at any opportunity. Some of the people believed that the Bible itself held magical properties and would touch it or rub it over their bodies so that good spirits might bless them. She also had some influence about the manner of dress, especially for the women who often walked about bare-breasted in the heat of summer. Elizabeth did not interfere with Eleanor's attempts to "civilize" the Croatan, but nor did she offer help. She reasoned that there were valuable aspects of each culture, and desired to find a way to blend them.

"Goodness," said Rose as she and Elizabeth worked a mixture of deer's brains into the freshly scraped hide, under the watchful eye of Poussu and Mamankanois, a lovely young woman who Elizabeth and Emme met the first day they'd arrived. She had washed their clothing and helped with the bathing ritual. The small group of women knelt in front of Poussu's *yeehaukan* around the stretched-out skin. "I did not realize this would be such a long, arduous task. It's unfortunate Emme could not be with us."

Emme was currently spending time in the menstrual hut. A practice Elizabeth and the other English women initially found absurd. The Croatan believed that a woman's power was strong during menstruation, and so she must live apart so as not to ruin the hunt, the fish catch, or the crops. No warrior would touch a woman during this time. She believed it to be a ridiculous custom until she spent time in the hut herself. It turned out to be quite a peaceful respite from the daily work. She was able to rest, read, write, and sew. After the week or so ended, she returned feeling renewed. Eleanor still balked at the idea, claiming it was superstitious, heathen nonsense.

"This hide will be soft and pliable as velvet by the time it's finished," Elizabeth said, as she determinedly rubbed the brain concoction into her section of the hide. "It will make a fine garment." She was not certain she could give up her few English dresses. She was not prepared for a complete change, though she did entertain the idea of sewing her own loose-fitting deerskin dress, for the Croatan women appeared comfortable, while she perspired in her heavy linen and wool skirts. It would be simpler than the tight, front-laced bodice, layered over a shift. She doubted she would ever be able to expose her breasts as many of the Croatan women did, but the desire for freedom from the restrictive clothing she wore became ever more tempting during the warm summer days. "It will be worth the effort, I think."

The skin soaked in water for a week. The flesh, fat, and sinew scraped off with a tool made from an animal horn or a shell. The skin would be washed again, twisted, and staked out, stretched tight as a drum on a wooden frame. Elizabeth and Rose began the tanning process. After they were finished, the hide would then be soaked again, wrung out and twisted. This process was then repeated.

Mamankanois knelt next to them, speaking in the Croatan dialect. Elizabeth listened attentively, wishing she would acquire the ability to understand every word. Their language was difficult for her, and unlike anything she had heard before. It frustrated her, since Poussu seemed to understand more English than Elizabeth understood Croatan. She felt as though she would never master the simplest conversation. She prided herself on her intelligence, and yet her efforts to learn the Algonquian dialect proved a humbling experience.

Mamankanois gestured, indicating that the skin should be soaked again. The women cleaned their hands in a clay pot filled with water.

At that moment, John Bridger strolled past. He nodded to them. "Ladies, what cheer?" he smiled in greeting.

"Good morrow," Elizabeth returned, drying her hands on her apron.

He smiled at the women again, attempting to keep his glance at Mamankanois appear casual. The young Croatan woman kept her eyes lowered, examining the hide, a shy smile on her lips.

After Bridger passed them, Rose and Elizabeth shared a look. "I've heard that Bridger has been bringing fresh meat and gifts to Mamankanois and her parents," Rose said. "I do believe he's smitten." Her lips quirked in a good-natured grin.

At the sound of her name, Mamankanois lifted curious eyes to the *Tosh shonte* women. Elizabeth touched her hand reassuringly. "Bridger," she said. "He is a good man, *winkapew*," her smile warm as she gestured toward him.

Mamankanois smiled in return indicating that if she did not understand Elizabeth's words, she understood the sentiment behind them. She continued to smile softly as she turned her head, a look of admiration in her eyes as she watched John Bridger's retreating form.

"I believe our friend here is equally smitten," Elizabeth commented amiably.

Poussu spoke to Mamankanois in their native tongue. "Will you accept the man with hair like the People and eyes like the sky?"

"*Kupi*," Mamankanois answered. "He spoke to Manteo, asking him how a Croatan man courts a woman he wishes to take as a wife. My family and I have accepted his gifts." Mamankanois rinsed her hands, shaking off the excess water. "I have seen the way one of our warriors looks at your new daughter," Mamankanois said, changing the subject.

Poussu grew serious. "Yes, I've also seen this."

"You are against it?" Mamankanois asked. "Your son Towaye, will join with Emme as his wife soon."

"I am not against it," Poussu sighed. She was not against it at all. In fact, she sent Elizabeth to Ompeu's *yeehaukan* with every evening meal when he was not away. Of course, she had done this purposefully. "But I believe Ompeu does not know his heart. He carries the burden of guilt over what happened to my daughter that was." She smiled sadly, thinking of her beautiful Sequan. "And while I miss her and my grandchild terribly, I do not hold the same anger in my heart for the *Tosh shonte*." She gestured to Elizabeth and Rose, who sat quietly, respectfully listening to Poussu, though they could not understand her words. "These good women here did not kill my daughter. Ompeu's anger is toward all *Tosh shonte*, not merely those responsible for what happened at Desamunkepeuc." She paused, shaking her head lightly. "If it could have happened differently, the Croatan would not have gone to Desamunkepeuc that day. But we cannot see the future, and we cannot change what is past, and we cannot live in either place for overlong. She and my grandson have been gone more than one full turn of the seasons. My daughter that was, would not wish for Ompeu to spend his days living with guilt and anger over things he could not foresee nor change until he is an old man. Perhaps in time he will come to know his heart again."

Poussu thought she knew something of Ompeu's dreams. He spoke of them in his sleep when she tended him after his mourning sacrifice on the dune. She continued to wonder over the connection between the doe and Elizabeth. How long before Ompeu would come to understand what the vision meant? When would he realize that it must be fulfilled?

"Perhaps the Green Corn Ceremony will help to restore balance," Mamankanois offered.

Poussu shrugged, uncertain yet hopeful. "Perhaps."

*   *   *

Manteo explained the Green Corn Ceremony to his English relatives. The ceremony took place every year when the early corn was ripe, and lasted seven days, including all preparations. It was a special occasion, a time of renewal. A time when old disputes were forgiven, and enemies reconciled. All debts and crimes were pardoned, except for murder. It was a time when all evil was purged, made ready by the purification of all for a new year. All fires in the village and in homes were extinguished and new, sacred fires were ignited. Many villagers fasted and prayed. Feasting and merriment followed. Sacrifices of food were made to appease the spirits. It was a time of giving thanks to the gods, reaffirming good intentions for the year to come, and renewing the belief in the sacredness of life.

Due to the lack of rains, the first harvest was not as plentiful. This however did not discourage preparations or dampen spirits. The Green Corn Ceremony would assure the fertility of the fields and the survival of the people.

Several villages on the island of Croatoan joined in this celebration. Elizabeth witnessed the joyous flurry of activity. On the second day, she and Emme helped Poussu sweep out the central fire of the longhouse. Old clothing, furnishings, or utensils would be taken to a bonfire constructed in the village hub, blessed by the holy man. All would be burned and replaced with new.

Surprisingly, Eleanor Dare added a packet of old belongings to the fire. Her expression was melancholy, and Elizabeth mentally promised to speak with her at the first opportunity. She and Eleanor did not often agree on many topics, but there was no ill-will between them. Life and work on Croatoan kept Elizabeth occupied, and Eleanor often kept herself apart.

Emme decided this was the perfect opportunity to rid herself of the English attire she had stored away. Her dress, undergarments, and shoes were tossed into the communal flames. She watched the last vestiges of her old life in England, burn. "Is it wrong t' feel unburdened?" she asked Elizabeth. They watched as countless villagers brought out their old items.

"You are leaving the old behind. Making ready for what is to come." Elizabeth caught sight of Ompeu, carrying a bundle. He tossed it into the bonfire. She could not take her eyes from his handsome form as he cast *uppowoc* into the flames and spoke silent words. She wondered what he prayed for. Elizabeth paused to accept a drink from Poussu, offering her thanks. She sniffed the foamy white concoction. A strong herbal scent wafted to her nostrils. It tasted bitter. Poussu urged her to drink all of it, causing Elizabeth's face to distort comically.

Emme laughed at her friend's facial expression. She placed a hand on Elizabeth's arm, holding it. "Why do ye not burn yours?" she suggested excitedly, her face luminous. "'Tis liberating. I cannot describe it!"

Elizabeth coughed, then smiled at her friend. "I have thought of it," she confessed. "But your heart is willing and eager." She cleared her throat. The bitterness of the drink stuck on her tongue. "I fear I am not yet inclined to divest myself of the last bit of home."

"Perhaps one day, ye will be," Emme replied.

Elizabeth coughed. "Perhaps."

The singing, dancing and feasting continued for some time. Elizabeth felt her stomach lurch unexpectedly. She began to sweat. Her heartbeat quickened. A wave of the jitters raced through her. Fearful that she would lose her most recent meal, her eyes darted frantically, searching for an unoccupied, hidden space. There were so many people. Her first thought was to run back to the longhouse. Instead she turned away from the festivities, walking briskly, then running outside the compound.

Ompeu had seen Poussu give Elizabeth the white drink. It was a drink that caused purging. It was part of the ritual of the Green Corn Ceremony, so that all on the inside of the body would be purified and cleansed for the new year. Usually women did not drink enough to cause the purging, only men did. He wondered if Elizabeth was unaccustomed to its effects.

She held her mouth closed as she ran, reaching a wooded area outside the village proper where there were few people. She could hold it no longer. She vomited. Bent at the waist, coughing and retching, Elizabeth did not hear the footsteps nearby, nor sense his presence until she stood upright, fighting for air. She turned to find Ompeu standing there, watching her.

Elizabeth hastily wiped her mouth with the apron of her skirt. Embarrassment flooded her. He was the last person she hoped to see. But even profound embarrassment could not stop the next wave. She turned from him and heaved once more. She felt a hand push her long hair aside, holding it away from her face. Another rubbed her back soothingly. He spoke a soft litany of Algonquian words, a quiet chant. Was he praying? Was she dying?

"Am I dying?" she choked. Elizabeth could not recall ever becoming this violently ill.

"You will not die."

You will not die. Something about the voice, the words, and the way they were spoken struck her. He must have said the words to her before. Another time. Another place. She pushed the thought aside as her gut convulsed again. When her stomach emptied, Elizabeth straightened, feeling much relieved. Ompeu released her and handed her a scrap of deerskin. She took it. "Forgive me," she rasped, her throat ached. Her head pounded in time to the drumbeat in the distance. Her eyes were watery, her nose plugged. She wiped her face, too mortified to look him in the eye. "I must have eaten something disagreeable," she said, collecting herself.

"White drink," he said. "You have much."

Did she detect a smile in his voice? He must find her predicament quite amusing. "White drink?" she spared him a glance. His handsome face was impassive, but his eyes betrayed a glint of humor. "What is white drink?"

"You drink. Poussu give you. Cere-mony to make new."

"Ugh." Elizabeth shivered, smoothing her hair, and gathering it away from her face. "I certainly do not feel new at present. I feel absolutely repulsive. Please remind me never to drink it again." She looked down at her soiled dress, thinking she may have to burn it after all. Removing her apron, she folded it, hiding the stains. She would wash it, and the dress as soon as possible.

Dusk was upon them. Ompeu extended his arm toward the village, indicating that they should return. Elizabeth walked a few unsteady feet toward the continuing festivities before turning to thank him for his care of her. He was gone. Her eyes scanned the surrounding woods to no avail. How did he disappear so effortlessly? How did he know Poussu gave her the drink? How did he know where she had gone? The realization that he must have been observing her for some time did not disturb or annoy her. Oddly, despite the humiliating circumstance, his nearness was comforting.

The following day the celebrations continued. Elizabeth felt revived, though she vowed never to go near the white drink again. She learned that the drink was black, but when shaken created a white froth. Information she would tuck away, for if she ever saw it again, she would know not to consume it. Sporting a clean, dark blue dress and dulled-white apron, she wrung out and hung the old gray one to dry. The drums started a steady rhythm. As she finished, she heard an exuberant voice.

"Must come!" Mamankanois ran toward her happily, pulling on Elizabeth's hand. She laughed as she guided her *Tosh shonte* friend to the ceremonial arena. Elizabeth joined Mamankanois and a group of women in the outer circle of the men's Feather Dance.

The men were a spectacle of colors, ornaments, and feathers. It seemed to Elizabeth that each man attempted to outdo the other, dressing in the most outrageous fashion. If there were a contest, Manteo's ceremonial dress would have outdone them all. Poussu watched her sons dance proudly, for the Feather Dance healed and rejuvenated the entire community. She was especially pleased that Ompeu was among the dancers. It meant that he was returning to them, and to himself.

Poussu showed Elizabeth and Emme how to keep the beat for the men. She gave them each gourd rattles, filled with seeds or stones, and demonstrated a two-step bouncing movement that women outside the circle performed. Rose ran to join them and laughed delightedly at the sights and sounds. "My own husband is among them!" she exclaimed, as she picked up the women's dance step. They watched Henry Darby, not lavishly costumed as the others, but just as enthusiastic in his dance movements.

"Oh my, and John Bridger as well!"

Mamankanois yipped and sang out her encouragement for Bridger. Her dark eyes beaming with love and pride, her beautiful smile was contagious. Emme hooted and hollered for her love, Towaye. Rose sang a quick chant of "Henry, Henry, Henry," before bursting into laughter.

Elizabeth could not remember the last time she laughed and smiled with this much joy. She peeked over her shoulder. The children formed a circle behind the women, mimicking the same steps, keeping the beat with rattles. Her gaze settled on her son, Phillip. No, she mentally corrected. His name is Onxe. Phillip was the quiet, withdrawn English boy. He shook the rattle in time, dancing, smiling and laughing with his friends. Her heart burst with love. It occurred to her, that in the months they lived among the Croatan she had never worked harder, but life here proved to be the most blessed she had ever experienced.

Turning forward, her eyes unexpectedly met Ompeu's. Her breath left her, for he was magnificent. Brown, blue and gray feathers adorned his crown. Similar feathers hung in multiple layers from a string belt that set low on his hips forming a kind of skirt that lifted and swayed with his movement. Fur wraps encased his calves, copper bands encircled his biceps, a copper disk hung from his neck. The lean muscles of his chest and torso rippled with each movement of his dance. He was beautiful. Elizabeth fought against sensuous thoughts of him. She recalled the night he held her in his arms, and the way her body reacted when they were pressed together. And now it seemed he was capable of arousing desires in her with a single look. Ompeu danced away. Elizabeth's cheeks burned hot.

Days later, when the Green Corn Ceremony ended, people went back to their villages and homes feeling renewed and replenished for the year to come.

*   *   *

September 1588

She convinced Ompeu to take her and Elizabeth, along with young Onxe to gather medicinal plants. He was reluctant since it meant being in the presence of the very woman he hoped to avoid. Poussu would hear none of his objections.

Elizabeth had never been aboard a canoe, but she had seen them float effortlessly over the water. After her initial concern that it would tip at the slightest movement, she was amazed at how smoothly the craft moved, gliding soundlessly. Her son handled the front end of the canoe like an experienced oarsman. Poussu sat in front of her, while Ompeu sat behind taking charge of the rear paddle, which he used expertly as a rudder.

Elizabeth gripped the side of the canoe, acutely aware of the man behind her. Today he wore his long hair bound up, tied in some intricate knot near the top of his head. Shell earrings dangled from his ears. He wore next to nothing, except for the deerskin apron that covered him from navel to knee. To avoid any further reaction he might evoke in her, she distracted herself with the opportunity to experience the view from the water. Red cedars, cypress, and dogwood trees stood in varying sizes and shapes against the sky. Their leaves had already begun to change, and soon would fall. Tiny insects buzzed and danced above the water's surface. A flock of herons rose suddenly from the bank as the canoe passed, the echo of their cries sounding as though a mass of people shouted all at once. Elizabeth was awestruck watching them take flight, a light joyous bubble of laughter rising from her throat.

Her face turned toward him as she followed the birds in flight, and Ompeu watched her expression, alight in wonder as she took in the beauty of their surroundings. Sights and sounds that amazed her, he sometimes took for granted. Ossomocomuck was a beautiful place, a land he loved, a home he would fight for. It was her home now as well. To see her appreciation for this land gave him an odd sense of pride.

"Take us to the ridge, over there," Poussu pointed to the left. Ompeu dipped his oar, pivoting the canoe in the direction she indicated.

When they reached the place Poussu selected, Ompeu leapt from the canoe as it slid partially up the sandy bank. Onxe jumped out as well and offered Poussu his hand. She took it gratefully, stepping out.

The canoe wobbled, and when Elizabeth stood to climb out, she lost her balance, nearly falling over; her long skirts hindering her efforts to remain upright. She felt strong hands fit around her waist to steady her and lift her out of the craft. "Thank you," Elizabeth said, embarrassed over the near mishap. The blush crept further up her cheeks as she realized her hands were placed on Ompeu's shoulders. They remained this way momentarily, as something sensuous stirred between them. She took an awkward step back, apologizing. Ompeu said nothing, yet held onto her arm, guiding her up the bank.

He spent the afternoon, eyes and ears vigilant, yet consistently nearby, ready with an English word for Poussu if he knew it. He tried to explain what he could about the properties of each plant and how it should be prepared. In some plants, the root, or the stem, not the leaf was used for healing. Poussu said that during the Harvest Moon, they must collect all they could, for soon the days would turn cold, and they would need medicines over the long winter. She urged Elizabeth to

190 ❦ Jen Caruso

sniff, touch, and examine every item presented to her, then looked to Ompeu for translation.

When they came upon a type of bluish-white clay, Poussu scraped some away, collecting it, and placing it into a separate deerskin pouch. She called it *wapeih* and Ompeu explained that it was a healing earth used to treat wounds. Elizabeth vaguely recalled hearing of a type of mineral-enriched earth that bore healing properties. Poussu reached for Elizabeth's hand, tugging her closer until she stood directly in front of the older woman. She took some of the healing clay, rubbed her fingers into it and then daubed streaks of damp, chalky-white onto Elizabeth's forehead, a line on each cheek and a circle above her left breast, near her heart. Poussu then took a pinch of *uppowoc* from one of her pouches and cast it into the air.

"*Wapeih*," she said, placing the flat of her palm between Elizabeth's breasts. "You will be like Wapeih that comes from our Mother, the Earth. You are a woman who is wounded, yet you will heal the deepest of wounds."

Elizabeth gave Poussu her full attention, not comprehending but understanding that something solemn and important was being conveyed. When Poussu stepped back, Elizabeth turned her gaze to Ompeu, a myriad of questions in her hazel eyes. He merely stared at her, his expression vaguely contemplative. He turned away.

"What did she say?" Elizabeth asked.

"You have new name," he said, stopping to look over his shoulder. "Wapeih." He turned then and strode purposefully back to the canoe.

Elizabeth followed him, brimming with more questions. Instead she helped him to retrieve the bundles of food they brought along. "Please tell Poussu that I thank her."

Ompeu handed her a wrapped deerskin bundle from the bow. "You tell. Say this, *kenah*," he said, still keeping his gaze averted, pretending to examine some flaw in the canoe.

Elizabeth's fingers grazed his as she took the pack. "*Kenah*," she repeated, then waited expectantly. "Is that good, *wingan*?"

Ompeu looked down into her golden eyes. "*Kupi.* Good."

She smiled up at him. He could not look away. She was strange, and beautiful, and Ompeu felt himself drowning. "Thank you, Ompeu... oh... I should say... *kenah*," she corrected. "I will tell Poussu. Are you hungry? I've packed victuals aplenty for us." Elizabeth turned her gaze away to take in the sky and the scenery along the bank. "Such a glorious day, would you not agree?" She realized she was making a feeble attempt at conversation. "I so love this time of year."

Ompeu said nothing, but took the bundle from her, leading her back to where Onxe and Poussu waited.

They ate mostly in amiable silence, the women on one side, the males on the other as was the Croatan custom. When they finished, Poussu took the boy away with her claiming she wished to show him something of interest.

Elizabeth busied herself putting away and clearing up their picnic area, realizing that this was the first time Ompeu shared a meal with them. She watched him covertly as she worked. He sat with his back against a tree, legs outstretched, crossed at the ankles. He chipped away at a piece of wood with his flint knife.

"Why do you not sup with us?" she asked without thinking. "Or retire at night with us in the longhouse?"

Ompeu lifted his head, black brows knit, as though confused by her sudden question. Still, he said nothing.

"Forgive me, I simply wonder. You are welcome to join us, of course. I thought it was a custom of the Croatan to eat together, and for extended families to live together. It seems you avoid people…," her voice trailed away, silenced by his reserved expression.

Ompeu's gaze fell to the carving in his hands, smoothing a rough spot with his thumb. He continued to work silently.

Elizabeth dropped down beside him, tying up the pack of remaining food. She thought to try a different tact. Encouraging him to speak and have a half-decent conversation was somehow becoming her mission. "Can you tell me what the poles are about? The ones in the center of the town with carved faces where the dancing took place. What are they? What about the *Kewás*, can you tell me of them? What does it mean? The carved statues? What is a *mantóac*? Are they gods? Spirits?"

Ompeu lifted his head, dark eyes moving over her, assessing her slowly from top to bottom. She was close enough to touch. "Why you come here?" he asked sincerely, without rancor.

Thinking he meant she was kneeling too closely, Elizabeth attempted to scoot back.

Ompeu grasped a fold of her skirt near her hip, tugging her. "*Matta.* Stay." He looked at her for an interminable time, as though he possessed the ability to see into the depths of her soul. Elizabeth became uncomfortable under his scrutiny and felt the warm rush of heat flush her cheeks. She was unlike any woman he had known. Inquisitive and unafraid of things she did not understand. Instead she wished to learn, hungry for knowledge. He was not annoyed with her questions, and would answer them in time, but since she pressed him for conversation, he had a few questions of his own. "Why you come *here*? This land?" he clarified, emphasizing with a gesture that encompassed their surroundings.

"I see. We are answering questions with questions." she mused aloud lightly, sitting now, with her legs folded aside, her skirts covering her.

Ompeu watched her arrange the long skirts around her, thinking to ask why she wore so many clothes.

"You have always question," he shrugged. "I have also," he defended amiably.

"Very well. I came here… well, because my husband wished it. To be free of his debt, and begin a new life, I suppose. We were promised a tract of land."

He shook his head. That was not entirely the answer he wanted. "Why *Tosh shonte* come?"

"*Tosh shonte* come because they… we seek new ways to trade," she answered as simply as she could. This man would not know or care about political intrigues in England, or an impending war with Spain, or Sir Walter Ralegh, or privateering, or any mission to Christianize the people here. Those reasons seemed complicated and moot at this point.

"Hmm." Ompeu continued to focus on working the piece of wood in his hands.

"Is that not a good reason?"

"Wish to trade but make enemy of the People."

"Not very intelligent, is it?" She could not argue his statement. The English forged enemies out of most of the neighboring tribes in the area. The Croatan were the last remaining friends who sheltered, protected, and cared for them. "Not very good."

He brushed away bits of wood from his lap. "You take by force. *Tosh shonte* come, take land that is for all. When you come, many sick, many die. Take gods away. Kill great Roanoac *werowance*. Take *pogatowr* in the night."

She swallowed, eyes downcast, staring at her folded hands. Elizabeth was aware of the illnesses that caused many deaths among the indigenous people, devastating their communities, yet sparing the English. She did not understand it. She did not believe that God would cause such heartbreak and calamity as punishment that many English posited. She also knew it was Master Lane's extreme violence against the Roanoac that made their entire existence here a perilous one. "The men who stole corn were punished severely and are no longer among us." And though difficult to speak, for the uncomfortable sense of helplessness the words evoked, she added, "I know we are allowed to live here due to the graciousness of your people. I am grateful." It was true. The Croatan, at great risk to themselves, welcomed the English. Were it not for this benevolence, the remaining colonists would not survive.

Ompeu looked up at her, dark eyes thoughtful. He reached up to gently graze a thumb over the clay stripe still present on her cheek. The action caused her to draw back slightly in mild surprise. Ompeu shook his head. "No hurt."

She blinked. "I know you would not."

Returning his hand to his lap, he rubbed his thumb and forefinger together, contemplating the clay, observing the way it smeared easily between his fingers, and recalling the words Poussu spoke of her. She would heal the deepest of wounds. "Why you have no man,

Wapeih?" he asked without looking at her, using her new name.

"Why do you not have a wife?" He sent her a brief glance, telling her it was a question he would not entertain. Elizabeth had clearly overstepped, as he had done. Ompeu returned to whittling away at the piece of wood.

Elizabeth's gaze slid down to watch his hands as they worked. Masculine hands that could wield a knife or a spear, catch fish, kill an enemy, comfort her child, caress a woman's body. She shivered lightly, remembering his hands at her waist and in her hair. "I have no man because he was among those responsible for stealing *pogatowr* in the night, among other transgressions. He is gone now. Hanged for his crimes," she admitted quietly. She did not tell him of her role in exposing her husband's scheme. It was a guilt she did not know how to process, nor speak of.

When he lifted his head, there was sympathy in his gaze, his dark eyes warming her. Ompeu gave her a slight nod of understanding. Her husband was a bad man. Was it wrong of him to think she was better off without him? Was it wrong of him to be glad her husband was dead? Ompeu looked away to stare out into the forest around them. He seemed pensive, not disturbed or angry. "She is gone. And my son."

Elizabeth studied his handsome profile and seemed to understand that his answer was akin to a gift. Something private he shared as a way to show her that they were not so different, and that the pain of his loss still cut him deeply. Sincere empathy made her reach for him, placing her hand atop his. "I am truly sorry," she whispered. "*Kenah*, Ompeu."

The surprise contact of her touch, gentle and comforting, stirred him. "For you, Wapeih," he murmured, taking her small, pale hand and turning it palm up. He placed the finished piece of wood there and rose to his feet.

Momentarily baffled, she realized what he had done. "I have nothing to give you in return," she said, knowing it was customary to reciprocate a gift. She did not wish to offend him, for generosity was important to the Croatan.

"I know you," he said solemnly. He then left her to gaze in amazement at his gift of a roughly carved, but unmistakable doe.

His words and his gift surprised her, not only for their sentiment, but for their odd familiarity, as though there were deeper meaning somewhere, hidden in a place she could not fully grasp. Elizabeth admired his handiwork, closed her fingers around the warm carving, and tucked Ompeu's gift into the pocket of her skirt.

The return trip was subdued and quiet until they were closer to home. The sun moved toward its destination across the sky, indicating late afternoon. Ompeu's attention shifted from mere observance of his surroundings to high alert, his eyes scanning the tree line along the bank. He saw something there, and spoke to Poussu in quiet, urgent tones, words Elizabeth could not understand. A whisper of unease teased her senses as she caught the scent of burning wood, and saw the billowing smoke, much too large to be a simple cook fire.

"Onxe, fast," he urged. The boy dipped his oar with more force, increasing the pace.

As they reached the bank, Ompeu hurdled over the water before the canoe hit the sand, racing into the woods toward their village.

Hiking her skirts to her thighs, Elizabeth was able to step out of the canoe without trouble. "Ompeu!" Elizabeth moved to follow him, but Poussu grasped her wrist, holding her back. "What is happening?" she asked the older woman, panic rising in her chest.

Poussu's words were imperative and insistent as she reached for Onxe, pulling on their hands, leading them both away from their village at a run that belied her age. They heard the harsh pop of musket fire in the distance.

"*Nek*," he said. "Our village is under attack!"

Sick fear coiled in the pit of her stomach. "We must go back!" Elizabeth pulled up short, attempting to run in the opposite direction, toward their homes and friends.

"*Matta!*" Poussu continued to pull on Elizabeth's hand. She spoke firmly, and Elizabeth became frustrated that she did not fully comprehend.

Onxe matched Poussu's urgency, pulling on his mother. "*Nek*, you must come. *Nunohum* wishes us to help her," he urged, using the Croatan term of respect for Poussu, referring to her as his grandmother.

Reluctantly, Elizabeth allowed herself to be pulled in Poussu's direction. They ran through the thick forest until they reached a section of the bank that appeared to be oddly overgrown with vegetation. Poussu scanned the area briefly, seemed to find what she was looking for, and began pulling away the overgrowth until Elizabeth saw the partially hidden canoe. It appeared to be large enough for twenty men.

She and her son helped Poussu uncover the canoe, but instead of climbing into it as Elizabeth thought she would, Poussu pushed it back into the water. The three of them pushed and shoved mightily until the large canoe floated on the water's surface, taken up by the current, and sent out on a slow journey across the sound. They uncovered two more canoes, and heaved them all into the water, the three of them winded from their frantic and difficult work.

"Secotan, Roanoac," Poussu said, leaning against a tree to catch her breath. Moments later she pushed herself away from the tree and led them further into the forest where they hid behind several large, fallen trees.

Elizabeth realized that Ompeu must have seen the hidden craft from the water. The Secotan and Roanoac camouflaged their canoes and crept toward their village in a surprise attack.

"What shall we do now?" Elizabeth asked worriedly.

"Wait. Ompeu come," Poussu answered, surprising Elizabeth with the English words.

"Are you well??" she asked her son.

"*Kupi*," he answered. "We will be safe, *nek*." He grasped her hand, reassuringly. "We must do what *nunohum* says."

Elizabeth squeezed her son's hand, silently proud of his ability to remain calm, and of his growing command of the language that proved difficult for her to learn. She leaned back against a fallen tree trunk, tipping her head back to rest against the rough, jagged bark until her breathing gradually slowed. Wait for Ompeu. But what if Ompeu did not come for them? What if he were harmed, or killed? Elizabeth pushed the thought from her mind, not wishing to consider it. He would come for them. He must.

The distant report of musket fire, the shouts of men, whooping and screeching reached her ears; the sounds of battle growing ever closer to their hiding place. Were the Roanoac and Secotan in retreat, heading in their direction?

Poussu gestured, urging them to dig. The three of them dug, frantically scooping up the soft, cool earth with their hands, creating a shallow hole, enough for them to slip partially beneath the fallen logs. She placed her arms around Elizabeth and Onxe, imploring them to flatten themselves against the sandy earth. She covered them with sand, dirt and rotting leaves, then broke off a few nearby lush branches. She returned to them, sliding as much of her body as possible into the crowded space, covering herself, and placing the branches in front of the hiding spot as added protection.

Voices grew closer. Elizabeth attempted to slow her breathing but found it impossible. Her heart pounded furiously. She looked over at her son in the cramped, semi-darkened space. He was still, his face a mask of calm, waiting, listening. The sound of rustling foliage and the pounding of feet against the earth passed close to their hiding place. She squirmed, shifting enough to be able to peek through a narrow slot between the logs. A ululating cry rent the air, causing Elizabeth's heart to jolt. It was Ompeu, outrunning and leaping onto another warrior, who attempted to sprint to where the canoes were left. More men flooded the scene blocking her view of him. There was more shouting and yelling, both in English and Algonquian.

Elizabeth felt as though she would burst out of her skin. She did not know how much longer she could remain still and silent. She lost sight of Ompeu in the melee, her fear for him causing a knot of panic to fill her chest. Elizabeth lowered her head and prayed it would end soon. She prayed for the safety of her friends, their faces appearing in her mind; Emme and Rose,

Mamankanois and John Bridger, Manteo and Towaye, Eleanor, Ananias and baby Virginia. Her heart wrenched in her chest, at the thought of the village children. Lastly, she thought of Ompeu; beautiful, angry, mysterious, proud. She closed her eyes and prayed for him as well.

Chapter Thirteen

The enemy was trapped between joint forces of the *Tosh shonte* and Croatan on one side and a body of water on the other. Without their canoes, they fled into the sound, its waters shallow for some distance.

Shouts and cheering at the retreat, caused Poussu to emerge from the hiding place and peer out cautiously. Before she could crawl out completely, Ompeu was there helping her to her feet. They spoke as they embraced warmly, Poussu's eyes closing in relief. Towaye jogged toward them shortly after, hugging her as well. They walked away together, continuing their conversation. The remaining men regrouped checking wounds, helping one another, removing usable possessions from dead enemies, dragging the bodies away, and tying up the few who lived, but were not fortunate enough to escape.

Most of the men began filtering back to the village to assess the damages at home and see about loved ones. Some remained behind performing a sweep of the area.

Onxe crawled out from beneath the logs, sprung up, and wrapped his arms around Ompeu's middle, squeezing his eyes shut. "I was not afraid," he said. "I'm glad you are here, Ompeu." Onxe squatted, peering into the shallow space under the logs. "Are you all right, *nek*?"

"I believe I am," Elizabeth responded, her voice strained as she attempted to wiggle a foot that was stuck. Her long skirts snagged on bark and branches as she scooted.

Ompeu placed a comforting hand on the boy's shoulder, then watched him run off to where Poussu spoke with her son, Towaye.

When Elizabeth poked her head out from beneath the logs, she was pulled out by her wrists, and set on her feet, Ompeu lifting her easily. Amusement danced in his eyes, as he plucked dead leaves from her hair. She was a sight to behold, covered in dirt. He silently thanked *Kiwasa* for keeping her, the boy, and Poussu safe.

Elizabeth brushed a few more leaves from her hair and dirt from her clothing. She thanked him, breathing a sigh of relief at the sight of him safe and alive. She caught a glimpse of red, her eyes widening. "You've been injured." She gestured to his upper arm where a gash oozed fresh blood.

Still energized after the fight, adrenaline rushed through his veins. He looked at the superficial wound, apparently unaware of it. He shrugged it away, not noticing the pain until now.

Poussu returned and bade him sit on the log, gesturing for Elizabeth to tend him. Ompeu thought to protest, then relented.

"It seems you are my first patient," Elizabeth shrugged apologetically.

He watched her hands on his skin as she cleansed the wound with water from a deerskin bag Poussu brought to her. Her touch was gentle and soothing. A tingling raced up his spine.

"You saw the hidden canoes, didn't you?" Elizabeth asked. Her soft voice warmed him.

"*Kupi*," was all he said, fidgeting. His knee bounced rhythmically.

Elizabeth thought he might jump out of his seat. "I saw you in the fight. I was worried."

He lifted dark, questioning eyes to her face. "Worried?"

Her gaze flitted to his briefly, then returned to his wound, staunching the blood with a folded piece of soft deerskin. "Concerned. For you, for your safety." She saw his uncertainty. "I was afraid for you," she said.

Understanding dawned. "I am a warrior. We fight well and the Secotan run. I am glad."

"I know. I know, 'tis just that... I'm glad you are not badly hurt."

He reached for her, pulling her wrist away from his wound, holding it. The knee bouncing stopped. "If I am hurt?" He waited for her response to his query, his eyes searching hers, daring her to answer.

Her heart skipped a beat. "I would be sad," she answered.

This he understood. He slowly released her wrist, looking away from her to stare straight ahead. She wondered if she had said something wrong. It was the truth. She could not help if he did not appreciate the sentiment.

She thought to change the subject. "Was anyone in the village harmed?" She continued to focus on her task, lifting the patch to check whether the bleeding had stopped.

"I know not." Ompeu remained restless.

"Hold you still," she instructed. He forced himself to lower his energy level. A few moments of silence passed before she asked tentatively, "Will you teach me to use the bow?"

He turned his head, black brows knit in question. "You wish to be warrior woman?"

"I wish to know how to defend myself and those I love. Does that make me a warrior?"

"Bow is good far away, not close fight." He took a moment to peruse her from head to toe. "You are small."

"I am strong," she defended, ignoring the warm sensations his look sent coursing through her body.

The remaining group of fighting men signaled an all clear and set out for home. Ompeu stood abruptly, not allowing her to finish her nursing. He startled her, picking her up and tossing her over his shoulder in a motion that induced head spinning. A loud, high-pitched yelp erupted from her throat. She dropped the cloth in her hand, grasping any part of him she could reach. She wondered what prompted this, thinking it must be a consequence of all the pent-up energy he needed to expend somehow.

She heard distant laughter and shouts of encouragement from the retreating men who must have turned about when they heard her scream. "Ompeu! Set me down!"

He chuckled softly, a husky draft of amusement as he walked casually around the fallen logs with a wiggling Englishwoman draped over his shoulder. "Small, I am wor-ried an enemy take you away."

She tried to suppress a smile at his use of the new word. "Very well, you've made your point," she said, bracing herself with her palms against his shoulder blades, attempting to arch her back. "And I am not that small."

Ompeu shifted her, allowing her to slide down his length until her feet touched the ground. His eyes darkened as they stood pressed together, the humor in them replaced by something that made her knees weaken. She felt his muscles tighten beneath her palms. Elizabeth found her gaze drifting to his sensuous mouth.

His expression stilled and grew serious. "It is no game. Ene-my have no care."

"Still, I wish to learn. Will you teach me?"

"*Kupi*, if you wish." He lifted his gaze, surveying their surroundings, then back to her. "We must go," he whispered. At last, reluctantly, they parted a few inches.

She nodded, clearing her throat, pretending not to be affected by him. There were much more serious, pressing concerns to attend. "We must see to our friends," she agreed, stepping away.

Ompeu picked up the deerskin water bag and draped the strap over her head. She slipped her arm through it so that it lay across her body. "Come, Wapeih." He extended a hand to her, waiting.

"But, your wound," she protested. Glancing at the proffered hand, she slipped her small, pale hand into his large, dark one without thought.

His hand closed around hers. "Come." He drew her close, then turned and wove his way through the forest, leading her home.

They did not see the dark eyes of Wanchese follow them from his hiding place. He watched them until they were out of sight.

The acrid smell of smoke became stronger as they approached their village. Elizabeth hoped that no one suffered major injuries. Burned out dwellings could be replaced, people she cared about could not. She heard the wailing before they entered the village. Elizabeth quickened her pace, letting go of Ompeu's hand. She ran into the circle of mourners, gathered in front of a partially burned, smoldering *yeehaukan*, squeezing past those who blocked her view. Ananias and Eleanor stood staring at the ground, bleary-eyed. Eleanor turned away, weeping softly into her husband's shoulder. Emme was on her knees, sobbing uncontrollably next to the fallen body of a light-haired woman, in English dress. She lay beside her husband Henry, who was gravely wounded, but alive.

A group of men, English and Croatan, picked him up, carrying him away to safety and to treat his wounds, "Rose!" he rasped weakly. "What of my Rose?"

Elizabeth gasped at the sight before her, a cold knot forming in her stomach. "No!" She fell upon her knees next to the body. Tears welled in her eyes clouding her vision and choking her voice. "No, no, no! My beautiful Rose!" She touched Rose's dirt-streaked face and tousled hair with trembling fingers. She gripped her friend's shoulders, shaking the lifeless body lightly as though the action would rouse her, and she would awaken. She leaned over the body, pressing her cheek to her friend's chest, heedless of the fresh blood stain there. "Please, please no. Rose, Rose!" Sobs wracked her body, the pain cut so deeply, her entire being seemed to cry out. Rose, her sweet Rose. Rose who had not judged her, who loved her, defended her, lent her courage, stood by her side, sat with her learning to read and write.

Elizabeth felt Emme beside her, clinging to her, weeping with her. "Dear God, she cannot be dead, she cannot," she wept, her throat aching with the words. "Who has done this? Why? Why?"

A flood of tears blurred her vision. Someone took Emme away. Strong arms wrapped around her waist, pulling her from Rose's body. She struggled futilely against a force greater than herself, reaching for her friend in vain. "No!" she growled. "No! I cannot leave her! I cannot leave her! She would not leave me!" Elizabeth wailed.

"*Sehe*," the masculine voice spoke gently in her ear. The strong arms around her pulled her to her feet, dragging her some distance away. He turned her in his embrace, and she wept uncontrollably into his chest, the warmth of his skin seeping into the cold empty places in her heart. He stroked her hair and caressed her shoulders and back, comforting her, soothing her with soft Croatan words until she quieted. "*Sehe*, Wapeih." His voice rumbled softly in his chest against her ear. Ompeu. She wrapped her arms around his waist and clung to him.

*   *   *

"The Lord is my shepherd; I shall not want. He maketh me to lie down in green pastures: he leadeth me beside the still waters."

The Croatan stood, heads bowed, along with their English relatives as they buried the dead English woman in their own ceremony. Ompeu watched from a distance as Elizabeth said the words, talking as she knew how to do from a book. She looked tired and worn from her tears over the death of her friend. The husband Henry would live, but he was unable to attend, for his wounds were severe. He mourned the loss of his wife, greatly. An unwanted pang of sympathy filled Ompeu's chest.

"He restoreth my soul: he leadeth me in the paths of righteousness for his name's sake. Yea, though I walk through the valley of the shadow of death, I will fear no evil: for thou art with me; thy rod and thy staff they comfort me."

Part of him wished to stay for her, but there was something he needed to do. They captured three enemy warriors, and their prize was the Roanoac, Nussacun. Ompeu knew the Roanoac and Secotan would possibly bargain for the release of the war leader, but before any negotiations took place, Ompeu wished to question him and to have his assurances that if he were released, the bloodshed would end.

Ompeu slipped away from the burial ceremony, heading for the village entrance. The captives were tied to posts, guarded and taunted by Croatan warriors. Manteo was there attempting to question Nussacun, who refused to speak. Nussacun's battered face lifted as Ompeu approached. His head was shaved in front, the hair long in back. He was shorter and stockier than Ompeu, but no less formidable.

Manteo stepped aside, acknowledging Ompeu and deferring to him, since he was better acquainted with the prisoner. They were allies and fought together. They attacked the English settlement last spring. Manteo wondered what Ompeu would do now.

Ompeu walked a predatory circle around Nussacun, noting the marks of his torture. Because he could be used as a pawn, he was not abused quite as harshly as the other two captives.

Nussacun spoke in his Algonquian dialect. "It is true then. The English white skins live among the Croatan, and they bring their women and children."

Ompeu stopped in front of him, silent. His jawline grew taut, a feral expression in his eyes.

Nussacun's voice erupted gravelly and dry for lack of water. "These *Wutahshuntar* are no better than dung. They are lower than dogs, and yet your people welcome them. Ompeu has forgotten what they have done."

He had not forgotten, but Ompeu refused to be goaded and responded by folding his arms over his chest.

Manteo remained silent, eying both men as the exchange unfolded before him. Nussacun worked up enough saliva to spit at Ompeu's feet. "I see that Ompeu's heart has changed. You were once an enemy of the *Tosh shonte*. You helped us attack their fort and burn their crops. You have wanted the English gone from here. And now you betray your family by protecting them. You once thirsted for English blood. I see now, you hunger for something else English."

Ompeu slipped the flint blade knife from his string belt. He studied it quietly, turning the blade over, then running his thumb along the edge, testing it. Let Nussacun believe what he liked. Whether it was true or not, it was not for him to know.

"The sobbing *Tosh shonte* woman you held in your arms; does she give you pleasure? Warm you in your bed?" Nussacun scoffed, "I cannot believe that a warrior such as yourself would lie between the legs of an English dog."

Ompeu took three slow steps toward Nussacun, placing the flat of the blade under his chin, and using it to lift his head. "Now you have seen the English are here," he said coolly. "Now you are done with your fighting. What is it that Nussacun wants?"

The two men stared at one another, their gazes battling for long moments. *"Tosh shonte* blood," Nussacun snarled.

Ompeu's lips quirked in a sardonic smile. He cast a glance toward Manteo and shook his head slightly. "That is not possible. Choose something else."

"Trade for the woman," Nussacun offered, more as a test of his suspicions about Ompeu's feelings toward the *Tosh shonte*, than any real interest in her. "Trade for her and all this ends."

"Matta. Try again."

"You have already planted your seed in her belly?"

Ompeu pressed the knife at Nussacun's throat until it pricked his skin. Blood drops appeared.

Manteo stepped forward. "My brother, no." he warned.

Nussacun realized he had discovered a crack in Ompeu's otherwise calm façade. "What say you, Ompeu? Trade for her," Nussacun urged, ever aware of the blade at his throat. "What is one *Tosh shonte* woman in exchange for the lives of the Croatan?"

"This is your trade for peace?" Ompeu stepped back, circling Nussacun once more. *"Matta.* This is nothing but empty, brave-talk from a man who is in no position to make trades or choices. I think you wish to have your freedom. You wish to go back to your people." He leaned in, speaking in Nussacun's ear, a quiet menace in his voice, "If we allow you to live." Ompeu moved in front of him again. "Perhaps I should let the woman decide your fate."

It was Nussacun's turn to seethe in silence.

Manteo asked his question again. "What of Wanchese? Where is he?"

"Wanchese says Manteo has filled your ears with lies." Nussacun continued to speak to Ompeu as though Manteo were not there. "Wanchese has no love for the *Tosh shonte*."

"Perhaps it is Wanchese who has lied," Manteo shot back. "The English treated him with kindness," he appealed to Ompeu. "Wanchese is bitter because they found favor with me. He refused to learn all he could from them, and so chooses to tell lies, instead."

"Wanchese has told the truth!" Nussacun turned on Ompeu once more. "Manteo no longer knows who he is. Is he English, or Croatan? Manteo thinks he is a big man, but he is nothing but a servant of the English. A tool they use as they wish, to gain what they wish. He saw the head of the Roanoac *werowance* displayed on a pike for all to see! Manteo knows the English kill with little cause, women and children, they have no care. *Tosh shonte* killed your family Ompeu, how can you abide them? You have grown soft living among them. You are a coward."

Manteo and Ompeu shared a brief look, recalling similar words Ompeu uttered not long ago. Manteo shook his head. "Wanchese knows the English have great power."

"Their power can be used against us. We must fight them, or be destroyed," Nussacun spat. "Did you not wonder why the Secotan, Roanoac, and Aquascogoc did not attend the peace meeting? It was Wanchese who warned the people. He told them there would be no peace meeting. Instead the English killed Croatans." A short derisive laugh escaped him. "Wanchese gave the order to abandon Desamunkepeuc."

"Then it is Wanchese who is responsible for Croatan deaths," Manteo said.

Ompeu's heart pounded at the revelation. Wanchese ordered the neighboring tribes to ignore the peace meeting invitation, and so they found Desamunkepeuc abandoned. But would he have known the Croatan would visit the town? Perhaps not, but he would have known nothing good would come from his treachery. Ompeu glared at both men, processing this new information. Finally, he spoke. "This is how it will be." He returned his attention to Nussacun and continued with deadly calm. "Your people will come to negotiate a peace. If they do not come, you will die. If they wish to continue the fight, you will die. And if your eyes look once at the *Tosh shonte* woman, I will kill you, myself."

Ompeu glared at the silent Nussacun for long moments before he and Manteo walked away together, leaving Nussacun to fume and struggle futilely against his bonds.

Nussacun stared at the two men as they retreated. He could not keep the demented smirk from his lips. He had his answer. Every man possessed a weakness, and he uncovered Ompeu's.

They walked some distance, out of Nussacun's sight as they rounded the nearest longhouse. "Now do you see?" Manteo asked, speaking their native tongue. "Wanchese is the cause of the deaths of our people. Your Secotan and Roanoac friends have attacked us for our protection of the English. They will not relent until all the English are dead, with no concern for Croatan lives. Are those the actions of honor? Of justice? Would you have Nussacun harm the boy or the Widow Cooke?"

Ompeu stopped abruptly, anger flashed in his eyes as he turned on his friend. "You do not know my heart," he ground out.

"Neither do you." Heated silence stretched between them before Manteo continued. "Tell me the woman and the boy are not important to you, and I will let Nussacun and his friends go free."

"You do not know," Ompeu growled, his ire rising.

Manteo continued to goad his friend, purposely. "Then allow Nussacun to take Mistress Cooke. You heard him. All this will end. Bring her to him to save your own people. Avenge the deaths of your wife and child. Is that not what you wanted?"

Ompeu turned to walk away. "I will not speak of this."

"Then I will do it, and end this." Manteo changed direction and strode toward the burial service where he knew Elizabeth to be.

Ompeu grabbed Manteo by the arm, spinning him around to face him. "*Matta!*"

"You are with us, or you are against us. You must choose." Manteo demanded. "There is no in-between path." The two men stood together, silence like an inferno stretched between them.

"You are one to speak of paths in-between," Ompeu countered.

"Not in this. The English are relatives. They live among us. They are Croatan."

Nussacun was correct in his assessment. Ompeu's heart had changed. The thought both pained and surprised him, for he knew not when the change occurred. As much as he initially abhorred the presence of the *Tosh shonte*, he had come to know and care for some of them. He would not allow the Secotan and their Roanoac friends to kill the English. Manteo knew this. Ompeu glared at his friend, hating him at this moment for forcing him to admit to a revelation he did not understand himself. He suffered greatly at the hands of the English, yet his insides recoiled at the thought of

Wapeih or Onxe harmed in any way. The knowledge that Wanchese deceived them proved to sway his allegiance. Ompeu relented, "Do not touch the woman," he said.

It was not the admission Manteo pushed for, but it was enough. Manteo relaxed visibly, relieved at his friend's choice. "I am glad," he said. "Come. We must speak to my mother of what Nussacun has revealed to us."

*   *   *

After the burial service, Elizabeth stood in front of the small, newly constructed wood cabin, thankfully spared during the attack. She knocked on the door. Eleanor opened it. Lovely brown eyes were red-rimmed. She had been crying.

"May I enter?" Elizabeth asked. Eleanor opened the door and stepped aside.

"To what do I owe this visit?"

Elizabeth went straight for the point. "I fear I have neglected our friendship. I know we have had our disagreements. But we are all that remain of our settlement."

"Rose is gone and now you come to grace my doorstep?"

"No. Please, that is not the way of it. I saw you at the Green Corn Ceremony. You were purging old items into the fire. You seemed distraught, and I promised then, that I would seek you out. Forgive me for not doing so, immediately."

Eleanor sighed, apparently accepting this explanation. She gestured for Elizabeth to take a seat at the small table. They had indeed grown apart, but it was not completely one-sided. "I fear I am also to blame for our lack of company."

Little Virginia was walking now, grasping the table leg. She cooed and babbled, having her own conversation, then dropped on her bottom. Elizabeth picked her up, setting the child on her lap. "You are rarely out and about. Rarely do you work with us in the fields. I have not seen you at the celebrations. I know you feel these are heathen rituals…"

"They are. But truthfully that is not why I have kept myself apart." Eleanor took the seat opposite, folding her hands on the roughly hewn wood of the table.

"Then why? We have lost our beloved Rose," Elizabeth paused, swallowing back tears, her voice thick with emotion. "I cannot bear to lose another friend. What is it that troubles you, Eleanor?"

Eleanor was silent for a time, watching her daughter play with the ties of Elizabeth's bodice. "In truth, I hold out hope that my father will come. I fear that I must hold onto all the parts of me that are English. I fear that I will become someone I no longer recognize. That my father will not know me." She lifted her eyes to

Elizabeth's. "If he arrived on the morrow, would you not wish to return to London?"

Elizabeth pondered the question. Virginia lay her head at Elizabeth's breast. The child's lids closed over. "Nay. Please do not think ill of me for saying it. There is nothing left for me in London. To live on my brothers' charity? To live as a servant? Or left to beg on the streets? I have but few choices." She gazed at the child falling asleep on her lap, stroking the soft brown hair. "Life here can be hard. But here, among the Croatan, I am my own woman. I am free. Had I a daughter, I would wish the same freedom for her."

"I have noted a change in you. 'Tis a good change. I fear it is one I am not prepared to make, and that is why I judged you for it."

"I understand. But that does not mean we cannot remain friends. Even if we disagree on occasion?"

Eleanor looked down at her hands, her lips pressed in a small smile. "I admit, I have missed our repartee."

Elizabeth returned the smile. Her expression then grew still. She had to ask the question. "Eleanor, what if your father does not return?"

"I will decide when I have waited long enough. Perhaps then, I will consider embracing this change."

Elizabeth rose from her chair and stealthily set the sleeping Virginia on the cot of furs.

Eleanor covered her daughter with a thin blanket. She reached for her friend and sometimes adversary. The women held fast to one another in a hug that spoke more than words could. "I know how important Rose was to you. My heart breaks with yours," she whispered.

"Thank you." They parted, eyes glittering with unshed tears. "If I may, I should like to come calling more often. I am always prepared for a lively debate," Elizabeth said as she made for the door.

"Elizabeth. I must confess something to you. The bundle you saw me purge in the fire. It contained some of my father's drawings and papers. I know it was wrong. I think a part of me is angry with him for not returning to us. I think I simply wanted to be rid of it. All of it."

"Did it help to rid you of the anger?"

"If you must know, it did."

"Then let your spirit be at ease."

*   *   *

Clearing out and rebuilding damaged homes became a priority. They salvaged what they could, for much time and effort went into making many of the daily items they used. Thankfully, the fires had not spread due to the efforts of people like Rose and Henry, who were working to put out the flames when Rose was killed.

Elizabeth threw herself into the work of helping those in need with a heavy heart, remaining mostly in a daze. She watched as the holy man chanted and prayed over the injured ones. She spent time with Poussu, helping her to formulate healing herbal teas and medicinal salves, and to treat the wounded; setting the bones of a child with a broken arm, brewing a concoction for an elderly man with breathing difficulties due to the smoke, bandaging a young woman with an arrow wound to the shoulder. Poussu instructed Elizabeth with each new patient they tended. It was work she could become lost in and gave her a sense of renewed purpose. Seeing to the well-being of others helped to keep Elizabeth from sinking into despair. She missed Rose, terribly.

Messengers were sent to the Secotan and Roanoac to arrange a meeting for peace. At the council meeting, the Englishmen and Croatan brothers vowed to fight alongside each other. More building materials were taken from Roanoke Island and brought to Croatoan via canoes and English longboats. Men began repairs to damaged homes and worked to construct new ones. A new home would be built for Emme, for she would soon share it with Towaye. The event would be simple. He gave gifts to Master Dare. Once her home was completed, there would be the ritual blessings of the home and the couple. Towaye would then move his belongings inside.

Ompeu returned from helping the men and thought to visit Poussu. The last few days left his heart unsettled. Thoughts of Wapeih and Onxe, thoughts of Sequan and

Waacoh. He felt it was time to speak to Poussu of his dreams and that which lay heavy on his heart.

When he arrived at the longhouse, there was no sign of Wapeih or the boy. He felt an odd sense of disappointment. Poussu welcomed him. "My son, my heart is glad to see you. Come." She bade him sit, and served up a bowl of warm, thick porridge made from ground *pogatowr*, flavored with sweet berries. She waited until he tasted it. "It is good?"

"*Kupi*," he answered. "*Winganouse*."

"I'm pleased with Wapeih. She can prepare a meal as well as any Croatan woman and now she is learning more about medicines."

He knew Elizabeth helped Poussu prepare most of what he had eaten over the past months.

Poussu's smile faded. She grew silent watching him as he ate. She shook her head sadly and sighed. "I am worried about her."

Ompeu swallowed a mouthful of porridge. "She is hurting over her friend's death."

"This is true. But I do not speak of her friend. I speak of Wapeih. I have sensed that Wapeih is a woman who has known much sadness. I have been asking questions. I learned from Manteo that her husband did horrible things to her. Once he beat her so badly that she lost the child she carried. Her friend that was, told this to Manteo in confidence after the beating, hoping he could help with our medicines for Wapeih to ease her pains. I asked him if he thought Wapeih dishonored her husband. Manteo said he knew that she spoke out against him, for he conspired to steal corn from the People. Speaking against an injustice is hardly dishonorable." Poussu shrugged. "It seems to me she has much spirit, which he tried to crush."

Ompeu recalled the day Onxe told him of the violence his father had done to Elizabeth. Evidently the boy was unaware of the child inside her, which meant that her pregnancy was not yet noticeable.

"I watch her among us, striving to be a part of the Croatan, and make the best life possible," Poussu went on. "She does not complain and works hard. She is curious and loves to learn. But in her eyes at times there is a sadness. I thought perhaps she missed her husband that was. But I no longer believe this. I think she lives with the scars he has made on her heart. She is a strong woman who lives but has not much joy in her life other than her son. The *Tosh shonte* are strange in their ways," she shook her head.

"He is dead. He can no longer harm her."

"Can't he? She wants no husband, ever. This is not good. She is not an old woman." She paused in order to underscore the weight of what she would say next. "It is a sad thing when the ghost of one who is dead has power over the living," she intoned.

Ompeu set his bowl aside, and his eyes moved to stare into the fire pit. "Do you speak of Wapeih? Or do you speak of me?"

"My daughter that is gone from us had a choice. She chose a good man for her husband."

"I failed her." He never lied to Sequan. He cared for her, provided for her, he was a good husband to her. She knew his feelings for her were not equal. That did not ease the burden of his guilt completely, but he also knew that carrying such a weight was no way for a man to live.

"My daughter knew how you felt. It was enough for her. She was content."

Ompeu looked up to protest. "But that does not..."

Poussu held her hand up to quiet him. "It was enough for her," she repeated. Silence passed between them. "All things come to pass for a purpose. Good as well as bad. We do not know the mind of *Kiwasa*, or what caused his displeasure. Perhaps my daughter went away to allow a place for another. I miss my daughter. I will mourn her for the rest of my days, but no amount of mourning will bring her back to me. Leave the dead to the land of the spirits. They are happy there. Think well on what I have said. Your answers will come."

"My answers have been in front of me since the day the *Tosh shonte* arrived here," he said. "I have not wished to see them. I am still not certain that I do."

"Life can be hard. Is it easier for you to live in darkness, or more difficult to live in the light? There is always a choice to be made. You needed time to mourn, time for your anger to ease. But never believe that you have no choices. One can take several paths, some longer than others, but the destination is the same. When we arrive, our eyes are opened."

"I can see we are the same, Wapeih and I."

"You have both been broken. But perhaps *Kiwasa* has seen these broken pieces and wishes to create a new whole that will be greater than each of you. I have seen the way you look at her. Somewhere in your heart you know this is true."

"I cannot deny that I care for her." At last, he said the words aloud.

"The doe has come to you again. If you care for her, then you will know what to do," Poussu reasoned.

He knew he used his anger for the English as a contrivance, a tool to shun and ignore her. Elizabeth did not kill his family. She was not responsible. She did not deserve his anger or hatred. She came to live among a people who were foreign to her, yet she adapted without complaint. She sought to question, and learn about things she did not understand, rather than judge harshly, or reach conclusions that led to misconceptions and false assumptions as most *Tosh shonte* did regarding the people of Ossomocomuck. She lived with the brutality of a cruel husband, yet Ompeu knew that she was unafraid of him, and he was witness to the fragments of her spirit that rose to the surface.

He thanked Poussu for her wise counsel and left the longhouse. He needed to return to his home to finish the repairs he had started. He needed to be alone, and to think. As he exited, he saw Wapeih and Onxe, walking together toward the longhouse. He turned away quickly, attempting to elude them.

Elizabeth paused mid-conversation with her son and lifted her head to watch Ompeu as he strode toward his dwelling. She directed her son to enter the longhouse and told him she would return later. Poussu appeared at the entrance, calling the boy to her with the promise of a good meal.

Elizabeth knew the fires caused extensive damage to Ompeu's *yeehaukan*. A section of domed roof and one wall were destroyed and partially repaired. After the burial of her friend, Rose, she had not seen Ompeu but once. He brought her a portion of fresh meat after returning from a day's hunt. They were both otherwise occupied; he with helping the men, meeting with the *werowansa* regarding the prisoners, and discussing plans for war, and she with caring for the wounded. Elizabeth knew there were enemy captives. She saw them tied to poles, but gave them a wide berth, avoiding them.

Perhaps it was his quiet strength, or the comfort he offered her, or simply the mysterious allure she felt in Ompeu's presence that drew her. She could not define why exactly, but some unknown force compelled her to follow him. Elizabeth found him standing inside his *yeehaukan* amid the destruction, surveying the repair work. She entered quietly. He turned and their eyes locked for long moments. He stared at her in mild surprise, wondering why she had come. She stared back in mild challenge, telling him to make something of her presence. She wanted to be here with him, and she would make no excuses. He seemed to accept her company. She said nothing, but her eyes broke away from his, scanning the *yeehaukan*. She launched into cleaning, picking up objects and sorting through the debris. He moved beside her, and together they separated household items, some charred and ruined, some usable. No words were spoken between them. No words were necessary.

Elizabeth moved to the opposite side of the *yeehaukan*, pulling apart the sleeping pallet to examine the stored items beneath. She picked up a dyed black deerskin object, turning it over in her hands. Her fingers splayed over the soft skin, rubbing it absently, until she brushed a section that was stiffened with a dried, crusted substance. She poked a finger through a ragged hole. She scratched the crusted part with a fingernail. Tiny flakes of what seemed to be old, browned, dried blood appeared on her fingertip. She could not be sure, but the object looked similar to the sort of wraps in which Croatan mothers carried their babies. "Ompeu, *ka ka torwawirocs yowo*?"

He looked over his shoulder at her question, wondering if she realized she asked it in his language.

Elizabeth held the black sling aloft for him to see. The look of shock on Ompeu's face spoke volumes. He walked over to her numbly and took the sling from her hand as though he were afraid to touch it. Crushing the deerskin in his fist, he lowered his head and brought the sling to his nose and lips. His eyelids closed over.

Elizabeth stood motionless in front of him. "Ompeu?"

He lowered the sling, gazing at it, and caressing it lovingly. "Smells of him," Ompeu said with a quiet sadness. "Burned all... cradleboard, all things. I not know why is here," he shook his head. "Per-haps I forget. Per-haps I not want forget."

He lifted his head to look at her. Elizabeth never witnessed his handsome face pinched with heart-rending sorrow. She had witnessed anger, humor, desire, and indifference in his expression, but never this. Elizabeth felt his pain wrench in her own breast, and casting her eyes downward, placed a gentle hand over the fist that clutched the baby sling.

"*Matta,*" he said abruptly, turning away from her, his voice low and raspy. He walked to the center of the *yeehaukan,* his back to her, hands on his hips, head bowed. "Woman must go." He did not want an Englishwoman's pity.

Elizabeth stared at his broad back, sudden realization flooding her like a tidal wave. She knew. She heard about what occurred at Desamunkepeuc. A young Croatan mother and baby were killed. Elizabeth's heart, already grieving the loss of her beloved friend, seemed to expand, for she felt this man's pain in her breast alongside her own. "Ompeu."

"Please, Eliz-abeth. Go now." He used her English name, his voice a mixture of pleading and annoyance. He had begun to accept what was past, she allowed him to think about possibilities of a future without darkness. The sling reminded him, and he did not want her here. Not at this moment.

Elizabeth moved toward him. She saw the sling fall from his fingers. Did he not comfort her days ago over her loss? He did not know Rose very well. He did not have to offer comfort, yet he did. She ached for him, for his loss and heartbreak, longing to give him that same comfort. "*Matta*," she said firmly. "*Matush*, I will not go." She reached out, touching his back.

Ompeu whirled on her suddenly, startling her. His hands gripped her shoulders, his voice harsh as he spoke. "Wo-man, go!" What he would say next, was forgotten. He heard the startled cry that escaped her, saw the unshed tears in her eyes for him, felt her small hands, the gentle, tender fingertips that reached to touch his chest, the sides of his neck, his jawline. The last thing he wanted was for this woman to think he would ever harm her. "Wapeih," he began, but no words would come.

"It was you." A tear slipped down her cheek. "I am sorry," she whispered. "I am so sorry. I understand now. I know why you hate the *Tosh shonte*," she wept, her voice catching on a breath.

He loosened his grip as her gentle hands caressed his skin, soothing him. His expression softened. His breathing resumed evenly. Once again, the thought came to him that Poussu named this Englishwoman wisely, for her touch was a healing balm.

She blinked, new tears staining her cheeks. "Ompeu," her breath shuddered. "Please," she whispered, not knowing what she was pleading for. Forgiveness? Absolution? She had not murdered his wife and child, but her people were responsible for their deaths. She was one of them.

His hands slid from her shoulders, falling to her waist. Their eyes met and held, each of them absorbed in silent communication. A fleeting recognition, something intangible yet potent passed between them. Sensing his acquiescence, Elizabeth shifted upward on her toes, her hands sliding to his neck beneath his heavy hair. Ompeu's only possible response, the one that existed at this moment was to enfold her, pulling her tight against him. He buried his face in her hair at the curve of her neck and breathed deeply of her. She afforded him permission to express and share this quiet anguish with her. He carried it with him for so long that he barely recognized the peace that fought to dwell inside him. Wapeih came to him, and the world shifted.

Elizabeth felt him shudder as he drew in a sharp breath. They held each other for long moments, until his memory of the hurt diminished. Until she relaxed against him, and he knew she had forgiven his outburst. Until the world fell away, and only the two of them existed, clinging to one another.

Ompeu lifted his head, stepping back. His eyes searched hers, moving over her face tenderly. He cupped her cheeks, wiping her tears away with gentle thumbs. "Come," he urged quietly. He then released her and turned to pick up the baby sling. She watched him as he searched the *yeehaukan* for a scrap of deerskin. He knelt, and wrapped the sling, tying it securely. Rising, bundle in hand he turned to her, "*Pyas*, Wapeih," he urged again, taking her hand and leading her out of the dwelling.

He walked purposefully. She quickened her pace to keep up with his long stride, but she held fast to his hand as they went, not stopping nor caring who saw them. Parts of the wooded path were dusty due to lack of rain, but he continued to lead her to higher ground. Neither of them spoke. He did not tell her where they were going. She did not ask him.

They reached a high dune, overlooking the sea. Elizabeth was struck by the beauty of the view. The roaring sound of the surf, the countless sea birds wheeling in the clear blue sky, and the sound of their shrill cries all felt oddly familiar. She had seen this before, but something about this place seemed to strike a chord in her soul. The sea breeze tossed their hair about gently, the salty air clung to her cheeks.

The strange feeling would not go away. "What is this place?" she asked, her voice full of wonder. "It seems I have been here before, though I know I have not." She looked up at Ompeu who stood beside her, still holding her hand.

He looked down at her. "Per-haps you dream it."

"Dreamed?" Elizabeth gazed back out over the sea, considering the possibility. He watched her reaction closely. She looked back at him, confusion clouding her features. "I do not remember."

He knew she did not remember being here with him when he fasted and prayed. Ompeu took a moment to answer, wanting her to understand, and to use the correct English words. "Each man, each woman have dream spirit. When sleep come, dream spirit goes and travels far. It goes where it must. It meets other dream spirits and talks to them. When we wake, we do not re-member where our dream spirit goes. Per-haps your dream spirit comes here, and that is why you have been here before."

Ompeu released her hand and walked the few feet away to where someone made a fire pit. She followed him.

"Someone has been here?"

Ompeu gathered up some of the dried, sparse grasses that grew nearby. He knelt in front of the pit and took out his fire making stones. "This place... the *mantóac* is strong. It is place to pray, find visions, to give thanks, to cry for ones lost."

"A holy place." Elizabeth turned slowly, her gaze scanning in every direction, unable to shake the feeling that she had been here before. "The *mantóac* are gods," she realized aloud.

He shook his head. "*Matta.* Two gods. One god, *Kiwasa.* One god, *Ahone*, creator of all things. But more spirits also. I tell you of them. *Mantóac* is spirit power. Much power, always, in all places. It live in us. In all things." He turned to her, inviting her to join him. Elizabeth knelt beside him. "You have much power, Wapeih. Is why husband feared you."

"I do?" Elizabeth asked, amazed that he thought this of her.

"*Kupi.* Here," he placed two fingers against his temple to indicate her mind, her intelligence. "And here," He moved his hand over his heart. Poussu once told him that because Elizabeth's compassionate heart and spirit endured the cruelty of a bad man, it made her capacity for empathy greater. It was why she felt his loss as though it were her own, why she tended the wounded and the sick, why she taught her friends to talk from a book, why a cruel husband could not break her.

It was why she would be a great healer and teacher. Ompeu realized, it was one of the many reasons he was drawn to this woman, but he also knew that if she were not careful, her power could be sapped away, drained by the burdens of others, or broken by cruelty. He would not allow that to happen.

Ompeu started a fire, and when it was to his liking, he dug into a small pouch at his belt, then sprinkled *uppowoc* over the flames, and tossed some into the wind. He chanted softly in his native tongue. Elizabeth watched in fascination as he picked up the deerskin bundle containing the baby sling and placed it reverently into the flames.

Elizabeth became silently enraptured as she watched him, listening to his song. Ompeu's face tilted toward the sky, his arms outstretched in supplication. Why the English thought the People were heathens and savages beneath them, she could not understand. Here was a man at prayer, simply praying for someone he loved and lost. Whether his gods or hers, no longer mattered. Perhaps they shared the same Creator who heard all prayers.

After some time, Ompeu stood before her. His expression was somber, but his eyes caressed her face tenderly. He extended an open hand, beckoning her. She placed her hand in his, and in one smooth movement he pulled her up and into the circle of his arms, cradling her head against his chest.

They gazed out over the sea and watched the flames of the fire pit dwindle to glowing embers, the smoke and ash carried away by the wind. "It is done," he said, as though a great weight was lifted from him. Ompeu took a cleansing breath, exhaling slowly. "It is done."

Elizabeth pressed her cheek to his warm skin, her palms placed at the small of his back. She wanted to give him comfort, yet it was she who found peace and contentment, nestled in the shelter of his arms at this moment. That odd sensation of familiarity crept into her consciousness. Safety, comfort, love. She felt the weight of all the heartbreak of the past week shifting. Somehow, she knew that despite the pain, there was hope. Ompeu's arms tightened around her, pressing her close, and Elizabeth's heart swelled with a kind of serenity. Here on this magical dune, she realized that as she grew to know this man, the more she cared for him. She did not wish to care for any man. She asked for his friendship, yet it seemed he had given her much more.

Ompeu gazed at the smoldering embers of the fire and watched the wind spirit take the smoke, causing it to float away and dissipate. Wapeih. She could take away his pain, ease it, and fill his heart. Ompeu felt her small hands on his back. Her tawny curls tossed about gently in the breeze, caressing his skin and mingling with the straight black of his hair. Unconsciously his arms tightened around her, holding her close. Here on the sacred dune, he realized that he could no longer deny his feelings for her. He desired her from the moment he saw her. He could not deny he had wanted to take her to his bed, bury himself inside her, and forget his pain. But taking her was no longer a vengeful, or simply lustful thought. The shift was a living thing inside him that he could not fight against.

Perhaps it pleased *Kiwasa* to bring this woman to him. Perhaps he and Wapeih were meant to come together to help one another grow and learn from one another. Each of them lost much. He understood that it was the fear of insurmountable loss that made them what they were. Two people who lived with closed hearts.

He knew he wanted her. It had nothing to do with a dream or a vision. Her light skin no longer mattered to him. He wanted to see and feel her skin beneath his hands. He wanted to lie with her and show her that a man's touch could bring pleasure, not pain. He wanted to lose himself deep inside her, forgetting all the anguish of the past in her arms. He wanted to offer his arms to her as a place of refuge, safety, and contentment. He wanted to erase the memory of her dead husband, take her to the height of passion and hear her moans and cries of pleasure, calling his name. He wanted her.

He knew the only peace he would find was in the arms of a small *Tosh shonte* woman, and the irony of this was not lost on him. But he also knew, that until she came to him willingly, until she chose him, he could do none of these things. She said that she did not seek a husband. She was content without a man. Ompeu thought that if he could, he would set her heart free. He would tear down the barriers she had erected, so that she would be free to choose him.

For now, there were pressing matters at hand to consider. It was an unusually dry spring and summer. There were concerns over the drying crops and possible lack of food stores for winter. Ompeu must push personal desires aside until the matter of the Secotan and Roanoac attack was settled. The council would decide the fate of Nussacun and the two prisoners, as well as whether to seek out their enemies to strike back at them.

Chapter Fourteen

Elizabeth shaded her eyes against the bright sunlight. He wore his hair tied up again, allowing her to watch the play of muscles under the smooth, bronzed skin of his back and arms as Ompeu demonstrated with several arrows. Each one hit the marked target with a faintly audible whoosh and thwack. Onxe ran to remove the arrows from the tree.

Ompeu turned to her. "Now you," he smiled faintly at her dazed expression. She had not been paying attention, and he knew it.

Elizabeth blushed, caught. "I'm certain I can manage," she set her shoulders, reaching for the bow.

He set it aside. "Not this. Too big. You need small bow." He moved to where another bow lay alongside several blunt arrows in the grass.

Elizabeth took the proffered bow, and gave the sinew a few practice stretches, testing it. She was paying attention after all.

Ompeu stood behind her and slipped his foot beneath her skirts, lifting the hem a few inches from the ground. "I not see feet," he quipped lightly. "You need Croatan dress."

She smiled easily then, lifting the bow into proper position. "They are indeed shoulder width apart; you have my word." She sent a conspiratorial wink to her son who stood watching nearby, ready with spare arrows. He beamed up at his mother, emitting a slight giggle.

"Turn," Ompeu adjusted her shoulders, then checked her hands. "Not hard," he instructed, having her loosen her grip. He placed the arrow between the index and third fingers of her other hand and nocked it. "*Matta.* Do not hold tight the arrow."

His voice in her ear created a tickling, tingling sensation down her spine. She let out with a short chuckle.

"Woman, you would laugh to enemy?" His voice floated from behind her head, the smile in it, evident. "Come. This way. Pull back. Use this to pull," he placed the flat of his palm against her back, indicating that she would use her back muscles as the pulling force. "Not arm." His arm came around her and his hand covered hers, pulling back the string so that the index finger of the pulling hand rested beneath her chin, and the string touched her nose and lips. He lifted her elbow slightly.

"Is this good?" Elizabeth squeaked, afraid to move, or breathe.

Ompeu's hands settled on the roundness of her hips, checking her stance. "*Winganouse*," he murmured. Was he speaking of her stance, or her hips? "Very good. Look down arrow. See mark on the tree."

"Yes," she whispered, focusing on aligning the arrow shaft with the indicated target.

"Now re-lease."

She relaxed her grip on the string and allowed her fingers to slip backward. The arrow took a nosedive a few feet away, far short of the target, causing raucous laughter to erupt from her son. She made a silly face, unable to keep her own laughter from bubbling up.

Onxe ran to retrieve the arrow. "Try again, *nek*. You can do it!"

Ompeu instructed her again, "Only move after release."

She shot the arrow again, this time it hit near the marked area and bounced off. "What happened?" She turned, encountering Ompeu's amused expression. His smile reached his eyes. Elizabeth was once again struck by the beauty of him. She had not seen him smile this way, genuinely relaxed and unburdened.

"Would I give true arrows to learn?"

"These are practice arrows, *nek*," Onxe supplied. "See?" He held one up to show her that the tips were dulled. "I helped Ompeu make them," he said proudly.

"You've done a fine job, too. Are these your arrows?"

Onxe nodded emphatically. "But you can use them."

Elizabeth smiled. "Thank you, love. I shall endeavor to return them unscathed."

"Here," Ompeu nocked a sharp, pointed tipped arrow. He repositioned her. "Again." His voice was silky in her ear.

This time when the arrow flew, it remained stuck in the tree. Onxe whooped with joy. Elizabeth turned to Ompeu, her face radiant. "I managed to hit the tree, if not the mark."

Ompeu's gaze was warm, dark eyes moving over her face. His lips turned upward in a soft smile. "Good." He retrieved the arrow, picking bits of wood from the grooves. "Again." He watched her nock the arrow and position herself. While he admired her efforts to learn, he hoped she would never have to use her newfound knowledge.

*   *   *

Days passed with no word from the enemy. One of the captive warriors died of his injuries. Wanchese waited, hiding in the woods where his allies fled during the fighting. He made his way to the Croatan village as the daylight faded. He surveyed the grounds noting that the central fire burned low. Several people were outdoors, some sitting by the fire, some walking through the village grounds. A lone sentry guarded the prisoners. Wanchese was uncertain of his next move. He could walk into the village and offer them a greeting and claim he was there to negotiate the release of Nussacun. Would they believe him? He had used the deception of friendship toward the *Tosh shonte* before. He did not think it was a plan he could repeat. He could attempt to steal his way inside and free Nussacun, but the war chief looked to be in no condition to make an escape. He saw the messenger sent by the Croatan, and knew that if there were no response soon, the Croatan along with their English brothers would kill Nussacun and attack the Secotan and Roanoac, if they could find them. He needed to devise a plan.

The skies threatened much-needed rain, the air thick and heavy with the promise of a violent storm to come. Perhaps a plan had come to him after all. Wanchese slipped back into the woods to seek nearby shelter and contemplate his next move.

The wind began to stir as Elizabeth made her usual visit to Ompeu's *yeehaukan* with food. Not even Ajax would follow her this evening as he seemed to sense the coming rain and preferred to beg food from Onxe in the comfort of the longhouse. Several fat drops of rain pattered against her skin, cooling her. Ompeu lifted the door-flap. She entered and set his bowl in the usual place near the fire pit. Rising, she turned, her eyes seeking and finding his in the dimness. They stood openly considering one another, each of them silent, lost in their own thoughts of the other.

He would leave in a few days with the available fighting men to find and confront those who attacked the village. He could be wounded or killed. Elizabeth worried her bottom lip as disquieting thoughts raced through her mind. Finally, she spoke, asking the obvious question. "Will you journey to fight the Roanoac and Secotan?" Elizabeth wiped her hands on her skirt, smoothing it.

"*Kupi.*"

She already knew the answer. Elizabeth continued, suddenly unsure of herself. "Will you take care for your safety?" she asked, her brows knit with concern. She looked away, attempting to disguise her anxiety.

"I will do what I must."

She met his gaze squarely. "What you must do is return, unharmed." *To me, to us*, she dared not add.

"Is it a wish?" Did she care for him enough to wish his safe return?

"It is. Very much." She tried to keep her focus on his beautiful face, but her eyes unwittingly drifted over a bare chest and lean torso, her gaze traveling to his breechclout, before she lifted her eyes quickly.

Ompeu remained stoically silent, his entire body seemed to be filled with waiting. But when Elizabeth stepped closer, so close he could touch her and gaze down into golden eyes that betrayed her every emotion, he knew her words to be true. She genuinely cared for him.

She reached out to touch him first. Lifting her eyes to his, she slipped her fingers into the cool, fragrant strands of dark, glossy hair that hung past his shoulders. Ompeu remained still and silent as she traced the contours of his face with gentle fingertips, exploring his cheekbones, the perfect black brows over dark, almond eyes, his angular, masculine jawline. His lips were full and sensual, and her fingers strayed to them. "Do you kiss?" she whispered, not entirely understanding what had come over her. She needed to touch him. Elizabeth paused to tame her rapid breathing and heartbeat as his fingers brushed errant strands of hair back from her face, threading into the softness behind her ear.

A ping of doubt erupted in his chest. Ompeu had seen the English do this kissing, and he wondered what it would be like to kiss her, but he had never done it. "Kiss?" He cupped her cheek in his palm, watching her swallow harshly as his hand touched her skin. A thumb stroked beneath her eye.

Her initial amusement at his slight anxiety was replaced by the hot blush that crept over her at the sudden caress of his opposite hand finding her waist. His fingers slid down the curve of her spine, settling at the small of her back, pulling her effortlessly against his length and holding her there.

Elizabeth could barely breathe or think a coherent thought. "*Kupi.* Kiss," she said. His lips were wonderfully shaped, made for kissing. It would be a sin not to kiss them. The hand that cupped her cheek, tipped her face up closer to his.

"Kiss me," he whispered. He lowered his mouth slowly, his lips slanting, hovering a scant inch above hers.

A low moan slipped past her lips, a husky helpless sound of want. Her fingers plunged into his hair, pulling his head closer. "Ompeu," she breathed.

His parted lips brushed against hers, barely touching them, softness and heat and unspoken promises, feather-touching her delicately. He took her top lip into his mouth, then her bottom lip, sucking gently, nipping it playfully. Taking her mouth completely, hungrily, he crushed his lips over hers. Starving, he dived deeper into her mouth, pouring everything he was into the kiss. It was the kiss of a man who knew exactly what he wanted, and he wanted Wapeih. The moment Ompeu's mouth took hers, he felt the invisible threads already binding them, tighten. Kissing her was a hundred times better than he imagined.

A groan, deep in his throat escaped him, as he dragged his mouth away. They were both breathless.

Ompeu brushed his nose against hers and held her tighter, closer, nearly lifting her off her feet.

"You frighten me, Ompeu," she breathed, visibly shaken by the intensity of the kiss.

"You are afraid? Tell me."

"I am afraid I will lose myself. I am unaccustomed to feeling this way about any man. I... I do not know if I possess the ability to... to surrender myself completely to someone, give all of myself. I wonder if I am worthy of anyone." For years she fought against and pushed back against a man who sought to control her every thought and action. She was not certain she could surrender the tiniest bit of herself to anyone. For years, the walls she built were fortifications she used for self-preservation. Now she wondered if they were a hindrance to something wondrous and beautiful. This man in her arms was not the same one who hurt and degraded her.

Ompeu did not understand every word she said, but thought he understood her hesitation. "I am same."

"You have lost someone. And I have just found myself."

"Your man that is gone, still hurts you." At her surprised expression, he added, "Onxe tells me it."

She pressed her lips together. "Sometimes I think, yes. He does still hurt me. It saddens me that my son has witnessed so much pain."

"Wounds not seen need more time."

"How is it that you can know me so well?"

"I am same."

"You miss your wife," she ventured, aware that speaking of the dead could be a touchy subject.

He paused a long moment. "Poussu daugh-ter. A good woman. She care much for me. I know her from a long time. As child-ren. I was friend to her. When she is gone, I have...," he closed his eyes, struggling for the English words. "She want me more but was happy with what I give. When she and my son die, I am very sad and angry."

"I believe I understand."

"Wapeih, when you come, I am angry at *Tosh shonte*, but more I am angry at you."

"Why?"

He shook his head. "I want you more than my wife that was. *Tosh shonte* kill her. I think then, is not good want *Tosh shonte* woman."

"Forgive me, Ompeu," she said, suddenly uneasy over her boldness toward him. "I do not mean to cause trouble for you. I know my people are responsible for your pain." She attempted a half-step out of his embrace but encountered resistance.

"*Matta*." He held her against him. His face became a mask of frustration not only at his seeming inability to express himself in her language, but also a result of the pent-up sexual energy boiling in his blood. He did not know the English words to explain his feelings, he did not know how to express his desires or his perceived transgressions against the memory of his wife. He held Elizabeth against his body and arched against her so that she would not misunderstand. "The want is strong. I think if I take you, the want can go away, but not so. I have dreams of you before you come across the great water."

She understood now that he must feel guilt over his desire for her. She decided to tell him the truth, thinking it might ease his conscience, and perhaps her own. "I want, desire you as well, Ompeu, but I have not... I never felt desire for my husband that was. Not once. He was cruel, and I was not happy in his bed." She put it as simply as she could, hoping he understood. Cooke seemed to enjoy the pain he inflicted, lending to his urgency and desire. Elizabeth tried to push thoughts of him aside, but she needed to unburden herself. Perhaps Ompeu would understand. "I also acknowledge guilt at my husband's death." She cast her eyes downward. "It was I who exposed him to the settlement for the theft of corn. I am to blame."

He lifted her chin with a thumb and forefinger so that she would look at him. "Wapeih, you not do bad thing."

"You have not either."

His eyes danced, searching her sweet face. "Stay with me now, Wapeih. The rain is hard. Stay. I will make you happy woman."

"But, Poussu..."

"Send you here. She wait for you to stay with me."

"I cannot believe she would…"

"It is true."

"She has told you this?"

"In her way, yes."

"Ompeu…"

"We want each other."

His simple statement stirred her desire in forbidden ways. She could not argue or deny the truth of his words.

He touched his forehead to hers. "Per-haps more."

"Perhaps more, yes. I need time, Ompeu. We both need time."

He lifted his head listening to the rain outside, suddenly heavier now. A flash of lightning was soon followed by the resounding boom of thunder. The wind picked up, whistling through the birch bark and reed mats of the *yeehaukan*. He left her side and she watched him as he moved to lower the smoke flap halfway with a long stick, then turned and went to his sleeping pallet, sitting upon it. "Come. Sit." He placed a hand on the space next to him, an invitation. "Wait when storm ends."

She swept her skirts aside to avoid the fire pit as she moved to sit next to him.

"You need Croatan dress," he remarked.

She smoothed her skirts, arranging them around her legs. "I've been thinking the same," she answered, glancing at him from the corner of her eye. He studied her intently, listening. "Poussu is helping me to make something that covers a bit more…," she gestured in the general area of her breasts.

He shifted sideways on the pallet, taking one of her hands from her lap. "You learn the bow, soon be true Croatan warrior woman." His slight smile warmed her.

She laughed lightly, thinking of all the near mishaps before she mastered the ability to hit a target. "You've been very patient with me. Though I am not certain I will ever master your language," she sighed. "You seem to learn English more quickly than I am able to learn Croatan." A short self-deprecating huff escaped her, shoulders lifting in a helpless gesture. "Poussu's English is better than my Croatan."

"She ask Manteo help her, and Onxe. As do I." His thumb stroked the back of her hand absently. "You talk from book. This I not do."

"I could teach you," she said. She became quiet, sadness clouding her features. "I was teaching Emme and Rose… my friend that was," she corrected.

He did not seem interested in learning how to read, slipping his fingers between hers, and studying them; hers small and pale, entwined with his, large and dark. Elizabeth studied the scars on his forearms. She knew he had cut himself in mourning for his wife and child. *Wounds not seen need more time.*

She changed the subject. "Tell me of these dreams."

"You have dreams."

"I barely remember them, nor do I understand them. They are simply dreams, nothing more."

"Dreams tell many things. I have same dream. You come to me."

"There are times when I'm certain someone is with me in my dreams, a man. It seems I know him, but I'm not certain."

"One day you know."

"Do you come to me? The way that dream souls visit one another, as you've said?"

He hesitated, unsure of her reaction. Would she consider what happened in the dream world to be wrong or evil? Would she not believe him? "*Kupi*, we share many dreams."

She did not censure him, instead her curiosity rose to fore. "What could it mean that we've dreamed of one another before ever meeting?" She could not deny that she was drawn to him from the start and wondered if the dreams were partly responsible for her attraction.

"I know not. I know dream is the same."

"What happens in the dreams?"

He did not tell her about the doe or the wolf. It did not matter. The dream ended the same. "We join bodies, and spirits also. You come to me. My heart is full."

256 & Jen Caruso

Elizabeth's eyes widened, and her cheeks colored slightly. "You mean, join our bodies, as in…ah… *join* our bodies?"

He smiled indulgently. "When man, woman want each other, they join. That is our way," he defended. "Is not so for *Tosh shonte*?"

"Yes, but… in England, it is far different. There are strict rules and conventions one must follow, and marriage of course."

"You here now. No bad in wanting. We both married before, joining not new. When man want woman, he give gifts of food. She will know he is good hunter. If she take his gift it is sign she want him also."

"Like Bridger did for Mamankanois and her family." Suddenly she thought about the deer meat Ompeu brought to her shortly after Rose's death. She accepted it with gratitude. "Are you courting me?"

He shrugged, having a vague idea of what the English word 'courting' meant. A hint of a grin played on his lips. He quirked a brow. "Is for you to choose."

Choose. Elizabeth never had the opportunity to choose anything in her life. She never made important choices and decisions. She had gone from her father's house to her husband's house. Many women were not afforded the luxury of choice back in England. Marriage was an institution borne of necessity, and the raising of children to ensure heirs. Affection between the parties was not necessarily part of the arrangement. Elizabeth knew this all too well. Croatan women chose their husbands. Well, she was a Croatan woman now. She should be able to choose. "What if I choose to share your bed as a lover, but do not wish to have a husband?" She surprised herself with the scandalous thought.

"If come share my bed, you not wish to leave."

Elizabeth saw the amused twitch of his mouth, her own lips curving into a shy smile. "You are very confident."

His brows furrowed in question.

"Certain. Sure of yourself," she explained, thinking that confidence was something he exuded in all things. "You know yourself very well."

The faintest trace of humor lit his eyes. "*Kupi.* You come to me, and you not wish to go."

She saw hints of his playful side after the Secotan battle, and during her lessons with the bow. She could not help but smile. She enjoyed seeing him this way, at ease, open and now teasing her about his apparent sexual prowess. She was not ready for a husband, not again, not yet. But part of her was ready to explore the sensations and desires Ompeu awakened in her. There were whisperings and gossip of women back home who took lovers, she rationalized. Sharing Ompeu's bed would be sinful. Elizabeth was not certain what she might be stepping into, but she could not deny that he seemed to cast a spell over her, causing all reasonable thought and good sense to fly out of her head.

She shifted in her seat, turning her body slightly so that she faced him. The hand that still held hers lifted slowly, inviting her to touch him. He brought her palm to his cheek, and she traced the line of his jaw, to the pulse at the base of his neck, and over the lines of his tattooed chest. His skin was smooth and warm, lean with hard muscle. He possessed the physique of one who led a highly active life outdoors, calling to mind her first thoughts of him as a sculpted work of art. He was young. She guessed him to be a few years younger than her own twenty-six.

He grasped her hand and held it against his chest, the action rousing her from her reverie. "*Iahcasomaw*...You are fire in me, Wapeih," he whispered. "I wish to give you same." His fingers traced hers gently.

Amber eyes lifted, seeking assurance in his expression. What she found there was intense longing and adoration. "Show me," she whispered, uncertain whether she was asking or urging. "I wish to know." She wished to feel something other than hurt and pain when a man touched her. It was selfish and went against every cultural and religious norm she grew up with, but Elizabeth knew Ompeu could offer a new and different experience. *'We want each other,'* he'd said. She was grateful that he had not spoken of love. She wasn't certain she was capable of loving Ompeu, for he would demand that she give herself to him whole-heartedly. No man had ever wanted her love. Her body, her obedience, yes; but never her love. She could not think of it now. All she knew at this moment was that she desired him, needed him to show her what could be between a man and a woman.

There was no challenge in her eyes when she asked him to show her, only curiosity and longing. She said that she was unhappy with her husband. Ompeu understood that she had not known pleasure. He would show her.

Ompeu rose from the sleeping pallet and stood to his full height, facing her. She gazed up at his bared chest and torso, the soft firelight emphasizing the sculpted bronze of his flesh. His long ebony hair fell over one shoulder in a luxuriant, glossy cascade down one arm. Her pulse leapt. He extended his hands to her, and she took them. "This must be as you wish. Say now."

The allure and overwhelming attraction she felt for him, overcame any apprehension she had. "I will stay with you. But only this night."

He released her hands and moved his own to her shoulders, easing her against the soft furs. He settled in beside her rising on an elbow, head resting in his hand. His free hand moved between her breasts, fingers splayed over the laces of her bodice. Elizabeth's heart pounded furiously as she remained motionless, uncertain what to do next. Lightning flashed and thunder sounded, the rain still heavy outside. She felt as though the same storm, swirled, raging inside her. Her fingers trembled slightly in nervous anticipation as she undid the laces, loosening the bodice, revealing more of the shift beneath. He pushed the bodice open, his hand finding her soft flesh still hidden beneath the thin fabric.

Her breast filled his hand perfectly. He caressed her over the shift, causing her nipples to perk and tighten. Still, he sensed some unease in her. He lowered his head to kiss her, and she responded, arching against him. Ompeu's hot mouth pressed a steaming rivulet of languid kisses over her cheek, jawline, and throat. "No hurt, Wapeih," he whispered in her ear.

"I know. I know you would not, Ompeu," she answered, inhaling deeply in an effort to relax. "I trust you. I do. Part of me still thinks of before, but...," her voice trailed off. She could not think clearly with his warm lips enticing her at the sensitive place between her neck and shoulder.

"Ompeu and Wapeih here now."

"Yes," she breathed. "No ghosts."

"Touch me," he invited softly, thinking that if she were in control and setting the pace, she would be more at ease, and go as far as she wished.

Elizabeth shifted, nudging him onto his back. He remained still and watched with barely controlled patience as her inquisitive hands explored his chest, shoulders, and down his abdomen as though she wished to discover every contour, every muscle. She saw him at the Feather Dance, his body moving in a sensuous rhythm, recalling how she wished to touch him as she was now. Her eyelids fluttered closed as she pressed her lips to his warm skin, her hot uneven breath grazing him, her tongue flicking over a male nipple.

Ompeu's hands came up, spearing his fingers into the hair at her temples. He made quick work of the fat twist at the back of her head, and ran his fingers through her long hair, letting it fall in tawny waves to drape over him. The heat of his eyes followed her movements, watching her kiss and caress him with her hands and mouth until he trembled with desire for her, and could no longer remain passive.

He switched their positions, rolling her beneath him before her mouth traveled too closely to his breechclout. This night was for her. He closed the distance between them swiftly, crushing his mouth to hers, kissing her hotly. Elizabeth gave herself over to the demand of his kisses as the whirling rush of heat surged through her veins, the winds and pelting rain outside the *yeehaukan* seeming to rise with her own desires.

They struggled with her skirts and smallclothes, untying and pushing the yards of fabric aside until she lay before him completely naked. Elizabeth waited, breathless, nervous. She attempted to cover her nakedness. What if he did not find her pleasing? What if he thought her repulsive? Years of degradation could not be erased in one night.

Ompeu would not allow it. He eased her hands away, warm lips pressing soft kisses to every part she tried to hide from him. His touches were both erotic and soothing at once. His eyes, dark with the heat of desire roamed over her. Hands wandered over her body to skim and caress her shoulders, her breasts, and the curve of her waist to the roundness of her hips. "When first I see you, I want you," he whispered.

Elizabeth warmed under his regard, shivering at the tendrils of awareness spiraling through her body at the words he spoke. Had she always wanted him as well? At this moment it seemed to be so. Ompeu's gentle hands on her body gratified and relaxed her, easing away her doubts and fears, remnants of another man, and another time. Thoughts of the past fought with her present. She wished to remain here and now with this man who touched her so tenderly and sweetly, it made her heart ache.

Her world spun as he moved over her, his arms on either side of her, his hair falling around her face, engulfing her in a shroud of black. She loved his hair and reached up to grasp thick handfuls of the stuff as his mouth took hers once again. He moaned in pleasure, his body hovering over hers as he kissed her, the warmth of his mouth, soft and pliant touching her throat and jaw line with languid gentleness. His slow, drugging kisses left her shaking, breathless and yearning for more. Elizabeth felt the heat and strength of his body radiating from him, his lean, muscular power surrounding her. Her arms wrapped around his neck, her thighs holding his hips, as she drew his body closer. Tilting her hips up, she nudged her pelvis against him, hard and swollen cupped by the soft buckskin of his breechclout.

Desire, a pulsing, throbbing need that made him rock hard, filled his every pore, even the air he breathed. Ompeu wondered what happened to his resolve to be patient. She pushed her hips against him, her heat permeating a layer of buckskin, causing him to lose all sense. She squirmed some more, rubbing herself against him, shifting so that the hot, hard ridge of his erection was cradled snugly against her slit. At her movement, a soft grunting-groaning sound escaped him, vibrating against her neck, his breath wobbling against her skin, catching in a sensual way.

Elizabeth gasped for breath, her heart hammering as his lips skimmed over her throat, blazing a trail to her breasts. His long hair brushed over her skin, adding to the exhilarating delight of her senses. No one, nothing, ever made her feel this way. Alive. So frightfully alive. She whispered his name.

"You are *wingaiuwh*, beauti-ful," he answered softly.

No one ever told her she was beautiful in any language. Elizabeth thought to deny or argue his statement, but could only grip his hair, as he took one enlarged nipple into his hot mouth, the gentle tugging sensations causing her to gasp with pleasure. His hand skimmed over her belly and moved between her thighs, his fingers touching her most intimate place. Her hips moved, pushing against his hand until she felt as though she were reaching for something beyond the edge of exhilaration. The sweet prickling warmth, kindling in her belly ignited to a burning flame, a soft cry escaping her. Her husband touched her in a similar manner, but rough and hurried, never concerned with her gratification, and never like this.

She was incredibly wet, his fingers slick with her woman's essence. "This is good, Wapeih."

"Yes," she whispered, helplessly.

Ompeu rose to his knees, straddling her. He took her hand and guided it to the tie at his hip. Dark eyes met amber ones. She saw the challenge there. "Choose, Wapeih," he urged, his voice raspy.

Elizabeth watched his expression and the intense heat of his eyes as he looked down at her. He was offering her one last opportunity to refuse him. Her hazel eyes lit with desire as she gazed up at him, the torture of wanting him becoming so great, she could bear it no longer.

She pulled. The breechclout fell away, and he tossed it aside. Ompeu stilled himself patiently as she explored his body. Tentatively, her hands moved over the smooth, rigid plane of his stomach, lower, her fingers pressing over his hard belly. Her eyes, bright with fascination and a hint of apprehension, met his burning ones as her fingers curved gently around the engorged male part of him.

At the touch of her hand cupping his warm, hard, silky flesh, his breath caught in his throat. His groin jerked in greedy expectation, every cell in his body erupting with need. She stroked him, thick and heavy from base to dripping wet tip, sliding her thumb over the head to test the slippery secretion there, delighting in the way his breath caught on a low groan. She watched his reactions, fully understanding her power over him. This is what it meant to give and receive pleasure. He was a revelation to her, for she never wished to give this same pleasure to her husband so willingly.

He reached for her, pulling her close and growling playfully as he moved over her once more, fitting himself between her thighs, and molding himself to her. His body was on fire – hot, hard and ready, aching with the need for release, and for the ease he knew he could find in her. Ompeu intended to bury himself deeply inside her until they were both mindless and spent. "I wish to give you every-thing," he breathed.

Her muddled brain wondered if his words held a deeper meaning. "I do not need everything. All I want…," Elizabeth gasped softly as she felt the iron heat of his erection pressing between her legs. "I simply want you, Ompeu. That is enough for me," she whispered, her body arching, thighs opening of their own volition, her heart beating erratically in anticipation. She needed him inside her.

Ompeu rocked his lower body against her, his thick ridge nudging against her clit with delicious friction, his gaze locked with hers, powerful and hot. Their skin seemed to sizzle where they pressed against one another. "You have me, Wapeih." Elizabeth tilted her hips beneath him, causing the tip of his manhood to slip between the folds of her slick entrance. The breath rushed out of him. Unable to keep himself apart from her any longer, he watched her eyes widen, and heard her sharp intake of breath as inch by sweet inch she slowly welcomed him into her body. "All of me," he whispered. He made a growling sound in the back of his throat as he sheathed himself further inside her heat, stretching and filling her. "*Winganouse*," he breathed erratically, his body shuddering with involuntary tremors of arousal, and passion. He had been a long time without a woman, and she felt so amazingly good, Ompeu was not certain he would last long.

He had barely gotten inside her before he felt her muscles spasming and gripping along his length. Sliding a hand to her hip, he lifted her, giving her more, taking all she had to offer and silently demanding that she give more. Her body was bombarded by sensation after sensation. Everywhere he touched her, it felt as though a current like the lightning outside, pulsed beneath her skin. He drove her as wild as the storm, the last of her inhibitions falling away. His slow, delicious rhythm rocked her hips, pumping and thrusting so deep inside it made her ache. She closed her eyes, taking every inch he gave, absorbing the heat of him. Thrill after thrill shot through her as he possessed her body. His passion swirled around her and raged through them both, the rhythm of their bodies moving together, increasing in intensity with every thrust. Her body vibrated with liquid fire. "Oh God," she moaned. "Ompeu." She opened her eyes to find him watching her, his gaze hot, his lids closing over in ecstasy. Grasping his hair, she pulled him down, kissing him hard, lips and teeth and tongues, commanding him. They breathed each other's labored breath, sighs and moans from each of them filling the *yeehaukan.*

Without warning, Ompeu rolled, pulling her with him so that she straddled his hips, still sheathed inside her warmth. If he did not give her control now, he would spill his seed too soon. She stilled above him, her breathing labored, her hair all around her. His hands reached for her, needing to touch her everywhere. He moved her hair aside to skim and cup her full breasts, kneading them. She was so beautiful and precious to him, he wished he could always have her this way. She only wanted this night, but he knew in this moment, he would never have enough of her.

Ompeu flexed his pelvis, nudging his hips upward. Elizabeth answered, moving above him tentatively at first, hips gyrating slowly, grinding her woman's mound against him. She varied the pace, rising and descending on his hard length, his hips meeting hers. He watched himself disappear inside her again and again, until his eyes rolled back, and a guttural sound, deep in his chest mingled with her cries. He drew her close, fingers threading through the tousled honey hair covering her face, kissing her, taking her mouth as he took her body, he groaned and came up off the sleeping pallet. "Wapeih… Wapeih…" he panted against her cheek; his voice strained in urgent warning.

Elizabeth knew he was on the precipice; this knowledge somehow edging her closer to completion. A cry of pleasure escaped her throat, and grinding herself on him, she tumbled over the last edge of ecstasy. Dizzying pulsing sensations coursed through her womb, radiating throughout her entire body. Elizabeth felt a spasmodic tightening of his muscles, his body shuddering. Ompeu clutched her hips, immersing himself deep, deeper, the heady rush and flow from his groin releasing inside her slick warmth.

Elizabeth slid down to him soft, boneless and limp, her body sprawled atop his, as she fought for air. She never knew passion could be this way, and suddenly the revelation washed over her, the emotions overwhelming. For too long she had endured the marriage bed of a cruel and indifferent man who merely sought his own pleasure. In one night, Ompeu gave her more than she could have ever imagined. Elizabeth swallowed against the rising urge to weep. She would not cry. She would not.

Ompeu held her tight against him as his heart continued to race, his blood simmering. He remained inside her, not wishing to leave her body. "You have me, Wapeih. All of me," he breathed erratically into the mass of soft tawny strands of hair that covered his face. "Know this."

They listened to the softening rain as the storm moved away, unable to keep wandering hands from caressing and sliding over one another in exquisite exploration as they spoke in quiet tones. She told him she never experienced anything remotely close to this. He told her it was the same for him. He listened when she told him how it was before with her husband, because he knew she needed to speak of it. When she broke, and could no longer keep her tears at bay, he brushed them away with gentle fingertips. In turn, he told her what occurred at Desamunkepeuc, of his anguish over the deaths of his wife and child. He spoke of his anger and reasons why he helped Nussacun and Wanchese attack the English settlement. With his telling, she seemed to understand the plight of his people, though different from hers, were merely attempting to live their lives in peace. Each of them spoke of things they never told another living soul, the experience both liberating, and binding them at once.

After a time, Elizabeth sensed his renewed arousal. Ompeu held her close, reveling in the feel of her as he cradled her with his body, craving her again. Desires rose, passion filling them, and after finding delicious completion in each other once more, breaths heaving, their eyes met, and they broke into sudden laughter from their utter exhaustion. When their laughter subsided, Ompeu pulled her close, and Elizabeth fell asleep immediately in the comfort and safety of his arms. He smoothed her hair between his fingers as she slept, warm and soft against him, pondering the many ways *Kiwasa* affected their lives. All things come to pass for a purpose. It was what the Croatan believed.

She shifted in his arms, snuggling closer to him. Having her in his arms evoked a sense of fulfillment and rightness. One night. That was all she asked of him. Emotions swept through him as he pushed concerns about the night's events away. They slept soundly, feeling warm and content, arms and legs entwined, wrapped in each other.

Hours later, Elizabeth awoke to the sound of distant voices, shouting, wailing, and camp dogs barking outside. Her lids fluttered, her mind still swimming around in a fog momentarily, wondering if it was all a dream. A strong arm around her waist, a large warm body curved protectively at her back, his soft, even breath at her neck confirmed it. It was no dream. She was in Ompeu's bed, wrapped lovingly in him. She lifted her eyes to the partially opened smoke flap. It was nearing dawn. Elizabeth attempted to leave his arms. Even as he slept, she felt his muscles constrict, resisting, not wishing to let her go.

She stroked his forearm. "Ompeu, something has happened."

"Mmm."

"Ompeu," she elbowed him gently.

He opened his eyes and rolled to his back, allowing her to rise from the pallet. She searched for her clothing strewn about haphazardly and began to dress. She needed to relieve herself and to bathe, the evidence of their lovemaking, sticky and slick between her thighs. Her body was sore, muscles ached, but for the first time, her mild discomfort was the result of the physical pleasure she experienced, not from physical harm.

Ompeu, fully awake now, listened intently to the voices outside. He rose suddenly, pulling on and tying his breechclout.

"What is it?" she asked worriedly, as she tightened the laces of her bodice.

He was nearly out the door. "Nussacun and the other gone in the night when storm come. My friend who guard is dead." He dropped the door flap and turned back, reaching for her. He pressed his lips to her temple, a quick kiss, then spoke urgently against her hair. "Go to Poussu. Stay with her and Onxe."

Elizabeth could only nod, shocked and wide-eyed before he was gone.

Chapter Fifteen

She had never seen his handsome face painted for war. Red ochre streaks like flames outlined in thin black were drawn from his forehead, over his cheeks, to his chin on either side of Ompeu's face. Croatan and English brothers alike prepared themselves, checking bows, arrows, spears, muskets and stores of powder and shot. Thanks to Henry Darby, many of their weapons were upgraded from metal he melted down and forged to make arrowheads, spears, and swords. John Bridger painted his face as well, choosing black horizontal lines across his forehead and cheeks, his startling blue eyes contrasting against the dark paint that matched his hair and sparsely bearded stubble. His wife Mamankanois stood quietly beside Elizabeth and Emme. Each woman watched a different man, but each felt the same mixture of worry and pride.

Towaye approached them, the top half of his face painted entirely red. He inclined his head as solemn greeting to the women before he took Emme's hand and led her a short distance away. He gently wiped tears from the young woman's cheeks, and she nodded as he spoke softly to her. They were newly married, the pain of parting unbearable. Manteo, standing by his mother's side, called to him. Towaye kissed his bride quickly, then bade her return to the other women.

When Emme returned to Elizabeth's side, she reached for her friend's hand. Elizabeth squeezed gently, offering silent comfort. Emme pressed her forehead to Elizabeth's shoulder. "It will be all right, love. He shall return to you." Elizabeth comforted Emme, but uttered the words for herself as well, her thoughts straying to Ompeu.

The women made sure the men carried food and full water pouches. Ensuring that the village was not entirely unprotected while most of the fighting men were gone, Ananias Dare and a handful of men stayed behind to fight.

Onxe broke away from the group of warriors, running toward his mother. His face was painted as well, in similar fashion to that of Ompeu's. "*Nek*!" He called out, halting in front of her. Elizabeth smiled at him and stroked his golden shoulder-length hair. "Ompeu says I must stay with you and *nunohum*."

"I believe that is wise," she answered. Something profound touched her heart to know that Ompeu painted her son's face.

"I wish to go with him."

"'Tis too dangerous. Ompeu is well-trained as a warrior."

"One day I shall be a warrior," he said.

"One day you shall," she answered. Wishing that he would never have to go off to fight, yet knowing that in all likelihood, he would grow to one day have to defend his loved ones. "But for now, we need you here to help us while many of the men are gone. *Kupi*?"

"*Kupi*," he answered reluctantly, though understanding he was too little to go with the men this time.

Poussu stepped up, taking the boy's hand. She spoke to him in the Algonquian dialect of the Croatan, leading him to where Eleanor and Ananias worked, prepping and taking inventory of weaponry laid out on a long, wooden table. She gestured to Elizabeth, indicating she should follow.

Elizabeth's eyes scanned the crowd of men before she left, unable to find Ompeu among them. She told Emme and Mamankanois that she would return, then followed Poussu.

Poussu said something to Onxe who went to join a group of boys who were gathering up rocks and sticks. She turned to Elizabeth, grasping her hand. "Go.

Ompeu," she said pointing in the direction of the village dwellings. At Elizabeth's questioning look, Poussu gestured once more. "Ompeu *yeehaukan*. Go. See."

"*Kenah*," Elizabeth said, before turning away from Poussu.

She walked through the village, past several homes and longhouses until she came to his dwelling. She scratched on the door flap. It opened, and a hand reached for her, pulling her inside.

Ompeu stood before her, frightfully painted for war. Oddly, it made him no less beautiful to her. "Wapeih, I wish to give you," he said, presenting her with a small flint blade knife.

She took it from his outstretched palm, studying it and testing its weight. He handed her a deerskin sheath with a strap to tie around her waist. Lifting her eyes to his she asked, "Why?"

"If enemy come," he touched her chin, the backs of his fingers straying to her cheek. "If your bow does not have good aim."

The corners of her mouth turned up slightly at his blaming the bow for her bad aim. "Thank you, Ompeu. Do you believe we are in danger here?"

"How Nussacun go in the night? Someone help him and the other."

It made sense, but whom? She reached up, her fingers curling around the hand that cradled her face gently. "Promise me you'll be careful."

His thumb caressed her cheek. "You will wait for me?" he asked quietly.

"I will," she replied, for it was the only answer in her head.

"I will be care-ful," he said, because he knew she needed to hear it.

All her fears and doubts were wiped away when his mouth closed over hers. The steady heartbeat of the drum sounded in the distance, and the women chanted a song to their departing warriors.

Ompeu reluctantly broke the kiss, studying her with solemn eyes, he gazed at her for an interminable time. "*Kuwumáras*," he whispered.

Elizabeth blinked up at him, slightly dazed from his kisses, not comprehending his words.

"I go," he said before she could ask him to translate. He took her hand, pulling her out of the *yeehaukan* and they walked together to where the crowd gathered. Ompeu trotted away from her side and joined the men traveling through the muddy path toward waiting canoes. The crowd of mostly women followed, continuing their chant, some shaking gourds filled with seeds and pebbles, keeping a steady rhythm. It was part of their war ritual, so their men would be victorious and return home safely. Elizabeth hoped *Kiwasa* would be pleased. She held back, watching Ompeu until she lost sight of him.

"*Wingan*. Is good, Wapeih."

Elizabeth turned her head to find Poussu beside her, also watching the men depart.

"Is good you go *yeehaukan* of Ompeu."

Elizabeth's cheeks burned, flooding with profound embarrassment. Of course, Poussu knew she spent the night with Ompeu, but did she suspect more?

"Ompeu plant seed in storm. Per-hap give Wapeih baby. Make Wapeih happy woman, make Wapeih *pommahaum,*" Poussu extended a hand in front of her belly to indicate a woman with child.

"Oh... no, I... *matta.*" Of course, Elizabeth had not considered the possibility of a child. For one so intelligent, she certainly did not think things through in this case. Horrified, she covered her face with her hands, completely distressed. "Forgive me, *nek...,*" she began, lowering her hands to cover her mouth, somehow too wrapped up in her own anguish and shame, not understanding Poussu's meaning. Elizabeth thought she'd gravely offended and disappointed the older woman, who had been nothing but kind to her.

Poussu noted the anguish of the younger woman and rubbed Elizabeth's shoulder vigorously. "Is good!" she said encouragingly, attempting to convince her daughter that she had done nothing wrong. What occurred between them was perfectly natural. Wapeih was not a maiden protected by parents. She had been a married woman with a child. She and Ompeu each lost spouses. Their coming together was as it should be. Poussu shook her head, wondering again over the strangeness of the *Tosh shonte* and how they thought things should be between men and women. "Ompeu need good *crenepo*... wo-man. Need you," she assured her. "Wapeih go with food. I send. I see Ompeu want Wapeih much. He is good for Wapeih."

Elizabeth lowered her hands, realizing that Poussu had indeed been sending her every night to Ompeu's dwelling, waiting for this to happen. She spent an impassioned night with Ompeu, and Poussu was happy about it. She searched her adoptive mother's kind face for any sign of censure. She found none. Relief flooded her, though her mind still fretted over a possible seed planted in a storm, her panicked brain struggling to recall her last visit to the menstrual hut.

Poussu smiled softly. "*Kupi.* Is good."

Elizabeth paused momentarily, unsure of herself, yet needing to say her next words. "*Nek*, I am sorry about your daughter. I know I cannot replace her, but I will be a good daughter to you."

Poussu pressed her lips together in a sad smile, her eyes pricked with the threat of tears. "Ompeu tell you. My heart happy. *Kenah, nunutánuhs.*" *Thank you, my daughter.*

Elizabeth released a small sigh of relief, worry still creasing her brow, she was unable to speak. Instead, she embraced her mother. When they parted, Poussu reached to wipe a bit of red ocher from Elizabeth's chin, remnants of war paint left from Ompeu's kisses.

Poussu eyes searched the crowd of people. "Emme sad for Towaye. Help find," she said, taking Elizabeth's hand, the two women walked off together.

*　　*　　*

Darkness settled on the island when Wanchese ran to where Nussacun and Watape remained hidden near the southern end of Croatoan, away from the main village and the other towns. They built a small fire and had skinned, roasted, and eaten two rabbits Wanchese caught earlier. "Most of the warriors have gone," he informed them. "They searched but did not find me."

Nussacun rested against a tree, in great pain over the wounds he suffered at the hands of the Croatan. The escape took the last bit of energy he possessed. "They will not find anyone in the Secotan town."

"They will search," Wanchese answered. "They will find someone."

"In a few days, I will be strong enough. With the warriors gone the village will have mostly women and children. The three of us will do as much damage as possible."

"Leave the Croatan. It is the *Tosh shonte* we wish to kill," Wanchese said. "They murdered the *werowance* who sheltered me. I will have recompense."

"Our Croatan brothers have too much affection for the *Wutahshuntar*. It is their weakness. The *Tosh shonte* have turned the Croatan against us." Nussacun shifted, wincing at the slight pain the movement caused. "Manteo, Towaye, and Ompeu have all been turned by the *Tosh shonte*."

Watape attempted to sit up. He collapsed twice during their escape in the violent storm. "There is a simple way to hurt them," he said quietly. He was in worse condition than Nussacun and unable to sit upright, he gave up the effort, his thin, lanky body sprawled on the ground. "The women and children. Towaye and Ompeu have taken *Tosh shonte* women to their sleeping mats. Take their women."

Nussacun recalled Ompeu's reaction at the mention of the *Tosh shonte* woman. "I have thought of this as well. Taking them will not be a simple thing. It also does not rid us of all the *Wutahshuntar*."

"Perhaps we will never be able to rid ourselves of the *Wutahshuntar*," Wanchese spoke. He moved to sit cross-legged near the fire. "I have been to their land across the sea. Their numbers are far greater than we imagine. They are a dirty, noisy people. Too many to count. If the great ships come, their people will flood our lands. Stealing two *Tosh shonte* women will mean nothing."

"It will mean something to the Croatan who shelter them and will serve as a warning to anyone who accepts them."

"It will simply anger them. The *Tosh shonte* have strong weapons, greater than ours. Towaye and Ompeu are both fierce warriors. You would start a war over women?"

"We've already started a war."

Wanchese countered boldly. "I see no point in taking their women to further our aim. If you wish to steal Ompeu's woman because you are angry with him for his change of heart, say it is so. Do not make your private war against him for all of us to fight."

"Ompeu threatened me with death if I looked at her. His threat alone has made her more valuable to me."

"To you alone. What action would he take if you stole her away? What would you do with her? Kill her?"

Nussacun shrugged. "Ompeu has made his choice. Now he must face what comes. We take women and children in war. That is our way. Weaken our enemies and strengthen ourselves. You know this."

"The Croatan were not our enemies until they accepted the *Tosh shonte* among them. The *Tosh shonte* are to blame."

"We will talk in circles," Watape interjected. "If stealing the women hurts them, we strike."

"Steal them if you wish, but be prepared for what follows", Wanchese warned. "Rest now, brothers. You will need all your strength. When the sun rises, I will travel to other towns and gather warriors. Stay hidden. Do not emerge until you hear my signal."

*   *   *

"Thank ye for staying the nights with me until Towaye returns, Elizabeth. Ye did not have to. I am grateful."

"'Tis no trouble. I understand," Elizabeth said as she made up a bed on the opposite side of the fire pit in Emme's *yeehaukan*.

Emme snuggled against the furs on the pallet she and Towaye shared. The nights were cooler now. In the coming months, winter would be upon them. It was Emme's first night without Towaye, and she asked Elizabeth to stay with her. "When I met Towaye in England, I'd only begun my indenture," she spoke wistfully, her fingers absently brushed the soft fur beneath her, as she stared up at the domed ceiling. "Master White wished to have a young woman to assist Eleanor and Master Dare, her bein' with child and all." She smiled fondly at the memories. "Towaye and Manteo were happy to be returning home again. He would tell me about this place, this land, his people. I could not imagine it. He asked me to help him with his

English, so he could learn our language quickly. Well, I was flattered. No one ever asked me to help them learn anythin'. Me, not knowing how to read or write. He thought I was something special, I suppose. And I felt special." Emme turned her head toward Elizabeth. "Once he asked me if I were an English lady. Can ye believe that? Me. An orphan girl, poor as a church mouse. He thought I was a lady." She chuckled lightly, before becoming thoughtful once again. "He made me feel as though I were a lady. When he understood I was a simple servant, he still treated me as though I were beautiful and special."

"You are beautiful and special," Elizabeth responded. She removed her dress, choosing to wear her thin shift as a sleeping gown. She lay upon the blankets and furs, attempting to find a comfortable position.

"We became close. There was the promise of more, but Towaye was afraid he would upset Master White. 'They look down on the People, but not you, you are different,' he said to me. At first I did not understand, but I would notice how those of the better sort spoke of and treated Towaye and Manteo. They were referred to as savages, paraded around as exotic oddities, somethin' that bothered me more than Towaye. When we arrived at the Roanoke settlement, Towaye left. He did not say good-bye, and I did not know what became of him. For a long time I wondered if I had done something to upset him. Later, I discovered that Master White told him that our friendship was inappropriate, that Towaye should not speak to me. Towaye loved me then, Elizabeth, but he did not wish to cause trouble for me."

"I'm glad he decided to return to us."

"I love him, so very much. I will pray every day for his safety. We'd like to start a family straight away." She placed her palm over her abdomen. "I pray I'm carrying Towaye's child even now, God willing."

"You deserve every happiness," Elizabeth smiled at her over the fire pit.

"My wish is for ye to be happy, Elizabeth." Emme rolled to her side to face her friend, resting her head in her hand. "I know you've had a hard time of it. I have seen you and Ompeu together. I see how he is with yer boy and with you. Mayhap, ye could be happy with him."

Elizabeth rolled to her back, peering up to the visible night sky through the smoke hole. She was silent, then blew out a breath. "I am happy with things as they are. When it comes to Ompeu, I do not know how to feel." She turned her head toward Emme. She would not tell the young woman of the night she spent with Ompeu. "Sometimes I fear I am incapable of such deep affection. For my son, yes. But for a man? I simply do not know. I do care for Ompeu, but I am afraid of anything more."

"Yer thinking of Cooke," Emme said. "Ye cannot compare one man with another."

"'Tis unfair. I know."

"What frightens ye so?"

"Losing my freedom. For the first time in many years, I feel unbound. I do not walk about in fear of what Cooke may say or do to me. There is no need for me to be defensive or defy him in small ways simply to keep that piece of myself I still have left."

"And ye think Ompeu will be the same?"

"No. And yes too. 'Tis difficult to explain. 'Tis that while Cooke demanded my obedience and my body, I fear Ompeu wishes my heart and soul. I know he would never demand these things of me. He would wait for me to give them freely and I'm afraid...."

"Yer afraid to love him, because ye think it means giving yer heart to him," Emme supplied.

"Aye. That's it."

"Ye must know by now that Croatan men see women a bit differently than Englishmen. The Croatan believe that woman was created first and all life comes from her. It seems to me that they hold women in higher regard. Least that is what Towaye says. He never saw me as a lowly servant."

"And you saw him as a young man worthy of your love, not as a savage."

"Do ye believe Ompeu is worthy of yours?"

"Truthfully, I am unworthy of his. I am nothing. No one."

"Those be Cooke's words. Not Ompeu's. Damn him for makin' ye believe them."

"When do the lies become truth? After hearing them, living with them for many years, they become accepted. The question is how to stop believing them. And so, I try to find my worth in small ways, and guard my heart, unwilling to give away any part of myself."

"Ye see it as giving something up, but what if ye gained so much more than ye could possibly imagine? What if ye gave love, opened yer heart a bit, and got so much more in return? I believe all love comes from God. We should embrace it where we find it. Loving someone, pure love, is never wrong, and worth the risk. Do ye not remember the poems? Perhaps ye must read them again."

"*'If these delights thy mind may move, then live with me, and be my love.'* Yes, I remember."

"Ompeu is not Cooke. Ye did not love Cooke, nor did he love ye. Love uplifts us, Elizabeth. It does not debase and degrade nor control. There is no fear, no jealousy. It is unselfish and immortal. Mayhap, Ompeu is worth the risk."

"How did you become such a wise young woman?" Emme was speaking truth. Ompeu was not Cooke. Elizabeth recalled his confession of guilt over his desire for her, a *Tosh shonte* woman. Until now, she did not fully comprehend the depth of his inner torment. Yet, despite what he had experienced at the hands of the English, he was willing to move past the pain and take the risk with her.

"I had a good tutor," Emme teased. "She read me spiritual love poems which I soaked up like a dried sponge. Gave me hope when I thought there was none. She simply needs time to sort herself out."

"Indeed." She told Ompeu that they both needed time. Neither of them experienced love such as the poets described. She wondered if such a love were possible. Emme seemed to have found it. "Thank you, Emme. You have given me much to consider."

"Yer welcome. *Winkan nupes*."

"*Winkan nupes*, my friend."

Chapter Sixteen

S couts returned to the Croatan war party encampment with information that the Secotan town appeared abandoned. "This is the way of it?" John Bridger asked. "They attack, then disappear just as the last, gone to ground like a fox. Cowards."

"We will find," Towaye said. "We will find, and they will tell us what they know."

The men gathered up the camp and trekked further inland, walking in a single-file line. Some of the warriors spread out evenly along each side of the line in search of any hidden dangers. The woods grew thicker as they traveled. Stillness pervaded the forest, but for the sound of birds, and rustling creatures, the eerie surroundings became more unnerving. It brought a sense of heightened awareness, the men ever on guard.

Distant shouts halted the group. Anxious men turned in every direction, searching for the source of the voices. *"Nipatas!"* The group spotted Ompeu through the trees, grasping what appeared to be a teen-aged boy by the neck, shoving him forward toward the line of Croatan warriors. "This one thinks he is a man. We will see how much of a man he is," he growled in his native tongue.

The frightened boy stood mouth slightly agape and wide-eyed at the warriors before him. Ompeu explained to the group, how the boy attempted to attack him, displaying the weapons he'd taken from the teen.

"What is your name?" Ompeu asked the youth. "No one will harm you. Tell us where the Secotan and Roanoac have gone."

"Nuturuwins Wutapantam," the boy said, lifting his head and standing proudly despite his fear. His eyes scanned the group of men gathered around him. There were many. Mostly Croatan, but some *Tosh shonte* were mixed with them. He had never seen a war party this large, nor seen some of the strange weapons or the body armor the *Tosh shonte* wore.

"Wutapantam, the Secotan and Roanoac have attacked our village without reason. We are here to speak to the *werowance*, but if no talking can be done, we are here to fight. You understand?"

Wutapantam nodded, then spoke to Ompeu. "Nussacun and Wanchese have told of the *Wutahshuntar* that live among you. They say the *Tosh shonte* are bad and urged everyone to kill them. Nussacun says the *Tosh shonte* have made the Croatan turn against their brothers. The Croatan have become lazy and weakened by the *Tosh shonte.*"

"We have not turned against them, it is they who have attacked us. Nussacun and Wanchese have twisted your minds with lies." Ompeu turned toward the crowd of men and in a gesture that encompassed them, he bade the boy look around him. "Do we appear weak to you?"

The teen shook his head. "*Matta.*"

"Where are your people?"

"Scattered. Wanchese said we must, for he knew you would come."

"Where is Wanchese?"

"I do not know. He and Nussacun never returned after the attack on your people. Some think they are dead."

"Nussacun is not dead. We have not seen Wanchese."

The boy looked Ompeu square in the eye, defiant. "Perhaps he is still on Croatoan. Perhaps he still plans to kill the *Tosh shonte.*"

Ompeu's expression was caustic, his eyes narrowing. The absence of Wanchese was of great concern. Wanchese could have helped Nussacun and the others escape. If this were true, the Croatan war party would need to return home as soon as possible. Ompeu thought of Wapeih. He longed to be with her now. "Perhaps you are right, brave boy. He can try." He motioned to Paukunnawaw to tie the boy's hands. "You will take us to your *werowance*."

The boy turned his face away to stare straight ahead as his hands were tied behind him. "I do not know where he stays."

Ompeu spoke calmly. "You dishonor yourself with the lie. We would prefer to keep the peace, but if no peace can be agreed upon, you will be the first to die. Tell us where he is."

Paukunnawaw tightened the bonds holding the boy's wrists, placing the attached rope around his neck, creating another knot. The youth swallowed visibly.

John Bridger approached. Startled, the youngster took a step back. The man before him possessed eyes like the sky, and a strange metallic covering over his chest and torso. An odd, stick-like weapon was perched on his shoulder. A long knife hung from a belt. "He's a mere lad. What does he know?"

Towaye explained what the boy told Ompeu.

"Tell him I've a Croatan wife I need t' return to." Bridger lowered the musket from his shoulder, balancing the barrel in his right hand. "Tell him that all we wish is t' live in peace. There's been enough bloodshed these last few years." He opened the primer pan tapping a bit of powder into it from a small pouch as Towaye translated. "Tell him I'm a Croatan man now and if his people choose t' take up arms against us, we'll be sure t' give them a good fight."

The boy watched in confounded fascination as the blue-eyed *Tosh shonte* blew lightly on the hemp rope match to keep it lit, poured some powder down the muzzle of the weapon, reached into a pouch at his waist, removed a ball, tamping it all into the muzzle with a long stick. The man then placed the thin, smoldering rope to light the weapon and aimed at a tree beyond the boy's shoulder. Fingers squeezed a trigger that touched the rope match to the powder. The teen jumped with fright when the loud booming sounded. Unable to cover his ears, he turned his face away and squeezed his eyes shut. Pieces of bark splintered away at the sound. When he looked back, he saw that a small chunk of tree was blown away.

Bridger thought to merely intimidate the lad into telling them what they needed to know with a display of the damage *Tosh shonte* weaponry could accomplish. "Ask him if he'd prefer t' live in peace, or t' die."

Ompeu relayed the question. The youth was too shaken to respond.

"Tell the lad I've no wish t' harm him, but we are wastin' time. His people need t' know what they're up against if they choose t' fight us."

Ompeu translated Bridger's statement, then asked, "Wutapantam, do you understand now? You must take us to the *werowance* so that there is peace among us."

The teen tore his eyes away from the weapon in the blue-eyed *Tosh shonte* warrior's hand. then nodded. "I will take you."

"You are wise," Ompeu said. "Perhaps you are more man than boy, after all."

Wutapantam led them further inland. When they grew closer to what appeared to be sparsely plotted dwellings, Bridger, Ompeu, and Towaye went ahead with the boy to speak to the *werowance*. The others remained behind, hidden among the trees and brush, fanning out around the small, hastily constructed village. They waited.

*   *   *

Elizabeth turned in a slow circle for her friend's perusal, then looked over her shoulder. "What do you think of it?" She smoothed the soft, café-colored doeskin down her body. The dress fit perfectly, loosely hugging and accentuating her petite, curvaceous form. "How I wish for a looking glass."

Emme giggled lightly. "'Tis lovely. The design on the yoke is most pleasing."

Elizabeth fingered the simple geometric design stitched there; little pearls dangled in evenly spaced formation. She smiled thoughtfully. "Poussu helped me with it." She gathered up her long hair at the nape and wound it, tying it securely with a leather strip. She had sewn in pockets, and her hand covered one, reassured that the small, carved deer she carried was tucked safely away. "I feel nearly unclothed, yet liberated from that constricting chemise, bodice, petticoat and skirt." Lifting a foot to gauge the length of her new dress, she wondered aloud, "Is the length agreeable? My ankles are exposed." The fringed edges fell mid-calf.

Emme helped Elizabeth secure a loose thin belt around her waist, tying it off so that the ends lay against her hip. Ompeu's gift of a flint knife completed the ensemble, tucked safely in its sheath. "As agreeable as mine. Besides, there is no need to be concerned about it. I'll wager, ye won't regret the wardrobe change."

"We need to convince Mistress Dare to trade her English dress." Elizabeth uttered absently, as she checked the shoulder ties to ensure nothing was exposed.

"Don't worry yerself," Emme chided. "She will come 'round. Though I've gone and married a savage against her wishes." Emme took a seat on her sleeping pallet.

Elizabeth frowned. "I should think by now that your indenture is null and void."

"I've continued to help her with little Virginia, but yes, Master Dare released me from my indenture when I married Towaye."

"Well then, you are your own woman now." Elizabeth offered her a reassuring smile, moving to where her English clothing lay on the floor of Emme's *yeehaukan*. She folded each piece and rolled up the entire collection into a bundle inside her gray outer skirt. "And one I gladly consider a friend. One day, Mistress Dare will realize that we are no longer in London, and never will be again. She will come to understand, that there are some facets of English society that have no place or usefulness here."

"Oh, I do not blame her," Emme emphasized with a wave of her hand. "She is attempting to hold on to the distant hope that her father will return. She is hangin' on to the last bit of home, and the life she has known. Not everyone has adjusted well to the changes."

"True. I suppose you and I were all too willing to cast off our old lives. I would do well to have patience with Eleanor." Elizabeth tied up the bundle of clothing, wondering if she should burn the lot at the next Green Corn Ceremony, then decided against it. The cloth could be cleaned and used to make various items.

Emme watched her, but her eyes betrayed her distant thoughts. "Do ye believe the men will return soon?"

Elizabeth's gaze drifted to the door. "It has been six days. I am certain they shall return posthaste."

Emme fell back upon the pallet, a sigh escaping her lips. "Six long days. I miss my husband." Neither of them wished to mention the possibility that the men encountered the Secotan in battle, though it weighed heavily on each of them.

"I know," was all Elizabeth could utter sympathetically. She truly did understand, unable to keep her thoughts from Ompeu, since the day he left. She wondered what he would think of her new doeskin dress, then dismissed her musings. When did it become important to her what he thought of her appearance? Still, she missed his quiet presence, and though she tried to rein in her emotions, the truth was, she yearned for him. It was merely a physical dalliance, of course, she reminded herself whenever her thoughts wandered. The pleasure she experienced in his bed, the way he filled her so deliciously and completely. She craved him. *'If come share my bed, you not wish to leave,'* he said. "Preposterous." Elizabeth muttered aloud.

"What is preposterous?"

"Nothing. I was merely thinking of burning this old dress, then thought the idea preposterous. I could use the cloth for bandages, or other things," Elizabeth recovered, smoothly.

"Yer becoming quite the medicine woman."

"Yes, well, I do not know nearly enough, but Poussu is a wonderful mentor and teacher."

"I could not ask for a better mother-in-law."

"She thinks of you as the daughter she lost."

"I wonder what happened to her," Emme pondered aloud.

"She and her infant were killed at Desamunkepeuc. She was Ompeu's wife."

Emme sat up abruptly. "Oh my, I was unaware! How dreadful! No wonder... poor Ompeu!"

"Aye."

"Towaye did not ever speak of the details of his sister's death. Only that he had a sister who passed on, but nothin' about Desamunkepeuc. I feel completely wretched about this. Why did he not tell me?"

"Perhaps he would have told you in time. He and Poussu seem to understand it was a painful and tragic accident, and you know it is not their custom to speak much about the dead."

"Has Ompeu spoken to ye?"

"He has. He told me all of it."

Knowing Ompeu's taciturn nature, Emme was impressed. Ompeu did not speak freely about much of anything. "He's placed his trust in ye, then."

Elizabeth pondered a moment at the revelation. "I suppose he has." *And I have placed my trust in him*, she thought, for she told him everything about her life with Cooke and how she came to marry him, as they lay skin to skin in Ompeu's bed. A sudden commotion outside prevented further thoughts of that night.

Emme jumped from her spot, lifting the door flap. "The men are returned!" she let out with delight before rushing through the door. Elizabeth followed, her heart racing.

She noted that none of the returning men were painted for war. She did not see Ompeu immediately, for her short stature prohibited a better view, but as the crowd opened to allow the men to enter the village proper, she caught sight of him leading a young man to where the previous prisoners were kept. Paukunnawaw helped him tie the lad to the post. She watched as Ompeu spoke to the prisoner briefly. Manteo stepped forward, speaking with them at length. The young man did not seem to be distressed and answered calmly. Elizabeth was relieved to see that he had not been tortured.

"What is happening?" she whispered to herself, attempting to squeeze her way through the milling crowd.

Ompeu caught sight of her, unable to keep the slight look of astonishment from invading his otherwise stoic façade. His eyes met hers briefly, the glint in them betraying his pleasure at her new choice of apparel. No one but Elizabeth noticed however, and he acknowledged her with the faintest of smiles. The look was fleeting, simmering with unspoken promise. He turned away then, walking with Manteo and the others to speak to the *werowansa*. Before he could take two steps, a joyous Onxe came running, leaping. Ompeu caught the boy up in his arms, carrying him a few steps before setting him on his feet and ruffling his hair. Warm, sweet emotion swept through her at the sight of them together. Elizabeth realized that her son loved Ompeu, and she envied him the ability to show such a public display of affection.

The crowd gradually dispersed, leaving the young man tied to the post, untroubled. Elizabeth watched as he slid to the ground sitting cross-legged, his wrists tied behind his back. She wondered why no one approached or taunted him.

Emme came running to her side. "He's the son of the *werowance*," she said, catching her breath. "Towaye told me they found him in the woods outside the Secotan town. He came with them willingly."

"Why is the lad tied up?" Elizabeth wondered aloud.

"Not certain. Towaye will tell me more, later. They're to council and talk about what they'll do next," Emme breathed a sigh of relief, and smiled. "I'm simply happy to have my husband safely returned. I must go and prepare supper.

Chapter Seventeen

The council meeting lasted well into the night. Elizabeth's curiosity and excitement over Ompeu's return would not allow her to sleep. She crept from her pallet and checked her sleeping son. She stroked his hair and pressed a kiss to his temple. Turning, she found Poussu watching her in the dim firelight. The older woman seemed to divine her thoughts, and silently encouraged her to go. Ajax had taken to sleeping near them. When he looked as though he would follow, she held her hand up, motioning for him to stay. He yawned, and changed sleeping positions, obeying her command.

Elizabeth exited the longhouse, but when she arrived at Ompeu's door, she stood motionless wondering if she had gone mad, creeping about in the night. She felt foolish, and considered turning back when he startled her, opening the door flap and pulling her inside. He swept her up in his arms, his lips finding hers, his kisses demanding and urgent. After her initial surprise, Elizabeth melded to him, returning his kisses with equal fervor.

Eager hands sought to rid one another of the coverings that impeded them, taking every opportunity to touch and caress as they did so. Ompeu made short work of the new dress, pulling the leather ties at her shoulders, opening the belt at her waist, pushing the doeskin past the fullness of her hips until it pooled at her feet.

"And I thought you would appreciate my new dress," she breathed against his lips, her hands pulling the tie at his hip, releasing his breechclout. Her fingers searched blindly for the part of him she wanted most, delighted to find him already hard, his warm flesh filling her hand.

His mouth traveled over her cheek to the column of her throat. "When I see you in the dress, I think... I want take it off."

They stood together naked, the caress of bodies brushing against one another. He did not want to wait. He wanted her now. Ompeu took her face in his hands, and lowering his head, he closed the distance between them, his lips capturing hers, covering her mouth, devouring the softness of her lips.

He lifted his head, his lips a mere inch away. "I think of you each day I am gone away," he whispered, then recaptured her mouth with his, this time more impassioned, telling her with his kisses, and the pressure of his body against hers, exactly what he wanted.

Instinctively, her body arched against him, her hands sliding and skimming over the muscles of his back, her soft curves and breasts, pressed against his lean body. "I know," she smiled, her voice a silky murmur against his lips. "It is the same for me," she admitted.

Ompeu lifted her, setting her upon the sleeping pallet, so that she was seated in front of him. He knelt before her, his fingers skimmed over her thighs to her knees, separating them. His mouth created a tantalizing trail moving lower, kissing, licking, and nipping his way down her body until his lips and tongue were working amazing magic between her thighs.

"Oh!"

Elizabeth rested her weight on the palms of her hands, leaning back to give him better access. The sensations were deliciously new, but she didn't want this. She wanted him. Inside her. She let him know without words what she wanted. His fingers grazed her thighs, sending tingling sensations through her, as he moved between her legs, his erection immediately seeking entrance, the tip of his manhood probing and rubbing against her wet slit.

"I am gone too long," he whispered. His lips found hers once again, his passion rising. "I want you, now," he panted lightly, his lips brushing against hers.

It had been the better of seven days since she'd felt Ompeu filling her, hot and hard inside her, and the way he kissed her and touched her, and whispered his need in her ear, drove her, the passion in his voice reverberating deep into the soft core of her body. His need became hers. His hands on her body caused shivers of delight to follow his every touch. How she missed his hands, and his mouth, and his skin against hers. Elizabeth surrendered to him completely. She threaded her fingers into his dark hair, pulling him toward her, drowning in his kisses as she tipped her hips to welcome his body.

Increasingly urgent sighs and moans mingled and filled the *yeehaukan*. Ompeu flexed his hips, gathering her against his body, hands grasping and sliding beneath her bottom. His fingers dug into her soft flesh, as he pushed himself further inside her, then partially withdrawing, entering again, easing his way into her slick warmth further with each rocking motion of his hips, inch by inch until she enveloped and surrounded him completely. He shuddered.

"Oh God," her voice quavered, trailing off as he drove a slow, delicious rhythm, plunging deeper, harder each time, filling her, overwhelming her, until there was nothing else that existed in the world but him. His movements quickened, his arduous pace increasing, mounting with every thrust. "Ompeu..." his name became a whispering moan.

A torturous, guttural sound escaped his lips in answer to his name, and he stilled himself momentarily, deep inside her, resting his forehead against hers. They breathed each other's erratic breaths. He licked his lips, wetting them. "*Matta*," he panted. He had to stop, or he would spill himself too quickly.

Elizabeth tipped her chin to capture his mouth with hers. "Don't stop, Ompeu. I don't care," she whispered between kisses. "We have all night," she breathed more kisses against his lips, and over his cheek. She whispered in his ear. "Don't stop." She wiggled her hips against his, making him groan. His mouth covered hers hungrily, and he moved against her, meeting her over and over, filling her again and again. Together they found the frantic tempo that bound their bodies together. "God…"

His raw sensuousness carried her to greater heights. He worried about her pleasure, wanting her to be satisfied, but his concern was needless. She missed him as much, and was as close to her own orgasm, a burning sweetness low in her belly, building with every thrust. Her desire for him consumed her as his passion swirled around her.

"More," she urged, her voice a heated whisper.

Ompeu's brows knit, then relaxed as his eyelids closed over. "Wapeih…" her name was a moan of ecstasy slipping through his lips, groaning sounds escaping him as involuntary tremors shook him, an arc of electricity passing through his body to hers. Ompeu came for her, with her, shuddering in his release. His head fell forward against her shoulder, his breath fanning her heated skin, his hands stroking her thighs, sliding up over her hips, around her back, pulling her closer.

Ompeu relaxed against her for a time, until he lifted his head, and his lips sought hers once more. He did not wish to leave her body. Not yet. She was still spasming around him. Tiny, involuntary tremors, clenching along his length, like aftershocks. He brushed the hair from her face with a gentle touch. Her hands roamed his body, soothing his heated skin. They could not seem to satisfy the desire to touch one another.

No words were needed between them. He pressed a warm, lingering kiss to her forehead before rolling away, falling beside her on the sleeping pallet. He drew her close, tucking her head beneath his chin, delighting in the way she threw a leg over his, in an effort to be closer to him. Her fingertips stroked his chest, tracing the lines of his tattoos.

Silence passed between them before he whispered, *"Sa kir winkan?"*

"Mmm," she mewed like a contented cat. *"Kupi.* More than fine. And you?"

Ompeu captured the small, pale hand on his chest and slipped his fingers through hers, silent as he studied their hands. "Enemy will come," he said quietly. "Wanchese and Nussacun are here. We must wait."

Elizabeth lifted her head from his shoulder, alarmed at his news. "Who is the young man tied to the post?"

Ompeu's hand caressed her bare shoulder and back. "He is called Wutapantam, son to Secotan *werowance*. He come with us."

"But why is he tied, as though he were a prisoner?"

"If Wanchese and Nussacun see him."

"He's being used as a pawn, then?"

Ompeu did not understand the word, but he guessed. "He know. He think of it. He want to stay here with us. He say if he is here, his people will not attack."

"Do you trust him?"

"*Kupi.* I must."

Ompeu attempted to explain how they came upon Wutapantam, and the display of weaponry Bridger showed. This prompted the youth to lead them to the Secotan *werowance*. They were initially unaware that Wutapantam was the chief's son. The Secotan were at first wary, but after several days of talking and feasting, Wutapantam bluntly asked him why he had changed his heart, for it was known that Ompeu abhorred the *Tosh shonte* for the killings at Desamunkepeuc. He told the young man that although much of what Wanchese told them was true, there were many things he lied about in order to stir up more hatred. Ompeu told him that he learned for himself of the *Tosh shonte* and grew to care for some of them. It was Ompeu's change of heart that intrigued the teen the most. He wished to understand how one so full of anger toward the *Tosh shonte*, could become a friend to them. Wutapantam wished to see for himself as well, and told them he would help to dissuade Nussacun and Wanchese in their attempt to harm the Croatan. Wutapantam reasoned that if he were among the Croatan, his presence would guarantee peace.

"Still, it does not seem acceptable to bind him to a post, when he's an ambassador of sorts."

The confusion displayed on Ompeu's handsome face told her, he did not understand all her words.

"It seems wrong to tie him when he wants to help," she explained.

"They watch us," Ompeu answered. "They will see him tied, and they will come."

This revelation unsettled her, and her expression grew fearful.

Noting her distress, he quickly replied. "They not hurt you. They not hurt Onxe. I keep you and boy safe with my life," he vowed.

"You mustn't speak so," she admonished gently.

"It is true. *Kuwumáras*."

"*Kuwumáras*," she repeated thoughtfully. "What does it mean?"

"You not know?" He released her hand, brushing gentle fingertips over her cheek. "I have great love for you, Wapeih."

"Ompeu... I...," Elizabeth stumbled. Why could she not tell him she loved him as well?

"*Sehe*, do not say the word Wapeih. Dream is ended, and vision is gone. You come to me be-cause you wish it, not be-cause I ask. For this, my heart is full." In his dreams, joining with the metaphorical doe turned she-wolf, turned woman brought him peace and contentment. Ompeu believed the dreams were a warning that to carry anger in his heart would be to destroy himself and his people. Joining with Elizabeth, loving her, helped him to heal. How could he not care for her? She was intelligent and beautiful. Her heart was good. She stirred his soul in ways he never expected. She was fire in his blood. "I know you," he whispered.

Elizabeth rose above him, straddling his hips. She kissed him, slowly and sweetly, until he was mindless with renewed desire for her. They made love again, this time gentle and unhurried. She could not say the words, but she could choose to share her body willingly with a man who vowed to protect her and her son with his life. He was not asking her to love him in return, he was not asking her to share his bed. He was asking her to make her own choices.

For now, it was enough, and he realized this must have been the way Sequan felt for many years.

*　　*　　*

"*Wingapo. Sa kir winkan? Nuturuwins Wapeih*," Elizabeth whispered to the young man seated near the central fire of the longhouse. She smiled reassuringly as she attempted her best Croatan dialect for an awestruck Wutapantam. Poussu slept nearby, snoring softly. The lad merely stared at Elizabeth, his dark eyes wide in wonder. Her long, curled, fawn-colored hair and amber eyes distracted him from realizing she spoke in his language. She knelt before him, offering him the bowl of sizzling venison and roasted tubers, noting the way he swallowed visibly as the aroma reached his nostrils. "Are you hungry?" she continued, using words he did not understand. "I've brought food. *Mincon,*" she gestured. "I'd also like to have a look at your wrists," she said, motioning toward his hands. "I have a salve for them." He looked at the red marks she indicated, then back up at her.

Ompeu entered the longhouse with a sleepy, giggling Onxe on his back, his small child's arms wrapped around Ompeu's neck. He set the boy down and Wutapantam watched the sun-haired child hug the *Tosh shonte* woman kneeling before him. She said something to the boy, placed her lips against his cheek with a smacking noise, and watched as the boy hopped onto a sleeping pallet. Ompeu covered the child with an English cloth blanket, then dropped beside the woman, sitting cross-legged.

"Ompeu," Elizabeth said, placing her hand on his arm. "Please explain to ….,"

"Is this your woman?" Wutapantam spoke in his native language before she could finish.

"This is Wapeih. She wishes to feed you and tend your wounds," Ompeu answered, clearly amused at the question.

"What did he say?" Elizabeth asked, her eyes moving from one man to the other.

"He wishes to know if you are my woman."

"Hmph," she responded with feigned indignation, noting Ompeu's dismal attempt at concealing a teasing grin. "Is it important to him whether I am or not?"

Ompeu shrugged, his eyes unable to contain his merriment at her unease. "If you wish to help him, perhaps."

"Very well," she said leaning into him, offering him a slight shoulder bump. "He likely witnessed my exit from your *yeehaukan* early this morning. Tell him whatever you wish, it matters not to me. He needs to eat."

Wutapantam watched the interplay between them, and though he did not understand their words, their expressions and body language were clear. He then reached for the bowl in Elizabeth's hands. "She is your woman," he pronounced, then proceeded to dip his fingers into the bowl, his hunger, obvious.

After he had eaten and washed it all down with several long gulps of fresh water, Wutapantam allowed Elizabeth to smooth a salve over his wrists where the rope burned his skin. Her touch was gentle. He studied her intently as she worked. "I have never seen such a woman before," he remarked. "I have seen *Tosh shonte* women here, but none this close."

"Her heart is good," Ompeu answered. "Not all *Tosh shonte* are as Wanchese has said."

"And the sun-haired boy?" Wutapantam indicated the sleeping child with a lift of his chin.

"Onxe is her son. Her husband is no more."

"Then *Kiwasa* has blessed you, my friend."

"Only a shaman can know the mind of *Kiwasa*."

Wutapantam shrugged. "If she has changed your heart, then her name suits her well."

Before he could respond, Elizabeth placed her hand on Ompeu's shoulder, using him to balance herself as she rose to her feet. "If you gentlemen are finished, I should like to retire, and I know you must tie him up again before the sun rises."

"*Kenah*, Wapeih," Wutapantam uttered sincerely before she turned away.

Elizabeth offered him a faint smile. "You are welcome, Wutapantam."

When Elizabeth left them to sleep in her own bed, Ompeu spoke. "They will come soon; we must be vigilant."

"I have heard their signals. They know I am here. When they come to release me, I will speak to them and tell them of the peace we have made. I wish to stay here and learn more of the *Tosh shonte* for myself. Manteo and Wanchese have been to their land, it is strange how one accepts them, and the other does not."

"There is truth in what Manteo and Wanchese see in the *Tosh shonte*," Ompeu replied. "There are two sides. They can be a violent people, driven by fear and greed. But they also possess great *mantóac* that we do not understand, yet desire for ourselves."

"At what cost? Many of us have died of sickness. Towns have suffered great losses. Different bands of people have come together to survive."

"This is true. But the English are men, not gods. There are no invisible bullets filled with sickness." Ompeu could not explain. Elizabeth told him she did not understand why so many people died quickly with illness after contact with the English. Perhaps they would never know. All things come to pass for a purpose. And some things could not be explained.

"Then perhaps it is our desire for the English *mantóac* that has displeased *Kiwasa*. We will lose ourselves, lose who we are. Perhaps the Roanoac *werowance* they killed knew this. And that is why he moved his people away and refused to help the *Tosh shonte*."

"Perhaps." Ompeu looked over his shoulder. Onxe and Wapeih were sleeping. The arrival of the *Wutahshuntar* could very well threaten the existence of his people. If more of them came from across the great water, there would be no way to stop the threat. Would helping the English, harm the people of Ossomocomuck? Would internal dissention among the People be their undoing? Each of these questions pointed to one root cause: contact with the English. He turned to Wutapantam. "We must do what we can to keep our people strong. We will always be here, as we have been since first woman emerged from the waters of Ossomocomuck."

"And what of your woman?"

Ompeu did not correct the teen's assumption that Elizabeth was his. He understood the underlying question. All troubles and tragedies of late stemmed from the English. Would his love for a *Tosh shonte* woman bring misfortune? Would his love for her threaten his own existence? He did not know the answers. "She is one of us, as is her son. They are Croatan."

Chapter Eighteen

October 1588

The hiding of women and children was imperative in war. Due to their immeasurable value in a community, the taking of women and children was an accepted war tactic. Women were givers and nurturers of life. They birthed and cared for children, they cultivated and sustained crops, they cared for and fed the village wolfdogs. Men took life away. They hunted, they fished, they killed enemies in hostile conflicts. Each role served one common purpose: survival.

At the first sign of impending attack, the women and children were moved to safety. Separated into small bands, they scattered. Some fled into the woods, others to the tall reeds. Poussu shepherded the women of her group. Babies and children were quieted. All were filled with waiting, huddled silently among the reeds. A cool breeze swept through the stalks, moving them in undulating waves, but the people hidden inside them were still.

Elizabeth's body jerked at the report of English musket fire. She prayed for Ompeu's safety, her heart pounding wildly. She glanced over at her son crouched beside her. He appeared anxious, fidgeting, holding tightly to the bow Ompeu made for him. The last time they hid from an enemy, her son was quiet and calm. More sounds of battle reached them. Shouts, shrieks, and whoops. The scent of burning wood and smoke. Elizabeth closed her eyes tightly. No doubt their homes were burning.

She felt movement beside her. When she opened her eyes, her son was gone, running toward the village. "No! Phillip... Onxe!" Elizabeth burst from her hiding place, running after him. Poussu called out to her. Elizabeth held her hand up urging her mother to stay hidden. "*Matta!*"

Onxe ran. He had to help Ompeu. He had to defend his home and his people. He did not understand why other tribes kept attacking them and burning their houses, but he needed to help stop it. Ompeu told him he was good with the bow. He carried sharpened arrows, and he would use them. He heard his mother call for him, but he was nine years old now, becoming a man, and it was time for him to do what men must do.

Wanchese had gathered warriors from several allied towns. In the mist of pre-dawn light, they converged on the Croatan town. Wutapantam shouted to Nussacun, attempting to quell any skirmishes. When he was ignored, Ompeu rushed to his side, cutting his bonds. He handed Wutapantam a war club and a hatchet. "I expect you are on my side. I am trusting in you." It was a risk.

"I am with you, brother." Wutapantam answered. He leapt to his feet and joined Ompeu in the melee.

Arrows flew past Onxe as he set his sights on an enemy warrior and took aim. Men were running, hiding, ducking, fighting all around him. His breath accelerated, heart pounding in his ears, his fingers unsteady. He had never used his bow against a man. He let the arrow fly. He watched, momentarily horrified as the enemy warrior fell. Onxe looked away then, surveying the chaos in his village. He darted off in search of Ompeu.

Ompeu thought he heard Elizabeth's voice calling for Onxe. His head swung around, eyes searching. A Roanoac ran toward him. Ompeu rid himself of the warrior, clubbing him as though he were a mere nuisance. A burning *yeehaukan* collapsed behind him. He heard her scream. When he saw her through the smoke, his heart stopped. Nussacun had her, was dragging her away. "Wapeih! *Matta!*"

Elizabeth screamed, kicked, and punched to no avail. Her captor gripped her about the waist, lifting her off her feet. Ajax, her favored wolfdog barked and snarled, his teeth bared. As he leapt forward, Nussacun kicked him, sending him sprawling. The dog yelped in pain, landing hard. "Ajax!" Ompeu ran to her. "No!" She screamed. "Get Onxe! Please save my son! Please, Ompeu!" She thrashed about, thrusting her arm out in the direction where Onxe was also being dragged away. She watched Ompeu stop in his tracks, indecision tormenting him.

Ompeu stood momentarily unsure. Elizabeth was carried away in one direction, Onxe in another. He could not save them both. His eyes scanned the grounds frantically for help from an ally. The enemy was in retreat and most followed, chasing them out of the village. She begged him to save her son. Before he could move toward Onxe, Ompeu felt the sharp pain of a blade to his back, then another in rapid succession. Before he could face his attacker, he fell to his knees, the world spinning wildly. His weapons fell from numbing hands. He thought he heard Elizabeth shriek, calling his name. She called to him as she did in his dreams. He tried to answer her, but his voice would not come. He fell forward. The sounds of a scuffle nearby, men fighting hand-to-hand. When it was ended, someone rolled him over. Wutapantam. Ompeu's breathing was shallow, his eyes glazed over.

"I killed the man who stabbed you, brother. It is over. The enemy has fled. Nussacun stole your woman. Another has taken her son."

It was the last thing Ompeu remembered.

Elizabeth watched helplessly as the enemy warrior appeared from nowhere. Ompeu, momentarily distracted by his indecision was an easy target. She screamed his name in warning, then saw Wutapantam rush to his aid. It was too late. Elizabeth ceased her struggling against Nussacun. "No!" she wailed; her arms outstretched as though she could reach the fallen Ompeu. Nussacun continued to drag her away. Ompeu lie face down in the dirt. He did not move. Elizabeth sobbed his name, and then saw him no more as they rounded a bend heading toward water.

Her wrists were tied in front of her, the rope then laced around her neck. They tossed her into a waiting canoe. "Where is my son? *Nuqisus!*" she demanded hoarsely, her throat raw. The question was met with laughter as the men navigated the canoe, the craft moving swiftly through the calm waters. Elizabeth turned back toward the village. Thick smoke filled the air, darkening the morning sky. Her chest constricted painfully, her body trembled uncontrollably. She turned away, pressing her lids shut against the horrific sight.

"You dress like Croatan, but Wanchese see you *Tosh shonte*," a voice uttered behind her.

She looked over her shoulder, eyeing the large warrior. He dipped his oar into the water forcefully. His hair was shaved and spiked in front. His face was painted black for war. "Wanchese. Where is my son? Please release me. I must help Ompeu!" she pleaded.

"Ompeu dead. You *Tosh shonte* wo-man not have think. Run into fight." He shook his head over her stupidity. "No talk now," he warned, pressing the tip of a blade against her back.

Ompeu was dead. Elizabeth faced forward, her head lowered. Ompeu was dead. Her son taken from her. She searched for that place inside herself. The place she often went to endure Phillip Cooke's cruelty. She despised that place, but if she felt nothing, then nothing would hurt. She gathered her defenses with several deep breaths. Numbness settled heavily upon her like a cloak. Nothing mattered.

They traveled for hours across the sound and up through a separate waterway, then portaged the canoes on land. Elizabeth hoped her son was with a separate war party and would be taken to the same location. She did not see him. They walked in a line headed by Nussacun at the front. A young warrior led her by the rope at her neck. She kept pace, while a jumble of emotions churned attempting to enter the place of numbness; terror, uncertainty, profound grief. She was unsure where they were headed. She did not care.

They camped at night, stretching her arms around the trunk of a wide tree, secured tightly. No one spoke to her. No one offered food or water. She tested the bonds several times while most of the camp slept, hoping to loosen them. At sunrise, she was allowed to relieve herself behind a bush. The warrior who led her, held a water pouch to her lips, offering a few precious gulps to allay her thirst. He stared at her in fascination. He reminded her of Ompeu. She closed her eyes, blocking him out. Ompeu was dead. The young man tightened the bonds before they traveled onward.

It was early evening when they reached a village. A crowd of mostly women, children and elders surrounded the war party. Some shouted and screamed in her face, slapping her, pulling her hair, hitting her with sticks. Angry faces filled her vision. Elizabeth endured every blow. She fell to her knees, dazed. She struggled to rise up defiantly on unsteady feet as the beating continued. She did not cry out, she did not move to defend herself. Nussacun stepped in, demanding the women leave her. He stared at her speculatively. Blood dripped from her nose and mouth, yet she remained unemotional. The only sign of distress was the trembling rise and fall of her breast heaving laboriously as she pulled in air. It was unusual for a prisoner to have no reaction. Elizabeth lifted her chin, staring back at Nussacun without apology. She had survived Phillip Cooke. She would survive this as well.

He led her to a dwelling, shoving her roughly inside. He pulled out a blade and held it in front of her face. Still she did not react, she simply stared at the weapon and watched as he lowered it. Nussacun was bewildered. Either this small *Tosh shonte* woman had courage, or she had not the sense to be afraid. He used the knife to cut her bonds, then motioned to the sleeping pallet, pushing her toward it, gesturing for her to sit. He left. Elizabeth's head pounded, her brain fogged. Her left eye swelled, closing off her vision. Blood from her nose and mouth dripped from her chin, landing on her lap, droplets seeping into her doeskin dress.

Voices outside indicated she was guarded. What would the Roanoac do to her? She told herself it no longer mattered. The world ceased to make sense. Nothing held meaning. She sat alone in the empty hut for hours. Long enough to think. Why did her son run toward the fighting? Where was he now? She did not wish to think. Did not wish to feel. Did not wish to play the horrible scene of her son carried away kicking and screaming, or Ompeu attacked from behind, his body dropping to the earth.

Ompeu. Was it just nights ago that she had lain in his arms? Felt his skin against hers? Welcomed him and held him inside her body? The memory caused a dry sob to burn her throat, but she refused to let it escape her. He loved her, yet she could not say the words. He loved her, despite his initial hatred of her people. He loved her, though he had lost a wife and child. Now, it was too late. Too late. She was cowardly. He was brave, unafraid to love her, a *Tosh shonte* woman.

Elizabeth's heart ached with a physical pain borne of intense grief. She leaned back against the frame of the sleeping pallet. Something pressed against her spine. Her knife! The knife Ompeu gifted her. Her captors, in their haste, had not inspected her for weapons. Elizabeth moved to a kneeling position, reached behind, found the handle tucked inside her belt and unsheathed it. She contemplated the flint blade, turning it over in her palm. It was not large, but it was sharp. It would do.

Gathering her disheveled, knotted hair, she brought the mass that fell past her waist over her shoulder. Elizabeth raised the knife with a trembling hand. She squeezed her eyes shut, heedless of the pain to her battered face. She sawed and hacked through the tawny strands, until it was done. Until her hair hung unevenly to her shoulders. Somehow the act infused her with relief. She tossed the discarded mane into the ashes of the empty firepit.

She was not finished. Holding the knife above her forearm, her hand shook as the blade hovered over her flesh. A tear slipped as she made the first long gash, then the second and third. She watched, through blurred vision as the blood seeped, dripping from her arm. For Onxe. For Ompeu. She slashed her other arm. Once, twice, three times. Yes. It felt good to bleed. To shed your life's blood, to stab the pain that gnawed at your heart, to grieve and weep for someone you loved. It was the ultimate pain of loving someone; living with the loss. It was the greatest hurt of all. She embraced it. The pain was life. Physical pain temporarily distracted her from the emotional, and was easier to bear.

"I love you, Onxe. I love you Ompeu. I will forever love you both," she whispered as she watched her blood flow, crimson soaking the front of her doeskin dress.

*   *   *

"She mourns someone."

"I do not care. Why should I bandage her? I do not know why Nussacun brought her here."

"Because you are his wife? Because she is his captive? I think it odd that a *Tosh shonte* woman would cut herself in mourning. I wonder who she mourns."

"Nussacun should bandage her. She is out cold. So much blood. She will be of no use to me this way."

Women's voices. Algonquian voices. Elizabeth had not the strength to open her eyes. She could not move. Morning birds sang cheerfully. Sunlight peeked through the opened door, pressing against her eyelids. Someone washed and bandaged her forearms. A cool, wet cloth wiped her tear-streaked face, cleansing the dried blood from her nose and mouth, a cool compress against her eye. A touch lit her shortened hair gently.

"Look at her hair. The color. See how it coils around?"

"All that matters is that she can work and help me care for the little ones."

"You are angry that your husband brought her here."

"I am angry that she is unable to work."

The women left. Elizabeth sank into sleep. She awoke to a darkening sky, visible through the smoke hole. Pushing herself up into a sitting position, her body rebelled painfully. Her head throbbed, only one eyelid opened completely. The wrappings on her arms were tight and pulsed with every heartbeat. She scanned the hut. It was smaller than most dwellings she had seen, unadorned with no paintings or drawings on the reed mats. Her discarded hair and her knife were gone. She saw that someone left food and water for her. She eyed the bowl suspiciously, but knew that if she were ever to escape this place, she would need her strength. She had to get out, had to find her son. Her hands trembled as she dipped fingers into the bowl, bringing a bite of venison to her sore and swollen lips.

The door flap opened, and a young Roanoac woman entered. She seemed surprised to find Elizabeth awake. A sourness entered her expression. A toddler peeked from behind the woman's leg, eyeing Elizabeth warily with beautiful dark eyes. The woman spoke, demanding Elizabeth's name.

"*Nuturuwins* Elizabe.... *Nuturuwins Wapeih,*" she corrected. "Do you know the whereabouts of my son? *Nuqisus?*"

"Wapeih," the woman repeated. She then assessed Elizabeth from head to toe. Her demeanor revealed disdain for the unwelcome captive. The woman left, little boy at her heels.

"No, please, wait! Where is my son?" Elizabeth called after her. The food forgotten, she fell back to the sleeping pallet.

Only the woman ever entered the hut where Elizabeth was kept, and for that she was grateful. Two days passed. The woman with the toddler brought a clean doeskin dress for her. Elizabeth continued to ask questions regarding the location of her son, but the woman would not speak to her. She continued to bring food, and tended Elizabeth's wounds in her cold, detached manner. Elizabeth was allowed to leave the dwelling to bathe and relieve herself, but always escorted by someone and closely watched.

A week passed. Elizabeth was put to gathering water and wood or performing menial tasks. She went about this work numbly, automatically. Only her body was present, just the shell of her, going through the motions of daily life, but not living. Rising in the morning was a chore. She did not care what happened to her. Her heart ached for her son. For Ompeu. The bruises on her face were now purple and green discolorations, the slashed forearms were healing. Her heart would not. '*Wounds not seen need more time.*' Ompeu once said. Yes, a lifetime.

The woman with the toddler was Sacquenuckot, the wife of Nussacun. There was another child, a girl of about five years. Elizabeth guessed at the reason for the woman's aloofness and quiet hostility. Thankfully, Nussacun appeared to have no interest in a *Tosh shonte* woman. She saw Wanchese but once. He did not acknowledge her presence and left the village soon after.

Elizabeth rarely spoke. Nor was she spoken to, other than the commands given to her. Shunned by most of the Roanoac, they talked of her in hushed tones, their restrained animosity felt as heavy as the blows she received the day she arrived. She yearned for home, to see Poussu, Emme, Eleanor, and Mamankanois. She prayed for their safety and longed to know how they fared. Thoughts of friends and her son gave her strength to endure. England and Phillip Cooke seemed a lifetime ago. The days were colder. If she did not escape soon, she would spend the winter among the Roanoac.

She had to find her son.

Chapter Nineteen

An involuntary growl of pain and frustration left Ompeu's lips.

"Forgive me. Be still," Poussu admonished.

"How much longer? I cannot stay here. I must help the men. I must search for Wapeih and Onxe." Ompeu lie prone on his sleeping pallet, his chin resting on his forearms, long hair in his face. Ajax was curled beside him, sleeping comfortably. Since Elizabeth's and Onxe's abductions, the dog rarely left Ompeu's side.

Poussu tended the stab wounds to his lower back. "One of the wounds was deep. You lost much blood. It is good that you are healing. You must give your body time." Poussu grew concerned that Ompeu would not recover at all. She feared internal wounds would cause his death. He was unconscious for days when fever set in.   Now the fever was gone, he was awake and a horrible patient, which meant he was returning to health.

Ompeu grunted.

"You must also wait until others can join you. It would be foolish of you to storm the Roanoac village alone. We have many things to do here since the attack. Homes need rebuilding, tools and weapons restored. We have suffered great losses. Our *Tosh shonte* brother is dead. His poor wife Eleanor mourns him greatly. Others were wounded as well. Have patience my son. You are not strong enough yet."

Ompeu learned of the killing of Ananias Dare just yesterday. The reminder sobered him. Ompeu knew he was fortunate to be alive. Still, his frustration at being incapacitated and unable to help his people, or search for those he loved grew with each passing day. "I cannot bear the thought of her in Nussacun's hands. I will kill him!"

"Not in your condition. You could not fight a rabbit and win today," she chuckled softly.

Ompeu grunted, unappreciative of Poussu's attempt at humor, even if her words were true.

"Think of it. Onxe and Wapeih are alive. If they were to be killed, it would have happened here. Instead they were taken as captives. We have done the same to our enemies."

"Nussacun is a dead man."

Poussu was silent for a time as she finished packing the wound. "You have much love for Wapeih, then?" she asked quietly.

Ompeu swept a hand over his forehead, fingers running through his hair, brushing the black mane away from his face. He turned his head to look into his adoptive mother's eyes. "I do not wish to live without her, or Onxe."

Poussu did not think he could bear the loss of another woman and child he cared for. She did not believe she could either. "We will make offerings to *Kiwasa* and seek his blessing. We will find them and bring them home."

*　　　*　　　*

Elizabeth spent her days helping to care for the children of Nussacun. The once shy toddler was now comfortable with her and would drop into her lap when he grew tired, or run to her when he sought comfort. If Sacquenuckot had any objections to this, she did not voice them. At times, it seemed she was grateful for the respite Elizabeth provided. The Roanoac woman was not unkind to her, but nor was she friendly.

Weeks passed, and still she had not found a way to escape. She did not know where to go, where her son was taken, or how to return home. She doubted anyone would come for her. After the devastation she witnessed during the attack, it would take time, resources, and great effort for the Croatan village to recover before winter set in. She helped Sacquenuckot and the Roanoac women harvest and store corn. She cooked, she cleaned, she cared for the children. Life here was not so different from life on Croatoan. But it was vastly different. There was no Onxe. No Ompeu. No friendly faces, English or native.

At the beginning of the Hunter's moon, or the Moon of Falling Leaves, Elizabeth experienced some lethargy along with mild nausea, her breasts tender and sore. She missed her woman's time for the second consecutive month. She knew. Ompeu had planted a seed in a storm. Bittersweet memories flooded her thoughts. And in the quiet of her prison dwelling, she wept for him and Onxe for she may never see her son again. She would protect and cherish this babe she carried, for it was all she had left.

Sacquenuckot suspected Elizabeth's pregnancy, for the captive *Tosh shonte* woman did not yet visit the menstrual hut. Through words and gestures, she questioned the one called Wapeih.

"*Kupi. Pommahaum,*" Elizabeth responded in a broken Algonquian dialect, but the thin thread of sadness in her voice needed no translation. She placed her palm over her still-flat belly. "*Nohsh Croatan.*" She knew she butchered the phrasing, but Sacquenuckot seemed to understand that she was carrying the child of a Croatan.

She expected Sacquenuckot to be angry. Instead a look of understanding and compassion infused her features. Her usual indifference toward Elizabeth shifted for reasons unknown. Until one day as they prepared the evening meal, Sacquenuckot told the story of how she came to be the wife of Nussacun. Elizabeth listened intently, grasping for words and phrases she understood. Through words and gestures, Sacquenuckot explained that years ago, she and several women were taken in a raid. Her husband was killed. She pointed to her first child, the five-year-old girl, Mayis. Apparently, this child was not Nussacun's, but her deceased husband's. Unbeknownst to Nussacun, Sacquenuckot was in the early stages of pregnancy. As the years passed, Sacquenuckot became an esteemed wife, with all rights and privileges afforded.

Elizabeth once again asked about her son, Onxe. Sacquenuckot told her she did not know where he was taken, only that a warrior named Watape had captured the sun-haired boy. Elizabeth tucked the piece of information away in her mind. She would remember the name Watape.

Not allowed to sleep in Sacquenuckot's *yeehaukan*, Elizabeth slept in a smaller outbuilding which served as a shed. That night as she undressed, preparing for sleep, she wondered briefly about the little boy, Apegwus. He did not look well today. He was listless, wanting to spend most of the day in either his mother's or

Elizabeth's arms. The burgeoning medicine woman in her decided to watch him closely the following day. She thought of possible illnesses, and remedies. She longed to speak to Poussu.

Settling under her blankets, she placed her palm over her womb, her mind filled with thoughts of Ompeu. In a month or so, her pregnancy would be noticeable. She ticked away the months in her mind. The first time they made love had to be early September. Unsure of the exact month, she guessed the babe would be born in late spring or early summer. After multiple mental calculations, she gave up, and dozed fitfully.

A high-pitched hum grew louder. Intense vibrations were followed by total body paralysis. She could not move. His presence permeated her entire being.

"Where are you?" her soul asked, desperate, crying out for him, reaching.

"I am here," he said wordlessly. His essence filled her, infusing her with peace and comfort. "Wait for me."

Nussacun delayed for some time, until he knew his wife and children slept soundly. He rose quietly, creeping stealthily out of his dwelling and into the night. He entered the shed where the *Tosh shonte* woman slept, careful to make no sound. He watched her sleep. The dim firelight danced, casting his shadow against the bark-mat wall.

Over the course of the past moon, he observed her from a distance. He wondered at the *mantóac* she possessed to capture the heart of Ompeu and turn him away from his hatred. There was nothing special about her. Other than her pale skin, and the unusual color of her hair and eyes. she was but a woman. She did the work of the women, she helped care for his children. She spoke little and did as she was told. She mourned her lover Ompeu, in the way of the People. Curiosity bade him step closer and crouch beside her. He lifted a hand to her hair.

Elizabeth sprung up suddenly, sensing the touch to her head. She had been dreaming of something, but... Wide-eyed, she found a male form had risen, stepping back. "*Matta*," she commanded, with more conviction and courage than she felt. Her insides roiled. Why was he here? Did he expect to share her bed? Elizabeth panicked, her eyes darting to the door, calculating her chances of escaping past him. They were slim to none.

Nussacun spoke a quiet string of words she did not understand.

"I do not know why you are here, but you must leave at once!" she said, pointing to the door, so that he would not mistake her meaning. The action caused her blanket to fall, exposing her nakedness.

Nussacun's eyes roamed hotly over her body in the dimness of firelight. He spoke again, soothingly, inching closer, carefully as though he approached a wild animal. He reached for her.

"*Matta!*" She shouted, holding up a hand to ward him off. He grasped her wrist, wrenching her arm to her side, pushing her down against the furs.

The door flap opened. "Leave the woman alone!" It was Nussacun's wife, gripping a woman's axe. "Move away from her and go back to my *yeehaukan*. You will not do to her what you did to me years ago," she growled in the Roanoac dialect.

Nussacun rolled away from Elizabeth. She understood few of Sacquenuckot's words, but thankfully they were effective. She hoped the woman would not strike her with the axe, thinking she encouraged Nussacun's behavior.

His wife raised the weapon. "Now!"

He rose from the pallet, spared a glance back at Elizabeth, who sat deathly still covering her nakedness, then at his wife. "She is a captive...," he began as though it excused his actions.

"She is with child. A Croatan is the father. You have shamed and dishonored yourself!"

The *Tosh shonte* woman carried Ompeu's child? Nussacun deflated, then shook his head in disbelief. He moved passed his wife to the door.

"Nussacun. Remove your belongings. You are not welcome in my home. And do not wake the children."

When he left, Sacquenuckot went to Elizabeth's side. She was trembling.

"*Sehe*," Sacquenuckot soothed. *"Sá kir winkan?"*

Elizabeth emptied her lungs of breath she did not realize she was holding and nodded affirmatively. "I am well. He did not hurt me. *Kenah*," she breathed. "Thank you."

Sacquenuckot spoke though she knew Wapeih would not understand every word. "I should have thrown him away and removed his things long ago. I do not know why I waited. I am sorry for what he has done. He will leave the village for a time but will return to me. It is all that can happen to him. To lie with a woman against her will is punishable by death. But since you are an enemy captive…," she shrugged, indicating there was not much that could be done.

Though Elizabeth could not formulate a response, surprisingly, she understood much of what Sacquenuckot said.

"Winter will be upon us soon. You must stay with us until the Worm Moon. I will find a way to help you return to Croatoan."

The following day, Sacquenuckot did not come for her. When Elizabeth arrived at the *yeehaukan*, she found the woman grief stricken. Elizabeth wondered if Nussacun had done something terrible. Sacquenuckot knelt next to a bundle indicating her sick child. Elizabeth fell beside her, moving the blanket aside. She touched the boy's brow with the back of her hand. "Fever."

The medicine man entered then, and the women stepped aside to allow him space. He burned *uppowoc* and waved the pungent smoke over the child with a fan made of turkey feathers. He chanted and prayed. Sacquenuckot's face was pinched with worry.

Knowing Nussacun was gone, Elizabeth stayed in the *yeehaukan* that night. She and Sacquenuckot took turns bathing Apegwus with cool water to keep his fever down and changed soiled bedding.

Knowing Sacquenuckot tried her own remedies, Elizabeth searched the home for medicinal items she knew to be stocked in every household. She and Poussu had experimented with varied mixtures of dried herbs, roots, and plants, testing their efficacy on patients. She opened containers and small leather pouches, sniffing the contents, and rubbing them between her fingers to test the identity of the herb. Whatever concoction she created might not cure Apegwus but would possibly alleviate his symptoms, and the small quantities she gave would not harm him.

Sacquenuckot watched as Elizabeth went about mixing the dried ingredients and set water to boil in a clay pot in the firepit. She made a tea, allowing it to steep and then cool. When Apegwus awoke, she fed him small sips.

On the second day, he ate a limited measure of thin, bland cornmeal porridge. After the fourth day, the boy showed great improvement. He was sitting up, and wishing to play with his sister, Mayis. Later that evening Elizabeth and Sacquenuckot sat quietly near the fire while the children slept. The women were exhausted.

"You must have loved the one you mourn greatly. The father of your child?" she ventured.

Elizabeth lifted tired eyes from the dancing flames. Sacquenuckot gestured to the scars on Elizabeth's forearms, she then touched a hand over her own heart. Elizabeth understood. "*Kupi,*" she replied quietly, though she never had the courage to tell him.

Chapter Twenty

March 1589

"There is food, water, and a blanket. The air still bites with cold," Sacquenuckot said, as she helped Elizabeth secure the items to her back. She tied the pack securely, then faced the *Tosh shonte* woman. "And this. This belongs with you."

The knife. The one she used to cut her hair and slash herself in mourning. The one Ompeu had given her months ago. "*Kenah.*" Elizabeth studied the blade, memories threatening to surge forth. She swallowed hard, holding them at bay. She slipped the knife into the belt at her growing waist. She was now visibly with child, but not yet near full term. Her best estimate was six or seven months. Sacquenuckot tried on numerous occasions to convince her to remain with the Roanoac until the child was born, but Elizabeth waited an entire winter. She needed to leave now, before Nussacun returned. She had to find her son. She had to return to Croatoan and seek the help of friends. Nothing would stop her.

"My brothers will take you to a village of the Tuscarora. They will explain all. There are people among them who will speak to you. They may have news of your sun-haired boy. You will seek passage to Croatoan from there." Sacquenuckot pressed a string of pearls into her hand as well as copper disk earrings, and several copper bracelets. "Use these wisely for trade, or gifts."

Elizabeth opened her fur wrap and slipped the valuable trinkets into the pouch slung across her body. Her understanding of the Algonquian dialect was improved, but she had difficulty producing the language. "*Kenah, nitáp.* I do not know how to repay thee."

"*Anath.*" *Farewell.* The women embraced warmly. Ones who were enemies, now parted as friends.

She took one last look at her surroundings at the edge of the Roanoac village. Apegwus clutched her long doeskin skirt and leggings. Mayis, grasped Elizabeth's hand. She would miss these beautiful children.

Elizabeth walked the wooded path in a single-file line among three silent Roanoac men. One, she simply knew as Nemat, his name was a variation of the word 'brother'. She was uncertain what his kinship was to

Sacquenuckot. They tended to address others as brother, sister, mother, father, grandmother, or grandfather as signs of respect, not necessarily as a result of any blood relation. Ohawas and Tindge volunteered for the journey as well, hoping to hunt and perhaps conduct trade along the way.

The ground beneath their feet was a spongy mixture of melting snow and ice mixed with rotting leaves. They trekked for an hour, until they came upon a riverbank where canoes were hidden. They stopped to read the river. When the men were satisfied that the frigid waters would carry them, they climbed into the canoe.

They traveled for some time. Elizabeth sensed they were being watched. Along the banks of the river, she spied figures hidden among the bare trees and thin brush.

"*Ska roh reh*," Ohawas murmured. He then shouted something to them, using hand gestures for added measure. Soon after, several warriors revealed themselves. One raised a hand in greeting, shouting and signing in response. They trotted to the river's edge, awaiting the arrival of the visitors.

The canoe slid up the embankment. Ohawas lent an arm to aid Elizabeth as she climbed out of the canoe. The four were surrounded and escorted to the village. Although these people were not hostile, Elizabeth was apprehensive, sensing the unease of her Roanoac travel companions. She clutched her fur wrap, pulling it closely against her body.

"Yeh kwah nee'st." She is handsome, one of the Tuscarora men commented as they walked through the village entrance. He stepped forward, then spoke directly to Elizabeth. *"Thah he syeah: heh hah ska roh reh?" Do you understand the Tuscarora language?*

Bewilderment clouded her features. She could not answer. Their language was unlike the Algonquian dialects she heard. Ohawas moved between Elizabeth and the man, signing as he spoke. Elizabeth did not understand a word, but what he said caused the Tuscarora to back away apologetically.

"Welcome!" A deep voice bellowed. Elizabeth could not believe her ears. Someone spoke English? She turned to discover the voice came from a tall, dark man. He did not appear to be indigenous. He smiled as he approached. Perfect teeth, stark white against the rich dark skin of his handsome face. He wore a sparse beard. His hair was thick and tied in a queue at the back of his head. He wore a cream-colored shirt made of a fibrous thread, as did most of the men here. "You speak English, do you not? *¿Quizas, habla usted castellano?*" The man asked a dumbfounded Elizabeth. Ohawas moved closer to her in a subtly protective maneuver. There was not trouble with the Tuscarora, but their peace was tenuous at times.

"Aye. English." She answered when she recovered from her shock. "It has been overlong since I have heard it. I fear my ears have grown unaccustomed."

He smiled at her indulgently. "I am Sumayl." He turned to his friend. "This is Farraj. We are Allah's forgotten ones. Welcome to our village." He lifted his hand in a gesture that encompassed the town. Most of the people had dispersed, continuing with daily activities. Elizabeth noted their homes were similar to most she had seen. There were several longhouses, much larger than anything she lived in.

She offered a guarded smile of greeting to each man. She wondered if the mention of Allah suggested that they were Moors. "Thank you, sirs for your kind welcome. I am... I do not understand. How did you come to be here? Were you among those left by Master Drake years before?"

"Demoiselle, there are no masters here. We are free men," Farraj answered. He was shorter than Sumayl. He too sported a beard, but his head was shaved in the manner of many native men.

"Forgive me... I do not wish to appear ill-mannered. I have been told my curiosity is a curse. I ask too many questions. You speak English. I thought perhaps...."

"Not at all," Sumayl rescued her. "If you must know, there are few of us that remain from Drake's ships. Most of the galley slaves, hundreds, were drowned in a storm along the coast. We are quite the blend of peoples here. Spaniards, Moors, Turks, West Africans. But now we have been embraced by the Tuscarora, and so we are Tuscarora."

A cursory glance around the village lent credence to his claim. There were indeed people of varied origins intermingled with the Tuscarora. "I understand."

Farraj, who seemed initially suspicious of the newcomers' presence, seemed assuaged by her sincerity. "My question is, if there is an English woman here, what became of your settlement?" he asked gently. "Ralegh sent subsequent voyages and planters no doubt, but you, my lady, appear to be lost."

"Our settlement was abandoned. Our Governor sailed to England for supplies and planters, but never returned. My home is Croatoan. Not England."

Sumayl seemed to notice Elizabeth's condition for the first time. He cast dark eyes to the protruded belly, peeking from beneath her fur wrap. "I understand."

"I was captured by Roanoac in an attack, during the Harvest Moon. These men are friends," Elizabeth indicated the three Roanoac men who stood silently beside her. "They agreed to escort me here in the hope that I could seek aid to return to Croatoan. They are unable to travel farther, for fear of reprisal. They want no continuation of war. I am also searching for my son who was taken that day. He has light hair and blue eyes. Do you know of such a boy?"

"I am afraid I do not." Sumayl paused, unsure whether to continue. He assumed the young Roanoac warrior most protective of her was her husband.

"Forgive me lady, for it is my turn to ask a delicate question...."

Elizabeth's eyes lowered. She placed her hand over her abdomen. "The father of my child is... was Croatan." She lifted her gaze to Sumayl. "Please, my name is Elizabeth, but you may call me Wapeih."

Sumayl noted her use of the past tense as well as her somber expression at the mention of the child's father. He chose not to comment further. "Wapeih, please allow us to welcome you and your companions as honored guests. My wives will bring you refreshment. We will speak again once you have rested."

Elizabeth glossed over the word 'wives'. Polygamy was an accepted practice, but many native men did not exercise it. A man had to possess wealth enough to keep more than one wife, as well as offspring. Some men chose monogamy simply to keep peace in the home. Jealousy and fighting among wives occurred on occasion. Others chose monogamy because one wife suited them best. "Are you the *werowance* of these lands?"

Sumayl smiled good-naturedly. "No, my lady, but I am a man of some importance. My knowledge of medicines and the healing arts has afforded me great esteem here. I am an advisor to the chief, and I shall speak to him on your behalf. He will wish to meet all of you."

A light entered the sadness of her eyes. "Healing arts?" Elizabeth returned his smile. "I too have an inclination. I am certain we shall have much to discuss. I thank you again for your kindness, and generosity."

Later as Elizabeth slept in the longhouse with the families of Sumayl and Farraj, three Roanoac men sat outside near the central fire. They were treated well, fed, and offered places to sleep. They met the elderly chief, who allowed them to stay for a short period. But the Roanoac men were anxious, eager to be on their way. It meant leaving Wapeih behind in the care of the Tuscarora. Ohawas thought this was unwise but kept this opinion to himself.

"If one wished for the *Tosh shonte* woman, one should have made an offer to Nussacun when he had the chance," Tindge commented to no one in particular, breaking the amiable silence.

Nemat remained quiet, his eyes darting from Tindge to Ohawas in the dimness. He wondered the same, but it was not for him to say.

Ohawas was silent for a time before answering. He was the one to lead Wapeih by the rope around her neck, all the way to the Roanoac village many months before. If she remembered, she gave no indication. He witnessed her initial beating by the women, and her defiance of Nussacun that day. Ohawas admired her. "Her heart cries for the father of her unborn child. She would not look upon me with love in her eyes," he lamented. The following morning, they were gone.

Elizabeth felt vulnerable and afraid among strangers without her Roanoac escort. The Tuscarora spoke an unfamiliar language. Thankfully, when she did use Algonquian words, they seemed to understand her. If it were not for Sumayl and Farraj, who acted as interpreters, Elizabeth would be lost. Days passed before she allowed herself to feel more at ease. The Tuscarora wives of Sumayl and Farraj treated her as an honored guest. She gave each of them a copper bracelet to express her gratitude. She helped with daily chores. This pleased them greatly.

Time elapsed too slowly as she awaited a decision regarding aid to return to Croatoan. No one seemed to sense her urgency, or if they did, chose to ignore it. It seemed to her, that native peoples did things in their own time, in their way. She was a guest among them, living on their good will, and could not press the issue overmuch. Elizabeth wondered if she would ever see her friends again.

*　　　*　　　*

After the death of Ananias, Eleanor was beside herself with grief for the loss of her husband and the capture of her friend, Elizabeth. In the months that followed, she was anchored only by Emme, little

Virginia and infrequent visits by Manteo to inquire after her well-being. Manteo and the men of their village repaired her burned out cabin before the onset of winter, adding a small extra room.

Manteo, uncertain of the timing or appropriateness of his actions, waited for the end of a long winter, until the final days of the Worm Moon. He hunted and fished. He brought his offerings to the door of the Widow Dare. Eleanor knew what it would mean to accept his gifts. She held on for as long as she could. She recalled telling Elizabeth that she would decide when she had waited long enough. She had to face stark realities. Her father would never return. Her beloved husband was gone. England was a distant place she no longer recognized.

They stood at the threshold of her cabin in the chill of a pre-dawn morning in March. Neither of them spoke, yet their eyes held a silent communication. Heartbreak, loss, understanding, comfort. A tentative hand reached for her, uncertain of her reaction. His fingers slipped through her hair at the back of her neck. He drew her close, his mouth slanting over hers breathless, waiting. She decided. Her lids fluttered closed as she rose to meet him. Her fingers crushed the velvety buckskin of his tunic. His kisses were inquisitive and sweet, then more sensual and demanding. Desires rising, they parted. Both were surprised and amazed at the promise of passions unleashed. For the first time in a long time, her lips pressed into a wistful smile. She took his hand. She took Manteo's gifts into her home and took Manteo to her bed.

They made love with quiet intensity, mindful of the sleeping toddler in the adjacent room. Afterward, they lay together, naked and spent. Manteo held her, whispering solemn vows between soft kisses. He promised they would marry before her God because he knew it was important to her. He promised to care for her and Virginia. He promised to give her more children. When he left with Ompeu to search for Elizabeth and her son, Eleanor treasured his promises like a mooring for her soul as she and the women of Croatoan watched the
men depart.

Chapter Twenty-One

April 1589

I t took longer than expected for Ompeu and those of his party to recover from their wounds and to restore the Croatan town. None of his friends would allow him to go alone. Henry Darby, now restored to health, fired up his forge. Since he was unable to fight, he poured himself into crafting weapons specifically for their long journey.

They searched for weeks. The hastily constructed town where Wutapantam lived months ago was gone. Ompeu surmised they moved inland for the winter and would relocate again before spring planting. They visited several towns, but no one had seen a sun-haired boy, or a small *Tosh shonte* woman with eyes the color of autumn honey. A *werowance* of the Aquascogoc told them of a village where they might find people who also came from across the great sea, located in distant Tuscarora lands east of the Chowan River. Intrigued by this news, the men of Croatoan set out to find this village. It was Ompeu's last hope.

The first sign of trouble came as their canoe left what the English called the Albemarle Sound, heading toward the Chowan River. The air was crisp, but the sun's rays beat down, dancing on the water's surface. As they reached the mouth of the river, shouts from the right bank sounded.

"Why do you come?"

"Strangers are far from home! See how they are armed. They wish to fight!"

"*Tosh shonte!*"

Manteo glanced at his companions. The younger ones, Wutapantam, Thomas Smart, and James Warren, looked wary. Manteo cupped his hands at the sides of his mouth. "We are friends! We search for captives taken from us!"

"Come friends, we will show you what we think of you!"

"You are no friends!" another shouted, followed by a volley of arrows.

The company rowed furiously across the wide expanse of water for the opposite bank. One arrow grazed Ompeu's forearm, another bounced off Bridger's armor, another stuck into the side of the canoe, numerous more splashed into the surrounding water. Towaye and Paukunnawaw shot back. Oars dipped and pushed against the river. No one broke rhythm.

As they reached the opposite bank, they continued rowing until it was deemed safe, the sun heading toward the west. They made camp near the water's edge, exhausted from the adrenaline rush and the exertion to make it this far at a steady pace. They ate around an evening fire in quiet companionship.

"If wish to go home, I go alone," Ompeu said using English words. Today was the first harrowing experience on the journey but would not be the last. This was his mission, and he had no desire to place his friends in further danger.

"I'll not go home yet," Bridger said, as he checked his store of powder. "Widow Cooke is a fine woman, she deserves t' be with her loved ones. And either we find her, or we do not, but I want no regrets."

Wutapantam picked up the few English words he recognized, answering Ompeu in their native language. "We will find your woman." He shrugged. "I had no plans to go elsewhere."

"We are near to Tuscarora lands. If we have no word of Widow Cooke or Onxe in the next village, we will travel home," Manteo said as he filled a pipe with *uppowoc*. He cast some crushed leaves into the flames, chanting a quiet prayer, seeking a blessing from *Kiwasa* and the Christian Heavenly Father, so that their journey would be successful. He offered the pipe to the four directions, then puffed the sacred tobacco, and smudged himself with the purifying smoke, before passing it to Paukunnawaw.

The two English adolescents, Thomas and James, trained with the Croatan since the first hunting trip and were baptized in the bloodshed of war. They, along with Wutapantam, Towaye, and John Bridger accompanied the search party. All shared in the passing of the pipe, receiving the sacramental smoke as brothers. In the morning they set off in search of the next village.

*   *   *

"Why, you have your own apothecary." Elizabeth stood in the center of a dwelling, taking in all that surrounded her. Various dried plants and herbs hung from the domed ceiling, small clay pot containers as well as pouches lined wooden shelves. A combination of earthy scents drifted in the air.

Sumayl followed her gaze, looking around the room. "I am quite proud of it." He moved toward the worktable. "Come. I wish to show you a most versatile plant." He raised a stalk. Its numerous leaves were thin with jagged edges. "Hemp." He pointed out the various parts of the plant as he explained. "The seeds are used to make oils and ointments. They may also be eaten. The leaves are dried and crushed, used to treat inflammation, minor pain, and insomnia. Here the stalk is used to create fibers for textiles. The shirts and clothing you see many of us wear are made from this. Even the root is used for medicinal purposes."

"Utterly fascinating," Elizabeth said as he offered her a stalk to examine. She turned the clipping over in wonderment. "Versatile, indeed. Where did you…?"

Elizabeth was about to ask where he studied the sciences and healing arts, when voices outside interrupted them. Sumayl strode to the door and lifted the flap, peering out. He turned to her. "Wait here, my lady. It appears we have visitors."

Her face broke into a grin. "Please, call me Wapeih." His use of the formal 'my lady' seemed out of place, and unnecessary. She was not of noble birth, and he was not a slave.

His smile was both boyish and roguish. He shrugged. "Some habits are difficult to break, Wapeih," he said, and left the apothecary.

Curious, Elizabeth drifted toward the entrance to peek through a slit in the doorway. The visitors were surrounded by Tuscarora. She caught a glimpse, a flash of metal, no, armor. Who were they? English? Spaniards? She watched as Sumayl and the elderly Tuscarora chief spoke to the newcomers. Movement in the crowd allowed a brief but better view. She froze. Her heart stopped, then started again with a thudding that pounded in her breast. No. It could not be.

Elizabeth lifted the door flap and stepped outside. She approached the crowd, senses reeling. Her body trembled, legs wobbly. "Ompeu," she whispered, then louder. "Ompeu!" Her head felt light, her limbs would not function. She could no longer stand upright.

Heedless of the Tuscarora surrounding them, Ompeu broke away from the group, pushing past the onlookers. He watched her sink to her knees, then fell beside her, enfolding her in his arms. "Wapeih!" He held her as she wept uncontrollably into his tunic. He stroked her hair, noting its shortened length. It once fell past her waist, but now touched over her shoulders. Her belly was swollen with child. His heart wrenched painfully. He could not imagine the horrors she endured in the many months they were apart. There would be time to talk later. For now, she was alive, and in his arms. Nothing else mattered.

"I thought I lost you," she sobbed. "I thought you were dead. They told me you were dead."

"I think same with you," he rasped, overcome with emotion, he could barely speak. "But not so. I am here, Wapeih." For the first time, he noticed the forearm wrapped around his middle. He caressed the pink scars lovingly, amazed that she had done such a thing for him. She thought him dead. She mourned him in the way of his people, cutting her hair, and slashing herself. She grieved for him in the way a woman who loved a man would. She never said the words to him. There was no need. It touched his heart in a way that nothing else did. Ompeu lifted his head, searching among the chattering people who gathered around them. "Where is Onxe?" he asked gently.

Elizabeth sniffled, wiping her eyes. "I know not. He was taken by a warrior called Watape. I have not seen my son since the day of the attack."

Sumayl and the Tuscarora chief approached them. "Come friends, let us find a more suitable place for our guest, Wapeih and her deliverers."

Ompeu helped her to her feet. When she lifted her eyes, she saw John Bridger. It was his worn and beaten armor that glinted in the sun. Manteo, Towaye, Paukunnawaw, Wutapantam and the English boys Thomas and James. Elizabeth, overjoyed at the sight of them, hugged each man in turn, happy and relieved to see each one. If any of them were surprised to see her state of pregnancy, they betrayed nothing. It was enough to find her alive and well after a long journey.

The chief spoke to Sumayl. He translated. "Our venerable chief asks that you consider remaining with us until the birth of Wapeih's child. It will ease her burden when traveling. She will have the help of my wives when her time comes."

Ompeu never saw a man such as this one, tall and dark. He appeared kind and was obviously a companion of the chief. A man of importance. "Tell *werowance* we thank him," he signed as he spoke so the chief would understand. "I talk to Wapeih and to friends," Ompeu indicated the rest of his group. "We will think on it."

"Please let us know of your decision," Sumayl replied. "You are welcome here."

Sumayl led them to an unoccupied section of a longhouse. While the others settled into their spaces, Ompeu sat next to Elizabeth on the sleeping pallet. She slipped her arm through his, sitting closely to maintain physical contact. He had to ask her. "Tell me of the child." He clasped her hand, threading their fingers. It did not matter to him whether the child was his or not. If she would have him, he would be her husband and raise the child as his own.

She leaned into him, pressing a soft kiss to his cheek. "You planted a seed in a storm," she whispered. "The child is yours."

Ompeu's lids closed over, her words affecting him. He turned to face her, touching his forehead to hers. His breath came unevenly. He placed a reverent hand over her distended abdomen, caressing her. He could not speak. He wanted to tell her he was sorry for all she had suffered. He wanted to ask her forgiveness for not protecting her and Onxe. He buried his face at her shoulder.

Elizabeth wrapped her arms around him as he quietly fell apart.

"I not save you, not save Onxe."

She cupped his face between her palms, lifting his head. *"Kurustuwes nir,* mark me well. You were badly wounded. You could have been killed, but you are here, now. We have found each other. We will find Onxe." She covered the hand that rested on her belly. "And now we will have a new babe to love. You did not fail us, Ompeu. All things come to pass for a purpose. We shall endure."

His lips met hers in a kiss full of love and hope.

"Kuwrumáras," she murmured between kisses. His lips traveled to her throat. She had to tell him. For all the days and nights she was unable to say the words, and wished she could. *"Kurwumáras, Kurwumáras.* I love you."

They sat around the fire after the evening meal. Elizabeth expressed her deep gratitude for the search they undertook on her behalf. They were all far from home. She told an abridged version of events that transpired since her abduction. The men offered congratulations on the impending birth to her and Ompeu. Her heart sank at the news of Ananias Dare's death during the attack. Poor Eleanor. She wished she could have been at her friend's side to offer comfort. The conversation meandered. Elizabeth asked after Emme, Poussu, and Mamankanois, relieved to hear that all were well, and that their village thrived despite the destruction.

"Tell the rest. Ye left somethin'," Bridger nudged Manteo good-naturedly.

Manteo pressed his lips together. "It is not... appropriate." He appeared flushed and embarrassed. Not usual for him.

"Do I detect bashfulness?" Elizabeth asked. "Do tell, Manteo," she urged. The friends joined in, encouraging him to speak of his newfound love.

Manteo relented. "When we return to Croatoan, the Widow Dare and I will wed."

The men cheered in approval. Elizabeth's jaw dropped open in surprise. "Oh my! That is unexpected and wonderful news." Eleanor had made her decision then, relinquishing the hope that her father would arrive. Abandoning England. "I wish you both, every happiness."

"She will forever have love for her husband that was. I will honor him. He was a friend to me." After a pause, Manteo changed the subject. "We must decide the next path to take. Do you wish to stay here until the child is born, or do we continue our search for Onxe on the morrow? There is not always peace between us and the Tuscarora. Some may not be happy because we are here."

"We have no idea where Onxe might be." The words caught in her throat.

"If Watape have him, I know," Ompeu interjected. He posed the translated question to Wutapantam who agreed.

"Watape?" Manteo mused.

"Aye. I learned the name of his captor from Nussacun's wife, Sacquenuckot," Elizabeth answered.

"This is good," Manteo thought aloud. "We can search for him on our way to Croatoan."

"If it is all the same to you, gentlemen, I would prefer to leave straightaway. I am anxious to find my son, and to return home, as I am certain you all are. Unless you would prefer to rest for a day or so, I am amenable."

"There is one problem," Manteo added. "We will have to go into Secotaóc. It will be dangerous."

Wutapantam asked for a translation. He thought he knew where Watape might hide. "I will enter the town."

They left two days later. Elizabeth gifted the string of pearls to the Tuscarora chief. She thanked Sumayl, Farraj and their wives for their hospitality. Sumayl's wives offered Elizabeth a baby sling, to carry the newborn.

Secotaóc was on the mainland, south and west of Croatoan. They would pass their home island on route. Ompeu sought to convince Elizabeth to return home while the men traveled on. She refused. Her stubbornness would slow their travel, but thankfully, none of the men complained. They traveled mainly by water, but due to Elizabeth's condition, they camped more frequently. It would take them twice as long to reach their destination.

The days grew longer and warmer, the evenings still brisk. New sprouts and tiny spring-green leaves appeared on the trees. Early flowers budded, waiting to awaken. She and Ompeu curled up together at night keeping some distance from the others for privacy. Amid the chirring of crickets and rustlings of nocturnal creatures, he held her, kissed her, caressed her. He did not make overt sexual advances. Elizabeth asked him why he went no further, since he was clearly aroused. She slid her palm over his body teasingly, reaching the male part of him.

He swallowed harshly as she caressed him. "Is not our way to join with woman when with child," he explained.

It never stopped Cooke from taking his husbandly rights. She wondered if the incident with Nussacun, and his apparent shame afterward had anything to do with this belief. She had not told Ompeu of that night.

"May hurt child or woman," his voice was strained, answering her unspoken question as to why this was so. She shifted to have better access to him, continuing her delicious strokes. Her belly was pressed against his side. He felt the kick and roll of the life inside her. "My child is strong," he smiled as his hand moved over her abdomen. "*Winganous.*"

She kissed him. "I love you," she whispered.

"I love you and this one," he caressed her middle. "We find Onxe. Take him home. We can be fam-ily. Everyone."

"*Kupi*," she whispered. "If you cannot join with a woman when she is with child, surely there are many ways to give pleasure to one you love?" she asked, flipping the covering over her head, and moving down his body before he could respond to her question.

It required every ounce of strength he possessed to remain silent, so as not to wake the camp, as she took him into the silken warmth of her mouth.

The following morning, they were near their destination. Elizabeth experienced excruciating pain that moved from her abdomen and spread like fiery tentacles throughout her body. Increased pressure surged through her lower back. Her water broke. They would have to stop and bank the canoe. She knew the delay was her fault for insisting on traveling. She knew it was selfish, but she had to see her son again. Had to hold him. She needed to be there when they found him, or to know whether he lived or died.

It was contrary for him to help her. Ompeu ran an agitated hand through his hair, his mind in turmoil. Birthing was a mystery for the realm of women. Woman's life-nurturing blood was powerful, and men should not be in its presence. To do so could weaken them or bring untold misfortunes. But there were no women here. Ompeu spoke to Manteo and Bridger who knew more about the ways of the *Tosh shonte*. Bridger assured him that no harm would come to him. Manteo suggested that a purification ceremony after the birthing, would hopefully appease the spirits. Both men offered to help.

Elizabeth was in so much pain, she no longer cared if they were present, or what they saw. She was about to give birth in the middle of the woods, in enemy lands, with a group of men. At this point, all propriety could surely be abandoned. She would be embarrassed afterward, or not, for another wave of contractions flooded her.

"Gentlemen, I pray you of your courtesy, please discuss this later," she groaned, as she paced restlessly between two trees, hand over her belly. "We will make offerings to *Kiwasa*. Perhaps the spirits will forgive us this one instance. I have done this before. I know what to expect."

"Tell us what to do, how t' help," Bridger urged gently.

She panted, her voice strained. "Build up the fire. Set some water to heat. We will need to wash the babe." She stopped momentarily in between steps to catch her breath while the men watched, helplessly alarmed. "Find some cloth or blankets for cleaning and swaddling the infant quickly. I will have need of clean water and cloths for myself." She paused, breathing through another contraction. She grunted. "A clean knife to cut the umbilical cord, and something for me to bite down on, a stick, anything. If there are enemies about, I will need to remain as silent as I am able."

All the men reacted, near frantic to do her bidding. Ompeu removed his shirt, cutting it into pieces with his knife. Manteo and Paukunnawaw ran to fetch water and search the canoe for any clay pots and blankets. Bridger gathered more wood. The rest of the company consisted of adolescents, who stood frozen, shocked and wide-eyed.

"Boys, best if ye stepped away. Keep a lookout, guard the camp," Bridger suggested. The three teens needed no further prompting and scattered.

Elizabeth hiked up her doeskin dress and sank to her knees, breathing through another contraction. Ompeu was approaching panic. Elizabeth would have laughed at his facial expression, for the calm unreadable mask he usually wore was nowhere in sight.

Hours passed. She could not find a comfortable position. After what seemed an eternity, Elizabeth took a few uneven steps to the nearest tree, gripping the knotty, rough bark with clenched fingers. The pressure of the infant waiting to be born became too great. It was time.

She motioned for Ompeu to get behind her. "You will have to reach for the babe," she breathed, moving herself into the least painful posture, she chose a squatting position. She clung to the tree trunk, bracing herself. Manteo covered her with a blanket for propriety, crouching beside her. Bridger placed a stick in her mouth, offering his hand for her to punish. Paukunnawaw, his back turned, kept watch over them.

Elizabeth made almost no sound, but several grunts and squeaks. Sweat beaded her brow, eyes watered in pain. She pushed several times, the final one causing a cry to erupt from her throat until the infant slid into Ompeu's waiting hands. A girl. A screaming, crying baby girl. Joy such as this did not exist for him until now. It was over, all were relieved, light laughter sounded, and smiles lit every face.

"Boy or girl?" Elizabeth rasped, resting her forehead against the rough bark, she collapsed against the tree, gasping for air.

"*Nunutánuhs.*" She heard Ompeu's voice, full of awe and wonder. She listened as he spoke to the newborn in soothing Algonquian words, as the babe wailed.

Elizabeth closed her eyes, unable to stop the urge to release a laughing sigh of joy. *My daughter.* Though exhausted, she instructed them to clean the baby's mouth and nose immediately. She pushed to expel the afterbirth. Ompeu washed the blood from the infant, cut the umbilical cord, and wrapped her securely while Elizabeth washed and packed herself with pieces of what was once Ompeu's tunic. They moved mother and child closer to the fire, using rolled up blankets of skins and fur to prop Elizabeth up into a sitting position. She coaxed her daughter to nurse. The babe had quieted but was uninterested. She was perfect. Heart-shaped face, black hair, tiny fingers and toes.

Ompeu sat beside his woman. He nuzzled her cheek, and whispered his love, his arm around her shoulders. "Women have much power. Men not strong to do this. Give life. It is sacred *mantóac*."

It was late, sunlight fading into dusk. A waxing moon hung in the sky, a sliver. While parents admired the newest family member, Manteo looked to the heavens, offering a silent prayer of thanks. "It is the Flower Moon," he said.

"Good name," Bridger added.

"Flower Moon," Elizabeth repeated thoughtfully. She looked at her daughter who rooted around at her mother's breast, understanding there was nourishment and comfort there. The infant latched on. "Flower Moon. 'Tis favorable you were not born in the Worm Moon, else we should think of a different name." Her gaze passed over the men who helped her. "I should like to call her Rose Flower Moon." She looked down again, speaking softly to her newborn. "Though Rose and Flower are a bit redundant, are they not? Aye. Let us settle with Rose Moon, or simply, Rose." She turned to Ompeu. "Rose. What say you?"

Ompeu smiled, still floating above the earth. "It will be as you wish."

"You have all acquitted yourselves quite admirably. I thank you, gentlemen. Little Rose could not ask for better godfathers." Her eyes fell on the man she loved. "Or a better father."

Three young men came ambling back to camp. Wutapantam spoke at length.

Manteo translated. "He has found the village of Secotaóc and scouted the area. If you are well enough, we can leave by mid-day on the morrow.

Chapter Twenty-Two

May 1589

S he washed soiled items in the nearby stream, grateful for the infant sling the wives of Sumayl had given her. Thankfully, they showed her how to use it to wrap her newborn securely. Little Rose slept next to the warmth and comfort of her mother's body. Elizabeth scrubbed vigorously, knowing it would be impossible to remove all the blood. She hoped the washed items would be dried in the sun by mid-day. She would need extra wrappings for changing and cleaning her child. Elizabeth's body ached, and she would bleed for a while, but she vowed there would be no more delays. They had all been away from home for too long.

"I pray that soon, we shall see your brother," she spoke to the infant at her back.

Ompeu and Manteo built a separate fire, and conducted a purification ritual, making offerings of food and burning *uppowoc* to appease *Kiwasa* and the spirits. They bathed in the stream, they prayed and asked for guidance.

At mid-day, the group trekked toward Secotaóc. Elizabeth wrapped her daughter in the sling, close to her breast. Rose nursed and slept, and apart from newborn squeaks and grunts, she was quiet. As they grew closer to the town, passing newly planted fields, the party knew their movements were tracked. Elizabeth became apprehensive, but Ompeu stepped closer. "Be brave," he said, before trotting toward the front of the line.

Wutapantam went ahead. These were his people. He was the son of a *werowance*. But as they reached the entrance of the village, they were surrounded by armed Secotan warriors. Elizabeth wrapped her arms around baby Rose, gasping and falling back a step, as the point of a spear entered her vision, directly in her face. Ompeu advanced in front of her, shepherding her behind him. He spoke harshly to the Secotan in their Algonquian dialect. "Is it your way to make targets of women and children? Or would you prefer to die honorably at the hands of another warrior?"

The Secotan eyed Ompeu, assessing him. Ompeu's caustic stare did not waver. He gave the warrior a piece of himself, daring him to say or do anything untoward. Elizabeth held her breath as she watched the display of barely contained male posturing. The moment of heightened tension was relieved when the Secotan withdrew at the sound of someone speaking. It was Manteo, asking to see the *werowance*. They were not here to provoke trouble, he assured them. They had a matter of utmost importance to discuss. The Secotan scouts eyed the *Tosh shonte* among the group with suspicion and disdain but led them to the central area of the town.

Elizabeth gaped in awe at the size and scope of Secotaóc. Not even the Tuscarora village loomed this large and impressive. Many smaller dwellings were spread around the anterior of the village, while several sizeable longhouses comprised the interior, all of which focused on the central circle. The Croatan village where she lived was a spit of a town in comparison.

Even the *werowance* was impressive. He strode toward the visitors surrounded by his advisors. Elizabeth observed a conjuror and a priest by their unusual dress. The *werowance* stood tall, an imposing figure. He wore a cape of feathers. A copper disk hung from his neck, copper bracelets adorned his wrists, and pearl earrings dangled from his ears. He wore a modest headdress, trimmed with several turkey feathers. He motioned to Wutapantam. "Nephew. Why do you bring these Croatan and *Wutahshuntar* among our people?"

"Uncle. These people are friends. Your brother, my father, sent me to live with them to learn of the ways of the *Wutahshuntar*. They have treated me kindly and well. We have searched and traveled a great distance to seek out the sun-haired child of this woman, Wapeih." He gestured toward Elizabeth. "He was taken from her in the fight at Croatoan."

"This boy wounded one of our men. Watape captured him. It is Watape you seek. It is for him to decide the boy's fate." He pinned Wutapantam with a look. "I have heard that my nephew struck against his own, that he killed a Secotan. I wonder if my nephew has forgotten that he is Secotan."

"I have not forgotten, uncle. I acted to defend my host, as he would have done for me." Wutapantam glanced back, acknowledging Ompeu. "I was honor bound to do so."

This reasoning seemed to appease the *werowance*. "Bring forth Watape and the boy." He gestured vaguely to one of the longhouses. A runner went to fetch them.

Elizabeth could not contain herself when she saw her son. He looked well and healthy. Had he grown since she saw him last? His blond hair grew past his shoulders, he was dressed in skins, his face a mask of confusion as Watape led the boy toward the crowd.

He caught sight of his mother and Ompeu but was held back from running to them. "*Nek!* Ompeu!"

"Onxe!" she called out.

Ompeu held her arm, preventing her from racing toward her son. "Be brave," he whispered once again. No one knew how this would unfold. Ompeu's senses were heightened, aware of every movement and sound around him. He glanced at his companions who also seemed on edge.

Watape jostled the *Tosh shonte* boy, who attempted to escape his grasp. "What is this?" he demanded when he reached the circle.

"Are you well?" Elizabeth asked her son, anxiously. How she longed to reach for him!

"Yes, I wish to go home!" he shouted before Watape yanked him backward.

Ompeu gave her arm a gentle squeeze. When she looked at him, he indicated with a subtle shake of his head that she was not to speak. Not yet.

"This woman has come to retrieve her son," the *werowance* indicated Elizabeth.

Watape smirked. "What is she willing to give in return?"

"Perhaps she will trade," a distant voice bellowed. "Perhaps she will give one child for another." All heads turned toward the sound. Nussacun approached them.

Ompeu's blood ran hot.

Nussacun gestured to the infant wrapped to Elizabeth's body. "What say you, woman?"

"*Matta!*" Ompeu shouted. "The infant is my daughter, newly born. You cannot take her from her mother."

Onxe understood most every word. His eyes widened at the statement, but he said nothing, seeming to notice the bundle wrapped to his mother's body for the first time.

Nussacun shrugged. "One life for another is hardly unreasonable. Watape has grown fond of the boy. He will be a great Secotan warrior. You have trained him well, Ompeu," he taunted, attempting to incite Ompeu's ire.

Elizabeth's eyes darted from Ompeu to Nussacun. She understood most of their words. She would not give up either of her children. They would have to kill her first.

"Let Watape speak for himself. Or does he allow Nussacun to speak for him?" Ompeu challenged. He faced Watape. "Does Watape not have his voice?"

"I will not give the boy without recompense," Watape said flatly.

"You stole him from his family!"

"He tried to kill one of us!"

"Let us settle this matter," the *werowance* intervened. The command silenced everyone. They would argue into the night if this continued. He addressed Ompeu and Elizabeth. "What have you to offer Watape for the boy?"

Elizabeth reached inside the pouch slung across her body, fumbling about, her fingers trembling. She pulled out the remaining copper bracelets and earrings Sacquenuckot had given her months ago. She held them out.

Watape laughed at her offering.

Nussacun eyed the trinkets. "You would give him stolen goods?" he accused. "Those belong to my wife."

"She give them to me," Elizabeth answered in not-so-perfect Algonquian. "To help go away from you!"

Nussacun had the decency to look ashamed for a fleeting moment. It explained why the *Tosh shonte* woman was here and not where he left her. Thoughts of Sacquenuckot filled his head. He missed her. He missed his children. He would return to his family. He would convince his wife to take him into her home once again.

Ompeu slipped a knife from his belt, newly forged by Henry Darby. The metal blade was sharp, the handle made of carved, smooth wood. It was a fine weapon, perfectly balanced. He held it out to Watape.

Watape took it, turning it over in his palm, then grasping the handle, moving it in varying slicing and stabbing motions, testing the weight and feel of it. He handed the blade back to Ompeu. "It is a fine knife, but it will not do. It is not enough for the boy. What else have you?"

"I have something that may please Watape." Manteo stepped forward. "It was given to me by Master Ralegh.

It is a prized possession. Very valuable." Manteo removed the matchlock hand-held pistol from his belt and cradled it in his palms. It was indeed a beautifully crafted weapon.

"No, Manteo. I cannot allow you to do this," Elizabeth pleaded, moving to his side. "There must be another way." She knew how much the musket meant to him. It was a symbol of the trust the English placed in him. A symbol of his standing among both peoples. A symbol of English *mantóac*.

He looked at her, his eyes warm and compassionate. "It is only metal and wood. Henry Darby can fashion a new one from old pieces." He passed the musket to Watape.

Watape fingered the weapon curiously. He looked at Manteo, thrusting the musket back at him. "Show me how to use it."

Manteo demonstrated, filling the firing pan with gunpowder, then more down the barrel of the musket. He tamped the ball and small wad of cloth with the scouring stick, blew on the match cord and attached it to the firing mechanism. He motioned for everyone to step aside. The crowd parted allowing Manteo to take aim at a nearby tree trunk. He raised his arm and fired. Gasps and sounds of awe emanated from the crowd as bits of wood flew away, leaving a deep gash in the tree.

Watape shoved Onxe toward his mother and Ompeu. The boy clung to them. "I accept," Watape pronounced.

His eyes lit with triumph as Manteo handed him the musket. "It is done," he said to the *werowance*.

"All is settled. Watape is satisfied. Go in peace," the *werowance* announced. "Let the visitors depart."

Manteo thanked the chief as well as by-standers in a most gracious manner. He turned to his friends. "Let us go. Make haste," he urged quietly, using English words. "Go, go." He rushed the Croatan party, along with Onxe and Wutapantam out of the village at a brisk pace. Manteo held up the rear, glancing backward from time to time.

Before they boarded the canoe, Elizabeth turned to her son. "I have missed you with all my heart," she caressed his cheek, brushing back blond locks. They held each other as she kissed his brow. "I will explain about the babe once we are home. This is your sister, Rose. She is my and Ompeu's daughter."

Onxe looked from her to Ompeu, bewilderment clouding his features.

"I be father to you, Onxe. If you wish."

Onxe held back tears. "I have missed you both. I would like that, Ompeu." The boy hugged Ompeu. "*Nohsh.*" *My father.*

"Come, come," Manteo rushed them, saying there would be time for explanations and reunions later. They needed to move.

It was not until they were gliding through the waters toward Croatoan, far from Secotaóc, that Manteo relaxed. A slow smile creased his face, and a low chuckle escaped his throat.

"What is amusing to you, my friend?" Ompeu asked in their native tongue. He dipped his oar into the still waters.

Manteo's laughter grew. He stopped rowing. The entire company watched as he doubled over, unable to keep from laughing, he could not speak. The canoe wobbled.

Understanding dawned as Bridger too, snorted and howled. "Very clever, Manteo," he blurted between guffaws.

"What is it? Please share," Elizabeth queried. Little Rose awoke, hungry. Her tiny fingers gripped Onxe's thumb as she nursed. The boy stared at his baby sister, his eyes lit with wonder.

"Manteo gave them his musket," Bridger chuckled. "But no powder and shot. The weapon is useless!" he burst into laughter once more. "Perhaps Watape can hang it 'round his neck as decoration!"

Elizabeth smiled. "What happens when he discovers the musket will not function?"

Manteo's laughter subsided. He shrugged, his smile still in place. "He did not trade for powder, only for the musket. If he wishes, he can make another trade for it."

Elizabeth needed reassurance. "And if he thinks you cheated him? Will he enact revenge?"

"He accepted. He will be too ashamed. He received no more than he deserved," Manteo said as he pushed his oar against the water.

"Thank you, Manteo."

"It is a small thing. Better to have one's family whole again."

Elizabeth glanced down at the infant at her breast, lifted her eyes to smile at her son, then turned her head to watch Ompeu behind her as he rowed. Yes. Her family was whole again.

Chapter Twenty-Three

Croatans left their dwellings at the call signifying the return of the search party. Eleanor stepped out of her cabin with Virginia in tow. Emme stared into the distance waiting to catch sight of them. Mamankanois, now visibly with child, held her breath. They had been gone two months.

Smiling friends and an exuberant Poussu converged upon them. Shouts and cheers filled the air. Elizabeth was deeply moved and overwhelmed at the outpouring of love. Emme, Eleanor, and Mamankanois hugged her and Onxe, crying tears of joy. They were shocked to see their friend carrying a newborn wrapped against her body. Poussu was not. Elizabeth promised to explain all to them as they were swept up in the moving crowd. The camp dogs barked and whined, tails wagging furiously. Ajax was among them, following Elizabeth wherever she went, curious about the tiny, squeaking human she carried.

Emme ran to Towaye, leaping into his arms. Mamankanois, no less excited to see her husband, waited patiently, until Bridger came to her and swept her up. He placed a hand on her abdomen and spoke lovingly to his unborn child. Mamankanois laughed as she led him into her *yeehaukan*.

Eleanor's eyes scanned the crowd, searching for him, but Manteo had already spotted her. He watched her from a short distance away, until their eyes met. She looked nervous and unsure, as though she wondered if he still felt the same. Did he still want her? Had his promises dissipated into thin air? She watched him drop the pack he carried right where he stood. Manteo strode toward her like the hunter he was. The sensuous yet playful, hungry look in his eyes erasing all her doubt. He took her breath away, enfolding her in the circle of his arms. His lips captured hers, kissing her in the village center for all to see. She did not care.

That night they celebrated with a feast. Ompeu held his daughter as Elizabeth once again told a shortened version of her story to her friends. Poussu commandeered baby Rose away from Ompeu to fawn over her new grandchild. Henry was at her side. He peered over Poussu's shoulder. Smiling sadly, he reached out to touch the baby's head, and stroke her fine, dark hair. "I hear you've named the little one Rose."

Henry looked as though he had aged since Rose's death and Elizabeth's capture. She knew that he and Rose shared a good marriage. Her heart went out to him. "I did. She was a special woman, someone I loved."

"That she was, and much loved, indeed. I am honored, Elizabeth. Rose would be as well."

"Thank you, Henry. That means a great deal to me."

"Blessings to you both," he said, with a look that encompassed Elizabeth and Ompeu.

Ompeu nudged her gently. They shared a knowing glance that reminded her. "Henry. May I ask a favor of you?"

"Anything."

She explained how Manteo relinquished his prized musket in order to obtain her son's freedom. She offered the remaining copper bracelets and earrings as payment for his work. Henry proposed fashioning a new musket free of charge, but Elizabeth insisted he take the items. It was settled. Manteo would have a new musket.

Later that night Elizabeth, Onxe, baby Rose, and Ompeu went to his *yeehaukan*. Elizabeth opened the door flap. She had forgotten someone. "Come Ajax, good boy." Once inside, the wolfdog was completely taken with sniffing little Rose. He curled up beside Elizabeth who petted the thick fur to calm him.

The family talked for hours. Onxe explained why he had run out from the protection of the tall reeds the day of the attack. He told them of his experience living among the Secotan. "At first, it was bad. Some people hated me because I shot one of the men with an arrow. But Watape said I was brave. Some people agreed with him. Watape was not ever cruel to me, but he could be quite stern. He did not have much patience. I was afraid because the man I shot was very angry. I thought he would hurt me, but he did not. I think Watape must have told him not to."

"I am grateful that you were not harmed," Elizabeth said.

"Not very much. At first, some boys would try to fight me, saying I was not as brave as all that. I am very happy to be home."

"This be home now." Ompeu said. "If you wish it." He turned to Elizabeth. "And mother, if she wish it." His dark eyes searched hers, even as Onxe spoke.

"I do. What do you say, *nek*? Does that mean you will marry Ompeu?"

"We marry?" he asked. A disarming grin curved his lips, dark eyes lit with challenge and invitation.

"We marry." she answered, holding his gaze. Challenge accepted. How could she not? She loved him. She mourned him when she thought him dead. He traveled for months with friends searching for her. He awakened her passion, showing her what ecstasy could be between a man and a woman. He was the father of her child. He had opened her heart, and in doing so, opened a new world to her. She had been a good wife to a man she did not choose, a man she did not love, a man who did not deserve her. Ompeu had not asked her for her love, he asked her to choose. Her eyes locked with his, full of love. "I will be your wife."

*   *   *

August 1590

Rough waters and fierce northeasterly winds kept Governor White and his companions from safe landings at the outer banks. Captain Spicer's boat overturned. Those who attempted to wade for shore were swept up by the sea. Spicer along with seven of his eleven men were drowned. The weight of this catastrophe caused many of the surviving crew to refuse to continue the search for the Roanoke colonists. Spicer's boat was recovered, and the men were persuaded to make their way into Roanoke Sound. Darkness fell. The crew spent the night on the boats. They could see a great fire burning in the distance, and assuming the planters were there, the men sang songs and sounded a trumpet.

It had been three years. White was unable to return to his planters. The war with Spain required available ships and men, delaying his return to Virginia. There were none to spare for a sea voyage to Roanoke, and during warfare the colony was not a priority to the crown.

In the morning, White and the crew set their feet on the island. To the north of the fort, he discovered a tree with the letters CRO carved into it. He found the settlement enclosed in wood palisades. On one of these the bark was removed and the words CROATOAN engraved. There was no signal of distress. The settlement was abandoned and had been for some time evidenced by overgrowth of vegetation, and disuse. The houses were taken down and stripped of anything usable.

White found buried chests dug up and looted, the valuables and papers within were damaged by wind and rain. His stored armor was eaten through with rust. The company weathered another intense, stormy night, and decided to head for Croatoan in the morning. This plan was thwarted by continued bad weather, a lost anchor, and lack of fresh water. They proposed to travel to the Caribbean for drinkable water, then return.

The winds did not cooperate. The ship sailed across the Atlantic to the Azores. By this time, the captain and crew became more interested in privateering than in any search for Roanoke colonists. White, at the mercy of the ship's captain was disappointed, yet his stresses were eased. After the loss of men, anchors, and fresh water barrels, all were relieved to return home. White took comfort in the knowledge that the colonists were among friends, Manteo's people, the Croatan.

There were rumors of ships spotted, navigating through an inlet at the northern end of Croatoan, but none stopped at Croatoan shores. A week after Governor White left for the Azores, the Croatan celebrated the Green Corn Ceremony. Villages on the island once again came together to share in a time of renewal and rebirth. The past year was relatively peaceful. The year brought more rainfall to quench the growing crops. There were no further attacks, and no sign or rumors regarding the whereabouts of Nussacun or Wanchese. Watape never appeared to trade for gunpowder, as Manteo predicted.

The communal bonfire burned brightly as people gathered, placing or tossing old items into the flames, watching them burn. Henry Darby bowed his head, a silent prayer on his lips as his wife's old clothing shriveled, incinerated by the heat. Eleanor, wearing a loose-fitting doeskin dress, with Manteo and three-year-old Virginia at her side, each tossed old items. Elizabeth recognized a few pieces that once belonged to Ananias. Eleanor's face was somber, yet peaceful. She smiled up at Manteo. He placed a comforting arm around her shoulders. Her head fell against him as they watched the blaze. Manteo kept every promise he made to Eleanor to the last, for she carried his child, now three months into her pregnancy.

Emme carried her infant son, Hunter, wrapped against her body. She stood back as Towaye threw two old sleeping mats into the fire. "Say fare thee well, mats. Ye served us well, but now we shall have new ones," she spoke to her child, old enough to sit upright on her hip and peer curiously up at his mother and smile a dimpled, toothless grin. Towaye kissed his wife, then both watched as the flames made quick work of their purged goods.

John Bridger carried his one-year-old son, Adam, on his shoulders, Mamankanois at his side. They strolled a safe distance away from the bonfire, stopping to speak with Manteo and Eleanor. Virginia stretched her little arms to Manteo, wanting to be lifted too. He obliged her, picking her up and setting her on his shoulders. She could not contain her joy.

A group of boys and teens sat around in a circle, playing a game of tossing marked stones. Fifteen-month-old Rose was scooped up by her father before she could toddle too closely to the bonfire. Ompeu held her upside down playfully, then raised her up over his head. She giggled with uncontrollable delight, a jubilant shriek bursting from her lips. Elizabeth marveled at the two of them. Rose was the perfect combination of her parents. Dark hair with a touch of curl, caramel complexion, brown doe-eyes. Ompeu handed his chortling bundle over to her mother. "She is like you," he laughed, shaking his head. "A cur-ious one."

"An admirable quality, yes Rose?"

"She will turn me old man."

Poussu and Henry came around with wooden cups filled with a white frothy drink. Poussu offered one to Elizabeth. Rose reached for it. Elizabeth swiveled her upper body away, keeping her daughter from grasping the cup. "If that is what I believe it to be, I must excuse myself."

"You not like white drink?" Ompeu asked. His mouth twitched at one end into a playful grin.

A smile quirked her lips, cheeks coloring at the memory. "*Matta*, nay, no, and absolutely not, never ever again."

A signal call sounded the arrival of new guests. Manteo set Virginia on her feet. Eleanor distracted her, handing her a gourd rattle, and leading her away. Ompeu turned, eyes narrowing. Nussacun and a small entourage were led into the village.

"What brings him?" It was Manteo's voice next to Ompeu.

"Sacquenuckot!" Elizabeth gasped in surprise, she made for the visitors with Rose in her arms before Ompeu could stop her. The women embraced. "My heart glad see you," Elizabeth fumbled with the Algonquian words. She looked at the two children she helped care for, not long ago. They had grown so much. "Mayis, Apegwus. *Wingapo*," she smiled, uncertain they knew her. Mayis seemed to remember and clutched Elizabeth's hand in greeting, a shy smile lifted the corners of the girl's mouth. As for Nussacun, she avoided him completely.

"May I see her?" Sacquenuckot reached for little Rose. "Ah, she is beautiful." She held the toddler, while Rose stared at the woman, her face unsure, but not upset. "My husband tells me your man is alive and well. I am happy."

"He is, and I am happy also." Elizabeth glanced at her husband, his expression guarded, distrust filling his eyes with reserve at Nussacun's approach.

While the women chatted, Nussacun stepped cautiously toward Ompeu and Manteo. He lifted his shoulders, opening his palms in a gesture of supplication. A small crowd gathered, Onxe and Wutapantam stopped their dice game to watch. Nussacun's face was solemn. "As is custom during the Green Corn Ceremony, I come to make amends. To ask forgiveness," he said with a slight bow of his head. "My wife's constant voice in my ears persuaded me. I heard the wisdom of her words. My wife bade us come to seek you out. She has great fondness for Wapeih. It was she who helped her escape our village. She told me of Wapeih's kindness toward our children. And while I still question the wisdom of sheltering the *Wutahshuntar*, and have not much trust in them, I wish to assure you that I will no longer seek vengeance against those who dwell among you, or the Croatan." Nussacun gestured to the remaining members of his group. "These men from our village who joined in the attack also wish to make amends."

Ohawas, Nemat and Tindge unburdened their packs, loaded with furs, trinkets, meat and assorted edibles. Ohawas's gaze followed as Elizabeth retrieved her daughter from Sacquenuckot and drifted to stand beside her husband. This did not go unnoticed by Ompeu. When their eyes met, Ompeu's hard, unflinching stare caused Ohawas to look away.

Nussacun presented the gifts. "Give these to your *werowansa* so that she may distribute them among the Croatan as she wishes."

"If your words be true, then you are welcome among us. Bring your wife and children, and your warriors. Come. Rest after your journey," Manteo said. "Join us in ceremony."

"One thing you must know," Nussacun continued. "Wanchese has traveled to the north, to Tsenacommacah. He seeks the ear of the powerful *werowance*, Wahunsenacawh, leader of the Powhatan."

Manteo's black brows knit. "For what purpose?"

"I believe he wishes to warn the great *werowance* of the presence of the *Tosh shonte* that left for the north. But what action he may take, is known only to himself."

This was unsettling news. The Powhatan Confederacy consisted of many tribes who provided military support and paid tributes to Wahunsenacawh. His power and influence grew with every passing year.

If Wanchese spoke against them, Manteo wondered what might become of the seventy or so English settlers who moved into the Chesapeake Bay area.

"*Kenah*, Nussacun. We shall keep our eyes and ears open. For now, let us celebrate."

Through the entire exchange, Ompeu remained silently skeptical, watching for any sign of treachery on Nussacun's part. He brought his wife and children. It would be foolish of him to attempt any action against the Croatan. As for the warrior unable to conceal the interest in his wife, Ompeu was unconcerned. Elizabeth was apparently oblivious to the man's attraction.

Nussacun and his group stayed for the remainder of the Green Corn Ceremony. They feasted and participated in the ceremonial dances with the Croatan. At their departure, Nussacun spoke to Ompeu. "I hope that we can set aside what is past. You and I were once allied in a common cause to protect our people from the *Wutahshuntar*."

"I will continue to protect our people from anyone, *Wutahshuntar* or otherwise. I hope you will do the same," Ompeu answered. The men parted in agreement, renewed and at peace for the coming year.

That night after Onxe and Rose fell asleep, Ompeu made love to his wife. She wanted another child. Ompeu was more than happy to oblige her wishes. As they lay entwined together, heartbeats settling in the ebb of afterglow, Elizabeth pressed a kiss to the pulse at his neck.

"All is well with Nussacun?"

"For now."

"I know we have been renewed by the Green Corn Ceremony, but there is a part of me that does not trust Nussacun. Do you expect trouble?"

"Not him. Wanchese, yes."

"What are your thoughts?"

"If Wanchese go to Wahunsenacawh, may be trouble."

"When we first arrived here, we were told of a king who could command a great army of many men. Would he be the same?"

"*Kupi.* Same." Ompeu's hand moved over her curves from breast to hip. He pressed warm lips to her forehead. "If trouble, we will go from here, cross to the mainland. Fight, run, hide. We are part of Ossomocomuck." Ompeu was uncertain how far the Powhatan reach would expand. Perhaps there was no cause for concern, though he could not help but form a vague plan of defense in his mind. There was no way of knowing what information Wanchese would give to the Powhatan *werowance*, or how he might be swayed to act.

Her lids felt heavy and she let them slide closed, snuggling against the man she loved whole-heartedly. "And Ossomocomuck is part of us," she whispered. "We shall endure."

The high-pitched hum sounded in her ears. The vibrations filled the air, radiating through her body. He reached for her. Together they flew where time and space did not exist, and souls spoke to one another without words.

ABOUT THE AUTHOR

Jen Caruso works in the field of education. She's a mom to two children, a horse, and dogs. She has written numerous published and unpublished short works. This is her first full-length novel.
Authors Note: The usage of terms such as "Indians", "savages", etc. are spoken or thought by characters representative of the era. Narrative sections of the book refrain from colonizer language, with more appropriate terms such as "natives", "aboriginal", "indigenous" or simply, "the People".
I'd love to hear your opinions. Honest reviews help other readers find books for their needs and interests. Thank you!

Algonquian Language Family

From Thomas Hariot's "A Briefe and True Report of the New Found Land of Virginia"

http://docsouth.unc.edu/nc/hariot/hariot.html

http://www.coastalcarolinaindians.com/coastal-algonquian-language-sampler/

Ahone – a benevolent god; giver of all good things. The Creator, who did not meddle in human affairs and therefore did not require offerings or worship.

Croatan – Native American group living in the coastal areas of what is now North Carolina, present-day Hatteras Island.

Croatoan is the English spelling of kurawoten pronounced (kuh-ra-woe-tain), which means 'talking or council town.'

Ka ka torwawirocs yowo? - What is this?/ How is this called?

Kiwasa – a god of mischief who must be appeased by rituals and offerings in order to avoid losses and other misfortunes.

kantokan - dance

kupi – yes

Kuwumáras [kuh-wuh-MAW-dahs] – I love you

Kurustuwes nir – Listen to me

macocqwer – pompions, melons, squashes

mantóac – force or power that exists in all things. It can impact human life for good or bad and can be harnessed or possessed with proper ritual.

matta – no

Manteo – to snatch, possible derivative of **mantóac** as

Manteo was one who lived "between worlds"

mincon - food

Nussacun – to bite

Mamankanois – Butterfly

nek - [neck] 'my mother'

nipatas - [NEE-pah-tahs] Stand up

nitáp - friend

nohsh - [noesh] my father ([oe] as in 'doe')

nunohum [nuh-NO-hum] 'my grandmother'

nunutánuhs – my daughter

nuqisus [nuh-KWEE-suhs] 'my son'

okindgier - beans

Ompeu – He is free, unbound (taken from northern Algonquian dialects)

yeehaukan – wigwam, dwelling, house

Paukunnawaw – He Who Goes in Dark of Night, also Great Bear

pogatowr – corn

Poussu – Big Bellied Woman

pyas – come here

Sá kir winkan? – Are you well/How are you?

sehe – hush

Sequan – Summer

Tosh shonte – English (man or woman)

wingapo – Hello/How are you?

wingan – good

winganouse – very good

Wutahshuntar– white people/people from Europe (pronounced [wuh-TAH-shun-tahs] – it actually meant "foreigners, strangers")

uppowoc – tobacco

Waacoh – Morning Star

Wapeih – Medicinal earth or clay used to heal and treat wounds.

Werowance/werowansa – a chief, leader (male/female)

Winkan nupes – sleep well

Wobsacuck – Eagle

Onxe - Fox

umpe (Nupuy) - water (pronounced [nuh-PEA])

www.ingramcontent.com/pod-product-compliance
Lightning Source LLC
Chambersburg PA
CBHW021425240626
47153CB00001B/29